A BRIDE FOR THE ITALIAN BOSS

BY
SUSAN MEIER

Printed and bound in Spain
by CPI, Barcelona

MILLS & BOON

Published in Great Britain 2015
by Mills & Boon, an imprint of Harlequin (UK) Limited,
Eton House, 18-24 Paradise Road, Richmond, Surrey, TW9 1SR

© 2015 Harlequin Books S.A.

Special thanks and acknowledgement are given to Susan Meier for her contribution to The Vineyards of Calanetti series

ISBN: 978-0-263-25149-4

23-0715

Harlequin (UK) Limited's policy is to use papers that are natural, renewable and recyclable products and made from wood grown in sustainable forests. The logging and manufacturing processes conform to the legal environmental regulations of the country of origin.

Susan Meier is an author of over fifty books for Mills & Boon. *The Tycoon's Secret Daughter* was a RITA® Award finalist, and *Nanny for the Millionaire's Twins* won the Book Buyer's Best award and was a finalist in the National Reader's Choice awards. She is married and has three children. One of eleven children, she loves to write about the complexity of families and totally believes in the power of love.

I want to thank the lovely editors at Mills & Boon for creating such a great continuity! Everyone involved LOVED this idea. Thank you!

CHAPTER ONE

ITALY HAD TO BE the most beautiful place in the world.

Daniella Tate glanced around in awe at the cobblestone streets and blue skies of Florence. She'd taken a train here, but now had to board a bus for the village of Monte Calanetti.

After purchasing her ticket, she strolled to a wooden bench. But as she sat, she noticed a woman a few rows over, with white-blond hair and a slim build. The woman stared out into space; the faraway look in her eyes triggered Daniella's empathy. Having grown up a foster child, she knew what it felt like to be alone, sometimes scared, usually confused. And she saw all three of those emotions in the woman's pretty blue eyes.

An announcement for boarding the next bus came over the public address system. An older woman sitting beside the blonde rose and slid her fingers around the bag sitting at her feet. The pretty blonde rose, too.

"Excuse me. That's my bag."

The older woman spoke in angry, rapid-fire Italian and the blonde, speaking American English, said, "I'm sorry. I don't understand a word of what you're saying."

But the older woman clutched the bag to her and very clearly told the American that it was her carry-on.

Daniella bounced from her seat and scurried over. She faced the American. "I speak Italian, perhaps I can help?"

Then she turned to the older woman. In flawless Italian, she asked if she was sure the black bag was hers, because there was a similar bag on the floor on the other side.

The older woman flushed with embarrassment. She apologetically gave the bag to the American, grabbed her carry-on and scampered off to catch her bus.

The pretty blonde sighed with relief and turned her blue eyes to Daniella. "Thank you."

"No problem. When you responded in English it wasn't a great leap to assume you didn't speak the language."

The woman's eyes clouded. "I don't."

"Do you have a friend coming to meet you?"

"No."

Dani winced. "Then I hope you have a good English-to-Italian dictionary."

The American pointed to a small listening device. "I've downloaded the 'best' language system." She smiled slightly. "It promises I'll be fluent in five weeks."

Dani laughed. "It could be a long five weeks." She smiled and offered her hand. "I'm Daniella, by the way."

The pretty American hesitated, but finally shook Daniella's hand and said, "Louisa."

"It's my first trip to Italy. I've been teaching English in Rome, but my foster mother was from Tuscany. I'm going to use this final month of my trip to find her home."

Louisa tilted her head. "Your foster mother?"

Dani winced. "Sorry. I'm oversharing."

Louisa smiled.

"It's just that I'm so excited to be here. I've always wanted to visit Italy." She didn't mention that her long-time boyfriend had proposed the day before she left for her teaching post in Rome. That truly would be oversharing, but also she hadn't known what to make of Paul's request to marry him. Had he proposed before her trip to tie her to him? Or had they hit the place in their relationship where marriage really was the next step? Were they ready? Was marriage right for them?

Too many questions came with his offer of marriage. So she hadn't accepted. She'd told him she would answer him when she returned from Italy. She'd planned this February side trip to be a nice, uncomplicated space of time before she settled down to life as a teacher in the New York City school system. Paul had ruined it with a proposal she should have eagerly accepted, but had stumbled over. So her best option was not to think about it until she had to.

Next month.

"I extended my trip so I could have some time to bum around. See the village my foster mother came from, and hopefully meet her family."

To Daniella's surprise, Louisa laughed. "That sounds like fun."

The understanding in Louisa's voice caused Danielle to brighten again, thinking they had something in common. "So you're a tourist, too?"

"No."

Dani frowned. Louisa's tone in that one simple word suddenly made her feel as if she'd crossed a line. "I'm sorry. I don't mean to pry."

Louisa sighed. "It's okay. I'm just a bit nervous. You were kind to come to my rescue. I don't mean to be such a ninny. I'm on my way to Monte Calanetti."

Daniella's mouth fell open. "So am I."

The announcement that their bus was boarding came over the loudspeaker. Danielle faced the gate. Louisa did, too.

Dani smiled. "Looks like we're off."

"Yes." Louisa's mysterious smile formed again.

They boarded the bus and Daniella chose a spot in the middle, believing that was the best place to see the sights on the drive to the quaint village. After tucking her backpack away, she took her seat.

To her surprise, Louisa paused beside her. "Do you mind if I sit with you?"

Daniella happily said, "Of course, I don't mind! That would be great."

But as Louisa sat, Daniella took note again that something seemed off about her. Everything Louisa did had a sense of hesitancy about it. Everything she said seemed incomplete.

"So you have a month before you go home?"

"All of February." Daniella took a deep breath. "And I intend to enjoy every minute of it. Even if I do have to find work."

"Work?"

"A waitressing job. Or maybe part-time shop clerk. That kind of thing. New York is a very expensive place to live. I don't want to blow every cent I made teaching on a vacation. I'll need that money when I get back home. So I intend to earn my spending money while I see the sights."

As the bus eased out of the station, Louisa said, "That's smart."

Dani sat up, not wanting to miss anything. Louisa laughed. "Your foster mother should have come with you."

Pain squeezed Daniella's heart. Just when she thought she was adjusted to her loss, the reality would swoop in and remind her that the sweet, loving woman who'd saved her was gone. She swallowed hard. "She passed a few months ago. She left me the money for my plane ticket to Italy in her will."

Louisa's beautiful face blossomed with sympathy. "I'm so sorry. That was careless of me."

Daniella shook her head. "No. You had no way of knowing."

Louisa studied her. "So you have no set plans? No schedule of things you want to see and do? No places you've already scouted out to potentially get a job?"

"No schedule. I want to wing it. I've done a bit of research about Rosa's family and I know the language. So I think I'll be okay."

Louisa laughed. "Better off than I'll be since I don't know the language." She held up her listening device. "At least not for another five weeks."

The bus made several slow turns, getting them out of the station and onto the street.

Taking a final look at Florence, Dani breathed, "Isn't this whole country gorgeous?" Even in winter with barren trees, the scene was idyllic. Blue skies. Rolling hills.

"Yes." Louisa bit her lip, then hesitantly said, "I'm here because I inherited something, too."

"Really?"

"Yes." She paused, studied Daniella's face as if assessing if she could trust her before continuing, "A villa."

"Oh, my God! A *villa*!"

Louisa glanced away. "I know. It's pretty amazing. The place is called Palazzo di Comparino."

"Do you have pictures?"

"Yes." She pulled out a picture of a tall, graceful house. Rich green vines grew in rows in the background beneath a blue sky.

It was everything Dani could do not to gape in awe. "It's beautiful."

Louisa laughed. "Yes. But so far I haven't seen anything in Italy that isn't gorgeous." She winced. "I hate to admit it, but I'm excited."

"I'd be beyond excited."

"I'm told Monte Calanetti developed around Palazzo Chianti because of the vineyard which is part of the villa I inherited. Back then, they would have needed lots of help picking grapes, making the wine. Those people are the ancestors of the people who live there now."

"That is so cool."

"Yes, except I know nothing about running a vineyard."

Daniella batted a hand. "With the internet these days, you can learn anything."

Louisa sucked in a breath. "I hope so."

Daniella laid her hand on Louisa's in a show of encouragement. "You'll be fine."

Louise's face formed another of her enigmatic smiles and Daniella's sixth sense perked up again. Louisa appeared to want to be happy, but behind her smile was something…

Louisa brought her gaze back to Daniella's. "You know, I could probably use a little help when I get there."

"Help?"

"I don't think I'm just going to move into a villa without somebody coming to question me."

"Ah."

"And I'm going to be at a loss if they're speaking Italian."

Dani winced. "Especially if it's the sheriff."

Louisa laughed. "I don't even know if they have sheriffs here. My letter is in English, but the officials are probably Italian. It could turn out to be a mess. So, I'd be happy to put you up for a while." She caught Dani's gaze. "Even all four weeks you're looking for your foster mom's relatives— if you'd be my translator."

Overwhelmed by the generous offer, Daniella said, "That would be fantastic. But I wouldn't want to put you out."

"You'll certainly earn your keep if somebody comes to check my story."

Daniella grinned. "I'd be staying in a villa."

Louisa laughed. "I *own* a villa."

"Okay, then. I'd be happy to be your translator while I'm here."

"Thank you."

Glad for the friendship forming between them, Daniella engaged Louisa in conversation as miles of hills and blue, blue sky rolled past them. Then suddenly a walled village appeared to the right. The bus turned in.

Aged, but well-maintained stucco, brick and stone buildings greeted them. Cobblestone streets were filled with happy, chatting people. Through the large front windows of the establishments, Dani could see the coffee drinkers or diners inside while outdoor dining areas sat empty because of the chilly temperatures.

The center circle of the town came into view. The bus made the wide turn but Dani suddenly saw a sign that read Palazzo di Comparino. The old, worn wood planks had a thick black line painted through them as if to cancel out the offer of vineyard tours.

Daniella grabbed Louisa's arm and pointed out the window. "Look!"

"Oh, my gosh!" Louisa jumped out of her seat and yelled, "Stop!"

Daniella rose, too. She said, *"Fermi qui, per favore."*

It took a minute for the bus driver to hear and finally halt the bus. After gathering their belongings, Louisa and Daniella faced the lane that led to Louisa's villa. Because Dani had only a backpack and Louisa had two suitcases and a carry-on bag, Daniella said, "Let me take your suitcase."

Louisa smiled. "Having you around is turning out to be very handy."

Daniella laughed as they walked down the long lane that took them to the villa. The pale brown brick house soon became visible. The closer they got, the bigger it seemed to be.

Louisa reverently whispered, "Holy cow."

Daniella licked her suddenly dry lips. "It's huge."

The main house sprawled before them. Several stories tall, and long and deep, like a house with suites not bedrooms, Louisa's new home could only be described as a mansion.

They silently walked up the stone path to the front door. When they reached it, Louisa pulled out a key and manipulated the lock. As the door opened, the stale, musty scent of a building that had been locked up for years assaulted them. Dust and cobwebs covered the crystal chandelier in the huge marble-floored foyer as well as the paintings on the walls and the curved stairway.

Daniella cautiously stepped inside. "Is your family royalty?"

Louisa gazed around in awe. "I didn't think so."

"Meaning they could be?"

"I don't know." Louisa turned to the right and walked into a sitting room. Again, dust covered everything. A teacup sat on a table by a dusty chair. Passing through that room, they entered another that appeared to be a library or study. From there, they found a dining room.

Watermarks on the ceiling spoke of damage from a second-floor bathroom or maybe even the roof. The kitchen was old and in need of remodeling. The first-floor bathrooms were outdated, as was every bathroom in the suites upstairs.

After only getting as far as the second floor, Louisa turned to Daniella with tears in her eyes. "I'm so sorry. I didn't realize the house would be in such disrepair. From the picture, it looked perfect. If you want to get a hotel room in town, I'll understand."

"Are you kidding?" Daniella rolled Louisa's big suitcase to a stop and walked into the incredibly dusty, cobweb-covered bedroom. She spun around and faced Louisa. "I love it. With a dust rag, some cleanser for the bathroom and a window washing, this room will be perfect."

Louisa hesitantly followed Daniella into the bedroom. "You're an optimist."

Daniella laughed. "I didn't say you wouldn't need to call a contractor about a few things. But we can clean our rooms and the kitchen."

Raffaele Mancini stared at Gino Scarpetti, a tall, stiff man, who worked as the maître d' for Mancini's, Rafe's very exclusive, upscale, Michelin-starred restaurant located in the heart of wine country.

Mancini's had been carefully crafted to charm customers. The stone and wood walls of the renovated farmhouse gave the place the feel of days long gone. Shutters on the windows blocked the light of the evening sun, but also added to the Old World charisma. Rows of bottles of Merlot and Chianti reminded diners that this area was the home of the best vineyards, the finest wines.

Gino ripped off the Mancini's name tag pinned to his white shirt. "You, sir, are now without a maître d'."

A hush fell over the dining room. Even the usual clink and clatter of silverware and the tinkle of good crystal wineglasses halted.

Gino slapped the name tag into Rafe's hand. Before Rafe could comment or argue, the man was out the door.

Someone began to clap. Then another person. And another. Within seconds the sophisticated Tuscany restaurant dining room filled with the sounds of applause and laughter.

Laughter!

They were enjoying his misery!

He looked at the line of customers forming beside the podium just inside the door, then the chattering diners laughing about his temper and his inability to keep good help. He tossed his hands in the air before he marched back to the big ultramodern stainless-steel restaurant kitchen.

"You!"

He pointed at the thin boy who'd begun apprenticing at Mancini's the week before. "Take off your smock and get to the maître d' stand. You are seating people."

The boy's brown eyes grew round with fear. "I…I…"

Rafe raised a brow. "You can't take names and seat customers?"

"I can…"

"But you don't want to." Rafe didn't have to say anything beyond that. He didn't need to say, "If you can't obey orders, you're fired." He didn't need to remind anyone in *his* kitchen that he was boss or that anyone working in the restaurant needed to be able to do *anything* that needed to be done to assure the absolute best dining experience for the customers. Everyone knew he was not a chef to be trifled with.

Except right now, in the dining room, they were laughing at him.

The boy whipped off his smock, threw it to a laundry bin and headed out to the dining room.

Seeing the white-smocked staff gaping at him, Rafe shook his head. "Get to work!"

Knives instantly rose. The clatter of chopping and the sizzle of sautéing filled the kitchen.

He sucked in a breath. Not only was his restaurant plagued by troubles, but now it seemed the diners had no sympathy.

"You shouldn't have fired Gino." Emory Danoto, Rafe's sous-chef, spoke as he worked. Short and bald with a happy face and nearly as much talent as Rafe in the kitchen, Emory was also Rafe's mentor.

Rafe glanced around, inspecting the food prep, pretending he was fine. Damn it. He *was* fine. He did not want a frightened rabbit working for him. Not even outside the kitchen. And the response of the diners? That was a fluke. Somebody apparently believed it was funny to see a world-renowned chef tortured by incompetents.

"I didn't fire Gino. He quit."

Emory cast him a condemning look. "You yelled at him."

Rafe yelled, "I yell at everybody." Then he calmed himself and shook his head. "I am the chef. I *am* Mancini's."

"And you must be obeyed."

"Don't make me sound like a prima donna. I am doing what's best for the restaurant."

"Well, Mr. I'm-Doing-What's-Best-for-the-Restaurant, have you forgotten about our upcoming visit from the Michelin people?"

"A rumor."

Emory sniffed a laugh. "Since when have we ever ignored a rumor that we were to be visited? Your star rating could be in jeopardy. You're the one who says chefs who ignore rumors get caught with their pants down. If we want to keep our stars, we have to be ready for this visit."

Rafe stifled a sigh. Emory was right, of course. His trusted friend only reminded him of what he already knew. Having located his business in the countryside, instead of in town, he'd made it even more exclusive. But that also meant he didn't get street traffic. He needed word of mouth. He needed every diner to recommend him to their friends. He needed to be in travel brochures. To be a stop for tour buses. To be recommended by travel agents. He couldn't lose a star.

The lunch crowd left. Day quickly became night. Before Rafe could draw a steady breath the restaurant filled again. Wasn't that the way of it when everything was falling apart around you? With work to be done, there was no time to think things through. When the last patron finally departed and the staff dispersed after the kitchen cleaning, Rafe walked behind the shiny wood bar, pulled a bottle of whiskey from the shelf, along with a glass, and slid onto a tall, black, wrought iron stool.

Hearing the sound of the door opening, he yelled, "We're closed." Then grimaced. Was he trying to get a reputation for being grouchy rather than exacting?

"Good thing I'm not a customer, then."

He swiveled around at the sound of his friend Nico Amatucci's voice.

Tall, dark-haired Nico glanced at the whiskey bottle, then sat on a stool beside Rafe. "Is there a reason you're drinking alone?"

Rafe rose, got another glass and set it on the bar. He poured whiskey into the glass and slid it to Nico. "I'm not drinking alone."

"But you were going to."

"I lost my maître d'."

Nico raised his glass in salute and drank the shot. "You're surprised?"

"I'm an artist."

"You're a pain in the ass."

"That, too." He sighed. "But I don't want to be. I just want things done correctly. I'll spread the word tomorrow that I'm looking for someone. Not a big deal." He made the statement casually, but deep down he knew he was wrong. It was a big deal. "Oh, who am I kidding? I don't have the week or two it'll take to collect résumés and interview people. I need somebody tomorrow."

Nico raised his glass to toast. "Then, you, my friend, are in trouble."

Didn't Rafe know it.

CHAPTER TWO

THE NEXT MORNING, Daniella and Louisa found a tin of tea and some frozen waffles in a freezer. "We're so lucky no one had the electricity shut off."

"Not lucky. The place runs off a generator. We turn it on in winter to keep the pipes from freezing."

Daniella and Louisa gasped and spun around at the male voice behind them.

A handsome dark-haired man stood in the kitchen doorway, frowning at them. Though he appeared to be Italian, he spoke flawless English. "I'm going to have to ask you to leave. I'll let you finish your breakfast, but this is private property."

Louisa's chin lifted. "I know it's private property. I'm Louisa Harrison. I inherited this villa."

The man's dark eyes narrowed. "I don't suppose you have proof of that?"

"Actually, I do. A letter from my solicitor." She straightened her shoulders. "I think the better question is, who are you?"

"I'm Nico Amatucci." He pointed behind him. "I live next door. I've been watching over this place." He smiled thinly. "I'd like to see the letter from your solicitor. Or—" he pulled out his cell phone "—should I call the police?"

Louisa brushed her hands down her blue jeans to remove the dust they'd collected when she and Daniella had searched for tea. "No need."

Not wanting any part of the discussion, Daniella began preparing the tea.

"And who are you?"

She shrugged. "Just a friend of Louisa's."

He sniffed as if he didn't believe her. Not accustomed to being under such scrutiny, Daniella focused all her attention on getting water into the teapot.

Louisa returned with the letter. When Nico reached for it, she held it back. "Not so fast. I'll need the key you used to get in."

He held Louisa's gaze. Even from across the room, Daniella felt the heat of it.

"Only if your papers check out." His frosty smile could have frozen water. "Palazzo di Comparino has been empty for years. Yet, suddenly here you are."

"With a letter," she said, handing it to Nico.

He didn't release her gaze as he took the letter from her hands, and then he scanned it and peered at Louisa again. "Welcome to Palazzo di Comparino."

Daniella let out her pent-up breath.

Louisa held his gaze. "Just like that? How do you know I didn't fake this letter?"

Giving the paper back to her, he said, "First, I knew the name of the solicitor handling the estate. Second, there are a couple of details in the letter that an outsider wouldn't know. You're legit."

Though Daniella would have loved to have known the details, Louisa didn't even seem slightly curious. She tucked the sheet of paper into her jeans pocket.

Nico handed his key to Louisa as he glanced around the kitchen. "Being empty so long, the place is in disrepair. So if there's anything I can do to help—"

Louisa cut him off with a curt "I'm fine."

Nico's eyes narrowed. Daniella didn't know if he was

unaccustomed to his offers of assistance being ignored, or if something else was happening here, but the kitchen became awkwardly quiet.

When Daniella's teapot whistled, her heart jumped. Always polite, she asked, "Can I get anyone tea?"

Watching Louisa warily, Nico said, "I'd love a cup."

Drat. He was staying. Darn the sense of etiquette her foster mother had drilled into her.

"I'll make some later," Louisa said as she turned and walked out of the kitchen, presumably to put the letter and the key away.

As the door swung closed behind her, Nico said, "She's a friendly one."

Daniella winced. She'd like to point out to Mr. Nico Amatucci that he'd been a tad rude when he'd demanded to see the letter from the solicitor, but she held her tongue. This argument wasn't any of her business. She had enough troubles of her own.

"Have you known Ms. Harrison long?"

"We just met. I saw someone mistakenly take her bag and helped because Louisa doesn't speak Italian. Then we were on the same bus."

"Oh, so you hit the jackpot when you could find someone to stay with."

Daniella's eyes widened. The man was insufferable. "I'm not taking advantage of her! I just finished a teaching job in Rome. Louisa needs an interpreter for a few weeks." She put her shoulders back. "And today I intend to go into town to look for temporary work to finance a few weeks of sightseeing."

He took the cup of tea from her hands. "What kind of work?"

His softened voice took some of the wind out of her sails. She shrugged. "Anything really. Temp jobs are temp jobs."

"Would you be willing to be a hostess at a restaurant?"

Confused, she said, "Sure."

"I have a friend who needs someone to fill in while he hires a permanent replacement for a maître d' who just quit."

Her feelings for the mysterious Nico warmed a bit. Maybe he wasn't so bad after all? "Sounds perfect."

"Do you have a pen?"

She nodded, pulling one from her purse.

He scribbled down the address on a business card he took from his pocket. "Go here. Don't call. Just go at lunchtime and tell Rafe that Nico sent you." He nodded at the card he'd handed to her. "Show him that and he'll know you're not lying."

He set his tea on the table. "Tell Ms. Harrison I said goodbye."

With that, he left.

Glad he was gone, Daniella glanced at the card in her hands. How could a guy who'd so easily helped her have such a difficult time getting along with Louisa?

She blew her breath out on a long sigh. She supposed it didn't matter. Eventually they'd become friends. They were neighbors after all.

Daniella finished her tea, but Louisa never returned to the kitchen. Excited to tell Louisa of her job prospect, Dani searched the downstairs for her, but didn't find her.

The night before they'd tidied two bedrooms enough that they could sleep in them, so she climbed the stairs and headed for the room Louisa had chosen. She found her new friend wrestling with some bedding.

"What are you doing?"

"I saw a washer and dryer. I thought I'd wash the bedclothes so our rooms really will be habitable tonight."

She raced to help Louisa with the huge comforter. "Our rooms were fine. We don't need these comforters, and the sheets had been protected from the dust by the comforters so they were clean. Besides, these won't fit in a typical washer."

Louisa dropped the comforter. "I know." Her face fell in dismay. "I just need to do something to make the place more livable." Her gaze met Daniella's. "There's dust and clutter...and watermarks that mean some of the bathrooms and maybe even the roof need to be repaired." She sat on the bed. "What am I going to do?"

Dani sat beside her. "We're going to take things one step at a time." She tucked Nico's business card into her pocket. "This morning, we'll clean the kitchen and finish our bedrooms. Tomorrow, we'll pick a room and clean it, and every day after that we'll just keep cleaning one room at a time."

"What about the roof?"

"We'll hope it doesn't rain?"

Louisa laughed. "I'm serious."

"Well, I have a chance for a job at a restaurant."

"You do?"

She smiled. "Yes. Nico knows someone who needs a hostess."

"Oh."

She ignored the dislike in her friend's voice. "What better way to find a good contractor than by chitchatting with the locals?"

Louisa smiled and shook her head. "If anybody can chitchat her way into finding a good contractor, it's you."

"Which is also going to make me a good hostess."

"What time's your appointment?"

"Lunchtime." She winced. "From the address on this card, I think we're going to have to hope there's a car in that big, fancy garage out back."

Standing behind the podium in the entry to Mancini's, Rafe struggled with the urge to throw his hands in the air and storm off. On his left, two American couples spoke broken, ill-attempted Italian in an effort to make reservations for that night. In front of him, a businessman demanded to be seated immediately. To his right, a couple kissed. And behind them, what seemed to be a sea of diners groused and grumbled as he tried to figure out a computer system with a seating chart superimposed with reservations.

How could no one in his kitchen staff be familiar with this computer software?

"Everybody just give me a minute!"

He hit a button and the screen disappeared. After a second of shock, he cursed. He expected the crowd to groan. Instead they laughed. *Laughed. Again, laughter!*

How was it that everybody seemed to be happy that he was suffering? These people—customers—were the people he loved, the people he worked so hard to please. How could they laugh at him?

He tried to get the screen to reappear, but it stayed dark.

"Excuse me. Excuse me. Excuse me."

He glanced up to see an American, clearly forgetting she was in Italy because she spoke English as she made her way through the crowd. Cut in an angled, modern style, her pretty blond hair stopped at her chin. Her blue eyes were determined. The buttons of her black coat had been left open, revealing jeans and pale blue sweater.

When she reached the podium, she didn't even look at Rafe. She addressed the gathered crowd.

"Ladies and gentlemen," she said in flawless Italian. "Give me two minutes and everyone will be seated."

His eyebrows rose. She was a cheeky little thing.

When she finally faced him, her blue eyes locked on his. Rich with color and bright with enthusiasm, they didn't merely display her confidence, they caused his heart to give a little bounce.

She smiled and stuck out her hand. "Daniella Tate. Your friend Nico sent me." When he didn't take her hand, her smile drooped as she tucked a strand of yellow hair behind her ear. But her face brightened again. She rifled in her jeans pocket, pulled out a business card and offered it to him. "See?"

He glanced at Nico's card. "So he believes you are right to be my hostess?"

"Temporarily." She winced. "I just finished a teaching position in Rome. For the next four weeks I'm sightseeing, but I'm trying to supplement my extended stay with a temp job. I think he thinks we can help each other—at least while you interview candidates."

The sweet, melodious tone of her voice caused something warm and soft to thrum through Rafe, something he'd never felt before—undoubtedly relief that his friend had solved his problem.

"I see."

"Hey, buddy, come on. We're hungry! If you're not going to seat us we'll go somewhere else."

Not waiting for him to reply, Daniella nudged Rafe out of the way, stooped down to find a tablet on the maître d' stand shelf and faced the dining area. She quickly drew squares and circles representing all the tables and wrote the number of chairs around each one. She put an X over the tables that were taken.

Had he thought she was cheeky? Apparently that was just the tip of the iceberg.

She faced the Americans. "How many in your party?"

"Four. We want reservations for tonight."

"Time?"

"Seven."

Flipping the tablet page, she wrote their name and the time on the next piece of paper. As the Americans walked out, she said, "Next?"

Awestruck at her audacity, Rafe almost yelled.

Almost.

He could easily give her the boot, but he needed a hostess. He had a growing suspicion about the customers laughing when he lost his temper, as if he was becoming some sort of sideshow. He didn't want his temper to be the reason people came to his restaurant. He wanted his food, the fantastic aromas, the succulent tastes, to be the draw. Wouldn't he be a fool to toss her out?

The businessman pushed his way over to her. "I have an appointment in an hour. I need to be served first."

Daniella Tate smiled at Rafe as if asking permission to seat the businessman, and his brain emptied. She really was as pretty as she was cheeky. Luckily, she took his blank stare as approval. She turned to the businessman and said, "Of course, we'll seat you."

She led the man to the back of the dining room, to a table for two, seated him with a smile and returned to the podium.

Forget about how cheeky she was. Forget about his brain that stalled when he looked at her. She was a very good hostess.

Rafe cleared his throat. "Talk to the waitresses and find out whose turn it is before you seat anyone else." He cleared his throat again. "They have a system."

She smiled at him. "Sure."

His heart did something funny in his chest, forcing his gaze to her pretty blue eyes again. Warmth whooshed through him.

Confused, he turned and marched away. With so much at stake in his restaurant, including, it seemed, his reputation, his funny feelings for an employee were irrelevant. Nothing. Whatever trickled through his bloodstream, it had to be more annoyance than attraction. After all, recommendation from Nico or not, she'd sort of walked in and taken over his restaurant.

Dani stared after the chef as he left. She wasn't expecting someone so young...or so gorgeous. At least six feet tall, with wavy brown hair so long he had it tied off his face and gray eyes, the guy could be a celebrity chef on television back home. Just looking at him had caused her breathing to stutter. She actually felt a rush of heat careen through her veins. He was *that* good-looking.

But it was also clear that he was in over his head without a maître d'. As she'd stood in the back of the long line to get into the restaurant, her good old-fashioned American common sense had kicked in, and she'd simply done what needed to be done: pushed her way to the front, grabbed some menus and seated customers. And he'd hired her.

Behind her someone said, "You'd better keep your hair behind your ears. He'll yell about it being in your face and potentially in his food once he gets over being happy you're here."

She turned to see one of the waitresses. Dressed in black trousers and a white blouse, she looked slim and professional.

"*That* was happy?"

Her pretty black ponytail bobbed as she nodded. "*Sì.* That was happy."

"Well, I'm going to hate seeing him upset."

"Prepare yourself for it. Because he gets upset every day. Several times a day. That's why Gino quit. I'm Allegra, by the way. The other two waitresses are Zola and Giovanna. And the chef is Chef Mancini. Everyone calls him Chef Rafe."

"He said you have a system of how you want people seated?"

Allegra took Daniella's seating chart and drew two lines dividing the tables into three sections. "Those are our stations. You seat one person in mine, one person in Zola's and one person in Gio's, then start all over again."

Daniella smiled. "Easy-peasy."

"*Scusi?*"

"That means 'no problem.'"

"Ah. *Sì.*" Allegra smiled and walked away. Daniella took two more menus and seated another couple.

The lunchtime crowd that had assembled at the door of

Mancini's settled quickly. Dani easily found a rhythm of dividing the customers up between the three waitresses. Zola and Gio introduced themselves, and she actually had a good time being hostess of the restaurant that looked like an Old World farmhouse and smelled like pure heaven. The aromas of onions and garlic, sweet peppers and spicy meats rolled through the air, making her confident she could talk up the food and promise diners a wonderful meal, even without having tasted it.

During the lull after lunch, Zola and Gio went home. The dining room grew quiet. Not sure if she should stay or leave, since Allegra remained to be available for the occasional tourist who ambled in, Daniella stayed, too.

In between customers, she helped clear and reset tables, checked silverware to make sure it sparkled, arranged chairs so that everything in the dining room was picture-perfect.

But soon even the stragglers stopped. Daniella stood by the podium, her elbow leaning against it, her chin on her closed fist, wondering what Louisa was doing.

"Why are you still here?"

The sound of Rafe's voice sent a surge of electricity through her.

She turned with a gasp. Her voice wobbled when she said, "I thought you'd need me for dinner."

"You were supposed to go home for the break. Or are you sneakily trying to get paid for hours you really don't work?"

Her eyes widened. Anger punched through her. What the hell was wrong with this guy? She'd done him a favor and he was questioning her motives?

Without thinking, she stormed over to him. Putting herself in his personal space, she looked up and caught his gaze. "And how was I supposed to know that, since you didn't tell me?"

She expected him to back down. At the very least to realize his mistake. Instead, he scoffed. "It's common sense."

"Well, in America—"

He cut her off with a harsh laugh. "You Americans. Think you know everything. But you're not in America now. You are in Italy." He pointed a finger at her nose. "You will do what I say."

"Well, I'll be happy to do what you say as soon as you say something!"

Allegra stopped dropping silverware onto linen-covered tables. The empty, quiet restaurant grew stone-cold silent. Time seemed to crawl to a stop. The vein in Rafe's temple pulsed.

Dani's body tingled. Every employee in the world knew it wasn't wise to yell at the boss, but, technically, she wasn't yelling. She was standing up to him. As a foster child, she'd had to learn how to protect herself, when to stay quiet and when to demand her rights. If she let him push her around now, he'd push her around the entire month she worked for him.

He threw his hands in the air, pivoted away from her and headed to the kitchen. "Go the hell home and come back for dinner."

Daniella blew out the breath she'd been holding. Her heart pounded so hard it hurt, but the tingling in her blood became a surge of power. He might not have said the words, but she'd won that little battle of wills.

Still, she felt odd that their communication had come down to a sort of yelling match and knew she had to get the heck out of there.

She grabbed her purse and headed for the old green car she and Louisa had found in the garage.

Ten minutes later, she was back in the kitchen of Palazzo di Comparino.

Though Louisa had sympathetically made her a cup of tea, she laughed when Daniella told her the story.

"It's not funny," Dani insisted, but her lips rose into a smile when she thought about how she must have looked standing up to the big bad chef everybody seemed to be afraid of. She wouldn't tell her new friend that standing up to him had put fire in her blood and made her heart gallop like a prize stallion. She didn't know what that was all about, but she did know part of it, at least, stemmed from how good-looking he was.

"Okay. It was a little funny. But I like this job. It would be great to keep it for the four weeks I'm here. But he didn't tell me what time I was supposed to go back. So we're probably going to get into another fight."

"Or you could just go back at six. If he yells that you're late, calmly remind him that he didn't give you the time you were to return. Make it his fault."

"It is his fault."

Louisa beamed. "Exactly. If you don't stand up to him now, you'll either lose the job or spend the weeks you work for him under his thumb. You have to do this."

Dani sighed. "That's what I thought."

Taking Louisa's advice, she returned to the restaurant at six. A very small crowd had built by the maître d' podium, and when she entered, she noticed that most of the tables weren't filled. Rafe shoved a stack of menus at her and walked away.

She shook her head, but smiled at the next customers in line. He might have left without a word, but he hadn't engaged her in a fight and it appeared she still had her job.

Maybe the answer to this was to just stay out of his way?

The evening went smoothly. Again, the wonderful scents that filled the air prompted her to talk up the food, the waitstaff and the wine.

After an hour or so, Rafe called her into the kitchen. Absolutely positive he had nothing to yell at her about, she straightened her shoulders and walked into the stainless-steel room and over to the stove where he stood.

"You wanted to see me?"

He presented a fork filled with pasta to her. "This is my signature ravioli. I hear you talking about my dishes, so I want you to taste so you can honestly tell customers it is the best food you have ever eaten."

She swallowed back a laugh at his confidence, but when her lips wrapped around the fork and the flavor of the sweet sauce exploded on her tongue, she pulled the ravioli off the fork and into her mouth with a groan. "Oh, my God."

"It is perfect, *si*?"

"You're right. It is probably the best food I've ever eaten."

Emory, the short, bald sous-chef, scrambled over. "Try this." He raised a fork full of meat to her lips.

She took the bite and again, she groaned. "What is that?"

"Beef *brasato*."

"Oh, my God, that's good."

A younger chef suddenly appeared before her with a spoon of soup. "Minestrone," he said, holding the spoon out to her.

She drank the soup and closed her eyes to savor. "You guys are the best cooks in the world."

Everyone in the kitchen stopped. The room fell silent.

But Emory laughed. "Chef Rafe is *one* of the best chefs in the world. These are his recipes."

She turned and smiled at Rafe. "You're amazing."

She'd meant his cooking was amazing. His recipes were amazing. Or maybe the way he could get the best out of his staff was amazing. But saying the words while looking into his silver-gray eyes, the simple sentence took on a totally different meaning.

The room grew quiet again. She felt her face reddening. Rafe held her gaze for a good twenty seconds before he finally pointed at the door. "Go tell that to customers."

She walked out of the kitchen, licking the remains of the fantastic food off her lips as she headed for the podium.

With the exception of that crazy little minute of eye contact, tasting the food had been fun. She loved how proud the entire kitchen staff seemed to be of the delicious dishes they prepared. And she saw the respect they had for their boss. Chef Rafe. Clearly a very talented man.

With two groups waiting to be seated, she grabbed menus and walked the first couple to a table. "Right this way."

"Any specialties tonight?"

She faced the man and woman behind her, saying, "I can honestly recommend the chef's signature ravioli." With the taste of the food still on her tongue, she smiled. "And the minestrone soup is to die for. But if you're in the mood for beef, there's a beef *brasato* that you'll never forget."

She said the words casually, but sampling the food had had the oddest effect on her. Suddenly she felt part of it. She didn't merely feel like a good hostess who could recommend the delicious dishes because she'd tasted them. She got an overwhelming sense that she was meant to be here. The feeling of destiny was so strong it nearly overwhelmed her. But she drew in a quiet breath, smiled at the couple and seated them.

Sense of destiny? That was almost funny. Children who grew up in foster care gave up on destiny early, and contented themselves with a sense of worth, confidence. It was better to educate yourself to be employable than to dally in daydreams.

As the night went on, Rafe and his staff continued to give her bites and tastes of the dishes they prepared. As she became familiar with the items on the menu, she tempted guests to try things. But she also listened to stories of the sights the tourists had seen that day, and soothed the egos of those who spoke broken Italian by telling stories of teaching English as a second language in Rome.

And the feeling that she was meant to be there grew, until her heart swelled with it.

* * *

Rafe watched her from the kitchen door. Behind him, Emory laughed. "She's pretty, right?"

Rafe faced him, concerned that his friend had seen their thirty seconds of eye contact over the ravioli and recognized that Rafe was having trouble seeing Daniella Tate as an employee because she was so beautiful. When she'd called him amazing, he'd struggled to keep his gaze off her lips, but that didn't stop the urge to kiss her. It blossomed to life in his chest and clutched the air going into and out of his lungs, making them stutter. He'd needed all of those thirty seconds to get ahold of himself.

But Emory's round face wore his usual smile. Nothing out of the ordinary. No light of recognition in his eyes. Rafe's unexpected reactions hadn't been noticed.

Rafe turned back to the crack between the doors again. "She's chatty."

"You did tell her to talk up the food." Emory sidled up to the slim opening. "Besides, the customers seem to love her."

"Bah!" He spun away from the door. "We don't need for customers to love her. They come here for the food."

Emory shrugged. "Maybe. But we're both aware Mancini's was getting to be a little more well-known for your temper than for its meals. A little attention from a pretty girl talking up *your* dishes might just cure your reputation problem. Put the food back in the spotlight instead of your temper."

"I still think she talks too much."

Emory shook his head. "Suit yourself."

Rafe crossed his arms on his chest. He would suit himself. He was *famous* for suiting himself. That was how he'd gotten to be a great chef. By learning and testing until he created great meals. And he wanted the focus on those meals.

The first chance he got, he intended to have a talk with Daniella Tate.

CHAPTER THREE

AT THE END of the night, when the prep tables were spotless, the kitchen staff raced out the back door. Rafe ambled into the dining room as the waitresses headed for the front door, Daniella in their ranks.

Stopping behind the bar, he called, "No. No. You…Daniella. You and I need to talk."

Her steps faltered and she paused. Eventually, she turned around. "Sure. Great."

Allegra and Gio tossed looks of sympathy at her as the door closed softly behind them.

Her shoulders straightened and she walked over to him. "What is it?"

"You are chatty."

She burst out laughing. "I know." As comfortable as an old friend, she slid onto a bar stool across from him. "Got myself into a lot of trouble in school for that."

"Then you will not be offended if I ask you to project a more professional demeanor with the customers?"

"Heck, no. I'm not offended. I think you're crazy for telling me not to be friendly. But I'm not offended."

Heat surged through Rafe's blood, the way it had when she'd nibbled the ravioli from his fork and called him amazing. But this time he was prepared for it. He didn't know what it was about this woman that got him going, why their arguments fired his blood and their pleasant encounters made him want to kiss her, but he did know he had to control it.

He pulled a bottle of wine from the rack beneath the bar and poured two glasses. Handing one of the glasses to her, he asked, "Do you think it's funny to argue with your boss?"

"I'm not arguing with you. I'm giving you my opinion."

He stayed behind the bar, across from her so he could see her face, her expressive blue eyes. "Ah. So, now I understand. You believe you have a right to an opinion."

She took a sip of the wine. "Maybe not a right. But it's kind of hard not to have an opinion."

He leaned against the smooth wooden surface between them, unintentionally getting closer, then finding that he liked it there because he could smell the hint of her perfume or shampoo. "Perhaps. But a smart employee learns to stifle them."

"As you said, I'm chatty."

"Do it anyway."

She sucked in a breath, pulling back slightly as if trying to put space between them. "Okay."

He laughed. "Okay? My chatty hostess is just saying okay?"

"It's your restaurant."

He saluted her with his wineglass. "At least we agree on something."

But when she set her glass on the bar, slid off the stool and headed for the door, his heart sank.

He shook his head, grabbed the open bottle of wine and went in the other direction, walking toward the kitchen where he would check the next day's menu. It was silly, foolish to be disappointed she was leaving. Not only did he barely know the woman, but he wasn't in the market for a girlfriend. His instincts might be thinking of things like kissing, but he hadn't dated in four years. He had affairs and one-night stands. And a smart employer didn't have a one-night stand with an employee. Unless he wanted trouble. And he did not.

He'd already had one relationship that had almost destroyed his dream. He'd fallen so hard for Kamila Troccoli that when she wasn't able to handle the demands of his schedule, he'd pared it back. Desperate to keep her, he'd refused plum apprenticeships, basically giving up his goal of being a master chef and owning a chain of restaurants.

But she'd left him anyway. After a year of building his life around her, he'd awakened one morning to find she'd simply gone. It had taken four weeks before he could go back to work, but his broken heart hadn't healed until he'd realized relationships were for other men. He had a dream that a romance had nearly stolen from him. A wise man didn't forget hard lessons, or throw them away because of a pretty girl.

Almost at the kitchen door, he stopped. "And, Daniella?"

She faced him.

"No jeans tomorrow. Black trousers and a white shirt."

Daniella raced to her car, her heart thumping in her chest. Having Rafe lean across the bar, so close to her, had been the oddest thing. Her blood pressure had risen. Her breathing had gone funny. And damned if she didn't want to run her fingers through his wavy hair. Unbound, it had fallen to his shoulders, giving him the look of a sexy pirate.

The desire to touch him had been so strong, she would have agreed to anything to be able to get away from him so she could sort this out.

And just when she'd thought she was free, he'd said her name. *Daniella.* The way it had rolled off his tongue had been so sexy, she'd shuddered.

Calling herself every kind of crazy, she got into Louisa's old car and headed home. A mile up the country road, she pulled through the opening in the stone wall that allowed entry to Monte Calanetti. Driving along the cobblestone street, lit only by streetlights, she marveled at the way her heart warmed at the quaint small town. She'd never felt so at peace as she did in Italy, and she couldn't wait to meet her foster mother's relatives. Positive they'd make a connection, she could see herself coming to Italy every year to visit them.

She followed the curve around the statue in the town square before she made the turn onto the lane for Palazzo di Comparino. She knew Louisa saw only decay and damage when she looked at the crumbling villa, but in her mind's eye Dani could see it as it was in its glory days. Vines heavy with grapes. The compound filled with happy employees. The owner, a proud man.

A lot like Rafe.

She squeezed her eyes shut when the familiar warmth whooshed through her at just the thought of his name. What was it about that guy that got to her? Sure, he was sexy. Really sexy. But she'd met sexy men before. Why did this one affect her like this?

Louisa was asleep, so she didn't have anyone to talk with about her strange feelings. But the next morning over tea, she told Louisa everything that had happened at the restaurant, especially her unwanted urge to touch Rafe when he leaned across the bar and was so close to her, and Louisa—again—laughed.

"This is Italy. Why are you so surprised you're feeling everything a hundred times more passionately?"

Dani's eyes narrowed. Remembering her thoughts about Monte Calanetti, the way she loved the quaint cobblestone streets, the statue fountain in the middle of the square, the happy, bustling people, she realized she did feel everything more powerfully in Italy.

"Do you think that's all it is?"

"Oh, sweetie, this is the land of passion. It's in the air. The water. Something. As long as you recognize what it is, you'll be fine."

"I hope so." She rose from the table. "I also hope there's a thrift shop in town. I have to find black trousers and a white blouse. Rafe doesn't like my jeans."

Louisa laughed as she, too, rose from the table. "I'll bet he likes your jeans just fine."

Daniella frowned.

Louisa slid her arm across her shoulder. "Your butt looks amazing in jeans."

"What does that have to do with anything?"

Louisa gave her a confused look, then shook her head. "Did you ever stop to think that maybe you're *both* reacting extremely to each other. That it's not just you feeling everything, and that's why it's so hard to ignore?"

"You think he's attracted to me?"

"Maybe. Dani, you're pretty and sexy." She laughed. "And Italian men like blondes."

Daniella frowned. "Oh, boy. That just makes things worse."

"Or more fun."

"No! I have a fiancé. Well, not a fiancé. My boyfriend asked me to marry him right before I left."

"You have a boyfriend?"

She winced. "Yeah."

"And he proposed right before you left?"

"Yes."

Louisa sighed. "I guess that rules out an affair with your sexy Italian boss."

Daniella's eyes widened. "I can't have an affair!"

"I know." Louisa laughed. "Come on. Let's go upstairs and see what's in my suitcases. I have to unpack anyway. I'm sure I have black pants and a white shirt."

"Okay."

Glad the subject had changed, Daniella walked with Louisa through the massive downstairs to the masterpiece stairway.

Louisa lovingly caressed the old, worn banister. "I feel

like this should be my first project. Sort of like a symbol that I intend to bring this place back to life."

"Other people might give the kitchen or bathrooms a priority."

Louisa shook her head. "The foyer is the first thing everyone sees when they walk in. I want people to know I'm committed and I'm staying."

"I get it."

It took ten minutes to find the black pants and white shirt in Louisa's suitcase, but Dani remained with Louisa another hour to sort through her clothes and hang them in the closet.

When it was time to leave, she said goodbye to Louisa and headed to the restaurant for the lunch crowd. She stashed her purse on the little shelf of the podium and waited for someone to unlock the door to customers so she could begin seating everyone.

Rafe himself came out. As he walked to the door, his gaze skimmed over her. Pinpricks of awareness rained down on her. Louisa's suggestion that he was attracted to her tiptoed into her brain. What would it be like to have this sexy, passionate man attracted to her?

She shook her head. What the heck was she thinking? He was only looking at her to make sure she had dressed appropriately. He was *not* attracted to her. Good grief. All they ever did was snipe at each other. That was not attraction.

Although, standing up to him did warm her blood…

After opening the door, Rafe strode away without even saying good morning, proving, at least to Dani, that he wasn't attracted to her. As she seated her first customers, he walked to the windows at the back of the old farmhouse and opened the wooden shutters, revealing the picturesque countryside.

The odd feeling of destiny brought Daniella up short again. This time she told herself it was simply an acknowl-

edgment that the day was beautiful, the view perfect. There
was no such thing as someone "belonging" somewhere.
There was only hard work and planning.

An hour into the lunch shift, a customer called her over
and asked to speak with the chef. Fear shuddered through
her.

"Rafe?"

The older man nodded. "If he's the chef, yes."

She couldn't even picture the scene if she called Rafe
out and this man, a sweet old man with gray hair, blue eyes
and a cute little dimple, complained about the food. So she
smiled. "Maybe I can help you?"

"Perhaps. But I would like to speak with the chef."

Officially out of options, she smiled and said, "Absolutely."

She turned to find Rafe only a few steps away, his eyes
narrowed, his lips thin.

She made her smile as big as she could. "Chef Rafe…"
She motioned him over. When he reached her, she politely
said, "This gentleman would like to speak with you."

The dining room suddenly grew quiet. It seemed that
everyone, including Daniella, held their breath.

Rafe addressed the man. "Yes? What can I do for you?
I'm always happy to hear from my customers."

His voice wasn't just calm. It was warm. Dani took a
step back. She'd expected him to bark. Instead, he was
charming and receptive.

"This is the best ravioli I've ever eaten." The customer
smiled broadly. "I wanted to convey my compliments to
the chef personally."

Rafe put his hands together as if praying and bowed
slightly. *"Grazie."*

"How did you come to pick such a lovely place for a
restaurant?"

"The views mostly," Rafe said, smiling, and Dani stared
at him. Those crazy feelings rolled through her again.

When it came to his customers he was humble, genuine. And very, very likable.

He turned to her and nodded toward the door. "Customers, Daniella?"

"Yes! Of course!" She pivoted and hurried away to seat the people at the door, her heart thrumming, her nerve endings shimmering. Telling herself she was simply responding to the happy way he chatted with a customer, glad he hadn't yelled at the poor man and glad everything was going so well, she refused to even consider that her appreciation of his good looks was tipping over into a genuine attraction.

She was so busy she didn't hear the rest of Rafe's conversation with the older couple. When they left, Rafe returned to the kitchen and Daniella went about her work. People arrived, she seated them, the staff served them and Rafe milled about the dining room, talking with customers. They gushed over the scene visible through the back windows. And he laughed.

He *laughed*. And the warmth of his love for his customers filled her. But that still didn't mean she was attracted to him. She appreciated him, yes. Respected him? Absolutely. But even though he was gorgeous, she refused to be attracted to him. Except maybe physically…the man *was* gorgeous. And having a boyfriend didn't mean she couldn't *notice* good-looking men… Did it?

When the lunch crowd emptied, and Gio and Zola left, Daniella turned to help Allegra tidy the dining room, but Rafe caught her arm. "Not so fast."

The touch of his hand on her biceps sent electricity straight to her heart. Which speeded up and sent a whoosh of heat through her blood.

Darn it. She *was* attracted to him.

But physically. Just physically.

She turned slowly.

Bright with anger, his gaze bored into her. "What in the hell did you think you were doing?"

With electricity careening through her, she pulled in a shaky breath. "When?"

"When the customer asked to speak with me!" He threw his hands in the air. "Did you think I did not see? I see everything! I heard that man ask to speak with me and heard you suggest that he talk to you."

She sucked in a breath to steady herself. "I was trying to head off a disaster."

"A disaster? He wanted to compliment the chef and you tried to dissuade him. Did you want the compliment for yourself?"

She gasped. "No! I was worried he was going to complain about the food." She took a step closer, now every bit as angry as he was. He was so concerned about his own agenda, he couldn't even tell when somebody was trying to save his sorry butt. "And that you'd scream at him and the whole dining room would hear."

He matched the step she took. "Oh, really? You saw how I spoke to him. I love my customers."

She held her ground. Her gaze narrowed on him. Her heart raced. "Yeah, well I know that now, but I didn't know it when he asked to speak with you."

"You overstepped your boundaries." He took another step, and put them so close her whole body felt energized—

Oh, no.

Now she knew what was going on. She didn't just think Rafe was handsome. She wasn't just *physically* attracted to him. She was completely attracted to him. And she wasn't yelling at him because she was defending herself. She was yelling because it was how he communicated with her. Because he was a stubborn, passionate man, was this how she flirted with him?

Not at all happy with these feelings, she stepped away

from him. Softening her voice, she said, "It won't happen again."

He laughed. "What? You suddenly back down?"

She peered over at him. Why hadn't he simply said, "Thank you," and walked away? That's what he usually did.

Unless Louisa was right and he was attracted to her, too?

The mere thought made her breathless. She sneaked a peek at him—he was distinguished looking with his long hair tied back and his white smock still crisp and clean after hours of work. The memory of his laughter with the customer fluttered through her, stealing her breath again. He was a handsome man, very, very good at what he did and dedicated to his customers. He could have his pick of women. And he was attracted to her?

Preposterous. She didn't for a second believe it, but she was definitely attracted to him. And she was going to have to watch her step.

She cleared her throat. "Unless you want me to hang out until the dinner crowd, I'll be going home now."

He shook his head. "Do not overstep your boundaries again."

She licked her suddenly dry lips. "Oh, believe me, I'll be very, very careful from here on out."

Rafe watched her walk away. His racing heart had stilled. The fire in his blood had fizzled. Disappointment rattled through him. He shook his head and walked back into the kitchen.

"Done yelling at Daniella?"

Rafe scowled at Emory. "She oversteps her place."

"She's trying to keep the peace. To keep the customers happy. And, in case you haven't noticed, they are happy. Today they were particularly happy."

He sniffed in disdain. "I opened the dining room to the view from the back windows."

Emory laughed. "Seriously? You're going with that?"

"All right! So customers like her."

"And no one seems to be hanging around hoping you'll lose your temper."

He scowled.

"She did exactly what we needed to have done. She shifted the temperament in the dining room. Customers are enjoying your food. You should be thrilled to have her around."

Rafe turned away with a "Bah." But deep down inside he *was* thrilled to have her around.

And maybe that wasn't as much of a good thing as Emory thought it was. Because the whole time he was yelling at her, he could also picture himself kissing her.

Worse, the part of him that usually toed the line wasn't behaving. That part kept reminding him she was temporary. She might be an employee, but she wasn't staying forever. He *could* have an affair with this beautiful, passionate woman and not have to worry about repercussions because in a few weeks, she'd be gone. No scene. No broken heart. No expectations. They could have a delicious affair.

CHAPTER FOUR

DANIELLA RETURNED HOME that night exhausted. Louisa hadn't waited up for her, but from the open cabinet doors and trash bags sitting by the door, it was apparent she'd begun cleaning the kitchen.

She dragged herself up the stairs, showered and crawled into bed, refusing to think about the possibility that Rafe might be attracted to her. Not only did she have a marriage proposal waiting at home, but, seriously? Her with Rafe? Mr. Unstable with the former foster child who needed stability? That was insanity.

She woke early the next morning and, after breakfast, she and Louisa loaded outdated food from the pantry into even more trash bags.

Wiping sweat from her brow, Louisa shook her head at the bag of garbage she'd just hauled to the growing pile by the door. "We don't even know what day to set out the trash."

Busy sweeping the now-empty pantry, Dani said, "You could always ask Nico."

Louisa rolled her eyes. "I'm not tromping over to his villa to ask about trash."

"You could call him. I have his card." She frowned. "Or Rafe has his card. I could ask for it back tonight."

"No, thanks. I'll figure this out."

"Or maybe I could ask the girls at the restaurant? Given

that we're so close to Monte Calanetti, one of them prob-ably lives in the village. She'll know what day the trash truck comes by."

Louisa brightened. "Yes. Thank you. That would be great."

But Dani frowned as she swept the last of the dirt onto her dustpan. Louisa's refusal to have anything to do with Nico had gone from unusual to impractical. Still, it wasn't her place to say anything.

She dressed for work in the dark trousers and white shirt Rafe required and drove to the restaurant. Walking in, she noticed that two of the chefs were different, and two of the chefs she was accustomed to seeing weren't there. The same was true in the dining room. Allegra was nowhere to be seen and in her place was a tall, slim waitress named Mila, short for Milana, who told Daniella it was simply Allegra's day off and probably the chefs', too.

"Did you think they'd been fired?" Mila asked with a laugh.

Dani shrugged. "With our boss, you never know."

Mila laughed again. "Only Chef Rafe works twelve hours a day, seven days a week."

"I guess I should ask for a schedule, then."

She turned toward the kitchen but Mila stopped her. "Do yourself a favor and ask Emory about it."

Thinking that sounded like good advice, she nodded and walked into the kitchen. Emory stood at a stainless-steel prep table in the back of the huge, noisy, delicious-smelling room. Grateful that Rafe wasn't anywhere in sight, she approached the sous-chef.

"Cara!" he said, opening his arms. "What can I do for you?"

"I was wondering if there was a schedule."

The short, bald man smiled. "Schedule?"

"I'm never really sure when I'm supposed to come in."

"A maître d' works all shifts."

At the sound of Rafe's voice behind her, she winced, sucked in a breath and faced him. "I can't work seven days a week, twelve hours a day. I want this month to do some sightseeing. Otherwise, I could have just gone back to New York City."

He smiled and said, "Ah."

And Daniella's heart about tripped over itself in her chest. He had the most beautiful, sexy smile she had ever seen. Directed at her, it stole her breath, weakened her knees, scared her silly.

"You are correct. Emory will create a schedule."

Surprised at how easy that had been, and not about to hang around when his smile was bringing out feelings she knew were all wrong, she scampered out of the kitchen. Within minutes, Rafe came into the dining room to open Mancini's doors. As he passed her, he smiled at her again.

When he disappeared behind the kitchen doors, she blew out her breath and collapsed against the podium. What was he doing smiling at her? Dear God, was Louisa right? Was he interested in her?

She paused. No. Rafe was too business oriented to be attracted to an employee. This wasn't about attraction. It was about her finally finding her footing with him. He hadn't argued about getting her a schedule. He'd smiled because they were beginning to get along as employer and employee.

Guests began arriving and she went to work. There were enough customers that the restaurant felt busy, but not nearly as busy as they were for dinner. She seated an American couple and walked away but even before she reached the podium, they waved her back.

She smiled. "Having trouble with the Italian?"

The short dark-haired man laughed. "My wife teaches Italian at university. We actually visit every other year. Though this is our first time at Mancini's."

"Well, a very special welcome to you, then. What can I help you with?"

He winced. "Actually, we were kind of hoping to just have soup or a salad, but all you have is a full menu."

"Yes. The chef loves his drama."

The man's wife reached over and touched his arm. "I am sort of hungry for this delicious-sounding spaghetti. Maybe we can eat our big meal now and eat light at dinner."

Her husband laughed. "Fine by me."

Dani waved Gio over to take their orders, but a few minutes later, she had a similar conversation with a group of tourists who had reservations that night at a restaurant in Florence. They'd stopped at Mancini's looking for something light, but Rafe's menu only offered full-course meals.

With the lunchtime crowd thinned and two of the three waitresses gone until dinner, Dani stared at the kitchen door. If she and Rafe really had established a proper working relationship, shouldn't she tell him what customers told her?

Of course, she should. She shouldn't be afraid. She should be a good employee.

She headed for the kitchen. "May I speak with you, Chef Rafe?"

His silver-gray eyes met hers. "Yes?"

She swallowed. It was just plain impossible not to be attracted to this guy. "It's... I... Do you want to hear the things the customers tell me?"

Leaning against his prep table behind him, holding her gaze, he said, "Yes. I always want the opinions of customers."

She drank in a long breath. The soft, seductive tone of his voice, the way he wouldn't release her gaze, all reminded her of Louisa's contention that he was attracted to her. The prospect tied her tongue until she reminded herself that they were at work. And he was dedicated to his diners. In this kitchen, that was all that mattered.

"Okay. Today, I spoke with a couple from the US and a group of tourists, both of whom only wanted soup or salad for lunch."

"We serve soup and salad."

"As part of a meal."

"So they should eat a meal."

"That was actually their point. They didn't want a whole meal. Just soup and salad."

Rafe turned to Emory, his hands raised in question as if he didn't understand what she was saying.

She tried again. "Look. You want people to come in for both lunch and dinner but you only offer dinners on the menu. Who wants a five-course meal for lunch?"

The silver shimmer in Rafe's eyes disappeared and he gaped at her. "Any Italian."

"All right." So much for thinking he was attracted to her. The tone of his voice was now definitely all business and when it came to his business, he was clearly on a different page than she was. But this time she knew she was right. "Maybe Italians do like to eat that way. But half your patrons are tourists. If they want a big meal, they'll come at dinnertime. If they just want to experience the joy that is Mancini's, they'll be here for lunch. And they'll probably only want a salad. Or maybe a burger."

"A burger?" He whispered the word as if it were blasphemy.

"Sure. If they like it, they'll be back for dinner."

The kitchen suddenly got very quiet. Every chef in the room and both busboys had turned to face her.

Rafe quietly said, "This is Italy. Tourists want to experience the culture."

"Yes. You are correct. They do want to experience the culture. But that's only part of why tourists are here. Most tourists don't eat two huge meals a day. It couldn't hurt to put simple salads on the lunch menu, just in case a tourist or two doesn't want to eat five courses."

His gray eyes flared. When he spoke, it was slowly, deliberately. "Miss Daniella, you are a tourist playing hostess. I am a world-renowned chef."

This time the softness of his voice wasn't seductive. It was insulting and her defenses rose. "I know. But I'm the one in the dining room, talking with your customers—"

His eyes narrowed with anger and she stepped back, suddenly wondering what the hell she was doing. He was her boss. As he'd said, a world-renowned chef. Yet here she was questioning him. She couldn't seem to turn off the self-defense mechanisms she'd developed to protect herself in middle school when she was constantly teased about not having a home or questioned because her classmates thought being a foster kid meant she was stupid.

She sucked in a long, shaky breath. "I'm sorry. I don't know why I pushed."

He gave her a nod that more or less dismissed her and she raced out of the kitchen. But two minutes later a customer asked to speak with Rafe. Considering this her opportunity to be respectful to him, so hopefully they could both forget about their soup and salad disagreement, she walked into the kitchen.

But she didn't see Rafe.

She turned to a busboy. "Excuse me. Where's Chef Rafe?"

The young kid pointed at a closed door. "In the office with Emory."

She smiled. "Thanks."

She headed for the door. Just when she would have pushed it open, she heard Emory's voice.

"I'm not entirely sure why you argue with her."

"*I* argue with *her*? I was nothing but nice to that girl and she comes into my kitchen and tells me I don't know my own business."

Dani winced, realizing they were talking about her.

Emory said, "We need her."

And Rafe quickly countered with, "You are wrong. Had Nico not sent her, we would have hired someone else by now. Instead, because Nico told her I was desperate, we're stuck with a woman who thinks we need her, and thinks that gives her the right to make suggestions. Not only do we not need her, but I do not want her here—"

The rest of what Rafe said was lost on Dani as she backed away from the door.

Rafe saying that she wasn't wanted rolled through her, bringing up more of those memories from middle school before she'd found a permanent foster home with Rosa. The feeling of not being wanted, not having a home, rose in her as if she were still that teenage girl who'd been rejected so many times that her scars burrowed the whole way to her soul.

Tears welled in her eyes. But she fought them, telling herself he was right. She shouldn't argue with him. But seriously, this time she'd thought she was giving a valuable suggestion. And she'd stopped when she realized she'd pushed too far.

She just couldn't seem to get her bearings with this guy. And maybe it was time to realize this really wasn't the job for her and leave.

She pivoted away from the door, raced out of the kitchen and over to Gio. "Um, the guy on table three would like to talk with Rafe. Would you mind getting him?"

Gio studied her face, undoubtedly saw the tears shimmering on her eyelids and smiled kindly. "Sure."

Dani walked to the podium, intending to get her purse and her coat to leave, but a customer walked in.

Rafe shook his head as Emory left the office with a laugh. He'd needed to vent and Emory had listened for a few minutes, then he'd shut Rafe down. And that was good. He'd been annoyed that Dani challenged him in front of his staff. But venting to Emory was infinitely better than firing her.

Especially since they did need her. He hadn't even started interviewing for her replacement yet.

He walked into the kitchen at the same time that Gio did. "Chef Rafe, there's a customer who would like to speak with you."

He turned to the sink, rinsed his hands and grabbed his towel, before he motioned for Gio to lead him to the customer.

Stepping into the dining room, he didn't see Dani anywhere, but before he could take that thought any further, he was beside a happy customer who wanted to compliment him on his food.

He listened to the man, scanning the dining room for his hostess. When she finally walked into the dining room from the long hall that led to the restrooms, he sighed with relief. He accepted the praise of his customer, smiled and returned to his work.

An hour later, Dani came into the kitchen. "Chef Mancini, there's a customer who would like to speak with you."

Her voice was soft, meek. She'd also called him Chef Mancini, not Chef Rafe, but he didn't question it. A more businesslike demeanor between them was not a bad thing. Particularly considering that he'd actually wanted to have an affair with her and had been thinking about that all damned day—until they'd gotten into that argument about soup and salad.

Which was why the smile he gave her was nothing but professional. "It would be my pleasure."

He expected her to say, "Thank you." Instead, she nodded, turned and left the kitchen without him.

He rinsed his hands, dried them and headed out to the dining room. She waited by a table in the back. When she saw him she motioned for him to come to the table.

As he walked up, she smiled at the customers. She said, "This is Chef Mancini." Then she strode away.

He happily chatted with the customer for ten minutes, but his gaze continually found Daniella. She hadn't waited for him in the kitchen, hadn't looked at him when he came to the table—had only introduced him and left. Her usually sunny smile had been replaced by a stiff lift of her lips. Her bright blue eyes weren't filled with joy. They were dull. Lifeless.

A professional manner was one thing. But she seemed to be...hurt.

He analyzed their soup-and-salad conversation and couldn't find anything different about that little spat than any of their disagreements—except that he'd been smiling at her when she walked in, thinking about kissing her. Then they'd argued and he'd realized what a terrible idea kissing her was, and that had shoved even the thought of an affair out of his head.

But that was good. He should not want to get involved with an employee. No matter how pretty.

When the restaurant cleared at closing time, he left, too. He drove to his condo, showered and put on jeans and a cable-knit sweater. He hadn't been anywhere but Mancini's in weeks. Not since Christmas. And maybe that was why he was having these odd thoughts about his hostess? Maybe it was time to get out with people again? Maybe find a woman?

He shrugged into his black wool coat, took his private elevator to the building lobby and stepped outside.

His family lived in Florence, but he loved little Monte Calanetti. Rich with character and charm, the stone-and-stucco buildings on the main street housed shops run by open, friendly people. That was part of why he'd located Mancini's just outside of town. Tourists loved Monte Calanetti for its connections to the past, especially the vineyard of Palazzo di Comparino, which unfortunately had closed. But tourists still came, waiting for the day the vineyard would reopen.

Rafe's boots clicked on the cobblestone. The chill of the February night seeped into his bones. He put up the collar of his coat, trying to ward off the cold. It didn't help. When he reached Pia's Tavern, he stopped.

Inside it would be warm from a fire in the stone fireplace in the back. He could almost taste the beer from the tap. He turned and pushed open the door.

Because it was a weekday, the place was nearly empty. The television above the shelves of whiskey, gin and rum entertained the two locals sitting at the short shiny wood bar. The old squat bartender leaned against a cooler beside the four beer taps. Flames danced in the stone fireplace and warmed the small, hometown bar. As his eyes adjusted to the low lights, Rafe saw a pretty blonde girl sitting alone at a table in the back.

Dani.

He didn't know whether to shake his head or turn around and walk out. Still, when her blue eyes met his, he saw sadness that sent the heat of guilt lancing though him.

Before he could really think it through, he walked over to her table and sat across from her.

"Great. Just what every girl wants. To sit and have a drink with the boss who yells at her all day."

He frowned. "Is that why you grew so quiet today? Because I yelled at you? I didn't yell. I just didn't take your suggestion. And that is my right. I am your boss."

She sucked in a breath and reached for her beer. "Yes, I know."

"You've always known that. You ignore it, but you've always known. So this time, why are you so upset?"

She didn't reply. Instead, she reached for her coat and purse as if she intended to go. He caught her arm and stopped her.

Her gaze dropped to his hand, then met his.

Confused, he held her blue, blue eyes, as his fingers slid against her soft pink skin. The idea of having an affair with her popped into his head again. They were both incredibly passionate people and they'd probably set his bedroom on fire, if they could stop arguing long enough to kiss.

"Please. If I did something wrong, tell me—"

An unexpected memory shot through him. He hadn't cared what a woman thought since Kamila. The reminder of how he'd nearly given up his dream for her froze the rest of what he wanted to say on his tongue and forced him back to business mode.

"If you are gruff with customers I need to know why."

"I'm not gruff with customers." Her voice came out wispy and smoky.

"So it's just me, then?"

"Every time I try to be nice to you, you argue with me." He laughed. "When did you try to be nice to me?"

"That suggestion about lunch wasn't a bad one. And I came to you politely—"

"And I listened until you wouldn't quit arguing. Then I had to stop you."

"Yes. But after that you told Emory I wasn't needed." She sniffed a laugh. "I heard you telling him you didn't even want me around."

His eyes narrowed on her face. "I tell Emory things like that all the time. I vent. It's how I get rid of stress."

"Maybe you should stop that."

He laughed, glad his feisty Dani was returning. "And maybe you should stop listening at the door?"

She shook her head and shrugged out of his hold. "I wasn't listening. You were talking loud enough that I could easily hear you through the door."

She rose to leave again. This time he had no intention of stopping her, but a wave of guilt sluiced through him. Her face was still sad. Her blue eyes dull. All because of his attempt to blow off steam.

She only got three steps before he said, "Wait! You are right. I shouldn't have said you weren't wanted. I rant to

Emory all the time. But usually no one hears me. So it doesn't matter."

She stopped but didn't return to her seat. Standing in the glow of the fireplace, she said, "If that's an apology, it's not a very good one."

No. He supposed it wasn't. But nobody ever took his rants so seriously. "Why did it upset you so much to hear you weren't wanted?"

She said nothing.

He rose and walked over to her. When she wouldn't look at him, he lifted her chin until her gaze met his. "There is a story there."

"Of course there's a story there."

He waited for her to explain, but she said nothing. The vision of her walking sadly around the restaurant filled his brain. He'd insulted hundreds of employees before, trying to get them to work harder, smarter, but from the look in her eyes he could see this was personal.

"Can you tell me?"

She shrugged away again. "So you can laugh at me?"

"I will not laugh!" He sighed, softened his voice. "Actually, I'm hoping that if you tell me it will keep me from hitting that nerve again."

"Really?"

"I'm not an idiot. I don't insult people to be cruel. When I vent to Emory it means nothing. When I yell at my employees I'm trying to get the best out of them. With you, everything's a bit different." He tossed his hands. He wouldn't tell her that part of the problem was his attraction. Especially since he went back and forth about pursuing it. Maybe if he'd just decide to take romance off the table, become her friend, things between them would get better? "It might be because you're American not European. Whatever the case, I'd like to at least know that I won't insult you again."

The bartender walked over. He gruffly threw a beer

coaster on the table, even though Dani and Rafe stood by the fireplace. "What'll it be?"

Rafe tugged Dani's hand. "Come. We'll get a nice Merlot. And talk."

She slid her hand out of his, but she did return to her seat. He named the wine he wanted from the bartender, and with a raise of his bushy brows, the bartender scrambled off to get it. When he returned with the bottle and two glasses, Rafe shooed him away, saying he'd pour.

Dani frowned. "No time for breathing?"

He chuckled. "Ah. So she thinks she knows wine?"

Her head lowered. "I don't."

His eyes narrowed as he studied her. The sad demeanor was back. The broken woman. "And all this rolls together with why I insulted you when I said you weren't wanted?"

She sighed. "Sort of. I don't know how to explain this so you'll understand, but the people I'm looking for aren't my relatives."

He smiled. "They're people who owe you money?"

She laughed. The first genuine laugh in hours and the tight ball of tension in Rafe's gut unwound.

"They are the family of the woman who was my foster mother."

"Foster mother?"

"I was taken from my mother when I was three. I don't remember her. In America, when a child has no home, he or she is placed with a family who has agreed to raise her." She sucked in a breath and took the wineglass he offered her. "Foster parents aren't required to keep you forever. So if something happens, they can give you back."

She tried to calmly give the explanation but the slight wobble of her voice when she said "give you back" caused the knot of tension to reform in Rafe's stomach. He imagined a little blue-eyed, blonde girl bouncing from home to home, hugging a scraggly brown teddy bear, and his throwaway comment about her not being wanted made his heart hurt.

"I'm sorry."

She sipped her wine. "And right about now, I'm feeling pretty stupid. You're a grouch. A perfectionist who yells at everyone. I should have realized you were venting." She met his gaze. "I'm the one who should be sorry."

"You do realize you just called me a grouch."

She took another sip of her wine. "And a perfectionist." She caught his gaze again. "See? You don't get offended."

He laughed.

She smiled.

Longing filled Rafe. For years he'd satisfied himself with one-night stands, but she made him yearn for the connection he'd had only once before. With her he wasn't Chef Rafe. She didn't treat him like a boss. She didn't talk to him like a boss…

Maybe because she had these feelings, too?

He sucked in a breath, met her gaze. "Tell me more."

"About my life?"

"About anything."

She set down her wineglass as little pinpricks of awareness sprung up on her arms.

She hadn't realized how much she'd longed for his apology until he'd made it. But now that he was asking to hear about her life, everything inside her stilled. How much to tell? How much to hold back? Why did he want to know? And why did she ache to tell him?

He offered his hand again and she glanced into his face. The lines and planes of his chin and cheeks made him classically handsome. His sexy unbound hair brought out urges in her she hadn't ever felt. She'd love to run her fingers through it while kissing him. Love to know what it would feel like to have his hair tumble to his face while they made love.

She stopped her thoughts. She had an almost fiancé at home, and Rafe wasn't the most sympathetic man in the world. He was bold and gruff, and he accepted no less than total honesty.

But maybe that's what appealed to her? She didn't want sympathy. She just wanted to talk to someone. To really be heard. To be understood.

"I had a good childhood," he said, breaking the awkward silence, again nudging his hand toward her.

She didn't take his hand, so he used it to inch her wine closer. She picked it up again.

"Even as a boy, I was fascinated by cooking."

She laughed, wondering why the hell she was tempting fate by sitting here with him when she should leave. She might not be engaged but she was close enough. And though she'd love to kiss Rafe, to run her fingers through that wild hair, Paul was stability. And she needed stability.

"My parents were initially put off, but because I also played soccer and roughhoused with my younger brother, they weren't worried."

She laughed again. He'd stopped trying to take her hand. And he really did seem to want to talk. "You make your childhood sound wonderful."

He winced. "Not intentionally."

"You don't have to worry about offending me. I don't get jealous of others' good lives. Once Rosa took me in, I had a good life."

"How old were you?"

"Sixteen."

"She was brave."

"Speaking from experience?"

"Let's just say I had a wild streak."

Looking at his hair, which curled haphazardly and made his gray eyes appear shiny and mysterious, Dani didn't doubt he had lots of women who'd helped his wild streak along.

Still, she ignored the potential to tease, to flirt, and said, "Rosa really was brave. I wasn't so much of a handful because I got into trouble, but because I was lost."

"You seem a little lost now, too."

Drat. She hadn't told him any of this for sympathy. She was just trying to keep the conversation innocent. "Seriously. You're not going to feel sorry for me, are you?"

"Not even a little bit. If you're lost now, it's your own doing. Something you need to fix yourself."

"That's exactly what I believe!"

He toasted. "To us. Two just slightly off-kilter people who make our own way."

She clinked her glass to his before taking another sip of wine. They finished their drinks in silence, which began to feel uncomfortable. If she were free, she probably would be flirting right now. But she wasn't.

Grabbing her jacket and purse, she rose from her seat. "I guess I should get going."

He rose, too. "I'll walk you to your car."

Her heart kicked against her ribs. The vision of a goodnight kiss formed in her brain. The knowledge that she'd be a cheat almost choked her. "There's no reason."

"I know. I know. It's a very peaceful little town. No reason to worry." He smiled. "Still, I've never let a woman walk to her car alone after dark."

Because that made sense, she said, "Okay." Side by side they ambled up the sidewalk to the old, battered green car Louisa had lent her.

When they reached it, she turned to him with a smile. "Thank you for listening to me. I actually feel better."

"Thank you for talking to me. Though I don't mind a little turmoil in the restaurant, I don't want real trouble."

She smiled up at him, caught the gaze of his pretty gray eyes, and felt a connection that warmed her. She didn't often tell anyone the story of her life, but he had really listened. Genuinely cared.

"So you're saying yelling is your way of creating the kind of chaos you want?"

"You make me sound like a control freak."

"You are."

He laughed. "I know."

They gazed into each other's eyes long enough for Dani's heart to begin to thrum. Knowing they were now crossing a line, she tried to pull away, but couldn't. Just when she was about to give one last shot at breaking their contact, he bent his head and kissed her.

Heat swooshed through her on a wave of surprise. Her hands slid up his arms, feeling the strength of him, and met at the back of his neck, where rich, thick hair tickled her knuckles. When he coaxed open her mouth, the taste of wine greeted her, along with a thrill so strong it spiraled through her like a tornado. The urge to press herself against him trembled through her. She'd never felt anything so powerful, so wanton. She stepped closer, enjoying sensations so intense they stole her breath.

His hands trailed from her shoulders, down her back to her bottom and that's when everything became real. What was she doing kissing someone when she had a marriage proposal waiting for her in New York?

CHAPTER FIVE

NOTHING IN RAFE'S life had prepared him for the feeling of his lips against Dani's. He told himself it was absurd for an experienced man to think one kiss different from another, but even as that thought floated to him, her lips moved, shifted, and need burst through him. She wasn't a weak woman, his Dani. She was strong, vital, and she kissed like a woman starving for the touch of a man. The kind of touch he longed to give her. And the affair was back on the table.

Suddenly, Dani jumped back, away from him. "You can't kiss me."

The wildness in her eyes mirrored the roar of need careening through him. The dew of her mouth was sprinkled on his lips. His heart pounded out an unexpected tattoo, and desire spilled through his blood.

He smiled, crossed his arms on his chest and leaned against the old car. "I think I just did."

"The point is you shouldn't kiss me."

"Because we work together?" He glanced to the right. "Bah! You Americans and your puritanical rules."

"Oh, you hate rules? What about commitments? I'm engaged!"

That stopped the need tumbling through him. That stopped the sweet swell of desire. That made him angry that she'd led him on, and feel stupid that he hadn't even suspected that a woman as pretty and cheerful as his Dani would have someone special waiting at home.

"I see."

She took three steps back, moving herself away from her own transportation. "I didn't mean to lead you on." She groaned and took another step back. "I didn't think I *was* leading you on. We were talking like friends."

He shoved off the car. "We were."

"So why'd you kiss me?"

He shrugged, as if totally unaffected, though a witch's brew of emotions careered through him like a runaway roller coaster. "It felt right." Everything about her felt right, which only annoyed him more.

She took another step away from him. "Well, it was wrong."

"If you don't stop your retreat, you're going to end up back in the tavern."

She sucked in a breath.

He opened her car door. "Get in. Go home. We're fine. I don't want you skittering around like some frightened mouse tomorrow. Let's just pretend that little kiss never happened."

He waited, holding open the door for her until he realized she wouldn't go anywhere near her car while he stood beside it. Anger punched up again. Still, keeping control, he moved away.

She sighed with relief and slid into her car.

He calmly started the walk to his condo, but when he got inside the private elevator he punched the closed door, not sure if he was angry with himself for kissing her or angry, *really angry*, that she was engaged. Taken.

He told himself not to care. Were they to have an affair, it would have been short because she was leaving, returning to America.

And even if she wasn't, even if they'd been perfect for

each other, he didn't do relationships. He knew their cost. He knew he couldn't pay it.

When the elevator doors opened again, he stepped out and tossed his keys on a convenient table in the foyer of his totally remodeled condo on the top floor of one of Monte Calanetti's most beautiful pale stone buildings. The quiet closed in on him, but he ignored it. Sometimes the price a man paid for success was his soul. He put everything he had into his meals, his restaurant, his success. He'd almost let one woman steal his dream—he wouldn't be so foolish as to even entertain the thought a second time.

The next day he worked his magic in the kitchen, confident his attraction to Dani had died with the words *I'm engaged*. He didn't stand around on pins and needles awaiting her arrival. He didn't think about her walking into the kitchen. He refused to wonder whether she'd be happy or angry. Or ponder the way he'd like to treat her to a full-course meal, watch the light in her eyes while she enjoyed the food he'd prepare especially for her…

Damn it.

What was he doing thinking about a woman who was engaged?

He walked through the dining room, checking on the tables, opening the shutters on the big windows to reveal the striking view, not at all concerned that she was late, except for how it would impact his restaurant. So when the sound of her bubbly laugher entered the dining room, and his heart stopped, he almost cursed.

Probably not seeing him in the back of the dining room, she teased with Allegra and Gio, a clear sign that the kiss hadn't affected her as much as it had affected him. He remembered the way she'd spoken to him the night before. One minute she was sad, confiding, the next she would say something like, "You should stop that." Putting him in his place. Telling him what to do. And he wondered, really, who had confided in whom the night before?

Walking to the kitchen, he ran his hand along the back of his neck. Had he really told her about his family? Not that it was any great secret, but his practice was to remain aloof. Yet, somehow, wanting to comfort her had bridged that divide and he'd talked about things he normally kept out of relationships with women.

As he approached a prep table, Emory waved a sheet of paper at him. "I've created the schedule for Daniella. I'm giving her two days off. Monday and Tuesday. Two days together, so she can sightsee."

His heart stuttered a bit, but he forced his brain to focus on work. "And just who will seat people on Monday and Tuesday?"

"Allegra has been asking for more hours. I think she'll be fine in the position as a stand-in until, as Daniella suggested, we hire two people to seat customers."

He ignored the comment about Daniella. "Allegra is willing to give up her tips?"

"She's happy with the hourly wage I suggested."

"Great. Fine. Wonderful. Maybe you should deal with staff from now on."

Emory laughed. "This was a one-time thing. A favor to Daniella. I'm a chef, too. I might play second to you, but I'm not a business manager. In fact, you're the one who's going to take this to Dani."

Ignoring the thump of his heart at having to talk to her, Rafe snatched the schedule sheet out of Emory's hands and walked out of the kitchen, into the dining room.

His gaze searched out Dani and when he found her, their eyes met. They'd shared a conversation. They'd shared a kiss. But she belonged to someone else. Any connection he felt to her stopped now.

He broke the eye contact and headed for Allegra.

"Emory tells me you're interested in earning some extra money and you're willing to be Dani's fill-in."

Her eyes brightened. *"Sì."*

"Excellent. You will come in Monday and Tuesday for Dani, then." He felt Dani's gaze burning into him, felt his face redden with color like a schoolboy in the same room with his crush. Ridiculous.

He sucked in a breath, pasted a professional smile on his face and walked over to Dani. He handed the sheet of paper to her. "You wanted a schedule. Here is your schedule."

Her blue eyes rose slowly to meet his. She said, "Thanks."

The blood in his veins slowed to a crawl. The noise in the dining room disappeared. Every nuance of their kiss flooded his memory. Along with profound disappointment that their first kiss would be their last.

He fought the urge to squeeze his eyes shut. Why was he thinking these things about a woman who was taken? All he'd wanted was an affair! Now that he knew they couldn't have one, he should just move on.

"You wanted time off. I am granting you time off."

He turned and walked away, satisfied that he sounded like his normal self. Because he was his normal self. No kiss…no *woman* would change him.

Lunch service began. Within minutes, he was caught up in the business of supervising meal prep. As course after course was served, an unexpected thought came to Rafe. An acknowledgment of something Dani had said. He didn't eat a multicourse lunch. He liked soup and salad. Was Dani right?

Dani worked her shift, struggling to ward off the tightness in her chest every time Rafe came out of the kitchen. Memories of his kiss flooded her. But the moment of pure pleasure had been darkened by the realization that she had a proposal at home…yet she'd kissed another man. And it had been a great kiss. The kind of kiss a woman loses herself in. The kind of kiss that could have swept her off her feet if she wasn't already committed.

She went home in between lunch and dinner and joined Louisa on a walk through the house as she mentally charted everything that needed to be repaired. The overwhelmed villa owner wasn't quite ready to do an actual list. It was as if Louisa needed to get her bearings or begin acclimating to the reality of the property she owned before she could do anything more than clean.

At five, Dani put on the black trousers and white blouse again and returned to the restaurant. The time went more smoothly than the lunch session, mostly because Rafe was too busy to come into the dining room, except when a customer specifically asked to speak with him. When she walked into the kitchen to get him, she kept their exchanges businesslike, and he complied, not straying into more personal chitchat. So when he asked for time with her at the end of the night again, she shivered.

She didn't think he intended to fire her. He'd just given her a schedule. He also wouldn't kiss her again. He seemed to respect the fact that there was another man in the picture, even if she had sort of stretched the truth about being *engaged*. But that was for both of their benefits. She had a proposal waiting. Her life was confusing enough already. There was no point muddying the waters with a fling. No point in leading Rafe on.

She had no idea why he wanted to talk to her, but she decided to be calm about it.

When he walked out of the kitchen, he indicated that she should sit at the bar, while he grabbed a bottle of wine.

After a sip, she smiled. "I like this one."

"So you are a fan of Chianti."

She looked at the wine in the glass, watched how the light wove through it. "I don't know if I'm a fan. But it's good." She took a quiet breath and glanced over at him. "You wanted to talk with me?"

"Today, I saw what you meant about lunch being too much food for some diners."

She turned on her seat, his reply easing her mind enough that she could be comfortable with him. "Really?"

"Yes. We should have a lunch menu. We should offer the customary meals diners expect in Italy, but we should also accommodate those who want smaller lunches."

"So I made a suggestion that you're going to use?"

He caught her gaze. "You're not a stupid woman, Dani. You know that. Otherwise, you wouldn't be so bold in your comments about the restaurant."

She grinned. "I am educated."

He shook his head. "And you have instincts." He picked up his wineglass. "I'd like you to work with me on the few selections we'll add."

Her heart sped up. "Really?"

"Yes. It was your suggestion. I believe you should have some say in the menu."

That made her laugh.

"And what is funny about that?" His voice dripped with incredulity, as if he had no idea how to follow her sometimes. His hazy gray eyes narrowed in annoyance.

She sipped her wine, delaying her answer to torment him. He was always so in control that he was cute when he was baffled. And it was fun to see him try to wrangle himself around it.

Finally she said, "You're not the big, bad wolf you want everybody to believe."

His eyes narrowed a little more as he ran his thumb along his chin. His face was perfect. Sharp angles, clean lines, accented by silvery eyes and dark, dark hair that gave him a dramatic, almost mysterious look.

"I don't mind suggestions to make the business better. Ask Emory. He's had a lot more say than you would think."

She smiled, not sure why he so desperately wanted to cling to his bossy image. "I still say you're not so bad."

* * *

Rafe's blood heated. The urge to flirt with Dani, and then seduce her, roiled like the sea before a storm. He genuinely believed she was too innocent to realize he could take her comments about his work demeanor as flirting, and shift the conversation into something personal. But he also knew they couldn't work together if she continued to be so free with him.

"Be careful what you say, little Dani, and how you take our conversations. Because I am bad. I am not the gentleman you might be accustomed to. Though I respect your engagement, if you don't, I'll take that as permission to do whatever I want. You can't have a fiancé at home and free rein to flirt here."

Her eyes widened. But he didn't give her a chance to comment. He grabbed the pad and pencil he'd brought to the bar and said, "So what should we add to this lunch menu you want?"

She licked her lips, took a slow breath as if shifting her thoughts to the task at hand and said, "Antipasto and minestrone soup. That's obvious. But you could add a garden salad, club sandwich, turkey sandwich and hamburgers." She slowly met his gaze. "That way you're serving a need without going overboard."

With the exception of the hamburger, which made him wince, he agreed. "I can put my own spin on all of these, use the ingredients we already have on hand, redo the menu tonight and we'll be ready to go tomorrow."

She gaped at him. "Tomorrow? Wow."

He rose. "This is my business, Dani. If a suggestion is good, there is no point waiting forever. I get things done. Go home. I will see you tomorrow."

She walked to the door, and he headed for the kitchen where he could watch her leave from the window above the sink, making sure nothing happened to her. No matter how hard he tried to stop it, disappointment rose up in him. At the very least, it would have been nice to finish a glass of wine with her.

But he couldn't.

Dani ran to her car, her blood simmering, her nerve endings taut. They might have had a normal conversation about his menu. She might have even left him believing she was okay with everything he'd said and they were back to normal. But she couldn't forget his declaration that he was bad. It should have scared her silly. Instead, it tempted her. She'd never been attracted to a man who was clearly all wrong for her, a man with whom she couldn't have a future. Everything she did was geared toward security. Everything about him spelled danger.

So why was he so tempting?

Walking into the kitchen of Louisa's run-down villa, she found her friend sitting at the table with a cup of tea.

Louisa smiled as she entered. "Can I get you a cup?"

She squeezed her eyes shut. "I don't know."

Louisa rose. "What's wrong? You're shaking."

She dropped to one of the chairs at the round table. "Rafe and I had a little chat after everyone was gone."

"Did he fire you?"

"I think I might have welcomed that."

Louisa laughed. "You need a cup of tea." She walked to the cupboard, retrieved the tin she'd bought in the village, along with enough groceries for the two of them, and ran water into the kettle. "So what did he say?"

"He told me to be careful where I took our conversations."

"Are you insulting him again?"

"He danced around it a bit, but he thinks I'm flirting with him."

Eyes wide, Louisa turned from the stove. "Are you?"

Dani pressed her lips together before she met Louisa's gaze. "Not intentionally. You know I have a fiancé."

"Sounds like you're going to have to change the way you act around Rafe, then. Treat him the way he wants to be treated, like a boss you respect. Mingle with the waitstaff. Enjoy your job. But stay away from him."

The next day, Rafe stacked twenty-five black leather folders containing the new menus on the podium for Dani to distribute when she seated customers.

An hour later, she entered the kitchen, carrying them. Her smile as radiant as the noonday sun, she said, "These look great."

Rafe nodded, moving away from her, reminding himself that she was engaged to another man. "As I told you last night, this is a business. Good ideas are always welcome."

Emory peeked around Rafe. "And, please, if you have any more ideas, don't hesitate to offer them."

Rafe said, "Bah," and walked away. But he saw his old, bald friend wink at Dani as if they were two conspirators. At first, he was comforted that Emory had also succumbed to Dani's charms, but he knew that was incorrect. Emory liked Dani as a person. While Rafe wanted to sleep with her. But as long as he reminded himself his desires were wrong, he could control them.

Customer response to the lunch menu was astounding. Dani took no credit for the new offerings and referred comments and compliments to him. Still, she was in the spotlight everywhere he went. Customers loved her. The waitstaff deferred to her. Her smile lit the dining room. Her laughter floated on the air. And he was glad when she said goodbye at the end of the day, if only so he could get some peace.

Monday morning, he arrived at the restaurant and breathed in the scent of the business he called home. Today would be a good day because Dani was off. For two glorious days he would not have to watch his words, watch where his eyes went or control hormones he didn't understand. Plus, her having two days off was a great way to transition his thoughts away from her as a person and to her as an employee.

And who knew? Maybe Allegra would work so well as a hostess that he could actually cut Dani's hours even more. Not in self-preservation over his unwanted attraction, but because this was a business. He was the boss. And the atmosphere of the restaurant would go back to normal.

As Emory supervised the kitchen, Rafe interviewed two older gentlemen for Dani's job. Neither was suitable, but he comforted himself with the knowledge that this was only his first attempt at finding her replacement. He had other interviews scheduled for that afternoon and the next day. He *would* replace her.

Allegra arrived on time to open for lunch. Because they were enjoying an unexpected warm spell, he opened the windows and let the breeze spill in. The scents of rich Tuscan foods drifted from the kitchen. And just as Rafe expected, suddenly, all became right with the world.

Until an hour later when he heard a clang and a clatter from the dining room. He set down his knife and stormed out. Gio had dropped a tray of food when Allegra had knocked into her.

"What is this?" he asked, his hands raised in confusion. "You navigate around each other every day. Now, today, you didn't see her?"

Allegra stooped to help Gio pick up the broken dishes. "I'm sorry. It's just nerves. I was turned away, talking to the customer and didn't watch where I was going."

"Bah! Nerves. Get your head on straight!"

Allegra nodded quickly and Rafe returned to the kitchen. He summoned the two busboys to the dining room to clean up the mess and everything went back to normal.

Except customers didn't take to Allegra. She was sweet, but she wasn't fun. She wasn't chatty. A lifelong resident, she didn't see Italy through the eyes of someone who loved it with the passion and intensity of a newcomer as Dani did.

One customer even asked for her. Rafe smiled and said she had a day off. The customer asked for the next shift she'd be working so he could return and tell her of his trip to Venice.

"She'll be back on Wednesday," Rafe said. He tried to pretend he didn't feel the little rise in his heart at the thought of her return, but he'd felt it. After only a few hours, he missed her.

CHAPTER SIX

AND SHE MISSED HIM.

The scribbled notes of things she remembered her foster mother telling her about her Italian relatives hadn't helped her to find them. But Dani discovered stepping stones to people who knew people who knew people who would ultimately get her to the ones she wanted.

Several times she found herself wondering how Rafe would handle the situation. Would he ask for help? What would he say? And she realized she missed him. She didn't mind his barking. He'd shown her a kinder side. She remembered the conversation in which he'd told her about his family. She loved that he'd taken her suggestion about a lunch menu. But most of all, she replayed that kiss over and over and over in her head, worried because she couldn't even remember her first kiss with Paul.

Steady, stable Paul hadn't ever kissed her like Rafe had. Ever. But he had qualities Rafe didn't have. Stability being number one. He was an accountant at a bank, for God's sake. A man did not get any more stable than that. She'd already had a life of confusion and adventure of a sort, when she was plucked from one foster home and dropped in another. She didn't want confusion or danger or adventure. She wanted stability.

That night when she called Paul, he immediately asked

when she was returning. Her heart lifted a bit hearing that. "I hate talking on the phone."

It was the most romantic thing he'd ever said to her. Until he added, "I'd rather just wait until you get home to talk."

"Oh."

"Now, don't get pouty. You know you have a tendency to talk too much."

She *was* chatty.

"Anyway, I'm at work. I've got to go."

"Oh. Okay."

"Call me from your apartment when you get home."

She frowned. Home? Did he not want to talk to her for an entire month? "Aren't you going to pick me up at the airport?"

"Maybe, but you'll probably be getting in at rush hour or something. Taking a taxi would be easier, wouldn't it? We'll see how the time works out."

"I guess that makes sense."

"Good. Gotta run."

Even as she disconnected the call, she thought of Rafe. She couldn't see him telling his almost fiancée to call when she arrived at her apartment after nearly seven months without seeing each other. He'd race to the airport, grab her in baggage claim and kiss her senseless.

Her breath vanished when she pictured the scene, and she squeezed her eyes shut. She really could not think like that. She absolutely couldn't start comparing Paul and Rafe. Especially not when it came to passion. Poor sensible Paul would always suffer by comparison.

Plus, her feelings for Rafe were connected to the rush of pleasure she got from finding a place in his restaurant, being more than useful, offering ideas a renowned chef had implemented. For a former foster child, having somebody give her a sense of worth and value was like gold.

And that's all it was. Attraction to his good looks and

appreciation that he recognized and told her she was doing a good job.

She did not want him.

Really.

She needed somebody like Paul.

Though she knew that was true, it didn't sit right. She couldn't stop thinking about the way he didn't want to pick her up at the airport, how he'd barely had two minutes to talk to her and how he'd told her not to call again.

She tried to read, tried to chat with Louisa about the house, but in the end, she knew she needed to get herself out of the house or she'd make herself crazy.

She told Louisa she was going for a drive and headed into town.

Antsy, unable to focus, and afraid he was going to royally screw something up and disappoint a customer, Rafe turned Mancini's over to Emory.

"It's not like you to leave so early."

"It's already eight o'clock." Rafe shrugged into his black wool coat. "Maybe too many back-to-back days have made me tired."

Emory smiled. "Ah, so maybe like Dani, you need a day off?"

Buttoning his coat, he ignored the dig and walked to the back door. "I'll see you tomorrow."

But as he was driving through town, he saw the ugly green car Dani drove sitting at the tavern again. The last time she'd been there had been the day he'd inadvertently insulted her. She didn't seem like the type to frequent taverns, so what if she was upset again?

His heart gave a kick and he whipped his SUV into a parking place, raced across the quiet street and entered the tavern to find her at the same table she'd been at before.

He walked over. She glanced up.

Hungrier for the sight of her than was wise, he held her

gaze as he slid onto the chair across from her. "So this is how you spend your precious time off."

She shook her head. "Don't start."

He hadn't meant to be argumentative. In fact that was part of their problem. There was no middle with them. They either argued or lusted after each other. Given that he was her boss and she was engaged, both were wrong.

The bartender ambled over. He set a coaster in front of Rafe with a sigh. "You want another bottle of that fancy wine?"

Rafe shook his head and named one of the beers on tap before he pointed to Dani's glass. "And another of whatever she's having."

As the bartender walked away, she said, "You don't have to buy me a beer."

"I'm being friendly because I think we need to find some kind of balance." He was tired of arguing, but he also couldn't go on thinking about her all the time. The best way to handle both would be to classify their relationship as a friendship. Tonight, he could get some questions answered, get to know her and see that she was just like everybody else. Not somebody special. Then they could both go back to normal.

"Balance?"

He shrugged. Leaning back, he anchored his arm across the empty chair beside him. "We're either confiding like people who want to become lovers, or we fight."

She turned her beer glass nervously. "That's true."

"So, we drink a beer together. We talk about inconsequential things, and Wednesday when you return to Mancini's, no one snipes."

She laughed.

He smiled. "What did you do today?"

"I went to the town where my foster mother's relatives lived."

His beer arrived. Waiting for her to elaborate, he took

a sip. Then another. When she didn't say anything else, he asked, "So did you find them?"

"Not yet. But I will."

Her smooth skin virtually glowed. Her blue eyes met his. Interest and longing swam through him. He ignored both in favor of what now seemed to be a good mission. Becoming friends. Finding a middle ground where they weren't fighting or lusting, but a place where they could coexist.

"What did you do today?"

"Today I created a lasagna that should have made customers die from pleasure."

She laughed. "Exaggerate much?"

He pointed a finger at her. "It's not an exaggeration. It's confidence."

"Ah."

"You don't like confidence?"

She studied his face. "Maybe it's more that I don't trust it."

"What's to trust? I love to cook, to make people happy, to surprise them with something wonderful. But I didn't just open a door to my kitchen and say, come eat this. I went to school. I did apprenticeships. My confidence is in my teachers' ability to take me to the next level as much as it is in my ability to learn, and then do."

Her head tilted. "So it's not all about you."

He laughed, shook his head. "Where do you get these ideas?"

"You're kind of arrogant."

He batted his hand. "Arrogant? Confident? Who cares as long as the end result is good?"

"I guess…"

"I know." He took another sip of beer, watching as she slid her first drink—which he assumed was warm—aside and reached for the second glass he'd bought for her. "Not much of a drinker?"

"No."

"So what are you?"

She laughed. "Is this how you become friends with someone?"

"Conversation is how everyone becomes friends."

"I thought it was shared experience."

"We don't have time for shared experience. If we want to become friends by Wednesday we need to take shortcuts."

She inclined her head as if agreeing.

He waited. When she said nothing, he reframed his question. "So you are happy teaching?"

"I'm a good teacher."

"But you are not happy?"

"I'm just not sure people are supposed to be happy."

He blinked. That was the very last thing he'd expected to hear from his bubbly hostess. "Seriously?"

She met his gaze. "Yeah. I think we're meant to be content. I think we're meant to find a spot and fill it. But happy? That's reserved for big events or holidays."

For thirty seconds, he wished she were staying in Italy. He wished he had time enough to show her the sights, teach her the basics of cooking, make her laugh, show her what happiness was. But that wasn't the mission. The mission was to get to know her just enough that they would stop arguing.

"This from my happy, upbeat hostess?"

She met his gaze again. "I thought we weren't going to talk about work."

"We're talking about you, not work."

She picked up her beer glass. "Maybe this isn't the best time to talk about me."

Which only filled him with a thousand questions. When she was at Mancini's she was usually joyful. After a day off, she was as sad as the day he'd hurt her feelings? It made no sense…unless he believed that she loved working in his restaurant enough that it filled her with joy.

That made his pulse jump, made his mind race with thoughts he wasn't supposed to have. So he rose.

"Okay. Talking is done. We'll try shared experience." He pointed behind her. "We'll play darts."

Clearly glad they'd no longer be talking, she laughed. "Good."

"So you play darts at home in New York?"

She rose and followed him to the board hung on a back wall. They passed the quiet pool table, and he pulled some darts from the corkboard beside the dartboard.

"No, I don't play darts."

"Great. So we play for money?"

She laughed again. "No! We'll play for fun."

He sighed as if put out. "Too bad."

But as they played, she began to talk about her search for her foster mother's family. Her voice relaxed. Her smile returned. And Rafe was suddenly glad he'd found her. Not for his mission to make her his friend. But because she was alone. And in spite of her contention that people weren't supposed to be happy, her normal state was happy. He'd seen that every day at the restaurant. But something had made her sad tonight.

Reminded of the way he had made her sad by saying she wasn't needed, he redoubled his efforts to make her smile.

It was easy for Dani to dismiss the significance of Rafe finding her in the bar. They lived in a small town. He didn't have a whole hell of a lot of choices for places to stop after work. So she wouldn't let her crazy brain tell her it was sweet that he'd found her. She'd call it what it was. Lack of options.

Playing darts with her, Rafe was kind and polite, but not sexy. At least not deliberately sexy. There were some things a really handsome man couldn't control. So she didn't think he was coming on to her when he swaggered over to pull the darts from the board after he threw them. She didn't think he was trying to entice her when he laughed at her poor attempts at hitting the board. And she absolutely made nothing of it when he stood behind her, took her arm and showed her the motion she needed to make to get the dart going in the right direction.

Even though she could smell him, feel the heat of his body as he brushed up against her back, and feel the vibrations of his warm whisper as he pulled her arm back and demonstrated how to aim, she knew he meant nothing by any of it. He just wanted to be friends.

When their third beer was gone and the hour had gotten late, she smiled at him. "Thank you. That was fun."

His silver eyes became serious. "You were happy?"

She shook her head at his dog-with-a-bone attitude. "Sort of. Yes. It was a happy experience."

He sniffed and walked back to their table to retrieve his coat. "Everyone is made to be happy."

She didn't believe that. Though she liked her life and genuinely liked people, she didn't believe her days were supposed to be one long party. But she knew it was best not to argue. She joined him at their table and slipped into her coat.

"I'll walk you to your car."

She shook her head. "No." Their gazes caught. "I'm fine."

He dipped his head in a quick nod, agreeing, and she walked out into the cold night. Back into the world where her stable fiancé wouldn't even pick her up at the airport.

CHAPTER SEVEN

WHEN DANI ENTERED the restaurant on Wednesday ten minutes before the start of her shift, Rafe stood by the bar, near the kitchen. As if he'd sensed her arrival, he turned. Their gazes caught. Dani's heart about pounded its way out of her chest. She reminded herself that though they'd spent an enjoyable evening together playing darts at the tavern, for him it had been about becoming friends. He hadn't made any passes at her—though he'd had plenty of chances— and he'd made a very good argument for why being friends was a wise move for them.

Still, when he walked toward her, her heart leaped. But he passed the podium to unlock the front door. As he turned to return to the kitchen, he said, "Good morning."

She cleared her throat, hoping to rid it of the fluttery feeling floating through her at being in the same room with him. Especially since they were supposed to be friends now. Nothing more. "Good morning."

"How did your search go for your foster mother's relatives yesterday?"

She shook her head. "Still haven't found them, but I got lots of information from people who had been their neighbors. Most believe they moved to Rome."

"Rome?" He shook his head. "No kidding."

"Their former neighbors said something about one of

their kids getting a job there and the whole family wanting to stay together."

"Nice. Family should stay together."

"I agree."

She turned to the podium. He walked to the kitchen. But she couldn't help thinking that while Paul hadn't said a word about her quest for Rosa's family, Rafe had immediately asked. Like someone who cared about her versus someone who didn't.

She squeezed her eyes shut and told herself not to think like that. They were *friends. Only friends.*

But all day, she was acutely aware of him. Anytime she retrieved him to escort him to a table, she felt him all around her. Her skin tingled. Everything inside her turned soft and feminine.

At the end of the night, the waitstaff and kitchen help disappeared like rats on a sinking ship. Rafe ambled to the bar, pulled a bottle of wine from the rack behind it.

The Chianti. The wine he'd ordered for them at the tavern.

Her heart trembled. She'd told him she liked that wine.

Was he asking her to stay now? To share another bottle of the wine she'd said she liked?

Longing filled her and she paused by the podium. When he didn't even look in her direction, she shuffled a bit, hoping the movement would cause him to see her and invite her to stay.

He kept his gaze on a piece of paper sitting on the bar in front of him. Still, she noticed a second glass by the bottle. He had poured wine in one glass but the other was empty—yet available.

She bit her lip. Was that glass an accident? An oversight? Or was that glass her invitation?

She didn't know. And things were going so well between

them professionally that she didn't want to make a mistake that took them back to an uncomfortable place.

Still, they'd decided to be friends. Wouldn't a friend want another friend to share a glass of wine at the end of the night?

She drew in a slow breath. She had one final way to get him to notice her and potentially invite her to sit with him. If he didn't take this hint, then she would leave.

Slowly, cautiously, she called, "Good night."

He looked over. He hesitated a second, but only a second, before he said, "Good night."

Disappointment stopped her breathing. Nonetheless, she smiled and headed for the door. She walked to Louisa's beat-up old car, got in, slid the key in the ignition…

And lowered her head to the steering wheel.

She wanted to talk to him. She wanted to tell him about the countryside she'd seen as she looked for Rosa's relatives. She longed to tell him about the meals she'd eaten. She yearned to ask him how the restaurant had been the two days she was gone. She needed to get not just the cursory answers he'd given her but the real in-depth stuff. Like a friend.

But she also couldn't lie to herself. She wanted that crazy feeling he inspired in her. Lust or love, hormones or genuine attraction, she had missed that feeling. She'd missed *him*. No matter how much she told herself she just wanted to be his friend, it was a lie.

A light tapping on her window had her head snapping up.

Rafe.

She quickly lowered the window to see what he wanted.

"Are you okay?"

Her heart swelled, then shrank and swelled again. Everything he did confused her. Everything she felt around him confused her even more.

"Are you ill?"

She shook her head.

Damn it. She squeezed her eyes shut and decided to just go with the truth. "I saw you with the wine and thought I should have joined you." She caught the gaze of his smoky-gray eyes. "You said we were going to be friends. And I was hoping you sitting at the bar with a bottle of wine was an invitation."

He stepped back. She'd never particularly thought of a chef's uniform as being sexy, but he'd taken off the jacket, revealing a white T-shirt that outlined muscles and a flat stomach. Undoubtedly hot from working in the kitchen, he didn't seem bothered by the cold night air.

"I always have a glass of wine at the end of the night."

So, her instincts had been wrong. If she'd just started her car and driven off, she wouldn't be embarrassed right now. "Okay. Good."

He glanced down into the car at her. "But I wouldn't have minded company."

Embarrassment began to slide away, only to be replaced by the damnable confusion. "Oh."

"I simply don't steal women who belong to other men."

"It wouldn't be stealing if we were talking about work, becoming friends like you said we should."

"That night was a one-time thing. A way to get to know each other so we could stop aggravating each other."

"So we're really not friends?"

He laughed and glanced away at the beautiful starlit sky. "We're now friendly enough to work together. Men only try to become 'real' friends so that they can ultimately become lovers."

The way he said *lovers* sent a wave of yearning skittering along her nerve endings. It suddenly became difficult to breathe.

He caught her gaze again. "I've warned you before to be careful with me, Dani. I'm not a man who often walks away from what he wants."

"Wow. You are one honest guy."

He laughed. "Usually I wouldn't care. I'd muscle my way into your life and take what I wanted. But you're different. You're innocent."

"I sort of liked being different until you added the part about me being innocent."

"You are."

"Well, yeah. Sort of." She tossed her hands in exasperation, the confusion and longing getting the better of her. "But you make it sound like a disease."

"It's not. It's actually a quality men look for in a woman they want to keep."

Her heart fluttered again. "Oh?"

"Don't get excited about that. I'm not the kind of guy who commits. I like short-term relationships because I don't like complications. I'm attracted to you, yes, but I also know myself. My commitment to the restaurant comes before any woman." He forced her gaze to his again. "This thing I feel for you is wrong. So as much as I wanted you to take the hint tonight and share a bottle of wine with me, I also hoped you wouldn't. I don't want to hurt you."

"We could always talk about the restaurant."

"About how you were missed? How a customer actually asked for you?"

She laughed. "See? That's all great stuff. Neutral stuff."

"I suppose you also wouldn't be opposed to hearing that Emory thinks that after the success of your lunch menu, we should encourage you to make suggestions."

Pride flooded her. "Well, I'll do my best to think of new things."

He glanced at the stars again. Their conversation had run its course. He stood in the cold. She sat in a car that could be warm if she'd started the darn thing. But the air between them was anything but cool, and she suddenly realized they were kidding themselves if they believed they could be just friends.

He looked down and smiled slightly. "Good night, Dani."

He didn't wait for her to say good-night. He walked away.

She sat there for a few seconds, tingling, sort of breathless, but knowing he was right. They couldn't be friends and they couldn't have a fling. She *was* innocent and he would hurt her. And though technically she'd stretched the truth about being engaged, it was saving her heartbreak.

After starting her car, she pulled out, watching in the rearview mirror as he revved the engine of his big SUV and followed her to Monte Calanetti.

Though Dani dressed in her usual black trousers and white blouse the next morning, she took extra care when she ironed them, making them crisper, their creases sharper, so she looked more professional when she arrived at the restaurant.

Rafe spoke sparingly. It wasn't long before she realized that unless she had a new idea to discuss, they wouldn't interact beyond his thank-you when she introduced him to a customer who wanted to compliment the chef.

She understood. Running into each other at the tavern the first time and talking out their disagreement, then playing darts the second, had made them friendly enough that they no longer sniped. But having minimal contact with her was how he would ignore their attraction. They weren't right for each other and, older, wiser, he was sparing them both. But that didn't really stop her attraction to him.

To keep herself from thinking about Rafe on Friday, she studied the customer seating, the china and silverware, the interactions of the waitresses with the customers, but didn't come up with an improvement good enough to suggest to him.

A thrill ran through her at the knowledge that he took her ideas so seriously. Here she was, an educated but simple girl from Brooklyn, being taken seriously by a lauded European chef.

The sense of destiny filled her again, along with Rafe's comment about happiness. This time her thoughts made her gasp. What if this feeling of rightness wasn't about Rafe or Italy? What if this sense of being where she belonged was actually telling her the truth about her career choice? She loved teaching, but it didn't make her feel she belonged the way being a part of this restaurant did. And maybe this sense of destiny was simply trying to point her in the direction of a new career when she returned to the United States?

The thought relieved her. Life was so much simpler when the sense of destiny was something normal, like an instinct for the restaurant business, rather than longing for her boss—a guy she shouldn't even be flirting with when she had a marriage proposal waiting for her at home.

Emory came to the podium and interrupted her thoughts. "These are the employee phone numbers. Gio called off sick for tonight's shift. I'd like you to call in a replacement."

She glanced up at him. "Who should I call?"

He smiled. "Your choice. Being out here all the time, you know who works better with whom."

After calling Zola, she walked back to the kitchen to return the list.

Emory shook his head. "This is your responsibility now. A new job for you, while you're here, to make my life a little easier."

She smiled. "Okay."

Without looking at her, Rafe said, "We'd also like you to begin assigning tasks to the busboys. After you say goodbye to a guest, we'd like you to come in and get the busboys. That will free up the waitresses a bit."

The feeling of destiny swelled in her again. The new tasks felt like a promotion, and there wasn't a person in the world who didn't like being promoted.

When Rafe refused to look at her, she winked at Emory. "Okay."

Walking back to the dining room, she fought the feeling that her destiny, her gift, was for this particular restaurant. Especially since, when returning to New York, she'd start at the bottom of any dining establishment she chose to work, and that would be a problem since she'd only make minimum wage. At Mancini's, she only needed to earn extra cash. In New York, would a job as a hostess support her?

The next day, Lazare, one of the busboys, called her "Miss Daniella." The shift from Dani to Miss Daniella caught on in the kitchen and the show of respect had Daniella's shoulders straightening with confidence. When she brought Rafe out for a compliment from a customer, even he said, "Thank you, Miss Daniella," and her heart about popped out of her chest with pride.

That brought her back to the suspicion that her sense of destiny wasn't for the restaurant business, but for *this* restaurant and these people. If she actually got a job at a restaurant in New York, she couldn't expect the staff there to treat her this well.

Realizing all her good fortune would stop when she left Mancini's, her feeling of the "destiny" of belonging in the restaurant business fizzled. She would go home to a tiny apartment, a man whose marriage proposal had scared her and a teaching position that suddenly felt boring.

"Miss Daniella," Gio said as she approached the podium later that night. "The gentleman at table two would like to speak to the chef."

She said it calmly, but there was an undercurrent in her voice, as if subtly telling Daniella that this was a problem situation, not a compliment.

She smiled and said, "Thank you, Gio. I'll handle it."

She walked over to the table.

The short, stout man didn't wait for Dani to speak. He immediately said, "My manicotti was dry and tasteless."

Daniella inclined her head in acknowledgment of his comment. "I'm sorry. I'm not sure what happened. I'll tell the kitchen staff."

"I want to talk to the chef."

His loud, obnoxious voice carried to the tables around him. Daniella peeked behind her at the kitchen door, then glanced at the man again. The restaurant had finally freed itself of people curious about Rafe's temper. The seats had filled with customers eager to taste his food. She would not let his reputation be ruined by a beady-eyed little man who probably wanted a free dinner.

"We're extremely busy tonight," she told the gentleman as she looped her fingers around his biceps and gently urged him to stand. "So rather than a chat with the chef, what if I comp your dinner?"

His eyes widened, then returned to normal, as if he couldn't believe he was getting what he wanted so easily. "You'll pay my tab?"

She smiled. "The whole meal." A quick glance at the table told her that would probably be the entire day's wage, but it would be worth it to avoid a scene.

"I'd like dessert."

"We'll get it for you to go." She nodded to Gio, who quickly put two slices of cake into a take-out container and within seconds the man and his companion were gone.

Rafe watched from the sliver of a crack he created when he pushed open the kitchen door a notch. He couldn't hear what Dani said, but he could see her calm demeanor, her smiles, the gentle but effective way she removed the customer from Rafe's dining room without the other patrons being any the wiser.

He laughed and Emory walked over.

"What's funny?"

"Dani just kicked somebody out."

Emory's eyes widened. "We had a scene?"

"That's the beauty of it. Even though he started off yell-ing, she got him out without causing even a ripple of trou-ble. I'll bet the people at the adjoining tables weren't even aware of what was happening beyond his initial grousing."

"She is worth her weight in gold."

Rafe pondered that. "Gio made the choice to get her rather than come to me."

Emory said, "She trusts Dani."

He walked away, leaving Rafe with that simple but loaded thought.

At the end of the night, the waitstaff quickly finished their cleanup and began leaving before the kitchen staff. Rafe glanced at the bar, thought about a glass of wine and decided against it. Instead, he walked to the podium as Dani collected her purse.

He waited for the waitresses on duty to leave before he faced Dani.

"You did very well tonight."

"Thank you."

"I saw you get rid of the irate customer."

She winced. "I had to offer to pay for his meal."

"I'll take care of that."

Her gaze met his, tripping the weird feeling in his chest again.

"Really?"

"Yes." He sucked in a breath, reminding himself he didn't want the emotions she inspired in him. He wanted a good hostess. He didn't want a fling with another man's woman.

"I trust your judgment. If not charging for his food avoided a scene, I'm happy to absorb the cost."

"Thanks."

He glanced away, then looked back at her. "Your duties just keep growing."

"Is this your subtle way of telling me I overstepped?"

He shook his head. "You take work that Emory and I would have to do. Things we truly do not have time for."

"Which is good?"

"Yes. Very good." He gazed into her pretty blue eyes and fought the desire to kiss her that crept up before he could stop it. His restaurant was becoming exactly what he'd envisioned because of her. Because she knew how to direct diners' attention and mood. It was as if they were partners in his venture and though the businessman in him desperately fought his feelings for her, the passionate part of him wanted to lift her off the ground, swing her around and kiss her ardently.

But that was wrong for so many reasons that he got angry with himself for even considering it.

"I was thinking tonight that a differentiation between you and the waitresses would be good. It would be a show of authority."

"You want me to wear a hat?"

He laughed. Was it any wonder he was so drawn to her? No one could so easily catch him off guard. Make him laugh. Make him wish for a life that included a little more fun.

"I want you to wear something other than the dark trousers and white blouses the waitresses wear. Your choice," he said when her face turned down with a puzzled frown. "A dress. A suit. Anything that makes you look like you're in charge."

Her gaze rose to meet his. "In charge?"

"Of the dining room." He laughed lightly. "You still have a few weeks before I give you my job."

She laughed, too.

But when her laughter died, they were left gazing into each other's eyes. The mood shifted from happy and businesslike to something he couldn't define or describe. The click of connection he always felt with her filled him. It was hot and sweet, but pointless, leaving an emptiness in the pit of his stomach.

He said, "Good night, Dani," and walked away, into the kitchen and directly to the window over the sink. A minute later, he watched her amble across the parking lot to her car, start it and drive off, making sure she had no trouble.

Then he locked the restaurant and headed to his SUV.

He might forever remember the joy in her blue eyes when he told her that he wanted her to look like the person of authority in the dining room.

But as he climbed into his vehicle, his smile faded. Here he was making her happy, giving her promotions, authority, and just when he should have been able to kiss her to celebrate, he'd had to pull back…because she was taken.

Was he crazy to keep her on, to continually promote her, to need her for his business when it was clear that there was no chance of a relationship between them?

Was he being a sucker?

Was she using him?

Bah! What the hell was he doing? Thinking about things that didn't matter? The woman was leaving in a few weeks. And that was the real reason he should worry about depending on her. Soon she would be gone. So why were he and Emory leaning on her?

Glad he had more maître d' interviews scheduled for the following Monday, he started his car and roared out of the parking lot. He would use what he had learned about Dani's duties for his new maître d'. But he wouldn't give her any more authority.

And he absolutely would stop all thoughts about wanting to swing her around, kiss her and enjoy their success. It was not "their" success. It was his.

It was also her choice to have no part in it.

Sunday morning, Dani arrived at the restaurant in a slim cream-colored dress. She had curled her hair and pinned it in a bundle on top of her head. When Rafe saw her his jaw fell.

She looked regal, sophisticated. Perfect as the face of his business.

Emory whistled. "My goodness."

Rafe's breath stuttered into his lungs. He reminded himself of his thoughts from the night before. She was leaving. She wanted no part in his long-term success. He and Emory were depending on her too much for someone who had no plans to stay.

But most of all, leaving was her choice.

She didn't want him or his business in her life. She was here only for some money so she could find the relatives of her foster mother.

The waitresses tittered over how great she looked. Emory walked to the podium, took her hands and kissed both of her cheeks. The busboys blushed every time she was near.

She handled it with a cool grace that spoke of dignity and sophistication. Exactly what he wanted as the face of Mancini's. As if she'd read his mind.

Laughing with Allegra, she said, "I feel like I'm playing dress up. These are Louisa's clothes. I don't own anything so pretty."

Allegra sighed with appreciation. "Well, they're perfect for you and your new position."

She laughed again. "Rafe and Emory only promoted me because I have time on my hands in between customers. While you guys are hustling, I'm sort of looking around, figuring things out." She leaned in closer. "Besides, the extra authority doesn't come with more money."

As Allegra laughed, Rafe realized that was true. Unless Dani was a power junkie, she wasn't getting anything out of her new position except more work.

So why did she look so joyful in a position she'd be leaving in a few weeks?

Sunday lunch was busier than normal. Customers came in, ate, chatted with Dani and left happy.

Which relieved Rafe and also caused him to internally scold himself for distrusting her. He didn't know why she'd taken such an interest in his restaurant, but he should be glad she had.

She didn't leave for the space between the last lunch customer and the first dinner customer because the phone never stopped ringing.

Again, Rafe relaxed a bit. She had good instincts. Now that his restaurant was catching on, there were more dinner reservations. She stayed to take them. She was a good, smart employee. Any mistrust he had toward her had to be residual bad feelings over not being able to pursue her when he so desperately wanted to. His fault. Not hers.

In fact, part of him believed he should apologize. Or maybe not apologize. Since she couldn't see inside his brain and know the crazy thoughts he'd been thinking, a compliment would work better.

He walked out of the kitchen to the podium and smiled when he saw she was on the phone. Their reservations for that night would probably be their best ever.

"So we're talking about a hundred people."

Rafe's eyebrows rose. A hundred people? He certainly hoped that wasn't a single reservation for that night. Yes, there was a private room in which he could probably seat a hundred, but because that room was rarely used, those tables and chairs needed to be wiped down. Extra linens would have to be ordered from their vendor. Not to mention enough food. He needed advance warning to serve a hundred people over their normal customer rate.

He calmed himself. She didn't know that the room hadn't been used in months and would need a good dusting. Or about the linens. Or the extra food. Once he told her, they could discuss the limits on reservations.

When she finally replaced the receiver on the phone, her blue eyes glowed.

Need rose inside him. Once again he fought the unwanted urge to share the joy of success with her. No matter how he sliced it, she was a big part of building his clientele. And rather than worry about her leaving, a smart businessman would be working to entice her to stay. To make *his* business *her* career, and Italy her new home.

Romantic notions quickly replaced his business concerns. If she made Italy her home, she might just leave her fiancé in America, and he could—

Realizing he wasn't just getting ahead of himself, he was going in the wrong direction, he forced himself to be professional. "It sounds like you got us a huge reservation."

"Better."

He frowned. "Better? How does something get better than a hundred guests for dinner?"

She grinned. "By catering a wedding! They don't even need our dishes and utensils. The venue is providing that. All they want is food. And for you that's easy."

Rafe blinked. "What?"

"Okay, it's like this. A customer came in yesterday. The dinner they chose was what his wife wanted to be served for their daughter's wedding at the end of the month. When they ate your meal, they knew they wanted you to cook food for their daughter's wedding. The bride's dad called, I took down the info," she said, handing him a little slip. "And now we have a new arm of your business."

Anything romantic he felt for Dani shrank back against the rising tide of red-hot anger.

"I am not a caterer."

He controlled his voice, didn't yell, didn't pounce. But he saw recognition come to Dani's eyes. She might have only worked with him almost two weeks, but she knew him.

Her fingers fluttered to her throat. "I thought you'd be pleased."

"I have a business plan. I have Michelin stars to protect. I will not send my food out into the world for God knows who to do God knows what with it."

She swallowed. "You could go to the wedding—"

"And leave the restaurant?"

She sucked in a breath.

"Call them back and tell them you checked with me and we can't deliver."

"But...I..." She swallowed again. "They needed a commitment. Today. I gave our word."

He gaped at her. "You promised something without asking me?" It was the cardinal sin. The unforgivable sin. Promising something that hadn't been approved because she'd never consulted the boss. Every employee knew that. She hadn't merely overstepped. She'd gone that one step too far.

Her voice was a mere whisper when she said, "Yes."

Anger mixed with incredulity at her presumptuousness, and he didn't hesitate. With his dream in danger, he didn't even have to think about it. "You're fired."

CHAPTER EIGHT

"Leave now."

Dani's breaths came in quick, shallow puffs. No one wanted to be fired. But right at that moment she wasn't concerned about her loss. Her real upset came from failing Rafe. She'd thought he'd be happy with the added exposure. Instead, she'd totally misinterpreted the situation. Contrary to her success in the dining room, she wasn't a chef. She didn't know a chef's concerns. She had no real restaurant experience.

Still, she had instincts—

Didn't she?

"I'll fix this."

He turned away. "This isn't about fixing the problem. This is about you truly overstepping this time. I don't know if it's because we've had personal conversations or because to this point all of your ideas have been good. But no one, absolutely no one, makes such an important decision without my input. You are fired."

He walked into the kitchen without looking back. Dani could have followed him, maybe even should have followed him, but the way he walked away hurt so much she couldn't move. She could barely breathe. Not because she'd angered him over a mistake, but because he was so cool. So distant. So deliberate and so sure that he wanted her gone. As if their evenings at the tavern hadn't happened, as if all those stolen moments—that kiss—had meant nothing, he was tossing her out of his life.

Tears stung her eyes. The pain that gripped her hurt like a physical ache.

But common sense weaved its way into her thoughts. Why was she taking this personally? She didn't love him. She barely knew him. She had a fiancé—almost. A guy who might not be romantic, but who was certainly stable. She'd be going home in a little over two weeks. There could be nothing between her and Rafe. He was passion wrapped in electricity. Moody. Talented. Sweet but intense. Too sexy for his own good—or hers. And they weren't supposed to be attracted to each other, but they were.

Staying at Mancini's had been like tempting fate. Teasing both of them with something they couldn't have. Making them tense, and him moody. Hot one minute and cold the next.

So maybe it really was time to go?

She slammed the stack of menus into their shelf of the podium, grabbed her purse and raced out.

When she arrived at the villa, Louisa was on a ladder, staring at the watermarks as if she could divine how they got there.

"What are you doing home?"

Dani yanked the pins holding up her short curls and let them fall to her chin, as she kicked off Louisa's high, high heels.

"I was fired."

Louisa climbed off the ladder. "What?" She shook her head. "He told you to dress like the authority in the dining room and you were gorgeous. How could he not like how you looked?"

"Oh, I think he liked how I looked." Dani sucked in a breath, fully aware now that that was the problem. They were playing with fire. They liked each other. But neither of them wanted to. And she was done with it.

"Come to Rome with me."

"You're not going to try to get your job back?"

"It just all fell into place in my head. Rafe and I are at-tracted, but my boyfriend asked me to marry him. Though I didn't accept, I can't really be flirting with another guy. So Rafe—"

Louisa drew in a quick breath. "You know, I wasn't going to mention this because it's not my business, but now that you brought it up… Don't you think it's kind of telling that you hopped on a plane to Italy rather than ac-cept your boyfriend's proposal?"

"I already had this trip scheduled."

"Do you love this guy?"

Dani hesitated, thinking of her last conversation with Paul and how he'd ordered her not to call him anymore. The real kicker wasn't his demand. It was that it hadn't affected her. She didn't miss their short, irrelevant conversations. In six months, she hadn't really missed *him*.

Oh, God. That was the thing her easy, intense attrac-tion to Rafe was really pointing out. Her relationship to Paul might provide a measure of security, but she didn't love him.

She fell to a kitchen chair.

"Oh, sweetie. If you didn't jump up and down for joy when this guy proposed, and you find yourself attracted to another man, you do not want to accept that proposal."

Dani slumped even further in her seat. "I know."

"You should go back to Mancini's and tell Rafe that."

She shook her head fiercely. "No. *No!* He's way too much for me. Too intense. Too *everything*. He has me work-ing twelve-hour days when I'm supposed to be on holiday finding my foster mother's relatives, enjoying some time with them before I go home."

"You're leaving me?"

Dani raised her eyes to meet Louisa's. "You've always known I was only here for a month. I have just over two weeks left. I need to start looking for the Felice family now." She smiled hopefully because she suddenly, fervently didn't want to be alone, didn't want the thoughts about Rafe that would undoubtedly haunt her now that she knew she couldn't accept Paul's proposal. "Come with me."

"To Rome?"

"You need a break from studying everything that's wrong with the villa. I have to pay for a room anyway. We can share it. Then we can come back and I'll still have time to help you catalog everything that needs to be fixed."

Louisa's face saddened. "And then you'll catch a plane and be gone for good."

Dani rose. "Not for good." She caught Louisa's hands. "We're friends. You'll stay with me when you have to come back to the States. I'll visit you here in Italy."

Louisa laughed. "I really could use a break from staring at so many things that need repairing and trying to figure out how I'm going to get it all done."

"So it's set. Let's pack now and go."

Within an hour, they were at the bus station. With Mancini's and Rafe off the list of conversation topics, they chit-chatted about the scenery that passed by as their bus made its way to Rome. Watching Louisa take it all in, as if trying to memorize the country in which she now owned property, a weird sense enveloped Dani. It was clear that everything was new, unique to Louisa. But it all seemed familiar to Dani, as if she knew the trees and grass and chilly February hills, and when she returned to the US she would miss them.

Which was preposterous. She was a New York girl. She needed the opportunities a big city provided. She'd never lived in the country. So why did every tree, every landmark, every winding road seem to fill a need inside her?

The feeling followed her to Rome. To the alleyways between the quaint buildings. To the sidewalk cafés and bistros. To the Colosseum, museums and fountains she took Louisa to see.

And suddenly the feeling named itself. *Home*. What she felt on every country road, at every landmark, gazing at every blue, blue sky and grassy hill was the sense that she was home.

She squeezed her eyes shut. She told herself she wasn't home. She was merely familiar with Italy now because she'd lived in Rome for months. Though that made her feel better for a few minutes, eventually she realized that being familiar with Rome didn't explain why she'd felt she belonged at Mancini's.

She shoved that thought away. She did not belong at Mancini's.

The next day, Dani and Louisa found Rosa's family and were invited to supper. The five-course meal began, reminding her of Rafe, of his big, elaborate dinners, the waitresses who were becoming her friends, the customers who loved her.The weepy sense that she had lost her home filled her. Rightly or wrongly, she'd become attached to Mancini's, but Rafe had fired her.

She had lost the place where she felt strong and smart and capable. The place where she was making friends who felt like family. The place where she—no matter how unwise—was falling for a guy who made her breath stutter and her knees weak.

Because the guy she felt so much for had fired her.

Her brave facade fell away and she excused herself. In the bathroom, she slid down the wall and let herself cry. She'd never been so confused in her life.

"Rafe, there's a customer who'd like to talk to you."

Rafe set down his knife and walked to Mila, who stood in front of the door that led to the dining room. "Great, let's go."

Pleased to be getting a compliment, he reached around

Mila and pushed open the door for her. Since Dani had gone, compliments had been fewer and farther between. He needed the boost.

Mila paused by a table with two twentysomething American girls. Wearing thick sweaters and tight jeans, they couldn't hide their tiny figures. Or their ages. Too old for college and too young to have amassed their own fortunes, they appeared to be the daughters of wealthy men, in Europe, spending their daddies' money. Undoubtedly, they'd heard of him. Bored and perhaps interested in playing with a celebrity chef, they might be looking for some fun. If he handled this right, one of them could be sharing Chianti with him that night.

Ignoring the tweak of a reminder of sharing that wine with Dani, her favorite, he smiled broadly. "What can I do for you ladies?"

"Your ravioli sucked."

That certainly was not what he'd expected.

He bowed slightly, having learned a thing or two from his former hostess. He ignored the sadness that shot through him at even the thought of her, and said, "Allow me to cover your bill."

"Cover our bill?" The tiny blonde lifted a ravioli with her fork and let it plop to her plate. "You should pay us for enduring even a bite of this drivel."

The dough of that ravioli had serenaded his palms as he worked it. The sweet sauce had kissed his tongue. The problem wasn't his food but the palates of the diners.

Still, remembering Dani, he held his temper as he gently reached down and took the biceps of the blonde. "My apologies." He subtly guided her toward the door. The woman was totally cooperative until they got to the podium, and then she squirmed as if he was hurting her, and made a hideous face. Her friend snapped a picture with her phone.

"Get it on Instagram!" the blonde said as they raced out the door. "Rafe Mancini sinks to new lows!"

Furious, Rafe ran after them, but they jumped into their car and peeled out of his parking lot before he could catch them.

After a few well-aimed curses, he counted to forty. Great. Just when he thought rumors of his temper had died, two spoiled little girls were about to resurrect them.

He returned to the quiet dining room. Taking another page from Dani's book, he said, "I'm sorry for the disturbance. Everyone, please, enjoy your meals."

A few diners glanced down. One woman winced. A couple or two pretended to be deep in conversation, as if trying to avoid his misery.

With a weak smile, he walked into the kitchen, over to his workstation and picked up a knife.

Emory scrambled over and whispered, "You're going to have to find her."

Facing the wall, so no one could see, Rafe squeezed his eyes shut. He didn't have to ask who *her* was. The shifts Daniella had been gone had been awful. This was their first encounter with someone trying to lure out his temper, but there had been other problems. Squabbles among the waitresses. Seating mishaps. Lost reservations.

"Things are going wrong, falling through the cracks," Emory continued.

"This is my restaurant. I will find and fix mistakes."

"No. If there's anything Dani taught us, it's that you're a chef. You are a businessman, yes. But you are not the guy who should be in the dining room. You are the guy who should be trotted out for compliments. You are the special chef made more special by the fact that you must be enticed out to the dining room."

He laughed, recognizing he liked the sound of that because he did like to feel special. Or maybe he liked feeling that his food was special.

"Did you ever stop to think that you don't have a temper with the customers or the staff when Dani's around?"

He didn't even try to deny it. With the exception of being on edge because of his attraction to her, his temperament had improved considerably. "Yes."

Emory chuckled as if surprised by his easy acquiescence. "Because she does the tasks that you aren't made to do, which frees you up to do the things you like to do. So, let's just bring her back."

Missing Dani was about so, so much more than Emory knew. Not just a loss of menial tasks but a comfort level. It was as if she brought sunshine into the room. Into his life. But she was engaged.

"Why should I go after her?" Rafe finally faced Emory. "She is returning to America in two weeks."

"Maybe we can persuade her to stay?"

He sniffed a laugh. Leaning down so that only Emory would hear, he said, "She has a fiancé in New York."

Emory's features twisted into a scowl. "And she's in Italy? For months? Without him? Doesn't sound like much of a fiancé to me."

That brought Rafe up short. There was no way in hell he'd let the woman he loved stay alone in Italy for *months*. Especially not if the woman he loved was Daniella.

He didn't tell Emory that. His reasoning was mixed up in feelings that he wasn't supposed to have. He'd gone the route of a relationship once. He'd given up apprenticeships to please Kamila. Which meant he'd given up his dream for her. And still they hadn't made it.

But he'd learned a lesson. Relationships only put the future of his restaurants at stake, so he satisfied himself with one-night stands.

Dani would not be a one-night stand.

But Mancini's really wasn't fine without her.

And Mancini's was his dream. He needed Daniella at his restaurant way too much to break his own rule about relationships. And that was the real bottom line. Getting involved with her would risk his dream as much as Kamila had. He needed her as an employee and he needed to put everything else out of his mind.

Emory caught Rafe's arm. "Maybe there is an opportunity here. If she's truly unhappy, especially with her fiancé, you might be able to convince her Mancini's should be her new career."

That was exactly what Rafe intended to do.

"But you can't have that discussion over the phone. You need to go to Palazzo di Comparino tomorrow. Talk to her personally. Make your case. Offer her money."

"Okay. I'll be out tomorrow morning, maybe all day if I need the time. You handle things while I'm gone."

Emory grinned. "That's my boy."

At the crack of dawn the next morning, Louisa woke Dani and said she was ready to take the bus back to Monte Calanetti. She was happy to have met Dani's foster mom's relatives, but she was nervous, antsy about Palazzo di Comparino. It was time to go back.

After grabbing coffee at a nearby bistro, Dani walked her friend to the bus station, then spent the day with her foster mother's family. By late afternoon, she left, also restless. Like Louisa, she'd loved meeting the Felice family, but they weren't *her* family. Her family was the little group of restaurant workers at Mancini's.

Saddened, she began the walk back to her hotel. A block before she reached it, she passed the bistro again. Though the day was crisp, it was sunny. Warm in the rays that poured down on a little table near the sidewalk, she sat.

She ordered coffee, telling herself it wasn't odd that she felt a connection to the staff at Mancini's. They were nice people. Personable. Passionate. Of course, she felt as if they were family. She'd mothered the waitresses, babied the customers and fallen for Emory like a favorite uncle.

But she'd never see any of them again. She'd been fired

from Mancini's. Rafe hated her. She wouldn't go home happy, satisfied to have met Rosa's relatives, because the connection she'd made had been to a totally different set of people. She would board her plane depressed. Saddened. Returning to a man who didn't even want to pick her up at the airport. A man whose marriage proposal she was going to have to refuse.

A street vendor caught her arm and handed her a red rose.

Surprised, she looked at him, then the rose, then back at him again. "*Grazie…* I think."

He grinned. "It's not from me. It's from that gentleman over there." He pointed behind him.

Dani's eyes widened when she saw Rafe leaning against a lamppost. Wearing jeans, a tight T-shirt and the waist-length black wool coat that he'd worn to the tavern, he looked sexy. But also alone. Very alone. The way she felt in the pit of her stomach when she thought about going back to New York.

Her gaze fell to the rose. Red. For passion. But with someone like Rafe who was a bundle of passion about his restaurant, about his food, about his customers, the color choice could mean anything.

Carrying the rose, she got up from her seat and walked over to him. "How did you find me?"

"Would you believe I guessed where you were?"

"That would have to be a very lucky guess."

He sighed. "I talked to your roommate, Louisa, this afternoon. She told me where you were staying, and I drove to Rome. Walking to your hotel, I saw you here, having coffee."

He glanced away. "Look, can we talk?" He shoved his hands tightly into the side pockets of his coat and returned his gaze to hers. "We've missed you."

"We?"

She almost cursed herself for the question. But she

needed to hear him say it so she'd know she wasn't crazy, getting feelings for a guy who found it so easy to fire her.

"*I've* missed you." He sighed. "Two trust-fund babies faked me out the other night. They insulted my food and when they couldn't get a rise out of me, they made it look like I was tossing one out on her ear to get a picture for Instagram."

She couldn't help it. She laughed. "Instagram?"

"It's the bane of my existence."

"But you hadn't lost your temper?"

He shook his head and glanced away. "No. I hadn't." He looked back at her. "I remembered some things you'd done." He smiled. "I learned."

Her heart picked up at the knowledge that he'd learned from her, and the thrill that he was here, that he'd missed her. "You're not a bad guy."

His face twisted around a smile he clearly tried to hide. "According to Emory, I'm just an overworked guy. And interviewing for a new maître d' isn't helping. Especially when no one I talk to fits. It's why I need you. You're the first person to take over the dining room well enough that I don't worry."

She counted to ten, breathlessly waiting for him to expand on that. When he didn't, she said, "And that's all it is?"

"I know you want there to be something romantic between us. But there are things that separate us. Not just your fiancé, but my temperament. Really? Could you see yourself happy with me? Or when you look at me, do you see a man who takes what he wants and walks away? Because that's the man I really am. I put my restaurant first. I have no time for a relationship."

Her heart wept at what he said. But her sensible self, the lonely foster child who didn't trust the wash of feelings that raced through her every time she got within two feet of him, understood. He was a gorgeous man, born for the limelight, looking to make a name for himself. She was a foster kid, looking for a home. Peace. Quiet. Security. They might be physically attracted, but, emotionally, they were totally wrong for each other. No matter how drawn she was to him, she knew the truth as well as he did.

"You can't commit?"

He shook his head. "My commitment is to Mancini's. To my career. My reputation. I want to be one of Europe's famed chefs. Mancini's is my stepping stone. I do not have time for what other men want. A woman on their arm. Fancy parties. Marriage. To me those are irrelevant. All I want is success. So I would hurt you. And I don't want to hurt you."

"Which makes anything between us just business?"

"Just business."

Her job at Mancini's had awakened feelings in Dani she'd never experienced. Self-worth. A sense of place. An unshakable belief that she belonged there. And the click of connection that made her feel she had a home. Something deep inside her needed Mancini's. But she wouldn't go back only to be fired again.

"And you need me?"

He rolled his eyes. "You Americans. Why must you be showered with accolades?"

Oh, he did love to be gruff.

She slid her hand into the crook of his elbow and pointed to her table at the bistro. "I don't need accolades. I need acknowledgment of my place at Mancini's…and my coffee. I'm freezing."

He pulled his arm away from her hand and wrapped it around her shoulders. She knew he meant it only as a gesture between friends, but she felt his warmth seep through to her. Longing tugged at her heart. A fierce yearning that clung and wouldn't let go.

"You should wear a heavier coat."

His voice was soft, intimate, sending the feeling of rightness through her again.

"It was warm when I came here."

"And now it is cold. So from here on I will make sure you wear a bigger coat." He paused. His head tilted. "Maybe you need me, too?"

She did. But not in the way he thought. She wanted him to love her. Really love her. But to be the man of her dreams, he would have to be different. To be warm and loving. To want her—

And he might. Today. But he'd warned her that anything he felt for her was temporary. He couldn't commit. He didn't want to commit. And unless she wanted to get her heart broken, she had to really hear what he was saying. If she was going to get the opportunity to go back to the first place in her life that felt like home, Mancini's, and the first people who genuinely felt like family, his staff, then a romance between them had to be out of the question.

"I need Mancini's. I like it there. I like the people."

"Ah. So we agree."

"I guess. All I know for sure is that I don't want to go back to New York yet."

He laughed. They reached her table and he pulled out her chair for her. "That doesn't speak well of your fiancé."

Hauling in a breath, she sat, but she said nothing. Her stretching of the truth to Rafe about Paul being her fiancé sat in her stomach like a brick. Still, even though she knew she was going to reject his marriage proposal, it protected her and Rafe. Rafe wouldn't go after another man's woman. Not even for a fling. And he was right. If they had a fling, she would be crushed when he moved on.

One of his eyebrows rose, as he waited for her reply.

She decided they needed her stretched truth. But she couldn't out-and-out lie. "All right. Paul is not the perfect guy."

"I'm not trying to ruin your relationship. I simply believe you should think all of this through. You have a place here in Italy. Mancini's needs you. I would like for you to stay in Italy and work for me permanently, and if you decide to, then maybe your fiancé should be coming here."

She laughed. Really? Paul move to Italy because of her? He wouldn't even drive to the airport for her.

Still, she didn't want Paul in the discussion of her returning to Mancini's. She'd already decided to refuse his proposal. If she stayed in Italy, it had to be for her reasons.

"I think we're getting ahead of ourselves. I have a few weeks before I have to make any decisions."

"Two weeks and two days."

"Yes."

He caught her hands. Kissed the knuckles. "So stay. Stay with me, Daniella. Be the face of Mancini's."

Her heart kicked against her ribs. The way he said "Stay with me, Daniella" froze her lungs, heated her blood. She glanced at the red rose sitting on the table, reminded herself it didn't mean anything but a way to break the ice when he found her. He wasn't asking her to stay for any reason other than her abilities in his restaurant. And she shouldn't want to stay for any reason other than the job. If she could prove herself in the next two weeks, she wouldn't be boarding a plane depressed. She wouldn't be boarding a plane at all. She'd be helping to run a thriving business. Her entire life would change.

She pulled her hands away. "I can't accept Louisa's hospitality forever. I need to be able to support myself. Hostessing doesn't pay much."

He growled.

She laughed. He was so strong and so handsome and so perfect that when he let his guard down and was himself, his real self, with her, everything inside her filled with crazy joy. And maybe if she just focused on making him her friend, a friend she could keep forever, working for him could be fun.

"I can't pay a hostess an exorbitant salary."

"So give me a title to justify the money."

He sighed. "A title?"

"Sure, something like general manager should warrant a raise big enough that I can afford my own place."

His eyes widened. "General manager?"

"Come on, Rafe. Let's get to the bottom line here. If things work out when we return to Mancini's, I'm going to be taking on a huge chunk of your work. I'm also going to be relocating to another *country*. You'll need to make it worth my while."

He shook his head. "Dear God, you are bossy."

"But I'm right."

He sighed. "Fine. But if you're getting that title, you will earn it."

She inclined her head. "Seems fair."

"You'll learn to order supplies, check deliveries, do the job of managing things Emory and I don't have time for."

"Makes perfect sense."

He sighed. His eyes narrowed. "Anything else?"

She laughed. "One more thing." Her laughter became a silly giggle when he scowled at her. "A ride back to Louisa's."

He rolled his eyes. "Yes. I will drive you back to Louisa's. If you wish, I will even help you find an apartment."

Leaving the rose, she stood and pushed away from the table. "You keep getting ahead of things. We have two weeks for me to figure out if staying at Mancini's is right for me." She turned to head back to the hotel to check out, but spun to face him again. "Were I you, I'd be on my best behavior."

The next morning, she called Paul. If staying in Italy was the rest of her life, the *real* rest of her life, she had to make things right.

"Do you know what time it is?"

She could hear the sleep in his voice and winced. "Yes. Sorry. But I wanted to catch you before work."

"That's fine."

She squeezed her eyes shut as she gathered her courage. It seemed so wrong to break up with someone over the phone and, yet, they'd barely spoken to each other in six months. This was the right thing to do.

"Look, Paul, I'm sorry to tell you this over the phone, but I can't accept your marriage proposal."

"What?"

She could almost picture him sitting up in bed, her bad news bringing him fully awake.

"I'm actually thinking of not coming back to New York at all, but staying in Italy."

"What? What about your job?"

"I have a new job."

"Where?"

"At a restaurant."

"So you're leaving teaching to be a waitress?"

"A hostess."

"Oh, there's a real step up."

"Actually, I'm general manager," she said, glad she'd talked Rafe into the title. She couldn't blame Paul for being confused or angry, and knew he deserved an honest explanation.

"And I love Italy. I feel like I belong here." She sucked in a breath. "We've barely talked in six months. I'm going to make a wild guess that you haven't even missed me. I think we were only together because it was convenient."

Another man's silence might have been interpreted as misery. Knowing Paul the way she did, she recognized it as more or less a confirmation that she was right.

"I'm sorry not to accept your proposal, but I'm very happy."

After a second, he said, "Okay, then. I'm glad."

The breath blew back into her lungs. "Really?"

"Yeah. I did think we'd make a good married couple,

but I knew when you didn't say yes immediately that you might have second thoughts."

"I'm sorry."

"Don't be sorry. This is just the way life works sometimes."

And that was her pragmatic Paul. His lack of emotion might have made her feel secure at one time, but now she knew she needed more.

They talked another minute and Dani disconnected the call, feeling as if a weight had been taken from her shoulders, only to have it quickly replaced by another one. She'd had to be fair to Paul, but now the only defense she'd have against Rafe's charms would be her own discipline and common sense.

She hoped that was enough.

CHAPTER NINE

HER RETURN TO the restaurant was as joyous as a celebration. Emory grinned. The waitresses fawned over her. The busboys grew red faced. The chefs breathed a sigh of relief.

Annoyance worked its way through Rafe. Not that he didn't want his staff to adore her. He did. That was why she was back. The problem was he couldn't stop reliving their meeting in Rome. He'd said everything that he'd wanted to say. That he'd missed her. That he wanted her back. But he'd kept it all in the context of business. He'd missed her help. He wanted her to become the face of Mancini's. He didn't want anything romantic with her because he didn't want to hurt her. He'd been all business. And it had worked.

But with her return playing out around him, his heart rumbled at the injustice. He hadn't lied when he said he didn't want her back for himself, that he didn't want something romantic between them. His fierce protection of Mancini's wouldn't let him get involved with an employee he needed. But here at the restaurant, with her looking so pretty, helping make his dream a reality, he just wanted to kiss her.

He reminded himself that she had a fiancé—

A fiancé she admitted was not the perfect guy.

Bah! That fiancé was supposed to be the key weapon in his arsenal of ways to keep himself away from her. Her admission that he wasn't perfect, even the fact that she was considering staying in Italy, called her whole engagement into question. And caused all his feelings for her to surface and swell.

She swept into the kitchen. Wearing a blue dress that highlighted her blue eyes and accented a figure so lush she was absolutely edible, she glided over to Emory. He took her hands and kissed the back of both.

"You look better than anything on the menu."

Rafe sucked in a breath, controlling the unwanted ripple of longing.

Dani unexpectedly stepped toward Emory, put her arms around him and hugged him. Emory closed his eyes as if to savor it, a smile lifted his lips.

Rafe's yearning intensified, but with it came a tidal wave of jealousy. He lowered his knife on an unsuspecting stalk of celery, chopping it with unnecessary force.

Dani faced him. "Why don't you give me the key and I'll open the front door for the lunch crowd?"

He rolled his gaze toward her slowly. Even as the businessman inside him cheered her return, the jealous man who was filled with need wondered if he wasn't trying to drive himself insane.

"Emory, give her your key."

The sous-chef instantly fished his key ring out of his pocket and dislodged the key for Mancini's. "Gladly."

"Don't be so joyful." He glanced at Dani again, at the soft yellow hair framing her face, her happy blue eyes. "Have a key made for yourself this afternoon and return Emory's to him."

She smiled. "Will do, boss."

She walked out of the kitchen, her high heels clicking on the tile floor, her bottom swaying with every step, all eyes of the kitchen staff watching her go.

Jealousy spewed through him. "Back to work!" he yelped, and everybody scrambled.

Emory sauntered over. "Something is wrong?"

He chopped the celery. "Everything is fine."

The sous-chef glanced at the door Dani had just walked through. "She's very happy to be back."

Rafe refused to answer that.

Emory turned to him again. "So did you talk her into staying? Is her fiancé joining her here? What's going on?"

Rafe chopped the celery. "I don't know."

"You don't know if she's staying?"

"She said her final two weeks here would be something like a trial run for her."

"Then we must be incredibly good to her."

"I gave her a raise, a title. If she doesn't like those, then we should be glad if she goes home to her *fiancé*." He all but spat the word *fiancé*, getting angrier by the moment, as he gave Dani everything she wanted but was denied everything he wanted.

Emory said, "I still say something is up with this fiancé of hers. If she didn't tell him she's considering staying in Italy, then there's trouble in paradise. If she did, and he isn't on the next flight to Florence, then I question his sanity."

Rafe laughed.

"Seriously, Rafe, has she talked to you about him? I just don't get an engaged vibe from her."

"Are you saying she's lying?"

Emory inclined his head. "I don't think she's lying as much as I think her fiancé might be a real dud, and her engagement as flat as a crepe."

Rafe said only, "Humph," but once again her statement that her fiancé wasn't the perfect guy rolled through his head.

"I only mention this because I think it works in our favor."

"How so?"

"If she's not really in love, if her fiancé doesn't really love her, we have the power of Italy on our side."

"To?"

"To coax her to stay. To seduce her away from a guy who doesn't deserve her."

Rafe chopped the celery. His dreams were filled with scenarios where he seduced Daniella. Except he had a feeling that kind of seducing wasn't what Emory meant.

"Somehow or another we have to be so good to her that she realizes what she has in New York isn't what she wants."

Sulking, Rafe scraped the celery into a bowl. Why did he have to be the one doing all the wooing? *He* was a catch. He wanted her eyelashes to flutter when he walked by and her eyes to warm with interest. He had some pride, too.

Emory shook his head. "Okay. Be stubborn. But you'll be sorry if some pasty office dweller from New York descends on us and scoops her back to America."

Rafe all but growled in frustration at the picture that formed in his head. Especially since she had said her fiancé wasn't perfect. Shouldn't a woman in love swoon for the man she's promised to marry?

Yes. Yes. She should.

Yet, here she was, considering staying. Not bringing her fiancé into the equation.

And he suddenly saw what Emory was saying.

She wasn't happy with her fiancé. She was searching for something. She'd gone to Rome looking for her foster mother's relatives—family! What Dani had been looking for in Rome was family! That was why she was getting so close to the staff at Mancini's.

Still, something was missing.

He tapped his index fingers against his lips, thinking, and when the answer came to him he smiled and turned to Emory. "I will need time off tomorrow."

Emory's face fell. "You're taking another day?"

"Just lunch. And Daniella will be out for lunch, too."

Emory caught his gaze. "Really?"

"Yes. Don't go thinking this is about funny business.

I'm taking her apartment hunting. Dani is a woman looking for a family. She thinks she's found it with us. But Mancini's isn't a home. It's a place of business. Once I help her get a house, somewhere to put down roots, it will all fall into place for her."

Rafe's first free minute, he called the real estate agent who'd sold him his penthouse. She told him she had some suitable listings in Monte Calanetti and he set up three appointments for Daniella.

When the lunch crowd cleared, he walked into the empty, quiet dining room.

Dani smiled as he approached. "You're not going to yell at me for not going home and costing you two hours' wages are you?"

"You are management now. I expect you here every hour the restaurant is open."

"Except my days off."

He groaned. "Except your days off. If you feel comfortable not being here two days every week, I am fine with it. But if something goes wrong, you will answer for it."

She laughed. "Whatever. I've been coaching Allegra. She'll be much better from here on out. No more catastrophes while I'm gone."

"Great. I've lined up three appointments for us tomorrow."

She turned from the podium. "With vendors?"

"With my friend who is a real estate agent."

"I told you we shouldn't get ahead of ourselves."

"Our market is tight. You must be on top of things to get a good place."

"I haven't—"

He interrupted her. "You haven't decided you're staying. I get that. But if you choose to stay, I don't want you panicking. Getting ahead of a problem is how a smart businessperson staves off disaster."

"Yeah, I know."

"Good. Tomorrow morning, Emory will take over lunch prep while you and I apartment hunt. We can be back for dinner."

Sun poured in through the huge window of the kitchen of the first unit Maria Salvetti showed Rafe and Dani the next morning. Unfortunately, cold air flowed in through the cracks between the window and the wall.

Dani eased her eyes away from the unwanted ventilation and watched as Rafe walked across a worn hardwood floor, his motorcycle boots clicking along, his jeans outlining an absolutely perfect behind and his black leather jacket, collar flipped up, giving him the look of a dangerous rebel.

For the second time that morning, she told herself she was grateful he'd been honest with her about his inability to commit. She didn't know a woman who wouldn't fall victim to his steel-gray eyes and his muscled body. She had to be strong. And her decision to stay at Mancini's had to be made for all the right reasons.

She faced Maria. "I'd have to fix this myself?"

"*Sì.* It is for sale. It is not a rental."

She turned to Rafe. "I wouldn't have time to work twelve-hour days and be my own general contractor."

"You could hire someone."

She winced as she ran her hand along the crack between the wall and window. "Oh, yeah? Just how big is my raise going to be?"

"Big enough."

She shook her head. "I still don't like it."

She also didn't like the second condo. She did have warm, fuzzy feelings for the old farmhouse a few miles away from the village, but that needed more work than the first condo she'd seen.

Maria's smile dipped a notch every time Dani rejected a prospective home. She'd tried to explain that she wasn't even sure she was staying in Italy, but Maria kept plugging along.

After Dani rejected the final option, Maria shook Rafe's hand, then Dani's and said, "I'll check our listings again and get back to you."

She slid into her car and Dani sighed, glad to be rid of her. Not that Maria wasn't nice, but with her decision about staying in Italy up in the air, looking for somewhere to live seemed premature. "Sorry."

"Don't apologize quite yet." He pulled his cell phone from his jacket and dialed a number. "Carlo, this is Rafe. Could you have a key for the empty condo at the front desk? *Grazie*." He slipped his phone into his jacket again.

She frowned at him. "You have a place to show me?"

He headed for his SUV, motioning for her to follow him. "Actually, I thought Maria would have taken you to his apartment first. It's a newly renovated condo in my building."

She stopped walking. "*Your* building?" She might be smart enough to realize she and Rafe were a bad bet, but all along she'd acknowledged that their spending too much time together was tempting fate. Now he wanted them to live in the same building?

"After Emory, you are my most valued employee. A huge part of Mancini's success. We need to be available for each other. Plus, there would be two floors between us. It's not like we'd even run into each other."

She still hesitated. "Your building's that big?"

"No. I value my privacy that much." He sighed. "Seriously. Just come with me to see the place and you will understand."

Dani glanced around as she entered the renovated old building, Rafe behind her. Black-and-white block tiles were accented by red sofas and chairs in a lounge area of the lobby. The desk for the doorman sat discreetly in a corner.

Leaning over her shoulder, Rafe said, "My home is the penthouse."

His warm breath tickled her ear and desire poured through her. She almost turned and yelled at him for flirting with her. Instead, she squelched the feeling. He probably wasn't flirting with her. This was just who he was. Gorgeous. Sinfully sexy. And naturally flirtatious. If she really intended to stay in Italy and work for him, she had to get accustomed to him. As she'd realized after she'd spoken to Paul, she would need discipline and common sense to keep her sanity.

He pointed at the side-by-side elevators. "I don't use those, and you can't use them to get to my apartment."

His breath tiptoed to her neck and trickled down her spine. Still, she kept her expression neutral when she turned and put them face-to-face, so close she could see the little flecks of silver in his eyes.

Just as her reactions couldn't matter, how he looked—his sexy face, his smoky eyes—also had to be irrelevant. If she didn't put all this into perspective now, this temptation could rule her life. Or ruin her life.

She gave him her most professional smile. "And I'd be a few floors away?"

"Not just a few floors, but also a locked elevator."

Dangling the apartment key, he motioned for her to enter the elevator when it arrived. They rode up in silence. He unlocked the door to the available unit and she gasped.

"Oh, my God." She spun to face him. "I can afford this?"

He laughed. "Yes."

From the look of the lobby, she'd expected the apartment to be ultramodern. The kind of place she would have killed to have in New York. Black-and-white. Sharp, but sterile. Something cool and sophisticated for her and distant Paul.

But warm beiges and yellows covered these walls. The

kitchen area was cozy, with a granite-topped breakfast bar where she could put three stools.

She saw it filled with people. Louisa. Coworkers from Mancini's. And neighbors she'd meet who could become like a family.

She caught that thought before it could take root. Something about Italy always caused her to see things through rose-colored glasses, and if she didn't stop, she was going to end up making this choice before she knew for certain that she could work with Rafe as a friend or a business associate, and forget about trying for anything more.

She turned to Rafe again. "Don't make me want something I can't have."

"I already told you that you can afford it."

"I know."

"So why do you think you can't have it?"

It was exactly what she'd dreamed of as a child, but she couldn't let herself fall in love with it. Or let Rafe see just how drawn she was to this place. If he knew her weakness, he'd easily lure her into staying before she was sure it was the right thing to do.

She pointed at the kitchen, which managed to look cozy even with sleek stainless-steel appliances, dark cabinets and shiny surfaces. "It's awfully modern."

"So you want to go back to the farmhouse with the holes in the wall?"

"No." She turned away again, though she lovingly ran her hand along the granite countertop, imagining herself rolling out dough to make cut-out cookies. She'd paint them with sugary frosting and serve them to friends at Christmas. "I want a homey kitchen that smells like heaven."

"You have that at Mancini's."

"I want a big fat sofa with a matching chair that feels like it swallows you up when you sit in it."

"You can buy whatever furniture you want."

"I want to turn my thermostat down to fifty-eight at night so I can snuggle under thick covers."

He stared at her as if she were crazy. "And you can do that here."

"Maybe."

"Undoubtedly." He sighed. "You have an idealized vision of home."

"Most foster kids do."

He leaned his shoulder against the wall near the kitchen. His smoky eyes filled with curiosity. She wasn't surprised when he said, "You've never really told me about your life. You mentioned getting shuffled from foster home to foster home, but you never explained how you got into foster care in the first place."

She shrugged. Every time she thought about being six years old, or eight years old, or ten years old—shifted every few months to the house of a stranger, trying unsuccessfully to mingle with the other kids—a flash of rejection froze her heart. She was an adult before she'd realized no one had rejected her, per se. Each child was only protecting himself. They'd all been hurt. They were all afraid. Not connecting was how they coped.

Nonetheless, the memories of crying herself to sleep and longing for something better still guided her. It was why she believed she could keep her distance from Rafe. Common sense and a longing for stability directed her decisions. Along with a brutal truth. The world was a difficult place. She knew that because she'd lived it.

"There's not much to tell. My mom was a drug addict."

He winced.

"There's no sense sugarcoating it."

"Of course there is. Everyone sugarcoats his or her past. It's how we deal."

She turned to him again, surprised by the observation. She'd always believed living in truth kept her sane. He seemed to believe exactly the opposite.

"Yeah. What did you sugarcoat?"

"I tell you that I'm not a good bet as a romantic partner."

She sniffed a laugh.

"What I should have said is that I'm a real bastard."

She laughed again. "Seriously, Rafe. I got the message the first time. You want nothing romantic between us."

"Mancini's needs you and I am not on speaking terms with any woman I've ever dated. So I keep you for Mancini's."

She looked around at the apartment, unable to stop the warm feeling that flooded her when he said he would keep her. Still, he didn't mean it the way her heart took it. So, remembering to use her common sense, she focused her attention on the apartment, envisioning it decorated to her taste. The picture that formed had her wrestling with the urge to tell him to get his landlord on the line so she could make an offer—then she realized something amazing.

"You knew I'd love this."

He had the good graces to look sheepish. "I assumed you would."

"No assuming about it, you *knew*."

"All right, I knew you would love it."

She walked over to him, as the strangest thought formed in her head. Maybe it wouldn't take a genius to realize the way to entice a former foster child would be with a home. But no one had ever wanted her around enough to figure that out.

"How did you know?"

He shrugged. His strong shoulders lifted the black leather of his jacket and ruffled the curls of his long, dark hair. "It didn't take much to realize that you'd probably lost your sense of home when your foster mother died."

She caught his gaze. "So?"

"So, I think you came to Italy hoping to find it with her relatives."

"They're nice people."

"Yes, but you didn't feel a connection to Rosa's nice relatives. Yet, you keep coming back to Mancini's, because you did connect with us."

Her heart stuttered. Even her almost fiancé hadn't understood why she so desperately wanted to find Rosa's family. But Rafe, a guy who had known her a little over two weeks, a guy she'd had a slim few personal conversations with, had seen it.

He'd also hit the nail on the head about Mancini's. She felt they were her family. The only thing she didn't have here in Italy was an actual, physical home.

And he'd found her one.

He cared about her enough to want to please her, to satisfy needs she kept close to her heart.

Afraid of the direction of her thoughts, she turned away and walked into the master bedroom. Seeing the huge space, her eyebrows rose. "Wow. Nice."

Rafe was right behind her. "Are you changing the subject on me?"

She pivoted and faced him. He seemed genuinely clueless about what he was doing. Not just giving her everything she wanted, but caring about her. He was getting to know her—the real her—in a way no one else in her life ever had. And the urge to fall into his arms, confess her fears, her hopes, her longings, was so strong, she had to walk away from him. If she fell into his arms now, she'd never come out. Especially if he comforted her. God help her if he whispered anything romantic.

"I think we need to change the subject."

"Why?"

She walked over to him again. For fifty cents, she'd answer him. She'd put her arms around his neck and tell him he was falling for her. The things he did—searching her out in Rome, making her general manager, helping her find a home—those weren't things a boss did. No matter how much he believed he needed her as an employee, he also had feelings for her.

But he didn't see it.

And she didn't trust it. He'd said he was a bastard? What if he really was? What if he liked her now, but didn't tomorrow?

"Because I'm afraid. Every time I put down roots, it fails." She said the words slowly, clearly, so there'd be no misunderstanding. Rafe was a smart guy. If she stayed in Italy, shared the joy of making Mancini's successful, no matter how strong she was, how much discipline she had, how much common sense she used, there was a chance she'd fall in love with him.

And then what?

Would she hang around his restaurant desperate for crumbs of affection from a guy who slept with her, then moved on?

That would be an epic fail. The very thought made her ill.

Because she couldn't tell him that, she stuck with the safe areas. The things they could discuss.

"For as good as I am at Mancini's, I can see us having a blowout fight and you firing me again. And for as much as I like the waitstaff, I can see them getting new jobs and moving on. This decision comes with risks for me. I know enough not to pretend things will be perfect. But I have to have at least a little security."

"You and your security. Maybe to hell with security and focus on a little bit of happiness."

Oh, she would love to focus on being happy. Touring Italy with him, stolen kisses, nights of passion. But he'd told her that wasn't in the cards and she believed him. Somehow she had to stop herself from getting those kinds of thoughts every time he said something that fell out of business mode and tipped over into the personal. That would be the only way she could stay at Mancini's.

When she didn't answer, he sighed. "I don't think it's an accident you found Mancini's."

"Of course not. Nico sent me."

"I am not talking about Nico. I'm talking about destiny."

She laughed lightly and walked away from him. It was almost funny the way he used the words and phrases of a lover to lure her to a job. It was no wonder her thoughts always went in the wrong direction. He took her there. Thank God she had ahold of herself enough to see his words for what they were. A very passionate man trying to get his own way. To fight for her sanity, she would always have to stand up to him.

"Foster kids don't get destinies. We get the knowledge that we need to educate ourselves so we can have security. If you really want me to stay, let me come to the decision for the right reasons. Because if I stay, you are not getting rid of me. I will make Mancini's my home." She caught his gaze. "Are you prepared for that?"

CHAPTER TEN

WAS HE PREPARED for that?

What the hell kind of question was that for her to ask?

He caught her arm when she turned to walk away. "Of course, I'm prepared for that! Good God, woman, I drove to Rome to bring you back."

She shook her head with an enigmatic laugh. "Okay. Just don't say I didn't warn you."

He rolled his eyes heavenward. Women. Who could figure them out? "I am warned." He motioned to the door. "Come. I'll drive you back to Louisa's."

But by the time they reached Louisa's villa and he drove back to his condo to change for work, her strange statement had rattled around in his head and made him crazy. Was he prepared for her staying? Idiocy. He'd all but made her a partner in his business. He *wanted* her to stay.

He changed his clothes and headed to Mancini's. Walking into the kitchen, he tried to shove her words out of his head but they wouldn't go—until he found the staff in unexpectedly good spirits. Then his focus fell to their silly grins.

"What's going on?"

Emory turned from the prep table. "Have you seen today's issue of *Tuscany Review*?"

In all the confusion over Daniella, he'd forgotten that today was the day the tourist magazine came out. He snatched it from Emory's hands.

"Page twenty-nine."

He flicked through the pages, getting to the one he wanted, and there was a picture of Dani. So many tourists had snapped pictures that someone from the magazine could have come in and taken this one without anyone in the restaurant paying any mind.

He read the headline. "Mancini's gets a fresh start."

"Read the whole article. It's fantastic."

As he began to skim the words, Emory said, "There's mention of the new hostess being pretty and personable."

Rafe inclined his head. "She is both."

"And mention of your food without mention of your temper."

His gaze jerked up to Emory. "No kidding."

"No kidding. It's as if your temper didn't exist."

He pressed the magazine to his chest. "Thank God I went to Rome and brought her back."

Daniella pushed open the door. Dressed in a sheath the color of ripe apricots, she smiled as she walked toward Rafe and Emory. "I heard something about a magazine."

Rafe silently handed it to her.

She glanced down and laughed. "Well, look at me."

"Yes. Look at you." He wanted to pull her close and hug her, but he crossed his arms on his chest. The very fact that he wanted to hug her was proof he needed to keep his distance. Even forgetting about the fiancé she had back home, she needed security enough that he wouldn't tempt her away from finding it. Her staying had to be about Mancini's and her desire for a place, a home. He had to make sure she got what she wanted out of this deal—without breaking her heart. Because if he broke her heart, she'd leave. And everything they'd accomplished up to now would have been for nothing.

"You realize that even if every chef and busboy cycles out, and every waitress quits after university, Emory and I will always be here."

Emory grinned at Daniella. Rafe nudged him. "Stop behaving like one of the Three Stooges. This is serious for her."

She looked up from the magazine with a smile for Rafe. "Yes. I know you will always be here." Her smile grew. "Did you ever stop to think that maybe that's part of the problem?"

With that she walked out of the kitchen and Rafe shook his head.

"She talks in riddles." But deep down he knew what was happening. He'd told her they'd never become lovers. She had feelings for him. Hell, he had feelings for her, but he intended to fight them. He'd told her anything between them was wrong, so she had to be sure she could work with him knowing there'd never be anything between them.

And maybe that's what she meant about being prepared.

Lately, it seemed he was fighting his feelings as much as she was fighting hers.

Two nights later, as the dinner service began to slow down, Rafe stepped out into the dining room to see his friend Nico walking into Mancini's. Nico's eyes lit when he saw Dani standing at the podium.

"Look at you!" He took her hand and gave her a little twirl to let her show off another pretty blue dress that hugged her figure.

Jealousy rippled through Rafe, but he squelched it. He put her needs ahead of his because that served Mancini's needs. It was a litany he repeated at least four times a day. After her comment about him being part of the reason her decision was so difficult, he'd known he had to get himself in line or lose her.

As he walked out of the kitchen, he heard Nico say, "Rafe tells me you're working out marvelously."

She smiled sheepishly. "I can't imagine anyone not loving working here."

Rafe sucked in a happy breath. She loved working at Mancini's. He knew that, of course, but it was good to hear her say it. It felt normal to hear her say it. As if she knew she belonged here. Clearly, keeping his distance the past two days had worked. Mancini's was warm and happy. The way he'd always envisioned it.

"We don't have reservations," Nico said when Dani glanced at the computer screen.

She smiled. "No worries. The night's winding down. We have plenty of space."

Seeing him approach, Nico said, "And here's the chef now."

"Nico!" Rafe grabbed him and gave him a bear hug. "What brings you here?"

"I saw your ravioli on Instagram and decided I had to try it."

"Bah! Damned trust-fund babies. I should—" He stopped suddenly. Half-hidden behind Nico was Marianna Amatucci, Nico's sister, who'd been traveling for the past year. Short with wild curly hair and honey skin, she was the picture of a natural Italian beauty.

"Marianna!" He nudged Nico out of the way and hugged her, too, lifting her up to swing her around. Rafe hadn't even seen her to say hello in months. Having her here put another piece of normalcy back in his life.

She giggled when he plopped her to the floor again.

"Daniella," he said, one hand around Marianna's waist, the other clasped on Nico's shoulder. "These are my friends. Nico and his baby sister, Marianna. They get the best table in the house."

She smiled her understanding, grabbed two menus and led Nico and Marianna into the dining room. "This way."

Rafe stopped her. "Not *there*. I want them by my kitchen." He took the menus from her hands. "I want to spoil them."

Nico chuckled and caught Dani's gaze. "What he really means is use us for guinea pigs."

She laughed, her gaze meeting Nico's and her cheeks turning pink.

An unexpected thought exploded in Rafe's brain. He'd told Dani he wanted nothing romantic between them. Her fiancé was a dud. Nico was a good-looking man. And Dani was a beautiful, personable woman. If she stayed, at some point, Dani and Nico could become lovers.

His gut tightened.

Still, shouldn't he be glad if Nico was interested in Daniella and that interest caused her to stay?

Of course he should. What he wanted from Daniella was a face for his business. If Nico could help get her to stay, then Rafe should help him woo her.

"You are lucky the night is nearly over," Rafe said as he pulled out Marianna's chair. He handed the menus to them both.

Smiling warmly at Nico, Dani said, "Can I take your drink orders?"

Nico put his elbow on the table and his chin on his fist as he contemplated Daniella, as if she were a puzzle he was trying to figure out.

Thinking of Dani and Nico together was one thing. Seeing his friend's eyes on her was quite another. The horrible black syrup of jealously poured through Rafe's veins like hot wax.

Unable to endure it, he waved Daniella away. "Go. I will take his drink order. You're needed at the door. The night isn't quite over yet."

She gave Nico one last smile and headed to her post.

Happier with her away from Nico, Rafe listened to his friend's wine choice.

Marianna said, "Just water for me."

Rafe gaped at her. "You need wine."

She shook her head. "I need water."

Rafe's jaw dropped. "You cannot be an Italian and refuse wine with dinner."

Nico waved a hand. "It's not a big deal. She's been weird ever since she came home. Just bring her the water."

Rafe called Allegra over so she could get Nico's wine from the bar and Marianna's water. All the while, Dani walked customers from the podium, past Nico, who would watch her amble by.

Rafe sucked in a breath, not understanding the feelings rumbling through him. He wanted Daniella to stay. Nico might give her a reason to do just that. He could not romance her himself. Yet he couldn't bear to have his friend even look at her?

"Give me ten minutes and I will make you the happiest man alive."

Nico laughed, his eyes on Daniella. "I sincerely doubt you can do that with food."

Jealousy sputtered through Rafe again. "Get your mind out of the gutter and off my hostess!"

Nico's eyes narrowed. "Why? Are you staking a claim?"

Rafe's chest froze and he couldn't speak. But Marianna shook her head. "Men. Does it always have to be about sex with you?"

Nico laughed.

Rafe spun away, rushing into the kitchen, angry with Nico but angrier with himself. He should celebrate Nico potentially being a reason for Daniella to stay. Instead, he was filled with blistering-hot rage. Toward his friend. It was insane.

To make up for his unwanted anger, he put together the best meals he'd ever created. Unfortunately, it didn't take ten minutes. It took forty.

Allegra took out antipasto and soups while he worked. When he returned to the dining room, there were no more people at the door. All customers had been seated. Tables that emptied weren't being refilled. Anticipating going home, the busboys cheerfully cleared away dishes.

And Dani sat with Nico and Marianna.

Forcing himself to be friendly—happy—Rafe set the plates of food in front of Nico and his sister.

Marianna said, "Oh, that smells heavenly."

Nico nodded. "Impressive, Rafe."

Dani inhaled deeply. "Mmm…"

Nico grinned, scooped up some pasta and offered it to Dani. "Would you like a bite?"

"Oh, I'd love a bite!"

Nico smiled.

Unwanted jealousy and an odd proprietary instinct rushed through Rafe. Before Daniella could take the bite Nico offered, Rafe grabbed the back of her chair and yanked her away from the table.

"I want her to eat that meal later tonight."

Nico laughed. "Really? What is this? A special occasion?"

Rafe knew Nico meant that as a joke, but he suddenly felt like an idiot as if Nico had caught his jealousy. He straightened to his full six-foot height. "Not a special occasion, part of the process. She's eaten bits of food to get our flavor, but tonight I had planned on treating her to an entire dinner."

Dani turned around on her chair to catch his gaze. "Really?"

Oh, Lord.

Something soft and earthy trembled through him, replacing his jealousy and feelings of being caught, as if they had never existed. Trapped in the gaze of her blue eyes, he quietly said, "Yes."

She rose, putting them face-to-face. "A private dinner?"

He shrugged, but everything male inside him shimmered. After days of only working together, being on his best behavior, he couldn't deny how badly he wanted time alone with her. He didn't want Nico to woo her. *He* wanted to woo her.

"Yes. A private dinner."

She smiled.

His breath froze. She was happy to be alone with him? He'd warned her…yet she still wanted to be alone with him? And what of her fiancé?

He pivoted and returned to the kitchen, not sure what he was doing. But as he worked, he slowed his pace. He rejected ravioli, spaghetti Bolognese. Both were too simple. Too common—

If he was going to feed her an entire meal, it would be his best. Pride the likes of which he'd never felt before rose in him. Only the best for his Dani.

He stopped, his finger poised above a pot, ready to sprinkle a pinch of salt.

His Dani?

He squeezed his eyes shut. Dear God. This wasn't just an attraction. He was head over heels crazy for her.

Dani alternated between standing nervously by the podium and sitting with Nico and Marianna.

The dining room had all but emptied, yet she couldn't seem to settle. Her fluttery stomach had her wondering if she'd even be able to eat what Rafe prepared for her.

A private dinner.

She had no idea what it meant, but when he emerged from the kitchen and walked to Nico's table, her breath stalled. He'd removed his smock and stood before the Amatuccis in dark trousers and a white T-shirt that outlined his taut stomach. Tight cotton sleeves rimmed impressive biceps and Dani saw a tattoo she'd never noticed before.

"I trust you enjoyed your dinners."

Nico blotted his mouth with a napkin, then said, "Rafe, you truly are gifted."

Rafe bowed graciously.

"And, Marianna." When Rafe turned to see her half-eaten meal, he frowned. "Why you not eat?"

She smiled slightly. "You give everyone enough to feed an army. Half was plenty."

"You'll take the rest home?"

She nodded and Rafe motioned for Allegra to get her plate and put her food in a take-out container.

Rafe chatted with Nico, calmly, much more calmly than Dani felt, but the second Allegra returned with the take-out container, Marianna jumped from her seat.

"I need to get home. I don't know what's wrong with me tonight, but I'm exhausted."

Nico rose, too. "It is late. Dinner was something of an afterthought. I promised Marianna I'd get her back at a decent hour. But I knew you'd want to see her after her year away, Rafe."

Rafe kissed her hand. "Absolutely. I'm just sorry she's too tired for us to catch up."

Dani frowned. Nico's little sister didn't look tired. She looked pale. Biting her lower lip, Dani realized she'd only known one other person who'd looked that way—

Rafe waved her over. "Say good-night to Nico and his sister."

Keeping her observations to herself, Dani smiled. "Good night, Marianna."

Marianna returned her smile. "I'm sure we'll be seeing more of you since Nico loves Rafe's food."

Nico laughed, took both her hands and kissed them. "Good night, Daniella. Tell your roomie I said hello."

Daniella's face reddened. Louisa had been the topic of most of Nico's questions when she'd sat with him and his sister, but there was no way in hell she'd tell Louisa Nico had mentioned her. Still, she smiled. Every time she talked to Nico, she liked him more. Which only made Louisa's dislike all the more curious.

"Good night, Nico."

After helping Marianna with her coat, Rafe walked his friends to their car. Dani busied herself helping the waitresses finish dining room cleanup. She didn't see Rafe return, but when a half hour went by, she assumed he'd come in through the back door to the kitchen.

Of course, he could be talking to beautiful Marianna. She might be with her brother, but that brother was a friend of Rafe's. And Nico had said he wanted to bring Marianna to Mancini's because he knew Rafe would want to see her. They probably had all kinds of stories to reminisce about. Marianna might be too young to have been his first kiss, his first love, but she was an adult now. A beautiful woman.

Realizing how possible it was that Rafe might be interested in Marianna, Dani swayed, but she quickly calmed herself. If she decided to stay, watching him with other women would be part of her life. She had to get used to this. She had to get accustomed to seeing him flirt, seeing beautiful women like Marianna look at him with interest.

She tossed a chair to the table with a little more force than was necessary.

Gio frowned. "Are you okay?"

She smiled. "Yes. Perfect."

"If you're not okay, Allegra and I can finish."

"I'm fine." She forced her smile to grow bigger. "Just eager to be done for the night."

As they finished the dining room, Rafe walked out of the kitchen to the bar. He got a bottle of wine and two glasses. As their private dinner became a reality, Dani's stomach tightened.

She squeezed her eyes shut, scolding herself. The dinner might be private for no other reason than the restaurant would be closed. Rafe probably didn't want to be alone with her as much as he wanted her to eat a meal, as hostess, so she could get the real experience of dining at Mancini's.

The waitresses left. The kitchen light went out, indicating Emory and his staff had gone.

Only she and Rafe remained.

He faced her, pointed at a chair. "Sit."

Okay. That was about as far from romantic as a man could get. This "private" dinner wasn't about the two of them having time together. It was about a chef who wanted his hostess to know his food.

She walked over, noticing again how his tight T-shirt accented a strong chest and his neat-as-a-pin trousers gave him a professional look. But as she got closer, Louisa's high, high heels clicking on the tile floor, she saw his gaze skim the apricot dress. His eyes warmed with interest. His lips lifted into a slow smile.

And her stomach fell to the floor. *This* was why she'd never quite been able to talk herself out of her attraction to him. He was every bit as attracted to her. He might try to hide it. He might fight it tooth and nail. But he liked her as more than an employee.

She reached the chair. He pulled it out, offering the seat to her.

As she sat, her back met his hands still on the chair. Rivers of tingles flowed from the spot where they touched. Her breath shuddered in and stuttered out. Nerves filled her.

He stepped away. "We're skipping soup and salad, since it's late." All business, he sat on the chair next to hers. He lifted the metal cover first from her plate, then his own. "I present beef *brasato* with pappardelle and mint."

When the scent hit her, her mouth watered. All thoughts of attraction fled as her stomach rumbled greedily. She closed her eyes and savored the aroma.

"You like?"

Unable to help herself, she caught his gaze. "I'm amazed."

"Wait till you taste."

He smiled encouragingly. She picked up her fork, filled it with pasta and slid it into her mouth. Knowing he'd made this just for her, the ritual seemed very decadent, very sensual. Their eyes met as flavor exploded on her tongue.

"Oh, God."

He grinned. "Is good?"

"You know you don't even have to ask."

He sat back with a laugh. "I was top of my class. I trained both in Europe and the United States so I could ascertain the key to satisfying both palates." He smiled slowly. "I am a master."

She sliced off a bit of the beef. It was so good she had to hold back a groan. "No argument here."

"Wait till you taste my tiramisu."

"No salad but you made dessert?"

He leaned in, studied her. "Are you watching your weight?"

She shook her head. "No."

"Then prepare to be taken to a world of decadence."

She laughed, expecting him to pick up his fork and eat his own meal. Instead, he stayed perfectly still, his warm eyes on her.

"You like it when people go bananas over your food."

"Of course."

But that wasn't why he was studying her. There was a huge difference between pride in one's work and curiosity about an attraction and she knew that curiosity when she saw it.

She put down her fork, caught in his gaze, the moment. "What are we really doing here, Rafe?"

He shook his head. "I'm not sure."

"You aren't staring at me like someone who wants to make sure I like his food."

"You are beautiful."

Her heart shivered. Her eyes clung to his. She wanted him to have said that because he liked her, because he was ready to do something about it. But a romance between them would be a disaster. She'd be hurt. She'd have to leave Monte Calanetti. She could not take anything he said romantically.

Forking another bite of food, she casually said, "Beauty doesn't pay the rent."

His voice a mere whisper, he said, "Why do you tease me?"

Her face fell. "I don't tease you!"

"Of course, you do. Every day you dress more beautifully, but you don't talk to me."

"I'm smart enough to stay away when a guy warns me off."

"Yet you tell me I must be prepared for you to stay."

"Because you…" *Like me.* She almost said it. But his admitting he liked her would be nothing but trouble. He might like her in the moment, but he wouldn't like her forever. It was stupid to even have that discussion.

She steered them away from it. "Because if I stay, no more firing me. You're getting me permanently."

"You keep saying that as if I should be afraid." He slid his arm to the back of her chair. His fingers rose to toy with the blunt line of her chin-length hair. "But your staying is not a bad thing."

The wash of awareness roaring through her disagreed. If she fell in love with him, her staying would be a very bad thing. His touching her did not help matters. With his fingers brushing her hair, tickling her nape, she couldn't move…could barely breathe.

His hand shifted from her hairline and wrapped around the back of her neck so he could pull her closer. She told herself to resist. To be smart. But something in his eyes wouldn't let her. As she drew nearer, he leaned in. Their gazes held until his lips met hers, then her eyelids dropped. Her breathing stopped.

Warm and sweet, his lips brushed her, and she knew why she hadn't resisted. She so rarely got what she wanted in life that when tempted she couldn't say no. It might be wrong to want him, but she did.

His hand slid from her neck to her back, twisting her to

sit sideways on her chair. Her arms lifted slowly, her hands hesitantly went to his shoulders. Then he deepened the kiss and her mind went blank.

It wasn't so much the physical sensations that robbed her of thought but the fact that he kissed her. He finally, finally kissed her the way he had the night he'd walked her to her car.

When he thought she was free.

When he wanted there to be something between them.

The kiss went on and on. Her senses combined to create a flood of need so strong that something unexpected suddenly became clear. She was already in love with Rafe. She didn't have to worry that someday she might fall in love. Innocent and needy as she was, she had genuinely fallen in love—

And he was nowhere near in love with her.

He was strong and stubborn, set in his ways. He said he didn't do relationships. He said he didn't have time. He'd told her he hurt women. And if he hurt her, she'd never be able to work for him.

Did she want to risk this job for a fling?

To risk her new friends?

Did she want to be hurt?

Hadn't she been hurt, rejected enough in her life already?

She jerked away from him.

He pulled away slowly and ran his hand across his forehead. "Oh, my God. I am so sorry."

"Sorry?" She was steeped in desire sprinkled with a healthy dose of fear, so his apology didn't quite penetrate.

"I told you before. I do not steal other men's women."

"Oh." She squeezed her eyes shut. Paul was such a done deal for her that she'd taken him out of the equation. But Rafe didn't know that. For a second she debated keeping up the charade, if only to protect herself. But they had hit the point where that wasn't fair. She couldn't let Rafe go on thinking he was romancing another man's woman. Especially not when she had been such a willing participant.

She sucked in a breath, caught his gaze and quietly said, "I'm not engaged."

Rafe sat up in his chair. "What?"

She felt her cheeks redden. "I'm not engaged."

His face twisted with incredulity. "You *lied*?"

"No." She bounced from her seat and paced away. "Not really. My boyfriend had asked me to marry him. I told him I needed time to think about it. I was leaving for Italy anyway—"

He interrupted her as if confused. "So your boyfriend asked you to marry him and you ran away?"

She swallowed. "No. I inherited the money for a plane ticket to come here to find Rosa's relatives and I immediately tacked extra time onto my teaching tour. All that had been done before Paul proposed."

"So his proposal was a stopgap measure."

She frowned. "Excuse me?"

"Not able to keep you from going to Italy, he tied you to himself enough that you would feel guilty if you got involved with another man while you were away." He caught her gaze. "But it didn't work, did it?"

She closed her eyes. "No."

"It shouldn't have worked. It was a ploy. And you shouldn't feel guilty about anything that happened while you were here since you're really not engaged."

"Well, it doesn't matter anyway. I called him after we returned from Rome and officially rejected his proposal."

"You told him no?"

She nodded. "And told him I might be staying in Italy." She sucked in a breath. "He wished me luck."

Rafe sat back in his chair. "And so you are free." He combed his fingers through his hair. Laughed slightly.

The laugh kind of scared her. She'd taken away the one barrier she knew would protect her. All she had now to keep her from acting on her love for him was her willpower. Which she'd just proven wasn't very strong.

"I should go."

His gaze slowly met hers. "You haven't finished eating."

His soulful eyes held hers and her stomach jumped. Everything about him called to her on some level. He listened when she talked, appreciated her work at his restaurant… was blisteringly attracted to her.

What the hell would have happened if she hadn't broken that kiss? What would happen if she stayed, finished her meal, let them have more private time? With Paul gone as protection, would he seduce her? And if she resisted… what would she say? Another lie? *I don't like you? I'm not interested? I don't want to be hurt?*

The last wasn't a lie. And it would work. But she didn't want to say it. She didn't want to hear him tell her one more time that he couldn't commit. She didn't want this night to end on a rejection.

"I want to go home."

His eyes on her, he rose slowly. "Let's go, then. I will clean up in the morning."

Finally breaking eye contact, she walked to the front of Mancini's to get her coat. Her legs shook. Her breaths hurt. Not because she knew she was probably escaping making love, but because he really was going to hurt her one day.

Heard morning.

She rejected him. He... *Then she'd...*

CHAPTER ELEVEN

THE NEXT MORNING, Rafe was in the dining room when Dani used her key to unlock the front door and enter Mancini's. Around him, the waitresses and busboys busily set up tables. The wonderful aromas of his cooking filled the air. But when she walked in, Dani brought the real life to the restaurant. Dressed in a red sweater with a black skirt and knee-high boots, she was just the right combination of sexy and sweet.

And she'd rejected him the night before.

Even though she'd broken up with her man in America.

Without saying good morning, without as much as meeting her gaze, he turned on his heel and walked into the kitchen to the prep tables where he inspected the handiwork of two chefs.

He waved his hand over the rolled-out dough for a batch of ravioli. "This is good."

He tasted some sauce, inclined his head, indicating it was acceptable and headed for his workstation.

Emory scrambled over behind him. "Is Daniella here?"

"Yes." But even before Rafe could finish the thought, she pushed open the swinging doors to the kitchen and entered. She strolled to his prep table, cool and nonchalant as if nothing had happened between them.

But lots had happened between them. He'd kissed her. And she'd told him she didn't have a fiancé. Then she'd run. Rejecting him.

"Good morning."

He forced his gaze to hers. His eyes held hers for a beat before he said, "Good morning."

Emory caught her hands. "Did you enjoy your dinner?"

She laughed. "It was excellent." She met Rafe's gaze again. "Our chef is extraordinary."

His heart punched against his ribs. How could a man not take that as a compliment? She hadn't just eaten his food the night before. She'd returned his kiss with as much passion and fervor as he'd put into it.

Emory glowed. "This we know. And we count on you to make sure every customer knows."

"Oh, believe me. I've always been able to talk up the food from the bites you've given me. But eating an entire serving has seared the taste of perfection in my brain."

Emory grinned. "Great!"

"I think our real problem will be that I'll start stealing more bites and end up fat as a barrel."

Emory laughed but Rafe looked away, remembering his question from the night before. *Are you watching your weight?* One memory took him back to the scene, the mood, the moment. How nervous she'd seemed. How she'd jumped when his hand had brushed her back. How her jitters had disappeared while they were kissing and didn't return until they'd stopped.

Because she had to tell him about her fiancé.

She wasn't engaged.

She *had* responded to him.

Emory laughed. "Occupational hazard."

Her gaze ambled to Rafe's again. All they'd had the night before was a taste of what could be between them. Yes, he knew he'd warned her off. But she'd still kissed him. He'd given her plenty of time to move away, but she'd stayed. Knowing his terms—that he didn't want a relationship— she'd accepted his kiss.

With their gazes locked, she couldn't deny it. He could see the heat in her blue eyes.

"From here on out, when we create a new dish or perfect an old one," Emory continued, oblivious to the nonverbal conversation she and Rafe were having, "you will sample."

"I want her to have more than a sample."

The words sprang from him without any thought. But he wouldn't take them back. He no longer *wanted* an affair with her. He now *longed* for it, yearned for it in the depths of his being. And they were adults. They weren't kids. Love affairs were part of life. She might get hurt, or because they were both lovers and coworkers, she might actually understand him. His life. His time constraints. His passion for his dream—

She might be the perfect lover.

The truth of that rippled through him. It might not be smart to gamble with losing her, but he didn't think he'd lose her. In fact, he suddenly, passionately believed a long-term affair was the answer to their attraction.

"And I know more than a sample would be bad for me." She shifted her gaze to Emory before smiling and walking out of the kitchen.

Rafe shook his head and went back to his cooking. He had no idea if she was talking about his food or the subtle suggestion of an affair he'd made, but if she thought that little statement of hers was a deterrent, she was sadly mistaken.

Never in his life had he walked away from something he really wanted and this would not be an exception. Especially since he finally saw how perfect their situation could be.

Dani walked out of the kitchen and pressed her hand to her jumpy stomach. Those silver-gray eyes could get more across in one steamy look than most men could in foreplay.

To bolster her confidence, which had flagged again, she

reminded herself of her final thoughts as she'd fallen asleep the night before. Rafe was a mercurial man. Hot one minute. Cold the next. And for all she knew, he could seduce her one day and dump her the next. She needed security. Mancini's could be that security. She would not risk that for an affair. No matter how sexy his eyes were when he said it. How deep his voice.

She walked to the podium. Two couples awaited. She escorted them to a table. As the day wore on, customer after customer chatted with her about their tours or, if they were locals, their homes and families. The waitstaff laughed and joked with each other. The flow of people coming in and going out, eating, serving, clearing tables surrounded her, reminded her that *this* was why she wanted to stay in Italy, at Mancini's. Not for a man, a romance, but for a life. The kind of interesting, fun, exciting life she'd never thought she'd get.

She wanted this much more than she wanted a fling that ended in a broken heart and took away the job she loved.

At the end of the night, Emory came out with the white pay envelopes. He passed them around and smiled when he gave one to Dani. "This will be better than last time."

"So my raise is in here?"

"Yes." He nodded once and strode away.

Dani tucked the envelope into her skirt pocket and helped the waitresses with cleanup. When they were done, she grabbed her coat, not wanting to tempt fate by being the only remaining employee when Rafe came out of the kitchen.

She walked to her car, aware that Rafe's estimation of her worth sat by her hip, half afraid to open it. He had to value her enough to pay her well or she couldn't stay. She would not leave the security of her teaching job and an apartment she could afford, just to be scraping by in a foreign country, no matter how much she loved the area, its people and especially her job.

After driving the car into a space in Louisa's huge garage, Dani entered the house through the kitchen.

Louisa sat at the table, enjoying her usual cup of tea before bedtime. "How did it go? Was he nice? Was he romantic? Or did he ignore you?"

Dani slipped off her coat. "He hinted that we should have an affair."

"That's not good."

"Don't worry. I'm not letting him change the rules he made in Rome. He said that for us to work together there could be nothing between us." She sucked in a breath. "So he can't suddenly decide it's okay for us to have an affair."

Louisa studied her. "I think you're smart to keep it that way, but are you sure it's what you want?"

"Yes. Today customers reminded me of why I love this job. Between lunch and dinner, I worked with Emory to organize the schedule for ordering supplies and streamline it. He showed me a lot of the behind-the-scenes jobs it takes to make Mancini's work. Every new thing I see about running a restaurant seems second nature to me."

"And?"

"And, as I've thought all along, I have instincts for the business. This could be more than a job for me. It could be a real career. If Rafe wants to risk that by making a pass at me, I think I have the reasoning set in my head to tell him no."

Louisa's questioning expression turned into a look of joy. "So you're staying?"

"Actually—" she waved the envelope "—it all depends on what's in here. If my salary doesn't pay me enough for my own house or condo, plus food and spending money, I can't stay."

Louisa crossed her fingers for luck. "Here's hoping."

Dani shook her head. "You know, you're so good to me I want to stay just for our friendship."

Louise groaned. "Open the darned thing already!"

She sliced a knife across the top of the envelope. When she saw the amount of her deposit, she sat on the chair across from Louisa. "Oh, my God."

Louisa winced. "That bad?"

"It's about twice what I expected." She took a breath. "What's he doing?"

Louisa laughed. "Trying to keep you?"

"The amount is so high that it's actually insulting." She rose from her seat, grabbed her coat and headed for the door. "Half this check would have been sufficient to keep me. This amount? It's—offensive." Almost as if he was paying her to sleep with him. She couldn't bring herself to say the words to Louisa. But how coincidental was it that he'd dropped hints that he wanted to have an affair, then paid her more money than she was worth?

The insult of it vibrated through her. The nerve of that man!

"Where are you going?"

"To toss this back in his face."

Yanking open the kitchen door, she bounded out into the cold, cold garage. She jumped into the old car and headed back to Monte Calanetti, parking on a side street near the building where Rafe had shown her the almost-perfect condo.

But as she strode into the lobby, she remembered she needed a key to get into the elevator that would take her to the penthouse. Hoping to ask the doorman for help, she groaned when she saw the desk was empty.

Maybe she should take this as a sign that coming over here was a bad idea?

She sucked in a breath. No. Their situation was too personal to talk about at Mancini's. And she wanted to yell. She wanted to vent all her pent-up frustrations and maybe even throw a dish or two. She had to talk to him now. Alone.

She walked over to the desk and eyed the phone. Luckily, one of the marked buttons said Penthouse. She lifted the receiver and hit the button.

After only one ring, Rafe answered. "Hello?"

She sucked in a breath. "It's me. Daniella. I'm in your lobby and don't know how to get up to your penthouse."

"Pass the bank of elevators we used to get to the condo I showed you and turn right. I'll send my elevator down for you."

"Don't I need a key?"

"I'll set it to return. You just get in."

She did as he said, walking past the first set of elevators and turning to find the one for the penthouse. She stepped through the open doors and they swished closed behind her.

Riding up in the elevator with its modern gray geometric-print wallpaper and black slate floors, she was suddenly overwhelmed by something she hadn't considered, but should have guessed.

Rafe was a wealthy man.

Watching the doors open to an absolutely breathtaking home, she tried to wrap her brain around this new facet of Rafe Mancini. He wasn't just sexy, talented and mercurial. He was rich.

And she was about to yell at him? She, who'd always been poor? Always three paychecks away from homelessness? She'd never, ever considered that maybe the reason he didn't think anything permanent would happen between them might be because they were so different. They lived in two different countries. They had two different belief systems. And now she was seeing they came from two totally different worlds.

Rafe walked around a corner, holding two glasses of wine.

"Chianti." He handed one to her and motioned to the black leather sofa in front of a stacked stone fireplace in the sitting area.

Unable to help herself, she glanced around, trepidation filling her. Big windows in the back showcased the winking lights of the village. The black chairs around a long black dining room table had white upholstered backs and cushions. Plush geometric-patterned rugs sat on almost-black hardwood floors. The paintings on the pale gray walls looked ancient—valuable.

It was the home of a wealthy, wealthy man.

"Daniella?"

And maybe that's why he thought he could influence her with money? Because she came from nothing.

That made her even angrier.

She straightened her shoulders, caught his gaze. "Are you trying to buy me off?"

"Buy you off?"

"Get me to stop saying no to a relationship by bribing me with a big, fat salary?"

He laughed and fell to the black sofa. "Surely this is a first. An employee who complains about too much money." He shook his head with another laugh. "You said you wanted to be compensated for relocating. You said you wanted to be general manager. That is what a general manager makes."

"Oh." White-hot waves of heat suffused her. Up until this very second, everything that happened with reference to her job at Mancini's had been fun or challenging. He pushed. She pushed back. He wanted her for his restaurant. She made demands. But holding the check, hearing his explanation, everything took on a reality that had somehow eluded her. She was general manager of a restaurant. *This* was her salary.

He patted the sofa. "Come. Sit."

She took a few steps toward the sofa, but the lights of the village caught her attention and the feeling of being Alice in Wonderland swept through her.

"I never in my wildest dreams thought I'd make this much money."

"Well, teachers are notoriously underpaid in America, and though you'd studied a few things that might have steered you to a more lucrative profession, you chose to be a teacher."

Her head snapped up and she turned to face him. "How do you know?"

He batted a hand. "Do I look like an idiot? Not only did I do due diligence in investigating your work history, but also I took a look at your college transcripts. Do you really think I would have given you such an important job if you didn't have at least one university course in accounting?"

"No." Her gaze on him, she sat on the far edge of the sofa.

His voice became soft, indulgent. "Perhaps in the jumble of everything that's been happening I did not make myself clear. I've told you that I intend to be one of the most renowned chefs in Europe. I can't do that from one restaurant outside an obscure Tuscan village. My next restaurant will be in Rome. The next in Paris. The next in London. I will build slowly, but I will build."

"You'd leave Mancini's?" Oddly, the thought actually made her feel better.

"I will leave Mancini's in Tuscany when I move to Rome to build Mancini's Rome." He frowned. "I thought I told you this." His frown deepened. "I know for sure I told you that Mancini's was only a stepping stone."

"You might have mentioned it." But she'd forgotten. She forgot everything but her attraction to him when he was around. She'd accused him of using promotions to cover his feelings for her. But she'd used her feelings for him to block what was really going on with her job, and now, here she was, in a job so wonderful she thought she might faint from the joy of it.

"With you in place I can move to the next phase of my business plan. But there's a better reason for me to move on. You and I both worry that if we do something about our attraction, you will be hurt when it ends and Mancini's will lose you." He smiled. "So I fix."

"You fix?"

"I leave. Once I start my second restaurant, you will not have to deal with me on a day-to-day basis." His smile grew. "And we will understand each other because we'll both work in the same demanding profession. You will understand if I cancel plans at the last minute."

This time the heat that rained down on her had nothing to do with embarrassment. He'd really thought this through. Like a man willing to shift a few things because he liked her.

"Oh."

"There are catches."

Her gaze jumped to his. "Catches?"

"Yes. I will be using you for help creating the other restaurants. To scout sites. To hire staff. To teach them how to create our atmosphere. That is your real talent." He held her gaze. "That is also why your salary is so high. You are a big part of Mancini's success. You created that atmosphere. I want it not just in one restaurant, but all of them, and you will help me get it."

The foster child taught not to expect much out of life, the little girl who learned manners only by mimicking what she saw in school, the Italian tourist who borrowed Louisa's clothes and felt as though she was playing dress up every day she got ready for work, that girl quivered with happiness at the compliment.

The woman who'd been warned by him that he would hurt her struggled with fear.

"You didn't just create a great job for me. You cleared the way for us to have an affair."

Rafe sighed. "Why are you so surprised? You're beautiful. You're funny. You make me feel better about myself. My life. Yes, I want you. So I figured out a way I could have you."

She sucked in a breath. It was heady stuff to see the lengths he was willing to go to be with her. And she also saw the one thing he wasn't saying.

"You like me."

"What did you think? That I'd agonize this much over someone I just wanted to sleep with?"

She smiled. "You agonized?"

He batted a hand in dismissal. "You're a confusing woman, Daniella."

"And you've gone to some pretty great lengths to make sure we can...see each other."

His face turned down into his handsome pout. "And you should appreciate it."

She did. She just didn't know how to handle it.

"Is it so hard to believe I genuinely like you?"

"No." She just never expected he would say it. But he said it easily. And the day would probably come when those feelings would expand. He truly liked her and she was so in love with him that her head spun. This was not going to be an affair. He was talking about a relationship.

Happiness overwhelmed her and she couldn't resist. She set her wineglass on the coffee table and scooted beside him.

A warm, syrupy feeling slid through Rafe. But on its heels was the glorious ping of arousal. Before he realized what she was about to do, she kissed him. Quick and sweet, her lips met his. When she went to pull back, he slid his hand across her lower back and hauled her to him. He deepened their kiss, using his tongue to tempt her. Nibbling her lips. Opening his mouth over hers until she responded with the kind of passion he'd always known lived in her heart.

He pulled away. "You play with fire."

Her tongue darted out to moisten her lips. Temptation roared through him and all his good intentions to take it slowly with her melted like snow in April. He could have her now. In this minute. He could take what he greedily wanted.

She drew a breath. "How is it playing with fire if we really, really like each other?"

She was killing him. Sitting so warm and sweet beside him, tempting him with what he wanted before she was ready.

Still, though it pained him, he knew the right thing to do.

"So we will do this right. When you are ready, when you trust me, we will take the next step."

Her gaze held his. "When I trust you?"

"*Si*. When I feel you trust me enough to understand why we can be lovers, you will come to my bed."

Her face scrunched as she seemed to think all that through. "Wait...this is just about becoming lovers?"

"Yes."

"But you just said you wouldn't worry that much about someone you wanted to sleep with." She caught his gaze. "You said you agonized."

"Because we will not be a one-night stand. We will be lovers. Besides, I told you. I don't do relationships."

"You also said that you'd never have a romance with an employee." She met his gaze. "But you changed that rule."

"I made accommodations. I made everything work."

"Not for me! I don't just want a fling! I want something that's going to last."

His eyebrows rose. "Something that will last?" He frowned. "Forever?"

"Forever!"

"I tried forever. It did not work for me."

"You tried?"

"*Si*."

"And?"

"And it ended badly." He couldn't bring himself to explain that he'd been shattered, that he'd almost given up his dream for a woman who had left him, that he'd been a ball of pain and confusion until he pulled himself together and realized his dreams depended on him not trusting another woman with his heart or so much of his life.

"*Cara*, marriage is for other people. It's full of all kinds of things incompatible with the man I have to be to be a success."

"You *never* want to get married?"

"No!" He tossed his hands. "What I have been saying all along? Do you not listen?"

She stood up. The pain on her face cut through him like a knife. Though he suddenly wondered why. He'd always known she wanted security. He'd always known he couldn't give it to her. He couldn't believe he'd actually tried to get her to accept less than what she needed.

He rose, too. "Okay, let's forget this conversation happened. It's been a long day. I'm tired. I also clearly misinterpreted things. Come to Mancini's tomorrow as general manager."

She took two steps back. "You're going to keep me, even though I won't sleep with you?"

"Yes." But the sadness that filled him confused him. He'd had other women tell him no and he'd walked away unconcerned. Her *no* felt like the last page of a favorite book, the end of something he didn't want to see end. And yet he knew she couldn't live with his terms and he couldn't live with hers.

CHAPTER TWELVE

AGREEING THAT HE was right about at least one thing—she was too tired, too spent, to continue this discussion—Dani walked to the elevator. He followed her, hit the button that would close the door and turned away.

She sucked in a breath and tried to still her hammering heart. But it was no use. They really couldn't find a middle ground. It was sweet that he'd tried, but it was just another painful reminder that she had fallen in love with the wrong man.

She squeezed her eyes shut. She'd be okay—

No, she wouldn't. She'd fallen in love with him. Unless he really stayed out of Mancini's, she'd always be in love with him. Then she'd spend her life wishing he could fall for her, too. Or maybe one day she'd succumb. She'd want him so much she'd forget everything else, and she'd start the affair he wanted. With the strength of her feelings, that would seal the deal for her. She'd love him forever. Then she'd never have a home. Never have a family. Always be alone.

She thought of the plane ticket tucked away somewhere in her bedroom in Louisa's house. Now that she knew he wanted nothing but an affair, which was unacceptable, she could go home.

But she didn't want to go home. She wanted to run Mancini's. He'd handed her the opportunity with her general managership—

And he was leaving. Maybe not permanently, but for the next several years he wouldn't be around every day. Most of the time, he'd be in other cities, opening new restaurants.

Wouldn't she be a fool to leave now? Especially since she had a few days before she had to use that ticket. Maybe the wise thing to do would be to use this time to figure out if she could handle working with him as the boss she only saw a few times a month?

The next day when she walked in the door and felt the usual surge of rightness, she knew the job was worth fighting for. In her wildest dreams she'd never envisioned herself successful. Competent, making a living, getting a decent apartment? Yes. But never as one of the people at the top. Hiring employees. Creating atmosphere. Would she really let some feelings, one *man*, steal this from her?

No! No! She'd been searching for something her entire life. She believed she'd found it at Mancini's. It would take more than unrequited love to scare her away from that.

When Emory sat down with her in between lunch and dinner and showed her the human resources software, more of the things she'd learned in her university classes tumbled back.

"So I'll be doing all the admin?"

Emory nodded. "With Rafe gone, setting up Mancini's Rome, I'll be doing all the cooking. I won't have time to help."

"That's fine." She studied the software on the screen, simple stuff, really. Basically, it would do the accounting for her. And the rest? It was all common sense. Ordering. Managing the dining room. Hiring staff.

He squeezed her hand. "You and me…we make a good team."

Her smile grew and her heart lightened. She loved Emory.

Even tempered with the staff and well acquainted with

Rafe's recipes, he was the perfect chef. As long as Rafe wasn't around, she would be living her dream.

She returned his hand squeeze. "Yeah. We do."

When she and Emory were nearly finished going over the software programs, Rafe walked into the office. As always when he was around, she tingled. But knowing this was one of the things she was going to have to deal with, because he wasn't going away permanently, she simply ignored it.

"Have you taught her payroll?"

Emory rose from his seat. "Yes. In fact, she explained a thing or two to me."

Rafe frowned. "How so?"

"She understands the software. I'm a chef. I do not."

Dani also rose from her chair. "I've worked with software before to record grades. Essentially, most spreadsheet programs run on the same type of system, the same theories. My boyfriend—" She stopped when the word *boyfriend* caught in her throat. Emory's gaze slid over to her. But Rafe's eyes narrowed.

She took a slow, calming breath. "My ex-boyfriend Paul is a computer genius. I picked up a few things from him."

Rafe turned away. "Well, let us be glad for him, then."

He said the words calmly, but Dani heard the tension in his voice. There were feelings there. Not just lust. So it wouldn't be only her own feelings she'd be fighting. She'd also have to be able to handle his. And that might be a little trickier.

"I've been in touch with a Realtor in Rome. I go to see buildings tomorrow."

A look passed between him and Emory.

Emory tucked the software manual into the bottom bin of an in basket. "Good. It's time to get your second restaurant up and running." He slid from behind the desk. "But right now I have to supervise dinner."

He scampered out of the room and Rafe's gaze roamed over to hers again. "I'd like for you to come to Rome with me."

Heat suffused her and her tongue stuck to the roof of her mouth. "Me?"

"I want you to help me scout locations."

"Really?"

"I told you. You are the one who created the atmosphere of this Mancini's. If I want to re-create it, I think you need to be in on choosing the site."

Because that made sense and because she did have to learn to deal with him as a boss, owner of the restaurant for which she worked, she tucked away any inappropriate longings and smiled. "Okay."

She could be all business because that's what really worked for them.

The next day, after walking through an old, run-down building with their Realtor, Rafe and Dani stepped out into the bright end-of-February day.

"I could do with a coffee right now."

He glanced at her. In her sapphire-blue coat and white mittens, she looked cuddly, huggable. And very, very, very off-limits. Her smiles had been cool. Her conversations stilted. But she'd warmed up a bit when they actually began looking at buildings.

"Haven't you already had two cups of coffee?"

She slid her hand into the crook of his elbow, like a friend or a cousin, someone allowed innocent, meaningless touches.

"Don't most Italians drink something like five cups a day?"

When he said, "Bah," she laughed.

All morning, their conversation at his apartment two nights ago had played over and over and over in his head. She wanted a commitment and he didn't. So he'd figured out a way they could be lovers and work together and she'd rejected it. He'd had to accept that.

But being with her this morning, without actually being allowed to touch her or even contemplate kissing her was making him think all kinds of insane things. Like how empty his life was. How much he would miss her when he stopped working at the original Mancini's and headquartered himself in Rome.

So though he knew her hand at his elbow meant nothing, he savored the simple gesture. It was a safe, nonthreatening way to touch her and have her touch him. Even if he did know it would lead to nothing.

"Besides, I love coffee. It makes me warm inside."

"True. And it is cold." He slid his arm around her shoulders. Her thick coat might keep her toasty, but it was another excuse to touch her.

They continued down the quiet street, but as they approached a shop specializing in infant clothing, the wheels of a baby stroller came flying out the door and straight for Daniella's leg. He caught her before she could as much as wobble and shifted her out of the way.

The apologetic mom said, *"Scusi!"*

Dani laughed. In flawless Italian she said, "No harm done." Then she bent and chucked the chin of the baby inside the stroller. "Isn't she adorable!"

The proud mom beamed. Rafe stole a quiet look at the kid and his lips involuntarily rose as a chuckle rumbled up from the deepest part of him. "She likes somebody's cooking."

The mom explained that the baby had her father's love of all things sweet, but Rafe's gaze stayed on the baby. She'd caught his eye and cooed at him, her voice a soft sound, almost a purr, and her eyes as shiny as a harvest moon.

A funny feeling invaded his chest.

Dani gave the baby a big, noisy kiss on the cheek, said

goodbye to the mom and took his arm so they could re-
sume their walk down the street.

They ducked into a coffeehouse and she inhaled deeply.
"Mmm...this reminds me of being back in the States."

He shook his head. "You Americans. You copy the idea
of a coffeehouse from us, then come over here and act like
we must meet your standards."

With a laugh, she ordered two cups of coffee, remembering his choice of brews from earlier that morning. She
also ordered two scones.

"I hope you're hungry."

She shrugged out of her coat before sitting on the chair
he pulled out for her at a table near a window. "I just need
something to take the edge off my growling stomach. The
second scone is for you."

"I don't eat pastries from a vendor who sells in bulk."

She pushed the second scone in front of him anyway.
"Such a snob."

He laughed. "All right. Fine. I will taste." He bit into
the thing and to his surprise it was very good. Even better with a sip or two of coffee. So tasty he ate the whole
darned thing.

"Not quite the pastry snob anymore, are you?"

He sat back. He truly did not intend to pursue her. He
respected her dreams, the way he respected his own. But
that didn't stop his feelings for her. With his belly full of
coffee and scone, and Daniella happy beside him, these
quiet minutes suddenly felt like spun gold.

She glanced around. "I'll bet you've brought a woman
or two here."

That broke the spell. "What?" He laughed as he shifted
uncomfortably on his chair. "What makes you say that?"

"You're familiar with this coffeehouse. This street. You
were even alert enough to pull me out of the way of the
oncoming stroller at that baby shop." She shrugged. "You

might not have come here precisely, but you've brought women to Rome."

"Every Italian man brings women to Rome." He toyed with his now-empty mug. He'd lived with Kamila just down the street. He'd dreamed of babies like the little girl in the stroller.

"I told you about Paul. I think you need to tell me about one of your women to even the score."

"You make me sound like I dated an army."

She tossed him an assessing look. "You might have."

Not about to lie, he drew a long breath and said, "There were many."

She grimaced. "Just pick one."

"Okay. How about Lisette?"

She put her elbow on the table, her eyes keen with interest. "Sounds French."

"She was."

"Ah."

"I met her when she was traveling through Italy…" But even as he spoke, he remembered that she was more driven than he was. *He* had taken second place to *her* career. At the time he hadn't minded, but remembering the situation correctly, he didn't feel bad about that breakup.

"So what happened?"

He waved a hand. "Nothing. She was just very married to her career."

"Like you?"

He laughed. "Two peas in a pod. But essentially we didn't have time for each other."

"You miss her?"

"No." He glanced up. "Honestly, I don't miss any of the women who came into and walked out of my life."

But he had missed Kamila and he would miss Dani if she left. He'd miss her insights at the restaurant and the way she made Mancini's come alive. But most of all he'd miss her smile. Miss the way she made *him* feel.

The unspoken truth sat between them. Their gazes caught, then clung. That was the problem with Dani. He felt for her the same things he had felt with Kamila. Except stronger. The emotions that raced through him had nothing to do with affairs, and everything to do with the kind of commitment he swore he'd never make again. That was why he'd worked so hard to figure out a way they could be together. It was why he also worked so hard to steer them away from a commitment. This woman, this Dani, was everything Kamila had been...and more.

And it only highlighted why he needed to be free.

He cleared his throat. "There was a woman."

Dani perked up.

"Kamila." He toyed with his mug again, realizing he was telling her about Kamila as much to remind himself as to explain to Dani. "She was sunshine when she was happy and a holy terror when she was not."

Dani laughed. "Sounds exciting."

He caught her gaze again. "It was perfect."

Her eyes softened with understanding. "Oh."

"You wonder how I know I'm not made for a relationship? Kamila taught me. First, she drew me away from my dream. To please her, I turned down apprenticeships. I took a permanent job as a sous-chef. I gave up the idea of being renowned and settled for being happy." Though it hurt, he held her gaze. "We talked about marriage. We talked about kids. And one day I came home from work and discovered her things were gone. *She* was gone. I'd given up everything for her and the life I thought I wanted, and she left without so much as an explanation of why."

"I'm sorry."

"Don't be." He sucked in a breath, pulled away from her, as his surety returned to him. "That loss taught me to be careful. But more than that it taught me never to do anything that jeopardizes who I am."

"So this Kamila really did a number on you."

"Were you not listening? There was no number. Yes, she broke my heart. But it taught me lessons. I'm fine."

"You're wounded." She caught his gaze. "Maybe even more wounded than I am."

He said, "That's absurd," but he felt the pangs of loss, the months of loneliness as if it were yesterday.

"At least I admit I need someone. You let one broken romance evolve into a belief that a few buildings and success are the answers to never being hurt. Do you think that when you're sixty you're going to look around and think 'I wish I'd started more Mancini's'? Or do you think you're going to envy your friends' relationships, wish for grandkids?"

"I told you I don't want those things." But even as he said the words, he knew they were a lie. Not a big pulsing lie, but a quiet whisper of doubt. Especially with the big eyes of the baby girl in the stroller pressed into his memory. With a world of work to do to get his chain of restaurants started, what she said should seem absurd. Instead, he saw himself old, his world done, his success unparalleled and his house empty.

He blinked away that foolish thought. He had family. He had friends. His life would never be empty. That was Dani's fear, not his.

"Let's go. Mario gave me the address of the next building where we're to meet him."

Quiet, they walked to his car, slid in and headed to the other side of the city. More residential than the site of the first property, this potential Mancini's had the look of a home, as did his old farmhouse outside Monte Calanetti.

He opened the door and she entered the aging building before him. Mario came over and shook his hand, but Dani walked to the far end of the huge, open first floor. She found the latch on the shutters that covered a big back window. When she flipped it, the shutters opened. Sunlight poured in.

Rafe actually *felt* the air change, the atmosphere shift. Though the building was empty and hollow, with her walking in, the sunlight pouring in through a back window, everything clicked.

This was his building. And she really was the person who brought life to his dining rooms. He'd had success of a sort without her, but she breathed the life into his vision, made it more, made it the vision he saw when he closed his eyes and dreamed.

Dani ambled to the center of the room. Pointing near the door, she said, "We'd put the bar over here."

He frowned. "Why not here?" He motioned to a far corner, out of the way.

"Not only can we give customers the chance to wait at the bar for their tables, but also we might get a little extra drink business." She smiled at him as she walked over. "Things will be just a tad different in a restaurant that's actually in a residential area of a city." Her smile grew. "But I think it could be fun to play around with it."

He crossed his arms on his chest to keep from touching her. He could almost feel the excitement radiating from her. While he envisioned a dining room, happy customers eating *his* food, he could tell she saw more. Much more. She saw things he couldn't bring into existence because all he cared about was the food.

"What would you play around with?"

Her gaze circled the room. "I'm not sure. We'd want to keep the atmosphere we've build up in Mancini's, but here we'd also have to become part of the community. You can get some really great customer relations by being involved with your neighbors." She tapped her finger on her lips. "I'll need to think about this."

Rafe's business instincts kicked in. He didn't know what she planned to do, but he did know whatever she decided, it would probably be good. Really good. Because she had the other half of the gift he'd been given.

He also knew she was happy. Happier than he'd ever
seen her. Her blue eyes lit with joy. Her shoulders were
back. Her steps purposeful. Confidence radiated from her.

"You want Mancini's to be successful as much as I want
it to be successful."

She laughed. "I doubt that. But I do want it to be the
best it can be." She glanced around, then faced him again.
"In all the confusion between us, I don't think I've ever
said thank-you."

"You wish to thank me?"

"For the job. For the fun of it." She shrugged. "I need
this. I don't show it often but deep down inside me, there's
a little girl who always wondered where she'd end up. *She*
needed the chance to be successful. To prove her worth."

He smiled. "She'll certainly get that with Mancini's."

"And we're going to have a good time whipping this
into shape."

He smiled. "That's the plan."

Her face glowed. "Good."

He said, "Good," but his voice quieted, his heart stilled,
as he suddenly realized something he should have all along.
Kamila had broken his heart. But Dani had wheedled her
way into his soul. His dream.

If he and Dani got close and things didn't work out, he
wouldn't just spend a month drinking himself silly. He'd
lose everything.

CHAPTER THIRTEEN

THE NEXT DAY in the parking lot of Mancini's, Dani switched off the ignition of Louisa's little car, knowing that she was two days away from D-day. Decision day. The day she had to use her return ticket to New York City.

Being with Rafe in Rome had shown her he respected her opinion. Oh, hell, who was she kidding? Telling her about Kamila had been his way of putting the final nail in the coffin of her relationship dreams. It hurt, but she understood. In fact, in a way she was even glad. Now that she knew why he was so determined, she could filter her feelings for him away from her longing for a relationship with him and into his dream. He needed her opinion. He wanted to focus on food, on pleasing customer palates. She saw the ninety thousand other things that had to be taken care of. Granted, he'd chosen a great spot for the initial Mancini's. He'd fixed the building to perfection. But a restaurant in the city came with different challenges.

Having lived in New York and eaten at several different kinds of restaurants, she saw things from a customer's point of view. And she knew exactly how she'd set up Mancini's Rome restaurant.

She *knew*.

The confidence of it made her forget all about returning to New York, and stand tall. She entered the kitchen on her way to the office, carrying a satchel filled with pictures she'd printed off the internet the night before using Louisa's laptop.

This was her destiny.

Then she saw Rafe entering through the back door and her heart tumbled. He wore the black leather jacket. He hadn't pulled his hair into the tie yet and it curled around his collar. His eyes were cool, serious. When their gazes met, she swore she could feel the weight of his sadness.

She didn't understand what the hell he had to be sad about. He was getting everything he wanted. Except her heart. He didn't know that he already had her love, but their good trip the day before proved they could work together, even be friends, and he should appreciate that.

Everything would be perfect, as long as he didn't kiss her. Or tempt her. And yesterday he'd all but proven he needed her too much to risk losing her.

"I have pictures of things I'd like your opinion on."

Emory looked from one to the other. "Pictures?"

Rafe slowly ambled into the kitchen. "Dani has ideas for the restaurant in Rome."

Emory gaped at him. "Who cares? You have a hundred-person wedding tomorrow afternoon."

Dani's mouth fell open. Rafe's eyes widened. "We didn't cancel that?"

"We couldn't," Emory replied before Dani said anything, obviously taking the heat for it. "So I called the bride's mother yesterday and got the specifics. Tomorrow morning, we'll all come here early to get the food prepared. In the afternoon Dani and I will go to the wedding. I will watch your food, Chef Mancini. Your reputation will not suffer."

Rafe slowly walked over to Dani. "You know we cannot do this again!"

"Come on, Chef Rafe." She smiled slightly, hoping to dispel the tension, again confused over why he was so moody. "Put Mr. Mean Chef away. I got the message the day you fired me over this." With that she strode into the office, dumped her satchel on the desk and swung out again. She thought of the plane ticket in her pocket and reminded herself that in two days she wouldn't have that option. When he yelled, she'd have to handle it.

"I'll be in the dining room, checking with Allegra on how things went yesterday."

Rafe sagged with defeat as she stormed out. He shouldn't have yelled at her again about the catering, but everything in his life was spinning out of control. He saw babies in his sleep and woke up hugging his pillow, dreaming he was hugging Daniella. The logical part of him insisted they were a team, that a real relationship would enhance everything they did. They would own Mancini's together, build it together, build a life together.

The other part, the part that remembered Kamila, could only see disaster when the relationship ended. When Kamila left, he could return to his dream. If Dani left, she took half of his dream with her.

He faced Emory. "I appreciate how you have handled this. And I apologize for exploding." He sucked in a breath. "As penance, I will go to the wedding tomorrow."

Emory laughed. "If you're expecting me to argue, you're wrong. I don't want to be a caterer, either."

"As I said, this is penance."

"Then you really should be apologizing to Dani. It was her you screamed at."

He glanced at the door as he shrugged out of his jacket. She was too upset with him now. And she was busy. He would find a minute at the end of the night to apologize for his temper. If he was opting out of a romance because he needed her, he couldn't lose her over his temper.

But she didn't hang around after work that night. And the next morning, he couldn't apologize because they weren't alone. First, he'd cooked with a full staff. Then he'd had to bring Laz and Gino, two of the busboys, to the wedding to assist with setup and teardown. They drove to the vineyard in almost complete silence, every mile stretching Rafe's nerves.

Seeing the sign for 88 Vineyards, he turned down the winding lane. The top of a white tent shimmered in the winter sun. Thirty yards away, white folding chairs created two wide rows of seating for guests. He could see the bride and groom standing in front of the clergyman, holding hands, probably saying their vows.

He pulled the SUV beside the tent. "It looks like we'll need to move quickly to get everything set up for them to eat."

Dani opened her door of the SUV. "Not if there are pictures. I've known brides who've taken hours of pictures."

"Bah. Nonsense."

Ignoring him, she climbed out of the SUV.

Rafe opened his door and recessional music swelled around him. Still Dani said nothing. Her cold shoulder stung more than he wanted to admit.

A quick glance at the wedding ceremony netted him the sight of the bride and groom coming down the aisle. The sun cast them in a golden glow, but their smiles were even more radiant. He watched as the groom brought the bride's hand to his lips. Saw the worship in his eyes, the happiness, and immediately Rafe thought of Daniella. About the times he'd kissed her hand. Walked her to her car. Waited with bated breath for her arrival every morning.

He reached into his SUV to retrieve a tray of his signature ravioli. Handing it to Laz, he sneaked a peek at Daniella as she made her way to the parents of the bride, who'd walked out behind the happy couple. They smiled at her, the bride's mom talking a million words a second as she pointed inside the tent. Daniella set her hand on the mom's forearm and suddenly the nervous woman calmed.

He watched in heart-stealing silence. A lifetime of rejection had taught her to be kind. And one failed romance had made him mean. Bitter.

As he pulled out the second ravioli tray, Dani walked over.

"Apparently the ceremony was lovely."

"Peachy."

"Come on. I know you're mad at me for arranging this. But at the time, I didn't know any better and in a few hours all of this will be over."

He sucked in a breath. "I'm not mad at you. I'm angry with myself—" *Because I finally understand I'm not worried about you leaving me, or even losing my dreams. I'm disappointed in myself* "—for yelling at you yesterday."

"Oh." She smiled slowly. "Thanks."

The warm feeling he always got when she smiled invaded every inch of him. "You're welcome."

Not waiting for him to say anything else, she headed inside the white tent where the dinner and reception would be held. He followed her only to discover she was busy setting up the table for the food. He and Laz worked their magic on the warmers he'd brought to keep everything the perfect temperature. Daniella and Gino brought in the remaining food.

And nothing happened.

People milled around the tables in the tent, chatting, celebrating the marriage. Wine flowed from fancy bottles. The mother of the bride socialized. The parents of the groom walked from table to table. A breeze billowed around the tent as everyone talked and laughed.

He stepped outside, nervous now. He'd never considered himself wrong, except that he'd believed giving up apprenticeships for Kamila had made him weak. But setback after setback had made Dani strong. It was humbling to realize his master-chef act wasn't a sign of strength, but selfishness. Even more humbling to realize he didn't know what to do with the realization.

Wishing he still smoked, he ambled around the grounds, gazing at the blue sky, and then he turned to walk down a cobblestone path, only to find himself three feet away from the love-struck bride and groom.

He almost groaned, until he noticed the groom lift the bride's chin and tell her that everything was going to be okay.

His eyebrows rose. They hadn't even been married twenty minutes and there was trouble in paradise already?

She quietly said, "Everything is not going to be okay. My parents are getting a divorce."

Rafe thought of the woman in pink, standing with the guy in the tux as they'd chatted with Dani at the end of the ceremony, and he almost couldn't believe it.

The groom shook his head. "And they're both on their best behavior. Everything's fine."

"For now. What will I do when we get home from our honeymoon? I'll have to choose between the two of them for Christmas and Easter." She gasped. "I'll have to get all my stuff out of their house before they sell it." She sucked in a breath. "Oh, my God." Her eyes filled with tears. "I have no home."

Rafe's chest tightened. He heard every emotion Dani must feel in the bride's voice. No home. No place to call her own.

A thousand emotions buffeted him, but for the first time since he'd met Dani he suddenly felt what she felt. The emptiness of belonging to no one. The longing for a place to call her own. And he realized the insult he'd leveled when he'd told her he wanted to sleep with her, but not keep her.

"I'll be your home." The groom pulled his bride away from the tree. "It's us now. We'll make your home."

We'll make your home.

Rafe stepped back, away from the tree that hid him, the words vibrating through him. But the words themselves were nothing without the certainty behind them.

The strength of conviction in the groom's voice. The promise that wouldn't be broken.

We'll make your home.

"Let's go inside. We have a wedding to celebrate."

She smiled. "Yes. We do."

Rafe discreetly followed them into the tent. He watched them walk to the main table as if nothing was wrong, as the dining room staff scrambled to fill serving bowls with his food and get it onto tables.

The toast of the best man was short. Rafe's eyes strayed to Daniella. He desperately wanted to give her a home. A real one. A home like he'd grown up in with kids and a dog and noisy suppers.

This was what life had stolen from her and from him. When Kamila left, she hadn't taken his dream. She'd bruised him so badly, he'd lost his faith in real love. He'd lost his dream of a house and kids. And when it all suddenly popped up in the form of a woman so beautiful that she stole his breath, he hadn't seen it.

Dear God. He loved her. He loved her enough to give up everything he wanted, even Mancini's, to make her dreams come true. But he wouldn't have to give up anything. His dream was her dream. And her dream was now his dream.

Their meal eaten, the bride and groom rose from the table. The seating area was quickly dismantled by vineyard staff, who left a circle of chairs around the tent and a clear floor on which to dance.

The band introduced the bride and groom and he took her hand and kissed it before he led her in their dance.

Emotion choked Rafe. He'd spent the past years believing the best way to live his dream was to hold himself back, forget love, when the truth was he simply needed to meet the right woman to realize his dream would be hollow, empty without her.

"Hey." Daniella walked up beside him. "Dinner is

over. We can dismantle our warmers, take our trays and go home."

He faced her. Emotions churned inside him. Feelings for Dani that took root and held on. He'd found his one. He'd fired her, yelled at her, asked her to become his lover. And she'd held her ground. Stood up to him. Refused him. Forced him to work by her terms. And she had won him.

But he had absolutely no idea how to tell her that.

She picked up an empty tray and headed for his SUV. Grabbing up another empty tray, he scurried after her.

"I've been thinking about our choice."

She slid the tray into the SUV. "Our choice?"

"You know. Our choice not to—"

Before he could finish, the busboys came out of the tent with more trays. Frustration stiffened his back. With a quick glance at him, Dani walked back to the noisy reception for more pans. The busboys got the warmers.

Simmering with the need to talk, Rafe silently packed it all inside the back of his SUV.

Nerves filled him as he drove his empty pans, warmers and employees to Mancini's. When they arrived, the restaurant bustled with diners. Emory raced around the kitchen like a madman. Daniella pitched in to help Allegra. Rafe put on his smock, washed his hands and helped Emory.

Time flew, as it always did when he was busy, but Rafe kept watching Daniella. Something was on her mind. She smiled. She worked. She teased with staff. But he heard something in her voice. A catch? No it was more of an easing back. The click of connection he always heard when she spoke with staff was missing. It was as if she were distancing herself—

Oh, dear God.

In all the hustle and bustle that had taken place in the past four weeks, she'd never made the commitment to stay.

And she had a plane ticket for the following morning.

The night wound down. Emory headed for the office to

do some paperwork. Rafe casually ambled into the dining room. As the last of the waitstaff left, he pulled a bottle of Chianti from the rack and walked around the bar to a stool.

He watched Dani pause at the podium, as if torn between reaching for her coat and joining him. His heart chugged. Everything inside him froze.

Finally, she turned to him. Her lips lifted into a warm smile and she sashayed over.

Interpreting her coming to him as a good sign, he didn't give himself time to think twice. He caught her hands, lifted both to his lips and said, "Pick me."

Her brow furrowed. "What?"

"I know you're thinking about leaving. I see it on your face. Hear it in your voice. I know you think you have nothing here but a job, but that's not true. I need you for so much more. So pick me. Do not work for me. Pick me. Keep me. Take *me*."

Her breath hitched. "You're asking me to quit?"

"No." He licked his suddenly dry lips. He'd known this woman only twenty-four days. Yet what he felt was stronger than anything he'd ever felt before.

"Daniella, I think I want you to marry me."

Dani's heart bounced to a stop as she yanked her hands out of his.

"What?"

"I want you to marry me."

She couldn't stop the thrill that raced through her, but even through her shock she'd heard his words clearly. "You said *think*. You said you *think* you want to marry me."

He laughed a bit as he pulled his hand through his hair. "It's so fast for me. My God, I never even thought I'd want to get married. Now I can't imagine my life without you." He caught her hand again, caught her gaze. "Marry me."

His voice had become stronger. His conviction obvious.

"Oh." She wanted to say yes so bad it hurt to wrestle the

word back down her throat. But she had to. "For a month you've said you don't do relationships. Now suddenly you want to marry me?"

He laughed. "All these years, I thought I was weak because I gave Kamila what she wanted and she left me anyway. So I made myself strong. People saw me as selfish. I thought I was determined."

"I understand that."

"Now I see I *was* selfish. I did not want to lose my dream again."

"I understand that, too."

He shook his head fiercely. "You're missing what I'm telling you. I might have been broken by her loss, but Kamila was the wrong woman for me. I was never my real self with her. I was one compromise after another. With you, I am me. I see my temper and I rein it back. I see myself with kids. I see a house. I long to make you happy."

Oh, dear God, did the man have no heart? "Don't say things you don't mean."

"I never say things I don't mean. I love you, Daniella." He reached for her again. "Do not get on that plane tomorrow."

She stepped back, so far that he couldn't touch her, and pressed her fingers to her lips. Her heart so very desperately wanted to believe every word he said. Her brain had been around, though, for every time that same heart was broken. This man had called Paul's proposal a stopgap measure…yet, here he was doing the same thing.

"No."

His face fell. "No?"

"What did you tell me about Paul asking to marry me the day before I left New York?"

He frowned.

"You said it was a stopgap measure. A way to keep me." He walked toward her. "Daniella…"

She halted him with a wave of her hand. "Don't. I feel

foolish enough already. You're afraid I'm going to go home so you make a proposal that mocks everything I believe in."

She yearned to close her eyes at the horrible sense of how little he thought of her, but she held them open, held back her tears and made the hardest decision of her life.

"I'm going back to New York." Her heart splintered in two as she realized this really was the end. They'd never bump into each other at a coffee shop, never sit beside each other in the subway, never accidentally go to the same dry cleaner. He lived thousands of miles away from her and there'd be no chance for them to have the time they needed to really fall in love. He'd robbed them of that with his insulting proposal.

"Mancini's will be fine without me." She tried a smile. "*You* will be fine without me." She took another few steps back. "I've gotta go."

CHAPTER FOURTEEN

DANI RACED OUT of Mancini's, quickly started Louisa's little car and headed home. Her flight didn't leave until ten in the morning. But she had to pack. She had to say goodbye to Louisa. She had to give back the tons of clothes her new friend had let her borrow for her job at Mancini's.

She swiped at a tear as she turned down the lane to Palazzo di Comparino. Her brain told her she was smart to be going home. Her splintered heart reminded her she didn't have a home. No one to return to in the United States. No one to stay for in Italy.

The kitchen light was on and as was their practice, Louisa had waited up for Dani. As soon as she stepped in the kitchen door, Louisa handed her a cup of tea. Dani glanced up at her, knowing the sheen of tears sparkled on her eyelashes.

"What's wrong?"

"I'm going home."

Louisa blinked. "I thought this was settled."

"Nothing's ever settled with Rafe." She sucked in a breath. "The smart thing for me is to leave."

"What about the restaurant, your job, your destiny?"

She fell to a seat. "He asked me to marry him."

Louisa's eyes widened. "How is that bad? My God, Dani, even I can see you love the guy."

"I said no."

"Oh, sweetie! Sweetie! You love the guy. How the hell could you say no?"

"I've been here four weeks, Louisa. Rafe is a confirmed bachelor and he asked me to marry him. The day before I'm supposed to go home. You do the math."

"What math? You have a return ticket to the United States. He doesn't want you to go."

Dani slowly raised her eyes to meet Louisa's. "Exactly. The proposal was a stopgap measure. He told me all about it when we talked about Paul asking me to marry him. He said Paul didn't want to risk losing me, so the day before I left for Italy, he'd asked me to marry him."

"And you think that's what Rafe did?"

Her chin lifted. "You don't?"

Rafe was seated at the bar on his third shot of whiskey when Emory ambled out into the dining room.

"What are you doing here?"

He presented the shot glass. "What does it look like I'm doing?"

Emory frowned. "Getting drunk?"

Rafe saluted his correct answer.

"After a successful catering event that could have gone south, you're drinking?"

"I asked Daniella to marry me. And do you know what she told me?"

Looking totally confused, Emory slid onto the stool beside Rafe. "Obviously, she said no."

"She said no."

Emory laughed. Rafe scowled at him. "Why do you think this is funny?"

"The look on your face is funny."

"Thanks."

"Come on, Rafe, you've known the girl a month."

"So she doesn't trust me?"

Emory laughed. "Look at you. Look at how you've treated her. Would you trust you?"

"Yeah, well, she's leaving for New York tomorrow. I didn't want her to go."

Emory frowned. "Ah. So you asked her to marry you to keep her from going?"

"No. I asked her to marry me because I love her." He rubbed his hand along the back of his neck. "But I'd also told her that her boyfriend had asked her to marry him the day before she left for Italy as a stopgap measure. Wanting to tie her to him, without giving her a real commitment, he'd asked. But he hadn't really meant it. He just didn't want her to go."

Emory swatted him with a dish towel. "Why do you tell her these things?"

"At the time it made sense."

"Yeah, well, now she thinks you only asked her to marry you to keep her from going back to New York."

"No kidding."

Emory swatted him again. "Get the hell over to Palazzo di Comparino and fix this!"

"How?"

Emory's eyes narrowed. "You know what she wants... what she needs. Not just truth, proof. If you love her, and you'd better if you asked her to marry you, you have to give her proof."

He jumped off the stool, grabbed Emory's shoulders and noisily kissed the top of his head. "Yes. Yes! Proof! You are a hundred percent correct."

"You just make sure she doesn't get on that plane."

Dani's tears dried as she and Louisa packed her things. Neither one of them expected to sleep, so they spent the night talking. They talked of keeping in touch. Video chatting and texting made that much easier than it used to be. And

Louisa had promised to come to New York. They would be thousands of miles apart but they would be close.

Around five in the morning, Dani shoved off her kitchen chair and sadly made her way to the shower. She dressed in her own old raggedy jeans and a worn sweater, the glamour of her life in Tuscany, and Louisa's clothes behind her now.

When she came downstairs, Louisa had also dressed. She'd promised to take her to the airport and she'd gotten ready.

But there was an odd gleam in her eye when she said, "Shall we go?"

Dani sighed, knowing she'd miss this house but also realizing she'd found a friend who could be like a sister. The trip wasn't an entire waste after all.

She smiled at Louisa. "Yeah. Let's go."

They got into the ugly green car and rather than let Dani drive, Louisa got behind the wheel.

"I thought you refused to drive until you understood Italy's rules of the road better."

Stepping on the gas, Louisa shrugged. "I've gotta learn some time."

She drove them out of the vineyard and out of the village. Then the slow drive to Florence began. But even before they went a mile, Louisa turned down an old road.

"What are you doing?"

"I promised someone a favor."

Dani frowned. "Do we have time?"

"Plenty of time. You're fine."

"I know I'm fine. It's my flight I'm worried about."

"I promise you. I will pull into the driveway and be pulling out two minutes later."

Dani opened her mouth to answer but she snapped it closed when she realized they were at the old farmhouse Maria the real estate agent had shown her and Rafe. She faced Louisa. "Do you know the person who bought this?"

"Yes." She popped open her door. "Come in with me."

Dani pushed on her door. "I thought you said this would only take a minute."

"I said two minutes. What I actually said was I promise I will be pulling out of this driveway two minutes after I pull in."

Dani walked up the familiar path to the familiar door and sighed when it groaned as Louisa opened it. "Whoever bought this is in for about three years of renovations."

Louisa laughed before she called out, "Hello. We're here."

Rafe stepped out from behind a crumbling wall. Dani skittered back. "Louisa! *This* is your friend?"

"I didn't say he was my friend. I said I knew him." Louisa gave Dani's back a little shove. "He has some important things to say to you."

"I bought this house for you," Rafe said, not giving Dani a chance to reply to Louisa.

"I don't want a house."

He sighed. "Too bad. Because you now have a house." He motioned her forward. "I see a big kitchen here. Something that smells like heaven."

She stopped.

He motioned toward the huge room in the front. "And big, fat chairs that you can sink into in here."

"Very funny."

"I am not being funny. You," he said, pointing at her, "want a home. I want you. Therefore, I give you a home."

"What? Since a marriage proposal didn't keep me, you offer me a house?"

"I didn't say I was giving you a house. I said I was giving you a home." He walked toward the kitchen. "And you're going to marry me."

She scrambled after him. "Exactly how do you expect to make that happen?"

She rounded the turn and walked right into him. He caught her arms and hauled her to him, kissing her. She made a token protest, but, honestly, this was the man she couldn't resist.

He broke the kiss slowly, as if he didn't ever want to have to stop kissing her. "That's how I expect to make that happen."

"You're going to kiss me until I agree?"

"It's an idea with merit. But it won't be all kissing. We have a restaurant. You have a job. And there's a bedroom back here." He headed toward it.

Once again, she found herself running after him. Cold air leeched in from the window and she stopped dead in her tracks. "The window leaks."

"Then you're going to have to hire a general contractor."

"Me?"

He straightened to his full six-foot-three height. "I am a master. I cook."

"Oh, and I clean and make babies?"

He laughed. "We will hire someone to clean. Though I like the part about you making babies."

Her heart about pounded its way out of her chest. "You want kids?"

He walked toward her slowly. "*We* want kids. We want all that stuff you said about fat chairs and good-smelling kitchens and turning the thermostat down so that we can snuggle."

Her heart melted. "You don't look like a snuggler."

"I'll talk you into doing more than snuggling."

She laughed. Pieces of the ice around her heart began to melt. Her eyes clung to his. "You're serious?"

"I wouldn't have told Louisa to bring you here if I weren't. I don't do stupid things. I do impulsive things." He grinned. "You might have to get used to that."

She smiled. He motioned for her to come closer and when she did, he wrapped his arms around her.

"I could not bear to see you go."

"You said Paul only asked me to marry him as a stop-gap measure."

"Yes, but Paul is an idiot. I am not."

She laughed again and it felt so good that she paused to revel in it. To memorize the feeling of his arms around her. To glance around at their house.

"Oh, my God, this is a mess."

"We'll be fine."

She laid her head on his chest and breathed in his scent. She counted to ten, waited for him to say something that would drive her away, then realized what she was really waiting for.

She glanced up at him. "I'm so afraid you're going to hurt me."

"I know. And I'm going to spend our entire lives proving to you that you have no need to worry."

She laughed and sank against him again. "I love you."

"After only four weeks?"

She peeked up again. "Yes."

"So this time you'll believe me when I say it."

She swallowed. Years of fear faded away. "Yes."

"Good." He shifted back, just slightly, so he could pull a small jewelry box from the pocket of his jeans. He opened it and revealed a two-carat diamond. "I love you. So you will marry me?"

She gaped at the ring, then brought her gaze to his hopeful face. When he smiled, she hugged him fiercely. "Yes!"

He slipped the ring onto her finger. "Now, weren't we on our way back to the bedroom?"

"For what? There's no bed back there."

He said, "Oh, you of no imagination. I have a hundred ways around that."

"A hundred, isn't that a bit ambitious?"

"Get used to it. I am a master, remember?"

"Yeah, you are," she said, and then she laughed. She was

getting married, going to make babies…going to make a
home—in Italy.

   With the man of her dreams.

   Because finally, finally she was allowed to have dreams.

* * * * *

"This isn't the first time you've acted like you want to call it off."

"Call it off?" she repeated in a stark whisper.

Will nodded. "I don't like it, but I can accept that maybe this just isn't something you're willing to do. You can move back to the boardinghouse. We'll tell everyone we realized it wouldn't work, after all. But then, if there's a baby, I want you to promise me that you'll come back."

Call it off…

Did she want that?

They'd been "married" for just three days. Not only did Jordyn Leigh have to deal with her guilt over the lies they were telling, but sometimes when she told a lie, it came out seeming way too much like the truth.

The stuff she'd just said to Cece, for instance. About how wonderful Will was, how superhot and protective, how when he kissed her, she melted…

Well, she found it easy to tell those lies because those lies felt so very true.

It didn't seem possible. She didn't know how it had happened. But somehow, Will Clifton was beginning to look like her dream man.

***

Montana Mavericks:
What Happened at the Wedding?
A weekend Rust Creek Falls will never forget!

THE MAVERICK'S
ACCIDENTAL BRIDE

BY
CHRISTINE RIMMER

Published in Great Britain 2015
by Mills & Boon, an imprint of Harlequin (UK) Limited,
Eton House, 18-24 Paradise Road, Richmond, Surrey, TW9 1SR

© 2015 Harlequin Books S.A.

Special thanks and acknowledgement to Christine Rimmer for her contribution to the Montana Mavericks: What Happened at the Wedding? continuity.

ISBN: 978-0-263-25149-4

23-0715

Harlequin (UK) Limited's policy is to use papers that are natural, renewable and recyclable products and made from wood grown in sustainable forests. The logging and manufacturing processes conform to the legal environmental regulations of the country of origin.

Printed and bound in Spain
by CPI, Barcelona

Christine Rimmer came to her profession the long way around. She tried everything from acting to teaching to telephone sales. Now she's finally found work that suits her perfectly. She insists she never had a problem keeping a job—she was merely gaining "life experience" for her future as a novelist. Christine lives with her family in Oregon. Visit her at www.christinerimmer.com.

For MSR,
Always.

Chapter One

"You remind me of a girl I used to know," said a way-too-familiar deep voice in Jordyn Leigh Cates's ear. "She was just a kid, really. Pretty little thing, always following me around..."

Jordyn whirled on the killer handsome cowboy she'd known all her life. "Will Clifton, you liar. I never, *ever* followed you around."

"Yes, you did."

"Did not."

"Did so."

She laughed. "You know we sound like a couple of overgrown brats, right?"

"Speak for yourself." Will gave her the sexy half smile that had broken more than one girl's heart back home in Thunder Canyon. "Never could resist teasing you."

Jordyn sipped from her paper cup of delicious wedding punch. "I heard that you were in town."

"Craig, Jonathan and Rob, too." Those were his brothers.

"We're staying out at Maverick Manor." Formerly known as Bledsoe's Folly, the giant, long-deserted log mansion southeast of town had been transformed the year before into an upscale hotel with a rustic flair.

She gave him a teasing look from under her lashes. "I also heard a rumor that *you* bought a place right here in Rust Creek Falls…?"

"As a matter of fact, I did." There was real pride in his voice, and his gorgeous blue eyes shone bright with satisfaction. "Beautiful spread in the Rust Creek Valley, east of town, not far from the Traub ranch. Escrow closes on Tuesday."

Jordyn was happy for him. It had always been Will's dream to have his own ranch. "Congratulations."

"Thanks."

They grinned at each other. She thought he looked even hunkier than usual in a white dress shirt, a coffee-colored Western-cut vest and a bolo tie. He'd polished his belt buckle to a proud shine, and his black jeans broke just right over his black dress boots.

He reached out a hand and tugged on a blond curl that trailed loose from her updo. "You're lookin' good."

A warm lick of pleasure stole through her. He was five years her senior, and he'd always treated her like a kid. But right now, the way he gazed at her? She didn't feel like a kid in the least. She dared to flutter her eyelashes at him. "Thank you, Will."

He tipped his black Stetson. "It's only the truth. You look great—not to mention, patriotic."

"Red, white and blue all the way." She flicked a glance down at her strapless knee-length chiffon bridesmaid's dress. It was Old-Glory Blue.

Just a couple of hours ago, Braden Traub, second oldest of the Rust Creek Traub boys, had married angelic blonde

Jennifer MacCallum, who had moved to town a year before. They'd decided on an outdoor wedding reception—an Independence Day picnic in Rust Creek Falls Park. Red-and-white-checked oilcloths covered all the picnic tables. Red, white and blue canopies provided shade from the summer sun.

Plus, they'd set up a portable oak dance floor not far from the punch table, where Jordyn and Will stood. The six-piece band wasn't half bad. Right then they were rockin' a great Brad Paisley song. Jordyn's sparkly blue high heels had a tendency to get stuck in the grass when she wasn't out on the dance floor, but she refused to let that slow her down. She kept her weight on her toes and had no trouble tapping a foot to the music as a certain tall cowboy in a big white hat two-stepped by with a curvy brunette. That cowboy gave Jordyn a wink.

And Jordyn winked right back at him. "Wahoo, cowboy!" She raised her bridesmaid's bouquet of red roses in a jaunty wave.

And of course, Will just had to demand, "Who's that?"

She sent him a glance of serene self-possession. "Just a guy I was dancing with a little while ago…" What she didn't say was that she intended to be dancing with that cowboy again soon. Very soon. Will could get way too big-brotherly, and she didn't need that. She lifted her paper cup for another sip—and Will snagged it right out of her hand. "Hey!" She brandished her bouquet at him. "Give me back my punch, Clifton. Or I won't be responsible for what happens next."

He smirked at her and sniffed the cup. "What's in this, anyway?"

"Oh, please. It's just punch."

"Spiked?"

She puffed out her cheeks with a disgusted breath.

"Hardly. Punch, I said. Fruit juice and mixers—and a small amount of sparkling wine—and don't give me that look. I asked the bride so I know whereof I speak. It's a public park, Will. No hard liquor allowed."

Being Will, he just had to argue the point. "I've spotted a hip flask or two in the crowd."

"Well, yeah. But on the down low. The punch is harmless, believe me. And if you're so worried about a teeny bit of sparkling wine, try the kids' punch table." With a flourish, she pointed her bouquet at the table several feet away, where the children and teetotalers were served.

Will was watching her, his expression annoyingly suspicious. "You seem to be having a really good time, Jordyn Leigh—maybe *too* good a time."

"There is no such thing as too good a time." She scowled at him. "And do not call me Jordyn Leigh."

"Why not? It's your name."

"Yeah, but when *you* say it, I feel like I'm eight years old. Wearing hand-me-down jeans and a wrinkled plaid shirt, with my hair in pigtails and my two front teeth missing."

Looking right next door to wistful, Will shook his head. "I really liked that little girl."

"Well, I'm not her. And I haven't been for seventeen years." Right then, that weird old guy, Homer Gilmore, hobbled by on the other side of the punch table. He gave Jordyn a great big snaggle-tooth grin. Homer was as sweet as he was strange, so she responded with a merry wave. "I'm all grown-up now," she reminded Will.

"Yes, you are." He toasted her with her own cup and then drank the rest, bold as brass.

She could almost get aggravated that he'd commandeered her punch. But no. Back at the church during the wedding, she'd been feeling a tad low to be a bridesmaid and not a bride for the umpteenth time. But it was a beautiful day, not a cloud in the wide Montana sky. And hadn't she already shared a dance with a handsome cowboy? Who knew what good things might happen next? Her dark mood had vanished. Will was right. She was having a wonderful time. No way was she letting Will Clifton harsh her lovely mellow.

Instead, she grabbed a fresh flag-printed paper cup and poured herself another full one. When he held out the cup that used to be hers, she good-naturedly served him, as well.

They tapped cups and drank.

For Jordyn, the rest of that fateful afternoon flashed by in soft-focus snapshots.

She and Will hung out. And it was good. Better than good.

Up until that day, he'd always treated her like a youngster he needed to boss around. But from the first wedding-punch toast they'd shared that day, it was different.

Suddenly, they were equals. She had fun with him. A lot of fun. They ate barbecue and wedding cake together. They visited with his brothers, with the bride and groom, and with Jordyn's Newcomers Club girlfriends, who were also her fellow bridesmaids.

They met a quirky married couple, Elbert and Carmen Lutello. Elbert, small and thin with dark-rimmed glasses, was the county clerk. Carmen, broad-shouldered, commanding and a head taller than her husband, was a district judge. Carmen and Elbert were so cute together, totally dewy-eyed over each other—and the wedding and love and romance in general. Jordyn adored them.

She and Will enjoyed more punch. They danced together. Several dances. Somehow, she never got around to another dance with the cowboy in the white hat. Truth to tell, she forgot all about that guy. It was just her and Will, together in a lovely, misty place. The park, the picnic reception, the music and laughter…all that got pleasantly hazy around the edges, became background to the magic happening between her and Will.

Will kissed her. Right there on the dance floor. Just tipped her chin up with a finger and settled that sexy mouth of his on hers. They swayed to the music and kissed on and on.

Sweet Lord, the man could kiss. He kissed like the prince in a fairy tale, the kind of kiss that could wake a girl up from a hundred years of sleep. It was something of a miracle, the way Will kissed her that day. At last. Just when she'd started to doubt that she would ever be on the receiving end of kisses like his.

And he told her she was beautiful.

Didn't he?

It seemed he did. But she wasn't sure…

Not completely, anyway. Because things got hazier and hazier as the afternoon turned to evening.

Once night fell, a few weird things happened. One of the Dalton sisters got thrown in jail for resisting arrest—after dancing in the newly dedicated park fountain.

At some point Jordyn and Will stood hand in hand in the parking lot between Rust Creek Park and Brooks's Veterinary Clinic. They stared into the lambskin-lined trunk of Elbert Lutello's pink 1957 convertible Cadillac Eldorado Biarritz. Elbert hauled out a leather briefcase and announced with great solemnity, "You never know when a legal order or some other official form might be needed. I am a public servant, and I like to be prepared…"

And then, in the blink of an eye, Jordyn and Will, still holding hands, were swept magically back to the park with all the party lights twinkling beneath the almost-full moon. People crowded around them, watching. Carmen Lutello stood before them, blessing them with a tender smile.

What happened next?

Jordyn wasn't sure.

But the party went on. Will gave her more of those beautiful endless kisses; he fed them to her, each one delicious and perfect, filling her up with delight and satisfaction.

Actually, a lot of folks were kissing. You couldn't walk beneath a tree without having to ease around an embracing couple. And why not? It was only natural for everyone to be feeling happy and affectionate at a wedding. High spirits ruled on this special, joyous, romantic night…

The next morning, in her bed at Strickland's Boarding House, Jordyn woke to discover that an army of mean little men with pickaxes had taken up residence in her brain.

For several minutes, she lay very still with her eyes closed, waiting for her stomach to stop lurching and the little men with the axes to knock off attacking the inside of her skull. Finally, breathing slowly and evenly through her nose, she opened her eyes and stared at the ceiling.

The *wrong* ceiling…

Her pained grimace became a frown.

With great care, she turned her head toward the nightstand at her side. It was rustic, that nightstand, of what appeared to be reclaimed, beautifully worked old wood. It bore no resemblance to the simple pasteboard one she had at the boardinghouse. A clock stood on that nightstand—not her clock.

And wait a minute. How could it possibly be past noon?

Her stomach did a forward roll. She swallowed down a spurt of acid and carefully, torturously, rolled her head the other way.

Dear, sweet Mary and baby Jesus. *Will*.

She blinked, looked away—and looked back again.

He was still there, still sound asleep beside her, lying on his stomach with his face turned away from her, his hair night black against the white pillow. His strong arms and broad, muscular shoulders were bare. So was his powerful back tapering down to his tight waist. Below that, she couldn't be sure. The sheet covered the rest of him.

The sight of Will Clifton possibly naked right next to her in the bed that was not her bed was the final straw. Her stomach rebelled.

With a cry of abject wretchedness and total mortification, she threw back the covers and raced for the open door that led to the bathroom.

The slamming of the bathroom door woke Will.

With a loud "Huh?" he flipped to his back and bolted to a sitting position. "What the…?" He pressed both hands to his aching head and groaned.

But then he heard the painful sounds coming from the bathroom.

"Huh?" he said again. Apparently, he wasn't alone. There was someone in the bathroom. Someone being sick.

"Ugh." Still only half-awake, he raked the sleep-scrambled hair off his forehead. His gaze skimmed past the bedside chair—and then homed right back in on it.

His clothes from last night were tossed in a wad across that chair. On top of them, the hem drooping toward the floor, lay a pretty blue dress topped by a woman's small sparkly purse and a wilted red bouquet. Will shut his eyes as the heaving noises continued in the other room.

But then, well, keeping his eyes shut wouldn't make the sounds from the bathroom go away. So he opened them again—opened them and let them track lower, to the foot of the chair and the pair of sexy, sparkly, red-soled blue bridesmaid's shoes that had toppled sideways beneath the filmy hem of the blue dress.

Will knew that dress, those shoes, that bouquet...

Jordyn?

Jordyn Leigh Cates, in the bathroom? Sweet Jordyn Leigh, in his hotel room without her dress on? Little Jordyn Leigh...had spent the night in his *bed*?

He clapped his hands to his head again and tried to think it through.

Okay, he remembered spending the afternoon and evening with her yesterday. They'd had a great time.

But what had happened later? How did they get here to his hotel room together?

Damned if he could remember.

He threw back the covers and saw he was wearing only boxer briefs. Did that mean...?

Damn it all to hell. He had no idea what it meant.

And poor Jordyn. The sounds coming from the bathroom were not good.

He jumped to his feet and whipped his black jeans out from under her pretty blue dress. He was pulling them on as he hopped to the bathroom door. Zipping up fast, he gave the door a cautious tap. "Jordyn, are you—?"

She let out a low groan, a sound of purest misery. "Leave me alone, Will. Don't you dare come in here."

"Let me—"

"No! Stay there. I'll be out in a minute."

His head drooped forward until his forehead met the door. Jordyn Leigh? He'd had *sex* with little Jordyn Leigh? He wanted to beat the crap out of himself. Her younger brother, Brody, probably *would* beat the crap out of him— and he would deserve every punch. And what about her parents, who were good friends with *his* parents? Dear

God, he should be tied down spread-eagled in the noon-day sun for the buzzards to peck to a million pieces. "Jordyn, I'm so sor—"

"Go *away*, Will!"

He raised his knuckles to knock again—but then just let them drop. "Uh. Just call. If you need me…"

She didn't bother to answer him that time. The heaving sounds continued.

He stood there, undecided, wanting to help, not knowing how. And that made him feel even more like a low-down dirty dog, because he couldn't help and he knew it.

And he had no business just standing there, his head against the door, listening to her being sick.

So he dragged his sorry ass back to his side of the tangled bed and sat on the edge of it. He braced his elbows on his spread knees and let his head hang low in shame.

And that was when he spotted the document on the floor.

"Huh?" He picked it up.

Then, for a long time, several minutes at least, he just stared at the damn thing in stunned disbelief.

But it didn't matter how long he stared, the document didn't magically become something else. Uh-uh. No matter how long he stared, it was still a marriage license, complete with the embossed seal of the county clerk declaring it a true certified copy.

The county clerk…

Last night there was a guy, wasn't there? A little guy in black-rimmed glasses. Yeah. Elton or Eldred, something like that. And the little guy was married to that big woman, the judge…

Will blinked hard and shook his head. It didn't seem possible. He had zero recollection of any actual ceremony.

But still. He was reasonably sure the county clerk had been there last night, the county clerk and his wife, the judge.

So it *could* have happened. It *was* possible...

More than possible.

Because he held the proof right there in his two hands.

Around about then, he spotted the gleam of gold on the third finger of his left hand. Or maybe that gleam was brass. He couldn't be sure.

But gold or brass, the ring looked a hell of a lot like a wedding band. And that signature on the marriage license? Definitely his own. His—and Jordyn's, too.

It wasn't possible. But it *had* happened.

Somehow, he and Jordyn Leigh had gotten married last night.

Chapter Two

Will heard a click when Jordyn opened the bathroom door.

He set the marriage license on the nightstand by his side of the bed and slowly rose, turning to face the woman he'd apparently married the night before.

Jordyn Leigh stood in the doorway. Her big blue eyes had dark shadows beneath them. Her peaches-and-cream skin looked slightly green, and her soft mouth trembled.

She'd put on the complimentary terry-cloth robe that had been hanging on the back of the bathroom door. Her hands were stuck in the pockets, and she kept her head pulled in, like a turtle trying to retreat into its shell. Her wheat-gold hair lay smooth and wavy across her shoulders. She must have used his comb before opening the door and facing him at last.

The sight of all that shining hair made him feel worse than ever. It sent random images of her, scenes from their shared past, sparking and flashing through his brain.

He saw her as a toddler with wispy yellow curls, running through the sprinklers in her front yard, wearing a bright orange bathing suit that tended to sag around her little bottom. And then he saw her in pigtails and busted-out jeans at nine or ten, astride one of the Traub horses.

And the night of her prom…

He couldn't recall why he'd dropped by the Cates's place that night, but he did remember Jordyn Leigh, her hand on the banister, slowly descending the front hall stairs, wearing a pink satin dress, her hair piled up high, held in place with sparkling rhinestone clips.

She was such a sweet thing. She deserved so much better than this.

He cleared his throat. "Jordyn, I—"

But she whipped a hand free of a pocket and held it up to him, palm out. "I'm getting dressed right now, Will Clifton," she muttered through hard-clenched teeth. "I'm getting dressed and going back to the boardinghouse. And if you know what's good for you, you'll never tell a soul about this."

Okay, he might be a low-down skunk for…whatever had happened last night, but she ought to know him better than that. "Jordyn, I would never—"

"Hush!" She raised her chin high and smacked the air between them with her palm. "Don't, okay? Just don't." And then she gathered the robe closer at the neck. She did that with her left hand. He saw she wore no ring. But before he had time to consider what that might mean, she hunched into herself again and made a beeline for the chair and that blue bridesmaid's dress.

He moved fast, skirting the end of the bed, to intercept her before she reached the chair. "Jordyn, wait."

Folding her arms protectively around herself, she glared up at him. "Out of my way, Will." Her breath smelled of toothpaste.

He felt another stab of mingled guilt and regret as he pictured her brushing her teeth in the bathroom mirror with her finger and a dab of toothpaste, trying to gather her dignity around her, trying to be strong. He told her gently, "Before you go, we need to talk."

"Talking with you is the *last* thing I need." She tried to dodge around him.

But he caught her by the shoulders. "Hey, come on…"

"Let me go, Will." Her slim arms felt so delicate, so vulnerable, in his grip.

"Damn it, you're shaking."

"I'm fine."

"You are not."

"Am, too." She shook all the harder. He wanted to gather her close, but he feared that putting his arms around her would only freak her out all the more.

They had to discuss this reasonably, with cool heads. But she looked so sick and frantic. He was afraid if he sprung the big news that they somehow got married on her right then, she might just drop to the rug in a dead faint.

Or maybe she already knew they were married. Maybe *she* remembered what had actually happened…

But they would get to that. First, he needed to settle her down, maybe get some food into her.

She jerked in his grip. "Damn you, Will Clifton. You let me go."

But he didn't release her. Instead, he turned her and walked her backward to the bed. "I mean it, Jordyn Leigh. You need to sit down before you fall down." He gave her a gentle push.

And what do you know? Her knees gave out and she sank to the side of the bed. "Oh, dear Lord…" Her fake bravado deserted her. She let her shoulders slump and buried her head in her hands. "Oh, Will. What's going on? I don't remember...I don't..."

"Shh, settle down," he soothed. "Come on, put your feet up on the bed. Put your head on the pillow. Just, you know, rest a little, take it easy, okay?" Damned if she didn't do what he said for once. Obedient as the child she kept insisting she wasn't, she swung her feet up and stretched out. "Good," he whispered, and pulled up the covers nice and cozy around her. "Water?"

Blue eyes wide and worried, she bit her lip and nodded. He got a bottle of water from the minifridge. She sat up, and he propped the pillows behind her as she sipped.

"I'm thinking aspirin and room service first," he suggested. "Then we talk."

She gulped down more water. "Okay," she said in a tiny voice. "I could use some aspirin. And you're right. We should probably talk."

When the food came, Will served her in the bed.

Jordyn managed to get some dry toast and tea down, along with the aspirin. He moved their clothing from the chair to the sofa in the sitting area. Then he sat in the chair with his tray on his lap, shoveling in eggs, bacon, potatoes and a muffin, along with several cups of excellent Maverick Manor Blend coffee. By the third cup, he was feeling almost human.

Neither of them said much of anything while they ate. She avoided his gaze as she sipped her tea and nibbled her toast.

"Finished?" he asked finally. At her nod, he took her tray and put it with his outside in the hallway. He returned to the chair.

She smoothed her hair, though it didn't need it. And

then fiddled nervously with the sheet. "I don't even know where to start, Will. I remember the wedding—"

He blinked. "My God. You do?"

She looked at him like he maybe had a screw loose. "You're kidding? You actually thought I might have blacked out on the fact that Braden Traub and Jenny Mac-Callum got married yesterday?"

His racing heart slowed. "Uh. Right. Of course you remember that."

"What? *You* don't?"

"Oh, no. I do."

"Will. You're acting strangely."

Yeah, and why wouldn't he? It was a damn strange situation, after all. He watched as she plucked at the sheet some more. "Tell me what else you remember."

She straightened the front of the terry-cloth robe and blew out a slow breath. "I remember the reception in the park, or most of it. I think. I remember what happened in the afternoon. I remember us dancing…" She twisted the sheet. "But the later it got, the more it all just becomes one weird, hazy blur."

A sinister thought occurred to him, and he went ahead and shared it. "Maybe someone put something in your punch."

She went straight to denial on that idea. "Oh, no. No. I don't think so. Why would anyone do a thing like that?"

He regarded her patiently. "Why do you think?"

She wrinkled up her nose at him. "Oh, come on."

"It happens, Jordyn. We all like to think it doesn't. But what about that smart-ass cowboy in the white hat, the one who danced by and winked at you when we were first standing there at the punch table together?"

"He wasn't a smart-ass. He was really nice."

"Seemed like a smart-ass to me," Will muttered.

But she shook her head. "No. Uh-uh. I don't believe he would do a thing like that." She stared off toward the window that looked out over the hotel grounds.

"Don't just blow me off," he insisted. "Think about it. I drank from your cup after you did, remember? So maybe both of us were drugged—Jordyn, are you even listening?"

She met his eyes then, but hers were a thousand miles away. "I don't believe that guy drugged me. I just don't. He was a great guy."

"And you know this, how?"

She glanced away. "Okay, fine. He *seemed* like a great guy—and he never even had a chance to put anything in my drink. I danced with him once. He was nowhere near me when I served myself the punch."

"Are you sure?"

"Of course I'm sure. *You'd* have been more in a position to put something in my drink than anyone."

He gaped at her in horror. "Jordyn. You really don't think I would—"

"Of course not. And I don't think that other guy did, either." She'd stopped mangling the sheet—and gone to work wringing her hands. "And frankly, I'm more concerned with—" she turned away again and cleared her throat "—the question of whether or not you and I…" And then she looked at him again, her eyes huge and haunted. "Did we have sex, Will?"

Damn. Direct question. He tried to think of a gentle way to tell her that he had no idea if they had or they hadn't.

But he took too long, and she went on. "I hope *you* know, because *I* don't. I don't know how we got here, Will. It's all just vague, cloudy images, flashes of us dancing. Of us laughing together. Of us kissing…" Her too-pale face colored slightly.

He remembered those kisses, too, remembered that she

smelled so good and tasted so sweet, that her slim body fit just right in his arms. "I remember kissing you, too."

"So then tell me. Please. Did we...?"

He was forced to confess, "I'm sorry, Jordyn. But I don't remember, either."

She stared at him as though he'd just slapped her across the face. "Oh, fabulous." More color flooded her soft cheeks—angry color now. "So I'm that forgettable, am I?"

"Jordyn, be fair. You don't remember, either." He said it roughly, letting his own frustration show—and then regretted his harsh tone when her eyes welled with tears. "Aw, come on, don't cry..."

Too late. Fat tears spilled over and trailed down her cheeks. She sniffed. "I...I can't help it. I'm a virgin." His mouth dropped open when she said that. She let out a sad little sigh. "Or I *was* a virgin." He gaped at her as she swiped furiously at the tears running down her face. "Can you just not look at me like that, please?" She squeezed her eyes shut, but the tears still leaked out. "Oh, I can't believe I just said that, just *told* you that..."

He tried to soothe her. "Jordyn, it's okay..."

"It is *not* okay, and don't you say that it is. Everything is very, very *not* okay."

He pleaded, "You have to believe me. I can't see how I would ever take advantage of you that way." But he couldn't be sure, damn it. Because he just plain did not remember.

Jordyn cried harder. "Oh, look at me. What a mess. And now I've said it. Now you know. I was a virgin—or I *am* a virgin. That's what's so awful. I don't know if I am, or just was, because I can't remember what happened." And with that, she buried her head in her hands again. Her slim shoulders shook with desperate sobs.

Will had no idea what he ought to do to comfort her, so

he just sat there and watched her cry. He felt lower than low. Not only had he possibly had sex with little Jordyn Leigh—if he had, she'd also been a virgin.

He didn't have sex with virgins. He knew better than that.

Still sobbing, Jordyn shoved back the covers, scooted aside and stared at the sheets. "Nothing, no blood," she said with a moan as she tugged on the hem of the robe. Then she whipped a few tissues from the box by the clock, blew her nose and declared, "I don't see any blood, and I don't *feel* like anything happened." She tossed the used tissues toward the wastebasket, flipped the covers over her again and folded her arms across her middle.

Silence. Jordyn gazed into space. Will had no idea what she might be thinking.

But he needed to comfort her. He needed to wipe that lost look off her pretty face. So in the interest of injecting a positive note into this train wreck of a situation, he blurted, "Listen, it could be worse. If we did make love last night, at least we were married first."

She missed the positive angle altogether and screeched, "Married? Have you lost your mind?" And she whipped one of the pillows from behind her and tossed it at his head. He put up both hands and caught it before it hit him in the face—at which point Jordyn screeched again. "Oh, my God! Will! Your finger!"

He peered cautiously around the pillow at her. "Huh?"

"You've got a ring on your ring finger, too!"

He just wasn't following. *"Too?"*

She muttered something discouraging under her breath, tossed back the covers again and jumped to her feet.

"Jordyn," he asked warily, "where are you going now?"

She didn't answer, just headed for the bathroom. A moment later she returned, plunked herself down on the side of the bed and held up a ring like the one he wore, only smaller. "It freaked me out when I saw it on my finger," she confessed glumly. "So I took it off and stuck it under a stack of extra towels." She dropped it on the nightstand. It spun for a moment and then settled. Jordyn cut her eyes to him again. "I don't remember getting married...though maybe, well, I do remember that little man with the black-rimmed glasses. He was the county clerk. Do you remember him?"

"I do. I remember him *and* his wife, the judge..."

She nodded, her eyes staring blankly into the middle distance again. "I stood beside you, Will. I remember that. I stood beside you under the moon. We were holding hands, and people were all around us, and Her Honor, the judge, was in front of us. And after that..."

"Yeah?"

A long, sad sigh escaped her. "After that, it's all a blank."

He couldn't bear to see her looking so dejected, so he got up and went to her. She didn't jump away when he sat down beside her, and that gave him the courage to wrap an arm around her. "You have to look on the bright side."

She made a doleful sound. "There's a bright side?"

"Yes, there is. Think about it. You saved yourself for marriage—and, well, *if* we had sex, we have proof that we were married at the time."

At first, she said nothing, only eased out from under his sheltering arm and faced him. Her expression was not encouraging. Finally, she demanded, "*That's* the bright side?"

He knew he'd stepped in it again. He gulped. "Er, it's not?"

Proudly, she informed him, "You don't get it, Will. It's not marriage I was waiting for. It's love. Or if not love, then at least *special*."

He nervously scratched the side of his neck. "Ahem. *Special?*"

"Yes. Special. That's what I waited for, something really special with a special, special man. And I have to tell you that having sex with you while unconscious is not the kind of special I was going for—plus, just because we woke up with rings on doesn't mean we're *really* married. Don't you need a license to be *really* married?"

He gave her a long look as he wondered if he should even go there. And then he threw caution to the wind and asked, "So if there was a license, you would believe that our marriage was real?"

She narrowed her eyes at him. "Is that a trick question?"

"Stay right there."

"Where are you going?" she demanded crossly as he got up, turned around and crawled across the mattress. "What are you *doing?*"

He crawled back, swung his legs to the floor so he was sitting beside her again—and held out the marriage license. "Believe it. It's real."

Jordyn read the document over several times before she could let herself believe what she was seeing.

Again, she remembered the skinny little clerk and his pink Cadillac, that briefcase where he kept those official documents. He could so easily have kept a box of cheap rings in there, too...

Will said, "So you see. I think it's real. I think we really are married."

Married. To Will Clifton.

She looked up into his worried eyes—and knew she couldn't bear another minute, another second of sitting there beside him trying to pin down what, exactly, had happened last night. "Here." She shoved the license at him.

"I've had enough." She jumped to her feet, ran to the sofa in the sitting area and snatched up her dress and shoes from where he'd set them before they ate.

"Jordyn, come on. We need to stay calm. We need to—"

"Stop talking, Will."

"But—"

"Stop. Please. I can't take any more. I've got to get dressed. I've got to get out of here." And with that, she ran into the bathroom and shut and locked the door.

"The county courthouse and offices are closed for the three-day weekend." Will eased his quad cab to the curb in front of Strickland's Boarding House. "They open again tomorrow. First thing in the morning, we'll head for Kalispell and straighten this craziness out. Maybe that license isn't even filed yet. Maybe we can make this whole thing just go away."

Jordyn stared out the windshield. For the moment, the street was quiet. No kids out playing, no neighbors working in their yards or walking their dogs. If she moved fast, she might get up the steps and in the front door before anyone spotted her going in wearing the same blue dress and high heels she'd been wearing the night before.

Will caught her arm as she leaned on the door handle. "Jordyn. Tomorrow?"

She gulped and nodded. "Yes. Tomorrow morning. Okay."

He stared in her eyes as though looking for a sign from her—but a sign of what? She had no clue. His cell started ringing, which was great because he let her go.

"Tomorrow," he said again, the phone already at his ear.

She made her escape, jumping to the sidewalk, shoving the door shut and then turning to sprint along the walk and up the stairs of the ramshackle four-story Victorian. She had her key out and ready when she hit the door. All she wanted was to get in and get up the two sets of stairs to her room on the third floor without having to talk to a soul.

But no.

As she fumbled to stick the key in the lock, the door swung open. Sweet old Melba Strickland, who owned and ran the boardinghouse, stood on the other side wearing one of those floral-patterned dresses she favored and a pair of very sensible shoes. Melba was at least eighty, but spry. She had a warm heart, a willing hand—and a staunch moral code.

Melba believed in the power of love. She also believed that sex should only occur between two people married in the sight of God and man. She'd made it way clear from Jordyn's first day at the rooming house almost two years ago now that there would be no hanky-panky on the premises. Yes, it was the twenty-first century, and Melba's old-fashioned ideas didn't stop her tenants from hooking up, anyway. They just did it discreetly.

Coming home in the middle of the afternoon in last night's bridesmaid's dress, looking like something the cat dragged in?

Not exactly discreet.

"Honey, are you all right?" Melba took Jordyn's hand and pulled her inside. "When you didn't come down for breakfast, I assumed you just needed a little extra sleep after the big party last night. By eleven or so, though, I began to worry. You're not the kind to sleep half the day away." Jordyn saw no judgment in Melba's eyes—nothing but affection and honest concern.

Again, the image of her and Will in front of Carmen Lutello last night rose up in her mind's eye. Had Melba been there?

No. If she had, she would have known why Jordyn didn't come down for breakfast. Plus, it had happened pretty late in the evening, hadn't it? Melba and her husband, Old Gene, rarely stayed up past ten.

Melba patted her hand. "Darling, what's wrong? What's happened? You look so pale."

"I'm all right," she baldly lied. "There's nothing wrong."

"Have you eaten?" The old woman started herding Jordyn toward the arch to the dining room.

"I had some tea and toast." Gently, Jordyn eased free of Melba's grip. "I'm not hungry."

"You sure, now?"

"Yes. I'll, um, be down later and get something then." She headed for the stairs and took them at a near run, never once pausing or glancing back until she'd reached the third-floor landing, where she halted, breathing fast, her stomach roiling, listening for the sound of Melba's sensible shoes coming up behind her.

But Melba stayed below. With a sigh of relief, Jordyn hurried along the third-floor hall to her room. She'd barely shut the door and sagged against it when her cell started ringing.

"What now?" She dug it out of her clutch and tossed the clutch on the dresser nearby. The display read *Will*. Just *Will*. She couldn't remember having Will's cell number— and if she had, she'd have programmed in his last name.

Which was now *her* last name.

"Oh, God." With an unhappy moan, she answered it. "How did you get my number?"

"I have no idea. I'm guessing we probably exchanged numbers last night."

"Of course." They'd exchanged so much last night. Phone numbers. Wedding vows. Possibly bodily fluids. She moaned again.

"Jordyn, are you okay?"

"No, I am not. Where *are* you, Will?"

"Out in front, in my pickup."

"Why aren't you gone yet?"

"Because I got a call from Craig." Craig was the oldest of Will's brothers.

"Why does that sound like very bad news?"

"Look. I just think you should know. Craig was there last night, when we got married. So was half the town, apparently."

Half the town? Lovely. Half the town knew more than she did about what she and Will had done last night. "I know there were people there. I told you that. This isn't news, Will."

"Yeah, it kind of is." He sounded scarily grim.

She kicked off her sparkly shoes and slid down the door till her butt hit the floor. "Just tell me."

"Craig says everyone's talking about it, about the ceremony in the park, about our, um, smoking-hot kiss—you know, the one that sealed our vows?"

Her headache had come back. With a vengeance. "So we kissed. Of course we kissed. That's what you do when you get married. Is that all?"

"Er, no."

"Then what else?"

"We made the *Rust Creek Falls Gazette*."

"What are you talking about, Will? I don't understand…"

"Apparently, there's this column called Rust Creek Ramblings written by some mystery gossip columnist. Does that ring a bell?"

Nobody knew who the columnist was, but he or she always had the scoop, was always outing the personal, intimate and romantic business of people in town. A low moan escaped Jordyn. "Oh, no…"

"Yeah. Craig says this morning's column is all about

you and me. All about our surprise wedding. It's, uh, not all that flattering, Craig says."

"Not all that flattering. What does that *mean*?"

"I'm not sure yet. I'm going to go get a copy of the *Gazette* and find out."

Jordyn cast a longing glance at her bed with its pretty white eyelet bedspread. All she wanted at that moment was to get in and pull the covers over her head.

"Jordyn, we really need to talk some more. We need to give careful consideration to how we want to handle this. We have to—"

"Will."

"Yeah?"

"I need some rest." She was going to take a hot shower, crawl under the covers and not come out for a year.

"All right," he said resignedly.

"Thank you."

And then he just *had* to remind her, "Tomorrow. First thing. We're going to Kalispell, remember? I'll pick you up at eight."

"I remember. I'll be ready." She hung up.

About then, it occurred to her that she was expected at work tomorrow. She would need the day off, and the sooner she called in, the better. She autodialed Sara, one of her two bosses at Country Kids Day Care Center.

"This is Sara Johnston."

"Hi, Sara, it's Jordyn Leigh."

"Hey! What a party yesterday, huh? I hear congratulations are in order…"

Jordyn, still on the floor in front of the door, put a soothing hand on her iffy stomach and wished her head would stop hurting. "I, um, yeah. Thank you. It was something, wasn't it?" she offered lamely.

"I just wish I'd been there. Suzie told me." Suzie Johnston was Sara's twin sister and her partner in the day care. "Suzie said it was so romantic, and you and your new husband looked so happy together. He's from Thunder Canyon, I understand. Just like you."

"Uh, yeah. I've known him since we were kids."

"He's one of Cecelia's brothers, right?" Cecelia Clifton Pritchett used to live at Melba's boardinghouse, too. So had Cece's new husband, Nick. Sara said, "His name's Will, right?"

"That's right—and Sara, listen, I called because I kind of need to take the day off tomorrow…" Jordyn's voice trailed off as she realized that she would have to tell Sara something about why she needed the day. She gathered her courage to explain everything.

But Sara believed that Jordyn was a real newlywed. "Take the week, if you need it. Be with your new hubby. Enjoy every minute. Have yourselves a honeymoon, for goodness' sake."

"You're an angel." *And I ought to have the integrity to tell you the truth.* But she didn't. She couldn't. Not right now. She'd deal with all that later. "I just need tomorrow. I'll be in Tuesday."

"You're sure?"

"Positive."

"If you change your mind, just call. We can manage if you need the time."

"Thanks so much."

"You're so welcome—and Jordyn Leigh, you be happy, you and your new husband, you hear? It all goes by so fast, believe me." Sara's voice held the weight of sadness now. She'd lost her husband in a car accident when their youngest was only a baby. "You need to treasure every moment the good Lord gives you together."

"Thanks, Sara. I will." The good Lord was probably up in heaven shaking His head.

Still, Jordyn let Sara believe what she wanted to. Eventually, the moment of truth would come, and Jordyn would face it. At least by then she'd be done with this awful hangover.

Sara said goodbye at last. Jordyn disconnected the call, dragged herself to her feet, grabbed her shower caddy and her robe and headed for the bathroom at the end of the hall.

Feeling pretty damn bad about everything, Will drove the two blocks to Crawford's General Store to get a copy of the *Rust Creek Falls Gazette*. The coin-operated rack by the entrance was empty, so he went inside to ask where else to get a paper.

Mrs. Crawford had a stack of them by the register. She took his money and congratulated him on his marriage. "I hope you and Jordyn Leigh will be very happy together." She seemed sincere enough.

Will thanked her, stuck the paper under his arm and turned to go. But he just happened to walk down the center aisle on his way out, the one lined with canned goods of every variety.

Two middle-aged ladies stood chatting in that aisle. One was tall and heavyset, the other thin with gray hair pulled back into a tight little bun. They didn't see him coming, they were so wrapped up in gossiping together.

The tall one clucked her tongue. "It's a disgrace is what it is. Two virtual strangers, that's what I heard." Will hesitated several feet away, dread creeping like a spider down his spine. Neither lady turned to see him standing there. The tall one went on, "They got married in a drunken stupor right there in Rust Creek Park at eleven o'clock last night."

The thin one said, "I heard that the *blushing* bride is one of those desperate Gal Rush women. Came to town looking for a husband during reconstruction after the flood."

"Well, and now she's caught one."

"Hah. But not for long, I'll bet. My guess is the groom's probably already running for the hills like his hair's on fire."

The tall one chortled merrily.

And Will knew he couldn't let that stand. So what if he and Jordyn *were* planning to end their unexpected marriage ASAP? Didn't matter. He wasn't standing by and having the sweet, spunky girl he'd grown up with disrespected.

"It's a disgrace to the institution of marriage," declared the thin one with an angry sniff.

That did it. Will walked right up to them. "Excuse me, ladies." He tipped his hat. Looking startled, they both turned to stare at him. He said, "It so happens that you are misinformed."

"Well, I never..." said the tall one.

"Really?" The thin one sneered.

"Yes," he said. "Really. You see, I'm the groom you were just now discussing." He offered the tall one his hand. "Will Clifton." She took it limply then quickly let go. "Pleased to meet you." He gave her his warmest smile and turned to the skinny one. "Ma'am." The thin one blinked several times in rapid succession before briefly taking his offered hand.

As soon as she released his fingers, Will swept off his hat and pressed it to his heart. "Have a good look now, ladies." He tipped his chin down so they had a clear view of every hair on his head. "Not a spark, not an ember, not one whiff of smoke. My hair is not on fire, so you got that all wrong. As a matter of fact, I'm a local now. I've bought the old Dodson place east of town. I'm going nowhere. Why would I want to? Rust Creek Falls is my home. And that's not all. I don't know where you've been getting your information, but someone has been telling you lies. Because my new wife and I did not marry impulsively."

Well, who was to say about that? Neither he nor Jordyn remembered their exact states of mind at the time they'd said their vows.

He continued, "Jordyn Leigh and I are both from Thunder Canyon. We are by no means strangers to one another. In fact, we've known each other since we were children. Our families are very good friends. I'm the happiest man in the world right now, because I love my wife with all my heart, and the day has finally come when she is mine." Yeah, all right. The love stuff was total crap. But so what?

It worked.

The tall lady sputtered out, "Well, I…erm…" and then couldn't figure out what to say next.

The thin one looked like she'd swallowed a lemon.

Will put his hat back on. "Real nice to meet you ladies. Have a great day, now." He took his *Gazette* out from under his arm, gave them a final wave with it and headed for the door.

Once back in his quad cab, he dropped the paper on the passenger seat and got the hell out of there. A few minutes later, he was pulling into the parking lot at Maverick Manor a few miles down the highway, southeast of town. He didn't open that paper until he was safe in his room.

The gossip column was a long one. It covered a lot more strange goings-on than what had happened between him and Jordyn. Others had behaved badly last night, and the mystery columnist hadn't hesitated to lay it all out there in black-and-white, including the waitress who went swimming in the park fountain and ended up in jail for it, and also a poker game at the local watering hole, where one of the Crawford boys won somebody's ranch.

The part about Will and Jordyn came last. Unlike those two awful ladies in Crawford's, the column was not cruel. Looked at objectively, he supposed the story of his spur-of-the-moment marriage might even seem romantic. But the fact remained that he hated to have a spotlight shone on the night he could barely remember—and he knew that Jordyn would hate it, too. In the end, what were they but two moonstruck idiots who'd lost their heads and tied the knot?

Frankly, reading it pissed Will off. No, it wasn't mean-spirited. But come on. Whoever wrote it should at least have had the guts to put their name to it. And didn't that columnist even wonder what had gotten into everyone last night?

Will did. He still suspected that cowboy in the white hat of spiking their punch. And beyond the issue of who put what in Jordyn's punch, the column and the encounter with the two ladies in Crawford's store had him rethinking what to do next.

Because they *were* married, and everyone seemed to know it. And in a town like Rust Creek Falls, people took their wedding vows seriously. If he and Jordyn didn't find the right way to deal with this accidental marriage of theirs, she would be shamed before the whole town, and he wouldn't look like much of a man.

The more he reconsidered their situation, the more certain he became that he and Jordyn needed a better plan than just to race off to Kalispell to see if they could call the whole thing off. Because it was too damn late for that.

Chapter Three

In the morning, when Will pulled up in front of the boardinghouse, Jordyn Leigh was waiting on the front steps
wearing faded jeans and a little white T-shirt. She jumped
up and ran down the steps to meet him, the morning sun
picking up glints of bronze and auburn in her pale gold
hair.

"Hey." She gave him a nod and a wobbly attempt at a
smile as she pulled the passenger door shut. A hint of her
scent came to him, that pleasing perfume he remembered
from Saturday night, like flowers and spring grass and
ripe, perfect peaches.

"Mornin'," he said.

She plunked her bag at her feet, hooked up her seat belt
and stared straight ahead.

He put it in gear and off they went. "You sleep okay?"

She sent him a look that said, *Are you kidding?* And
then she went back to her intense study of the street ahead
of them.

Once they got to the highway, he tried to get her talking—about harmless things. About the weather and her job at the local day care. But she was having none of it. Her answers consisted of as few words as possible. She volunteered nothing.

He went ahead and asked her if she'd seen the *Gazette*. "I saw it," she answered. That was it. Nothing more.

He kept trying. "I talked to Craig again last night. He had more on the Brad Crawford story—Brad's the guy who won that ranch in the poker game." He waited for a nod or a grunt from her to tell him she was listening. Nothing. He soldiered on. "Well, now the ranch belongs to Brad, and the former owner has vanished into thin air. Nobody's seen him since Saturday night. Some folks are thinking there's been foul play."

Jordyn only shrugged and stared out the windshield.

Will gave it up. For the time being, anyway. They rode the rest of the way in silence.

In Kalispell, it only took a few minutes to get to the county justice center. Will parked in the lot, and they went in together. The county clerk's office was on the third floor. They waited their turn in line and quickly learned that the clerk himself wasn't in the office right then.

At that news, Jordyn muttered, "Thanks a bunch, El-bert."

The woman who helped them told them that yes, their license was on file and they were indeed married. As Jordyn stood wide-eyed and silent at his side, Will went ahead with the original plan and asked about the possibility of an annulment.

The woman clucked her tongue as if in sympathy and then patiently explained that it would actually be very difficult for them to get an annulment. "In Montana, an annulment requires proof that there has been no sexual intercourse between the married couple. You can imagine how complicated proving that can be."

Jordyn made a strangled sound. Will fully expected her to burst into tears, and he braced to deal with that.

But somehow she held it together, and the woman went right on, "What you want is a joint dissolution—joint dissolution meaning that you two file jointly for your divorce. It's simple and straightforward and also fair." She gave them the large packet of documents they would need and said that the same documents were also available to print off online.

"Fill them out completely and bring them back," she said. "When you return all the needed documentation—in person, together—you'll be given a hearing date a maximum of twenty days out. The hearing is a formality. Bottom line, twenty days from filing jointly, you will be divorced."

They went back downstairs and out the door. Back in the quad cab, Jordyn remained scarily subdued.

Will tried again to get through to her. "Jordyn. I think we really need to talk some more about all this."

But she only shook her head. "Just take me back to the boardinghouse, please."

He drove north on Main and turned right on Center. Two blocks later, he pulled into the parking lot of a cute little café. The tidy building was painted white, and there were cheerful geraniums in cast-iron boxes at each of the wide windows. He switched off the engine and stuck his key in his pocket.

Jordyn shook off her funk long enough to send him a scowl. "What are you doing, Will?"

"I need some breakfast. Did you eat?"

Her eyes flashed with annoyance. "I told you, I want to go back to the boardinghouse."

He slid his arm along the back of the seat and leaned a little closer to her. "So you didn't eat."

She just stared at him, her soft lower lip beginning to quiver.

He wanted to reach out and pull her close and tell her it was going to be all right. But he had a very strong feeling that if he so much as touched her, she would shatter. So he kept his hands to himself and said reasonably, "We need to eat. And we also need to talk."

She bit her lip. And then at last, she nodded. "Okay," she said in a voice that only shook a little. "We'll eat. And you're right. We should talk."

Jordyn followed Will into the cheery little restaurant. She really didn't want to be there. She felt so awful about everything, and Will was being so wonderful and calm and reasonable and understanding.

She wanted to grab him and hug him tight and tell him how great he was. But if she did, she would only end up blubbering like a big baby, and that would only make it all crappier than ever.

Dear Lord, they were *married*. They were really, truly married. And now they would have to get divorced. Jordyn didn't believe in divorce. In her family, marriage was forever.

It was all so wrong.

She felt caught in some awful nightmare, one she couldn't seem to make herself wake up from.

Will chose a table in the corner. The waitress came and poured them coffee. He ordered steak and eggs, and Jordyn opened her mouth to say she only wanted the coffee. But Will's beautiful blue eyes were on her, giving her that look, both stern and gentle, so she ordered a pancake sandwich.

They sipped their coffee in silence until the food came.

He dug right in. She drizzled syrup on her pancakes and nibbled at the bacon and felt a ray of hope that maybe he'd given up on the idea that their accidental marriage demanded further discussion.

But he hadn't given up. Once he'd worked his way through half his steak and two of his three eggs, he leaned across the table toward her and said, low-voiced so it stayed just between the two of them, "We need a better plan."

She set down her half-eaten strip of bacon. "Better, how?"

He ate more steak, sipped his coffee. "I know you're upset about this, Jordyn, and I don't want to make it any worse than it already is for you, but have you thought about what to do if it turns out you're pregnant?"

Her stomach lurched. She pushed her barely touched plate away and confessed in a whisper, "No. I... Oh, my God." The thought that she might be pregnant hadn't even occurred to her.

"I'm going to just lay it out there." He held her gaze, steadily.

She coughed into her hand weakly, trying to clear the sudden lump from her tight throat. "All right."

"I carry a condom in my wallet. It's still there."

"Oh," she said, because she had no idea what else to say.

One black eyebrow lifted. "You're not by any chance on the pill?" When she shook her head, he suggested, "So maybe you want to get that Plan B pill, just in case?"

Jordyn shook her head again. "I don't believe I'm pregnant. And as for that Plan B pill...no. Just no. I'm not going there."

Now Will wore his most patient expression. "All right. But you have to see that we can't be sure about anything. It's possible we had sex Saturday night. And if we did, then it's possible that you're pregnant."

Her cheeks suddenly felt on fire. She pressed her hands against them to cool the flash of heat. "What do you want from me, Will?"

"You really want to know?" He waited for another nod from her before he said, "I think we need to stay married for a while."

"But I don't—"

"Wait. Hear me out."

She pulled her coffee mug closer and wrapped her hands around it, seeking comfort from the warmth of it, from its curving, firm shape. "Go on."

"Jordyn, if you're having my baby, there will be no divorce. If there's a baby, I want your agreement that we'll find a way to make this marriage work."

Oh, she did long to argue—that it was all a crazy nightmare, that a baby wasn't possible.

But no. She needed to snap out of this numb state of denial she'd been dragging around in since she woke up in Will's bed yesterday. They'd done…whatever they'd done on Saturday night. And if there was a baby, well, she and Will shared the same values. If there was a baby, they *would* make it work. "Okay, you're right. I agree. About the baby. I mean, if there is one, we'll stay married."

He let out a slow breath. "Good."

"But I'm sure there's not."

"Be sure all you want, Jordyn. It's still possible, and we have to accept that."

She longed to make him—to make *somebody*—understand. "I…well, I do have plans, Will. I know people think I just came to Rust Creek Falls to get myself a man—and maybe I did. A little. Because the truth is I am sort of a hopeless romantic."

He slathered strawberry jam on a triangle of toast.

"There's nothing the least bit hopeless about you, Jordyn Leigh."

His rueful words warmed her, deep down, where she needed warmth most right then. "Not hopeless, then." She dared a smile. He gave her a grin in return. "But I *am* a romantic. I believe in love and marriage and family and forever. I believe in waiting for that one special man. And I guess that's why what we did Saturday night—whatever it was—has me wanting to climb in my bed and hide under the covers. What we did flies hard in the face of everything I believe."

"I know that." He held her gaze in that unwavering way he had. "But we still have to deal with it the best way we can."

"I know. I agree. And what I'm trying to say is, yes, I'm a romantic. I want real love and a true marriage. I'm... disappointed that I haven't found the right guy when all four of my sisters are married and settled down, when everyone else seems to be coupled up and getting on with their lives. I'm disappointed, but I'm not giving up living over it. I haven't been just sitting around waiting for some guy to show up and give my life meaning. I have plans of my own. Career plans."

He ate another bite of steak. "Tell me about those plans."

She sent him a sideways look. "You really want to know?"

"I do, absolutely."

Did he mean that? He seemed to. She took him at his word. "Okay, then. I've been taking classes online, and I'm only a couple of semesters away from a degree in child development. I thought, well, okay. It didn't work out for me in Rust Creek Falls. I've made good friends there and I've loved living there. But the true, forever love I hoped to find when I moved to town never showed up. So I decided it was time to try something new, you know? Time to get out in the big world and make my mark."

"So…?"

"So I'm off to Missoula, to UMT, in the fall. I'm all enrolled and ready to go. I have a little money from Grandpa Cates, and I've saved enough to manage it, as long as I find a job once I get there. So I do have a plan. I have a dream, Will, I really do. I want to get my degree and have a meaningful, productive career. I'm leaving Rust Creek Falls at the end of August. And I don't care what a few small-minded people there say."

He set down his knife and fork and slowly shook his head. "I don't believe you. I think you do care. And *I* care. I don't accept that you should ever have to feel shamed or embarrassed by what happened Saturday night. And even if you're leaving, *I* live in Rust Creek now. I want to be known as a man who honors his commitments."

"But if it's not a *real* commitment—"

"It *is* a real commitment." He said it roughly, almost angrily. "We *are* actually married. No, it's probably not going to last forever. But it is a commitment that we should both take seriously, that we need to treat with respect and dignity. I've said it before. We need a better plan. And I have one, a plan that will keep other people out of our business, a plan that doesn't necessarily have to interfere with your going to college."

She gulped. "You do?"

"Yeah. When did you say your fall term starts?"

"Orientation is second-to-last week of August."

"That should work fine."

"Uh, it should?"

"We'll stay married through the summer. You'll move in with me at my new place."

That had her sitting up good and straight. "Tell me you didn't just say that I would move in with you."

"That is exactly what I said. You'll move in at the ranch, and if anyone asks about your college plans, you'll tell them all about how proud and supportive I am of you, how I've insisted you have your education, that it's your lifetime dream, and I intend for you to have your dream."

She tried to make a joke of it. "Gee, what a guy. I think you're my hero."

He didn't miss a beat. "You'll say how, even though you're going to UMT this fall, you'll be coming home often, because we hate to be apart."

"I will?"

He nodded. "How long until you know if you're pregnant?"

"You know, I think we ought to slow down a little here and—"

"How *long*, Jordyn?"

She knew that mulish look. He would be keeping after her until she answered him. "Oh, fine. A couple of weeks, I guess. I'm, um, pretty regular. Or I can probably take a home test sooner than that."

"Say a couple of weeks, then, just for a reference point. If you *are* having a baby, we'll figure out a way to make the marriage work. If not, we'll file the papers at the end of July, and we'll be divorced by the time you leave for Missoula."

She fiddled with the salt shaker. "I'm just not sure this is such a good idea."

"Well, *I* am. Questions?"

She had a powerful urge to bop him upside his thick head. "As a matter of fact, I do have a question."

"Hit me with it."

Oh, I wish. "Do you mean for us to share a room?"

He looked vaguely offended. "Jordyn. You know me better than that. I'm trying to *help* you, not put a move on you."

"I think I would be better off just to be honest with everyone and deal with the fallout—and move on."

The man did not miss a beat. "Well, you're wrong. *My* way is better for both of us—and where was I? Oh, yeah. Separate rooms. But everywhere except in bed, we would be together, making it work."

"But it would be a lie, Will. We would be lying to everyone."

"No, we wouldn't. Because we really are married. And it's nobody's business but ours how we choose to *be* married. And if it did turn out that you were pregnant, we would already have a life together. Think about that. Think about our innocent child."

A wild laugh bubbled up inside her, and she couldn't quite hold it back.

Those black brows drew together. "What's so funny?"

"It's just...*you*, Will. Determined to protect my reputation, so set on doing what you consider the right thing. I mean, we don't even know if we had sex, yet you're already talking about protecting the baby."

He looked a tad insulted. "Exactly. On all counts. What of it?"

"So...I would pay you rent?"

He scowled. "Of course not."

"But if I'm going to be staying at your place—"

"You mind doing some of the cooking, keeping things tidy, generally helping out around the house?"

"Of course I don't mind, but I should still pay you—"

He cut her right off again. "You help out where needed. That's more than enough payment for me. Believe me, there will be plenty of work to do. And the house has three bedrooms. I can only use one myself."

A minute ago she'd been laughing. She wasn't laughing now. She held his gaze across the table and silently admitted to herself that she really had been dreading facing everyone alone, being a joke, a laughingstock. "Some people will still gossip," she warned.

"So what? Let 'em talk. They'll get bored with it pretty quick when they see that we're just a nice, happily married couple. They'll have to find something else to talk about."

"I just…"

The waitress appeared. She refilled their coffee mugs. "Can I get you two anything else?"

"A check." Will waited as the woman pulled the bill from her apron and set it on the table. She scooped up his empty plate and moved on. He regarded Jordyn silently for a second or two before prompting, "You just, what?"

She forked her fingers through her hair. "Are you sure you really want to do this?"

"It's *my* plan. You bet I'm sure."

Jordyn marveled at him. She thought back to all those years growing up, when he used to thoroughly annoy her with his overbearing know-it-all big-brother act. She probably should have appreciated him more. If she had to be accidentally married to someone, it helped that she'd chosen a guy who'd always looked out for her, a guy who wanted the best for her, one who intended to stand up for her, stand up *with* her, until she left Rust Creek Falls behind. "You're one of the good guys, Will, a real hero. And I mean that sincerely this time."

"Just say that you'll do it." His quiet voice was gruff.

And even though she still had her doubts, the possibility that there might be a baby had tipped the scales for her. "All right, yes. Let's do it. Let's go ahead with your plan."

There was a silence. They stared into each other's eyes. Finally, he said, "Give me your hand."

She reached across the table to him.

"Uh-uh. Your *left* hand." He dipped into the breast pocket of his Western-style shirt—and came out with the wedding band she'd abandoned on the nightstand in his room the day before.

Tears burned behind her eyes at the sight of it. Suddenly, the moment seemed filled with meaning. Her heart ached—but in a good way, really. "Leave it to you to think of everything."

His fine mouth quirked. "Your hand, Jordyn Leigh."

So she held out her hand, and he slipped that ring back on her finger. And then she found she was reaching with her other hand, too. He met her halfway. They held hands across the table.

"Thank you," she whispered in a voice that only wobbled a little bit.

Chapter Four

On the way back to Rust Creek Falls, he kept shooting her glances out of the corner of his eye.

She knew he was working up to something. "Okay, Will. Whatever it is, you might as well just say it."

He shot her another glance then stared at the road again.

She gave it a mental count of ten before she prodded, "Still waiting. Better just tell me."

"Ahem. About tonight…"

She folded her arms across her middle. "What about it?"

A swift, measuring glance, then, "This is my last night at the Manor. Tomorrow I take possession of my ranch."

"Right. You told me that Saturday—before we did a whole lot of crazy stuff and then forgot about half of it."

"I think you need to stay with me."

"We already agreed on that."

"No, Jordyn. I mean tonight. In my room. We're married, remember? We need to play to that."

She thought about arguing—that she'd slept at the

boardinghouse last night, that one more night wouldn't matter that much. That they'd agreed on separate rooms and they wouldn't have that at the Manor, not and keep up the fiction that they were blissful newlyweds.

But then again, well, she'd already spent one night in his bed. At least this time she would remember whatever happened there. "All right. I'll stay with you at Maverick Manor."

She got him to drop her off at the boardinghouse and promised to meet him at the Manor in an hour and a half.

Upstairs in her room, Jordyn got right to work packing an overnight bag. Once that was done, she started gathering the rest of her things together for tomorrow. After work she would pile everything into her old Subaru and follow Will out to the ranch.

The door to her room stood ajar as she packed. She'd left it that way on purpose for Melba, who appeared just as Jordyn was tucking a stack of T-shirts into one of the suitcases spread open on the bed.

"So it looks like you're leaving us earlier than you planned," Melba said, huffing a little from the climb up the stairs.

Jordyn went to her. The old woman wrapped her in a hug. Jordyn breathed in her comforting scent. Melba always seemed to smell of lemon polish and cinnamon cookies.

Melba stroked her hair. "I heard the news that you married Cecelia's brother. Congratulations, honey. I know you'll be very happy."

Jordyn felt a sharp stab of guilt at deceiving Melba, who had always been kind and generous to her. "Thank you. I've known Will forever. He's a wonderful man." She stepped back from the old woman's embrace. "I'm sorry I didn't tell you yesterday. It was all kind of sudden."

"Sometimes love is like that."

"Uh, yeah. Yeah, it is—and listen, I'll come back to-morrow, after work, to pick up everything and turn in my key, if that's okay." Melba took her hand and pressed a small piece of paper into it. It was a check, the amount Jordyn had paid ahead for her July rent, plus her original deposit. "Oh, no. Melba, I didn't even give you notice."

"Shh, now." Melba patted her cheek. "Consider it a wedding present from Old Gene and me—and don't you dare be a stranger, you hear? You come back and see me now and then. I want to know all about how married life is treating you."

"I will definitely be back to visit." Until August, anyway, when she would be leaving for good.

Melba gave a pleased little laugh. "And didn't I tell you to have faith, that the perfect man for you would come along?"

More than once in the past two years, Jordyn had cried on Melba's kindly shoulder because everybody else was coupling up and getting married, but she'd yet to meet the guy for her. "Yes, you did."

"And just look at you now."

Jordyn put on a big, fat smile. "You're right. It all worked out in the end." And it had. Just not in the way that Melba assumed. Jordyn *was* married, as she'd dreamed of being. But by the third week in August, barring the slim chance that she might be pregnant, she would be divorced.

Also, when she'd dreamed of marriage, what she'd really been longing for was that special, special man and true love to last a lifetime.

Will was special, all right. And he loved her—as an honorary baby sister he felt he had to take care of.

It was a long, long way from what she'd been dreaming of.

*** *** ***

When she knocked on Will's door at the Manor, he answered with his cell phone at his ear.

He ushered her in and went on with his conversation—with his mother, Carol. "Yeah, Mom. I know. I should have called. Sorry. It is a big, big deal, and I know you hate being left out of the loop…Yeah. Absolutely. You had a right to be here. It's just that, well, when I swept Jordyn Leigh off her feet, I needed to make her mine before she came down to earth and had second thoughts." He glanced Jordyn's way, arching a dark eyebrow and grinning, as if to say, *Boy, do I know how to make this crap up.* And he did. He went on, "I wanted that ring on her finger before she had a chance to think twice. Couldn't have her changing her mind on me, now, could I?" His mother said something and he replied, "Tomorrow, that's right. We'll be moving in then…Thanks. I will…" And then, "Yeah, she's here…"

Jordyn dropped her overnighter on the floor, scowled at Will for putting her on the spot—and then gave in and took the phone. "Hi, Carol."

"Jordyn Leigh, I am so happy." Will's mom had been crying. She sniffled. "I have to say, I always wondered about you two, always suspected there was more going on between you than any of us realized."

Seriously? "And you were so right," she lied. "Just look at us now." She sent Will another scowl. He put on a big smile and gave her a thumbs-up.

"I have to tell you," Will's mom said in her just-between-us-girls voice. "I was beginning to think Will would never find the right woman and settle down. But now I get it. He was waiting to get to Rust Creek Falls—and you. I just… Words fail me. They do. Your mother and I have always dreamed that someday our families would be joined together. And now it's happened. It's really happened. You're my own daughter now. I only wish we could get up there to see you this summer."

"Well, that would be wonderful…" And awkward. And strange.

"But even if we don't make it to visit before the end of summer, we'll see you here at home for Thanksgiving." They would? "Will says you're off to Missoula at the end of August, but he promised to bring you home to us over your Thanksgiving break. And then you'll both be coming down for Christmas, of course."

"Erm, of course…"

"Oh, sweetie, I can't wait."

Jordyn played her part. She said she couldn't wait, either. And Carol Clifton babbled happily on for another ten minutes.

Finally, she asked for Will again. "I have a few more things I need to tell him, and then his father will want to congratulate him."

Jordyn tossed Will the phone as if it was a scalding hot potato, scooped up her overnighter and made a beeline for the bathroom, which gave her a door to shut on Will as he told more brilliantly detailed lies to his own mother.

Determined not to go back out there until Will had finished his call, Jordyn set her toiletry case on the shelf, ran a comb through her hair and put on some lip gloss. She was just peeking around the door to make sure the coast was clear when her own phone rang. It was her mother, who was crying happy tears just like Will's mother had been.

Jordyn emerged into the main room and dropped to the sofa as Evelyn Cates said how thrilled she was about the marriage. She was also hurt that she hadn't been there to see her youngest daughter say *I do* to the man of her dreams. Jordyn talked to her for fifteen minutes, in the course of which her mom got past her hurt and confessed that she was over the moon at the news.

"I've always favored Will over his brothers," her mother confided in an excited whisper. "Though make no mistake, I do love his brothers, too."

"I know you do, Mom."

"And your father and I are going to see what we can do, see if we can make it up there to the Rust Creek Valley for a visit this summer..."

"It would be so great to see you." *Except for how I'll have to lie straight to your face the whole time that you're here.*

"Well, I can't promise anything. Things are always crazy here at home—and you'll be here in Thunder Canyon for Thanksgiving, anyway, won't you?"

She cast a reproachful glance in Will's direction. "That's the plan."

"Wonderful." Her mother sighed. "Just wonderful. I'm so happy for you—and Will is a lucky, lucky man."

Her father came on the phone next. He told her he loved her and he was proud of her and he thought she'd made a damn fine choice in Will for a husband. "And is he there with you? I would like a word with him."

Jordyn passed Will her phone. He got congratulated by her father and then her mother. Twenty minutes later, they finally said goodbye to the Cates parents.

And five minutes after that, Jordyn's sister Jasmine called. Jazzy had come to Rust Creek Falls with Jordyn, but had found love in no time with the local veterinarian, Brooks Smith.

"I've called twice before this and sent more than one text, too, since I heard the news Sunday morning," Jazzy chided in a wounded tone. "I was getting worried."

Jordyn apologized and settled her down and told all

the right lies. Already they were starting to come way too smoothly, those lies. And that seemed somehow a whole new kind of wrong. Bad enough that she kept lying, even worse that the untruths were starting to rise so easily to her tongue.

After she got rid of Jazzy, she looked up to find her new husband watching her. "I would really love it if I didn't have to tell another lie today." She tossed her phone on the low table and sank to the sofa in the room's small living area.

"Hey." He came to her in long strides, dropping down beside her and throwing an arm across the back of the couch. Faintly, she could smell his aftershave, like saddle soap and spice. He had a scruff of black beard on his fine, square jaw, and his eyes really were beautiful, surrounded by long, black lashes that any girl would envy, his irises light as blue frost in the center, the outer circle rimmed in cobalt. "Don't think of it as lying," he advised in that know-it-all tone he'd been using on her practically since she was in diapers.

"Of course I think of it as lying. It *is* lying."

"Because you're approaching it the wrong way. Strictly speaking, nothing we've told them is untrue."

"Strictly speaking," she shot back, "now you're lying to me, too."

"That's not so."

"Think back, Will. You told your parents that you're bringing me home to Thunder Canyon for Thanksgiving—and at Christmas, too."

A muscle in that square jaw twitched. "It could happen."

"If I'm pregnant, which I'm not."

"It's going to be fine. I promise. We just need to stick with the plan."

"Yeah. Our Divorce Plan," she said sourly, already

thinking of it as requiring capital letters, something huge and looming, dishonest and wrong that she'd somehow let Will convince her was right. "And not only are there all the lies we're telling now. Think about how fun it's going to be having to also explain to everyone we love that it 'didn't work out.'"

He studied her for a long, uncomfortable moment and then asked too quietly, "Do you want to call it off now? If you do, just say so."

She should say yes and she knew it. *Yes, Will. Let's put an end to this craziness now.* But she didn't want to call it off. She wanted...

She didn't know for sure what she wanted. But calling it off wasn't it.

His eyes had a hard light in them. "Are you going to answer my question, Jordyn Leigh?"

"I, um..."

"Answer my question."

"Fine. No, then. I don't want to call it off."

His expression gentled. "What do you say we not borrow trouble?" He caught a lock of her hair and rubbed it slowly between his fingers.

She wrapped her fingers around his wrist. "Don't."

They stared at each other. She was pinching up her mouth at him, and she knew it. His skin was so warm against her palm. She found herself remembering the other night—before it all got so crazy and misty and they did things she could no longer recall.

It had been wonderful, that night. She'd loved being with him. And his kisses had thrilled her, just set her on fire...

She didn't know quite how it had happened, but she was staring at his mouth. So soft, that mouth, especially in contrast to the general hardness of him.

Her stomach chose that moment to rumble. That made him grin.

It also broke the strange spell she'd somehow fallen under. "Don't make me smile." She let go of his wrist and pretended to sulk. "I'm too annoyed with you."

"What you are is hungry. We need to get a decent meal into you."

He was right. She really should eat. "They have room service here, I hope."

He shook his head. "I think we need to get out."

"Maybe you do. Find me a menu. I'll hang around here."

"Jordyn, we can't just hide in the room."

"You're the one who's calling it hiding." At that, he simply stared at her disapprovingly until she began to feel like a bit of a brat. Grudgingly, she confessed, "And I've told enough lies for one day."

He shrugged. "Okay. I can understand that. How about this? I know of a really good Italian place in Kalispell."

"We're going back to Kalispell?" She whined the words and almost winced at the grating sound of her own voice.

"Look at it this way. No one there will ask you any questions, and that means you'll be telling no lies."

Will thought that the afternoon went pretty well, overall.

At the Italian place, they shared an antipasto. He ordered three-meat lasagna and she had veal *piccata*. Jordyn asked for a second basket of bread and cleaned her plate.

When they left the restaurant, she seemed in a much better mood. She asked about the ranch.

He told her about the great views of the mountains and the good water access. "It's just what I always wanted, mostly prime grassland and quality bottom land where I can grow alfalfa. But I've also got a few pretty cottonwood groves and pines higher up. The house, bunkhouse, foreman's cottage and the barn—well, just about all of the buildings—need work. I'll be getting to that, but it's livable in the meantime. I've bought cattle, and they'll be showing up within the week, to get me going on my herd. And I've hired a married couple to help out. They'll be coming up from Thunder Canyon, bringing my horses and all the furniture I own, on Thursday or Friday."

"Do I know them?"

"I doubt it. Pia and Myron Stevalik?"

'Nope. Don't think I've met them. You haven't told me what you're going to call the place."

"Shangri-La?"

"Hah. That is so totally *not* you, Will."

"How about the Flying C?"

At that, she nodded. "I like it." And then she sent him a smile.

He felt pleased—with himself, with the sunny afternoon outside the quad cab, with just about everything. "That settles it, then. I'm calling it the Flying C."

She bent and got something from her purse—an elastic band, he saw a moment later, when he glanced her way again. With her gaze on the road ahead, she put her hair up in a ponytail. The action lifted her small, firm breasts even higher.

About then, he realized he was staring. Before she could catch him at it, he faced front again and told himself to quit drooling over her and drive the damn truck.

She said, "So tell me your secret. How'd you get your ranch so soon? I remember when you used to talk about it back home, you always said you hoped that you might swing it by the time you were in your forties." Apparently, she had no clue he'd been staring at her breasts.

Good. "Yeah. That was the plan. But maybe you remember my great-aunt Wilhelmina?"

"Of course. You were named after her, right? And she made it big in real estate in San Diego…"

"That's Aunt Willie. About six months ago, she passed on."

"Oh, Will. I'm so sorry. I hadn't heard." She reached across the console and gave his shoulder a light squeeze then quickly retreated to her side of the cab again. He wouldn't have minded at all if she'd held on for a moment or two longer. The impression of her soft hand seemed to linger through the fabric of his shirt. "How old was she?"

"In her eighties, and she'd been frail for a couple of years. It happened peacefully."

"I'm glad for that."

"She went to sleep one night and never woke up. Aunt Willie had married five times, but never had any children."

"And she doted on you…"

"She was the greatest. I miss her. She left me a generous nest egg and a final letter that told me to 'live my dream' and 'follow my heart.'" He sent her a grin.

"Oh, I like that." Jordyn's eyes got that shine to them. She was a pretty woman. But that shine in her eyes made her downright beautiful. "Your aunt Willie was a romantic."

He chuckled. "To you, everyone's a romantic." They passed the Manor. He didn't turn in.

And Jordyn's eyes went from shining to guarded. "What's up, Will?"

He kept his tone casual. "I just thought we'd go on into town for a little, take a walk in the park."

She was pinching up her mouth again. "I told you. I've done enough lying for one day."

"If we see anyone, we'll just smile, say thank-you when they congratulate us—and walk on by."

She muttered something unpleasant under her breath. He had the good sense not to ask her to say that again.

Will stopped his quad cab in the lot between the park and the veterinary clinic. It was the same lot where Jordyn vaguely remembered Elbert Lutello pulling a briefcase from his pink Cadillac on Saturday night.

Jordyn tried again to get through to her temporary husband. "I don't feel like a walk right now, Will."

"It'll be good for you, a little fresh air, some exercise." He said it so cheerfully, as though he had nothing more on his mind than a late-afternoon stroll.

Bull. "I've known you all my life. You think I can't tell when you're playing me?"

He turned off the engine and adjusted his straw Stetson on his handsome head. "Okay, Jordyn. The truth is I was kind of hoping that a walk in the park might jog loose a few memories of what happened Saturday night."

"But we already know the main points of what happened in the park. The mystery is how we got to your hotel room and what we did once we were in there."

"I admit I don't remember what we did when we got there, but I know we drove there in this pickup." He tapped the steering wheel for emphasis. "That's easy to figure out because I left the pickup here in this lot for the wedding and the party—and the next morning, it was at the Manor."

"Listen to yourself. *That* is scary. We're lucky we made it to the hotel that night without ending up in a wreck."

"Exactly. Another reason that whoever drugged us needs to be called to account for it."

"That's assuming we were drugged in the first place."

"Jordyn, would you just walk in the park with me? Please?" He said it so nicely.

She knew she was weakening. She grumbled, "Anyone

ever tell you that you're like a dog with a bone once you get fixated on something?"

He tugged on the brim of his hat again. "Humor me?"

She cast a glance toward the headliner and puffed out her cheeks with a hard breath. "Oh, fine."

He rewarded her for giving in with a slow, way-too-sexy grin. "You're the best wife I ever had, you know that?"

"You silver-tongued devil, you." She shoved open her door and climbed down to the blacktop. He went around the rear of the truck to meet her. When she started off toward the park, he caught her hand and twined his fingers with hers. She slanted him a wary look.

"We're newlyweds, remember? Newlyweds should hold hands." His hat shadowed his eyes, and she couldn't really read his expression.

But hey. It felt good, his big, warm hand all wrapped around hers. As if she wasn't alone. As if...they really *were* married. Or at least, intimate. Close...

Better not to overthink it. She squeezed his fingers. "Let's go."

They set off. "I think we should start at the beginning," he said, "at that spot by the gazebo, where they set up the punch table and the portable dance floor."

A half an hour later, they'd strolled through most of the small park hand in hand, stopping at any spot either of them could recall from Saturday night. They'd waved and smiled and said hi to a couple of young mothers and some kids tossing a ball.

And neither of them had remembered anything new from the night in question.

"Well, it was worth a shot," Will said as they started across the parking lot on their way back to the quad cab.

"If you say so." They were still holding hands. She

slanted him a smile. "And the walk actually turned out to be kind of nice."

"I knew you'd enjoy it."

"Don't get smug, Clifton."

"I am never smug."

"Yeah, right."

He tugged on her hand, pulling her closer. "And see? No one asked you a single question."

She beamed wider. "True. It was fine."

"Told you so." He tipped his head down to her.

They stopped walking and just stood there, on the edge of the blacktop, grinning at each other. She caught herself on the verge of going on tiptoe to press her lips to his.

Oh, a girl could get so confused in a situation like this. Married for the world to see, both of them playing their parts.

Maybe too well.

Gently, and much too regretfully, she pulled her hand free of his. "I, um, have some homework I should get busy on…"

He frowned, puzzled at first. But then he remembered. "Right. Those online classes you've been taking." He took off his hat, smoothed his black hair and slid the hat back in place. "So. Back to the Manor?"

"That would be great. I'll get out my laptop and get to work."

Will seemed kind of quiet on the drive to the hotel. But then, Jordyn was quiet, too, thinking about how she'd almost tried to kiss him, about how she had to watch herself with him.

That walk in the park had failed to spark any lost memories from Saturday night. But lost memories weren't the only kind. What about the things she *hadn't* forgotten from Saturday night?

Like for instance, Will's kiss. Ironic? Oh, yeah. She couldn't recall if she'd had sex with him or not. But kissing him? She remembered that just fine. And she might as well be honest with herself. She wouldn't mind at all if he kissed her again.

However, given their situation, kissing Will probably fell directly into the "things *not* to do" category. Their situation was plenty complicated already. No need to make it more so.

At the Manor, he walked her to the room and then went off to find his brothers, suggesting she order up room service if she got hungry and promising to be back by ten or so. That gave her four hours on her own. She got out her laptop and went to work.

Once she'd caught up with her assignments, she grabbed a quick shower and put on a comfy pair of terry-cloth shorts and a Grizzlies T-shirt suitable for sitting around in—and sleeping in, when the time came. She had a chicken sandwich and a soda then brushed her teeth and stretched out on the bed to watch a little TV.

The next thing she knew, she heard the shower running. She opened her eyes to the end of a *Scandal* rerun and realized that Will must have come in while she was sleeping.

She switched off the TV and sat up against the pillows and wondered why her heart had started racing a thousand miles a minute. There was nothing to get all excited about. Yeah, it was weird, her and Will in one room with one bed.

But come on. They'd already spent a night together, even if she couldn't remember a thing about what had happened when they did. He was…just Will. They'd known each other forever, and it was not a big deal.

Eventually the shower stopped. She sat there staring

at the bathroom door, ordering her silly heart to slow the heck down.

He came out on a cloud of steam, wearing sweats and a soft gray T-shirt that clung to the hard muscles of his chest and outlined those corrugated abs of his. His feet were bare, and his hair was wet, and her mouth was suddenly desert dry. "Sorry," he said. "I didn't mean to wake you up."

"Oh! You didn't. I was…I didn't mean to fall asleep." Lame. Utterly, completely lame. If she *wasn't* a virgin, she certainly sounded like one—a virgin from way back in the day, one who knew nothing about sex or pleasure or what to do with a man in her room.

Well, she did know. She'd read plenty of books about pleasing her special guy—as well as herself. She was ready and then some for whenever *he* finally bothered to come along.

True, she lacked experience at being intimate with a man and she would be counting on her special guy to help her with that. But she wasn't afraid of her own desires. She was a healthy, normal grown woman who took care of herself in every way, including sexually.

He studied her for a moment. "You okay, Jordyn?"

"Sure. Fine. I mean, all things considered."

His mouth quirked at the corners. "Tell you what. Just give me a pillow. I'll take the couch, and you can turn off the light."

That wasn't right. "No." It kind of popped out without her actually planning to say it. "I mean, come on. It's a big bed, and we've already spent one night together in it."

"I'm taking the sofa."

"But it's too short for you, hardly more than a love seat, really. You won't be comfortable on that."

He had that look, the one she'd always thought of as his

noble look. When she was younger and he got that look, it always meant he was about to start telling her what to do. But now that noble look seemed more directed at himself. He said grimly, "I promised you separate rooms. Tomorrow we'll have them. Tonight the couch will do me fine."

She folded her arms across her breasts and executed a serious eye roll. "This is ridiculous."

"It's not right that you should have to—"

"Shush," she commanded. He surprised her and actually shut up. She wasted no time jumping from the bed, pulling back the covers and climbing in. "There's a blanket in the closet. Grab that. You can sleep outside the covers. I promise not to try and put a move on you."

He chuckled at that and then looked at her sideways. "You sure?"

"Absolutely. Come to bed."

Chapter Five

Will was stretched out beside her in the dark.

She could smell him—all clean and masculine and freshly showered. She stared at the shadows up near the ceiling and wondered if she would ever get back to sleep.

"Jordyn Leigh?" His voice kind of filled up the darkness, so deep and manly and just rough enough to make her wish...

Well, never mind about what she might wish. "Yeah?"

"What's the matter?"

She should tell him there was nothing. But suddenly she felt so safe in the dark, in the bed, with Will. She wanted to share her thoughts, to tell him the thing that kept preying on her mind. "It's just too strange, that's all."

When she said no more, he gently prompted, "What's strange? Tell me."

"Well, I mean, to wait all these years for that special night. And then, not to know if it happened or not."

"It really gets to you, huh?" His voice just wrapped around her, soothing and comforting and wonderfully deep.

She let out a sigh into the darkness. "Yeah, it gets to me."

"You could go to a doctor, get an exam, find out for sure?"

"But see, that's just it…"

A silence. She matched her breathing to his. And then he encouraged her in a near whisper, "Come on. You can tell me."

She thought what a great guy he was. All those years she'd found him so annoying. How wrong she'd been. She confessed, "I looked it up online yesterday while I was trying to get my mind around the whole idea that I can't even remember if we did or we didn't."

"Looked what up, exactly?"

"You know, about hymens."

Another silence from him. He didn't even breathe. She suspected he might be trying not to laugh.

And strangely enough, that he might be holding back a chuckle didn't bother her. Why wouldn't he chuckle over the idea of her madly searching the web for the scoop on her possibly lost virginity? It *was* kind of funny, she supposed.

Just not to her.

Finally, he asked, "Hymens, huh?"

"Mmm-hmm. Turns out they're something of a myth."

"Wait. You're trying to tell me there's no such thing as a hymen?"

"No. They do exist."

"Whew." His voice was teasing now. She smiled to herself in response to the sound of it. "Had me worried there for a minute."

"The thing is some women hardly have one, even when they're really young. And it can get thin and slowly disappear if a woman is an athlete, thus the old wives' tale that women should ride sidesaddle to preserve the proof of their virginity. And by my age, even if a woman's never had sex, she very well might not have much of one left, anyway—and also, a woman can actually have sex and her hymen can stretch, but still be there. So it's a problem, because whether or not I have one wouldn't necessarily tell a doctor anything, unless there was scarring or bleeding or some kind of injury. I don't feel as though I've been injured. And Sunday morning, there was no blood, and I wasn't the least bit sore."

She stared into the darkness, waiting for him to say something else. But he didn't.

So she finished in a small, sad voice, "The plain fact is the most reliable way to find out if a woman's a virgin is to ask her—unless she got drunk off her ass and can't remember, that is."

She waited again, hoping for a few more words of support and comfort from him. But he remained totally silent beside her.

Had he dropped off to sleep?

Not that she'd blame him if he had. What guy wanted to lie in the dark with his clothes on next to his wife who wasn't *really* his wife and listen to her babble endlessly about hymens?

"TMI, huh?" she asked in a trembling whisper.

And that was when she felt his hand, down between them, next to hers. His warm fingers brushed her cool ones. She gave him her hand. He twined their fingers together and lifted their joined hands toward his face. She felt his breath across her knuckles, followed by the soft brush of his lips on her skin.

Jordyn let out the breath she hadn't realized she was holding. Her eyes drifted shut. She fell asleep thinking that as temporary husbands went, she could have done a whole lot worse.

* * *

She woke to daylight and the smell of fresh coffee.

"Mornin'." Will was already up, sitting on the sofa, eating eggs delivered from room service. He indicated a still-covered dish on the tray on the coffee table. "I ordered you the breakfast scramble, wheat toast. Hope that'll work."

She sat up and stretched. "Perfect."

He gave her a look that made her empty tummy feel warm. "Come on, then. Dig in before it gets cold."

So they ate, sitting side by side on the sofa.

After breakfast, he let her hog the bathroom. She had to hurry to get ready for work.

He followed her to the door and pulled it open for her as she juggled her purse and her laptop. "What time will you be through for the day?"

"About three."

"I'll meet you there. We can go by the boardinghouse and get your things. Then you can follow me out to the ranch."

"You don't have to—"

He waved away her objections. "Three o'clock. I'll be there."

She clutched her laptop to her chest. "Wow. Today's the day, huh?"

He looked so pleased with himself. "Closing is at ten."

"Allow me to congratulate you again on the total fabulousness of having your own place at last."

He gave a modest little snort. "I'll be knee-deep in cow crap before you know it."

"But it will be your *own* cow crap." She moved past the threshold into the hallway, but she was leaning up toward him.

And he leaned down to her, his eyes alight with excitement at what the day would bring. "I like a woman who understands the dreams of a ranching man."

She waited for him to kiss her.

And then she realized she was doing it and quickly stepped back. "Well, see you at three, then."

"Three. Right. See you then."

She whirled and headed off down the hall, feeling the heat flooding her cheeks, hoping she'd turned away in time, before he saw her blush.

Will stood in the doorway, staring after Jordyn's excellent backside as she hurried away from him.

He'd almost kissed her.

And from the wide, welcome look in her eyes and the softness of that tempting mouth of hers, he guessed that she would have let him do it. He wished he had, even though the side of him that had always looked out for her wanted to punch his lights out for having such thoughts.

Which made zero sense. He'd kissed her Saturday night, and more than once. He'd likely done *more* than just kiss her. The horse had left the barn for him and Jordyn, kissingwise.

And besides, they were married. Why shouldn't they kiss?

Don't go there, you idiot. Keep yourself in line.

He pulled his head back into the room and shut the door and told himself he wouldn't think about sharing kisses with his adorable accidental wife. It should be easier to keep his hands and his mouth to himself after today. At the ranch, they would have separate bedrooms.

Not like last night, when he'd lain beside her in the dark and listened to her breathing even out into sleep and tried to block out the softness of her body, the sweet scent of her skin—all of her, right there beside him.

And this morning? He woke up spooning her, sporting wood. Lucky for him, she was still asleep. He'd managed to ease himself away from her, slide out of the bed and make it to the bathroom without her waking up and discovering how very happy he was to have her around. It could have been damned embarrassing.

But then again, he *was* a man. Morning wood happened. No big deal.

And anyway, today he would take possession of his ranch. He'd have his room, and she'd have hers.

Problem solved.

"Don't you dare peek, Miss Jordyn," said little Sophie Lundergren.

It was half past noon. They'd all just finished their sack lunches. Sophie sat beside Jordyn at the long picnic table under the giant oak in the play yard at Country Kids Day Care.

"I'm not peeking, I promise," Jordyn vowed, and kept her hands on the tabletop, away from the blindfold Sophie's older sister, Delilah, had tied around her head moments before.

There were giggles from the kids all around her.

And lots of whispering. Someone brushed by her and set something on the table.

One of the boys said, "Shh. Hurry."

And one of her bosses, either Sara or Suzie—she couldn't be sure which—said, "Careful, now. Yes..."

And then, finally, Sara's oldest daughter, Lindy, said, "Ahem. We're ready. Remove the blindfold."

Quick hands untied the bandanna wrapped around Jordyn's head and whipped it away.

And everyone, kids and Sara and Suzie together, cried, "We love you, Miss Jordyn!"

Jordyn blinked and stared—at the leaning stack of brightly wrapped packages piled on one end of the table, at the obviously homemade cake with "Jordyn and Will" printed in lopsided pink letters on top. "Oh!" she exclaimed, and pressed her hands to her mouth. "Oh, my!"

"It's a wedding shower!" exclaimed nine-year-old Lily Franklin. "We're giving you a wedding shower!"

"Yeah!" said Bobby Neworth, who was almost eight. "Because all that lovey-dovey stuff is kind of icky, but cake and presents are good!" The other boys hooted and whistled in noisy agreement.

Jordyn gulped down the huge knot of mixed emotions that had suddenly formed high up in her chest and told herself not to think about the lies, to put her focus on the total sweetness of the moment. "Oh, this is beautiful. Thank you. Thank you, all."

"You're welcome, Miss Jordyn," the kids said, again pretty much in unison.

Lily proudly announced, "We baked the cake yesterday. It's called red velvet. And the frosting is buttercream."

"I did the frosting letters!" Bobby declared. "And Mrs. Suzie only had to help me a teeny-tiny bit."

Jordyn nodded in appreciation. "It looks so good."

"It's a little bit crooked," Delilah allowed.

"It's the best cake I ever had," declared Jordyn, and everybody beamed.

"And we made all the presents, too!" chimed in six-year-old Theodore Brickman.

"You're gonna love them," Sophie decreed.

"Oh, I know that I will." Across the table, Suzie and Sara stood side by side grinning. Jordyn mouthed a teary-eyed *thank you* at both of them and tried not to think how much she would miss them when she left for Missoula.

"Our pleasure," said Sara, pressing a kiss to the plump

cheek of the beautiful eight-month-old baby cradled in her arms. The baby, Bekka Wyatt, was Melba Strickland's great-granddaughter and a new addition as of yesterday to the Country Kids roster.

Delilah turned suddenly wide eyes to Jordyn. "Miss Jordyn, are you *Mrs.* Jordyn now?"

"She certainly is," Sara answered for her.

And all the kids chimed in with, "Mrs. Jordyn."

"Mrs. Jordyn!"

"She's Mrs. Jordyn now!"

Suzie laughed. "So, *Mrs.* Jordyn. Time to cut the cake."

A happy chorus of agreement followed that suggestion. "Yeah!"

"Cake!"

"Cut the cake, Mrs. Jordyn."

"Cut the cake *now*!"

So Jordyn made the first slice and then Suzie took over, cutting kid-sized slices and passing them around. Jordyn got to work opening her presents.

The kids had done well. Each gift was an art project, and each one delighted her. She admired a watercolor of a stick-figure bride and groom holding hands on a patch of green beneath a bright yellow sun. Another present consisted of bits of yellow crepe paper and white lace glued to a paper plate, with a red-lipped, blue-eyed face drawn in the center. "That's you, Miss—er, *Mrs.* Jordyn—the bride," Sophie explained. "See?" She caressed the lace with her little hand. "It's your wedding veil."

Jordyn put her arm around Sophie and gave her a quick hug. "How beautiful. Thank you, Sophie."

"You're welcome," Sophie shyly replied.

There were construction-paper hearts decorated with rickrack and lace, creations in clay molded to form flowers and butterflies, any number of glittery caterpillars made of egg cartons with pipe-cleaner antennae, plus several bright and cheerful finger paintings of nothing recognizable. Jordyn admired each one and thanked each child, after which she had her cake, which was really quite delicious.

They all pitched in to clean up. The kids got a half hour to work off steam on the playground equipment and then they filed inside for story time. Next, there would be naps for the younger ones and a quiet period for the older children.

Once they went in, Jordyn left Suzie and Sara with the children and went to the office at the front of the house. It was Sara's house. They'd added on rooms to either side in front to accommodate the growing day care. It was a great old house, comfortable and sprawling. Jordyn enjoyed working there.

She loved dealing with the kids, but she also found satisfaction in developing new projects for the day care's curriculum. She helped keep the accounts, and she wrote a mean grant application. Suzie and Sara both claimed they didn't know how they'd ever gotten along without her. A few months before, when Jordyn had told them she planned to head for Missoula in the fall, they'd been supportive of her plans for her future, but unhappy at the prospect of losing her. Jordyn hated to leave them. Yes, she wanted a new start. But the twins were a joy to work for—and the kids were the best.

Jordyn opened up the accounting software and then just stared at the screen for a few minutes, torn between getting all choked up with guilty emotion and a big, fat grin. A wedding shower, so beautifully and lovingly planned and executed off-the-cuff yesterday, while she was away for her "honeymoon" day.

Only at Country Kids…

She heard a light tap on the open French doors behind her. "Excuse me?" said a woman's voice. "Jordyn Leigh?"

Jordyn swiveled her chair to find Claire Strickland Wyatt standing in the entry hall behind her. Claire, who always looked beautiful and pulled together with her long hair just so, was baby Bekka's mom, and Melba Strickland's granddaughter. Claire and her family lived in Bozeman, but now and then she and her husband, Levi, would bring the baby to town and stay with her grandparents at the boardinghouse. They'd arrived last Friday, as a matter of fact, for the wedding and the Fourth of July weekend. "Claire! I heard this morning that you were still in town."

Claire gestured vaguely toward the front door. "Sara told me to just come right in during day-care hours…"

"Perfect. Suzie said you'd signed Bekka up with us. She's been a little darling, seems to be settling right in—in case you were wondering."

Claire's gaze slid away. And then she seemed to catch herself. She met Jordyn's eyes again with a brittle smile. "Well, I, um, decided that Bekka and I would stay in Rust Creek Falls for a little while. Levi went on back home. It's work, you know." Claire let out a sad little chuckle. "He's always got work he has to get back for."

By then, Jordyn had no doubt that something was off with Claire. Way off. Undecided whether to mind her own business or ask Melba's granddaughter if something was bothering her, Jordyn volunteered lamely, "I hear you."

Claire's smile seemed stretched to the breaking point. "They needed him at the store."

"Nice for you, though, to get away for a while."

"Oh, it is, yes. Just great. To get away…"

Ugh. Maybe Claire had read that gossip column in the *Gazette* and couldn't make up her mind if she ought to congratulate Jordyn—or offer her condolences.

And whatever Claire might think about Jordyn getting married out of the blue, something else was going on with Melba's granddaughter. Jordyn felt awful for her. She looked totally miserable.

"So, did you hear my big news?" Jordyn went for lighthearted, with a touch of humor, and thought she succeeded pretty well. "Jenny and Braden weren't the only ones who got married on Saturday."

Claire gulped—and then pasted on another uncomfortable smile. "Yes! I did hear. Congratulations. I...don't think I've met him. I..." She seemed to run out of words.

Jordyn offered, "His name is Will Clifton. I've known him forever. He's from Thunder Canyon, like me. We grew up together."

"Ah. Well, Will Clifton is a lucky, lucky man. I hope you'll be very happy together."

"Oh, we definitely will," Jordyn assured Claire with a blithe wave of her hand. What was another lie—or ten— anyway? "It was sudden, our marriage, but so what? I don't care what they say about marrying in haste, sometimes you just know when the right man comes along."

"Of course you do," Claire replied with real feeling. Jordyn dared to think they were getting past whatever awkwardness had charged the air a moment before.

And then Claire burst into tears.

For an awful string of endless seconds, Jordyn just sat and gaped at her.

Claire slapped her hands to her mouth. "Oh, God. I'm so sorry. I don't know what's—" the words caught on a sob "—come over me..." The tears ran down her cheeks and trickled through her fingers.

Jordyn finally stopped gaping and lurched into action. She grabbed the tissue box from the corner of the desk and jumped from her chair. "Claire. Oh, honey..."

"I'm such a complete, hopeless fool…"

"No. No, you are not. Not in the least," Jordyn insisted. "Now, come on. Come and sit down." She passed the other woman the tissue box. Claire took it and clutched it to her chest like a lifeline. Jordyn wrapped an arm around her and guided her over to the love seat opposite the desk. "Sit right here…"

Still sobbing, Claire dropped to the cushions, whipped out a few tissues and dabbed unhappily at her streaming cheeks. "I'll have my mascara all over the place. And you know what? Right this minute, I don't even care."

"Don't worry about your makeup. You just cry."

"It's so embarrassing…"

"No. It's how you feel, and that is never embarrassing." Jordyn sat beside her and patted her shoulder.

"Would you mind if we shut the doors?"

"Not in the least." Jordyn rose again and went over to close and latch the doors. Anyone in the hall could still see them through the glass panes, but the sounds of poor Claire's distress would be mostly muffled.

"I'm so sorry," Claire insisted again. "I don't know what's the matter with me…"

"Shh, now." Jordyn went back and sat with her. "It's okay. It's only you and me. Whatever it is, you just cry it out." Jordyn sympathized with Melba's granddaughter. She'd been there herself on Sunday morning, when she sobbed her heart out over her possibly lost virginity while Will tried to tell her that somehow, the night before, she'd become his wife. "Sometimes it's just all you can do, you know? Sometimes you need that, to let go and let it out."

Claire took a fresh tissue and blew her nose. "I can't believe I'm doing this. You shouldn't have to deal with this…"

"It's okay. Really. I do understand."

Claire dabbed at her eyes. "It was when you mentioned getting married in haste. I, well, the tears just came, and I couldn't stop them."

"Is this about your marriage?" Jordyn dared to ask. "Are you saying that you think you and Levi got married too soon?"

"No." Claire swiped at her wet cheeks. "We didn't rush. We dated for two years before we got married."

"So then what is it? What's got you hurting like this?"

"I don't know, Jordyn." Another hard sob escaped her and she shook her head, hard. "No. That's not true. I *do* know why I'm crying. I know why, exactly."

Jordyn cleared her throat and guessed, "This *is* about Levi, right?"

"Oh, yeah. Levi. Jordyn, I knew the day I met him that he was the one. I knew we would live happily ever after."

The born romantic in Jordyn just had to chime in on that. "Oh, that is beautiful, Claire. I believe in that, I do. In happily-ever-afters. In love at first sight."

"Sometimes," Claire said glumly, "happily-ever-after isn't all it's cracked up to be."

"I'm so sorry…"

"I thought I knew it all, Jordyn. I thought I had love and forever all figured out. But now, well, I have to face the cold, hard truth. I *don't* know. I had it wrong, messed it up. I don't even know how to *talk* to him anymore. The issues keep piling up, and I don't know how to address them."

Jordyn reassured her, "It happens. And I'm sure all married couples have issues." Look at her and Will. They had issues. Like the fact that they'd never planned to get married in the first place, for starters.

"Yes, yes." Claire bobbed her head. "I know you're right. But see, I thought we were better than that, Levi and me. I thought we would get through the tough times, get through the challenges that come with a new baby, get through the loneliness I've been feeling with Levi working all the time. I thought we were managing. But then, Saturday night, after the wedding, I had to get back to Grandma's to relieve the sitter."

"Of course you did."

"I had to get back, and Levi wanted to stay. He was having a good time, he said, and he'd be home soon. For once, couldn't I just let him enjoy himself?"

"That was a little harsh of him."

"I thought so, too. I was hurt. I just turned around and left him without another word. I went back to the boardinghouse, relieved the sitter. And waited. I waited and waited. He'd *said* he'd be home soon. But no. He didn't come staggering in until dawn. And then he tried to tell me he'd hardly had a thing to drink. I mean, what is it Judge Judy says? 'Don't pee on my leg and tell me it's raining?'"

Jordyn couldn't hold back a chuckle. "That Judge Judy, she tells it to them straight."

"Yes, she does. And so did I. I said I knew he was lying. He said no, he wasn't. He didn't even have the integrity to tell me the truth. Well, I wasn't about to stand there and take it while he lied in my face. I said a few things I shouldn't have. And it all went downhill from there. We had a big fight. And…" She paused to blow her nose again. "He *left* me, Jordyn."

"Oh, no…"

"Yes. He did. He left me—well, sort of."

"Sort of?"

Claire drew back her shoulders and aimed her chin high. "Well, all right. I kicked him out. I yelled at him that I didn't want to be married anymore. I yelled at him and kicked him out—and he went. He went back to Bozeman." The waterworks started again. Claire swayed toward Jordyn.

Jordyn gathered her close. "It's okay. You know that." She patted Claire's back. "Just cry…" She stroked Claire's hair and made sympathetic noises as Claire let it all out.

Finally, her sobs faded to sniffles, and Claire straightened from Jordyn's arms. "I simply can't believe he got so drunk. Levi *never* gets drunk."

"I think a lot of people got drunk that night." *Yours truly, among them.*

"He swore up and down that he'd only had a few glasses of punch. I didn't believe him, and I told him so in no uncertain terms. I mean, please. That would be insane, for Braden and Jenny to spike the punch and get everybody falling-down drunk for their wedding reception. Where's the sense in that?"

"There's none," Jordyn agreed, thinking about Will. He was so sure that a certain cowboy had spiked *her* punch. But what if someone had put something right in the punch bowl itself? A lot of people had behaved way out of character that night. Bizarre things had happened. Maybe that punch was at least partly to blame.

Or maybe not. Maybe it was just a case of people kicking over the traces, letting loose and getting crazy on a beautiful summer's night.

Claire heaved a shaky sigh, smoothed a hand down her long sable hair and slowly shook her head. "I can't believe I just unloaded all over you."

Jordyn patted her hand. "It's okay. Believe me, I get it. Sometimes you just need a good cry."

Claire pressed her fingers under her tear-puffy eyes. "I look terrible, don't I?"

"No, you don't. You look like a woman who needed to get something difficult off her chest."

Claire actually smiled then, a trembling smile, but a sincere one. "Grandma adores you. I can see why."

"Aw. I love her right back."

"Do you think I could use the bathroom to freshen up a little?"

Jordyn stood and pulled the doors wide again. "Right this way…" She led Claire to the half bath off the foyer. "I'm guessing you came to pick up Bekka?"

"I did, yes. I'm taking her into Kalispell. Thought I'd do a little shopping, get my mind off my problems."

"Sounds like a great plan. I'll get her for you, why don't I?"

"That would be perfect."

Ten minutes later Claire left with the baby. Jordyn worked on the books for a while then got going on future lesson plans.

At three she got up, went into the entry and peeked out through the sidelight next to the door.

Will was there at the curb in his quad cab, right on time as promised. She smiled at the sight of him. He really was one of the good guys.

She pulled open the door and waved him inside, where she introduced him to Suzie and Sara and the kids. He took it all in stride, answering any and all prying questions, admiring the pile of handmade wedding presents and helping her carry the big box of artistic treasures out to her Subaru.

He put the box in the back, closed the hatch and asked, "So what are you going to do with all those clay butterflies and egg carton caterpillars?"

"I haven't decided yet—maybe decorate my bedroom at the ranch." She grinned at him. "So how *is* the new homestead?"

"The main thing is it's mine." He looked so proud.

"I'm happy for you." She said it softly, with feeling. "Way to go, Will."

He resettled his Stetson, tipping the brim at her. "'Preciate that."

She led the way to the boardinghouse and parked on the street in front. He pulled in behind her.

She started to open her door, but he jogged over and slid into the passenger seat, pulling the door shut behind him. "What?" she asked.

He sent her a guarded glance. "Jordyn…"

"Go ahead. I'm listening."

"I just think I ought to warn you up front that at first, we'll definitely be roughing it. The main house needs work. All the buildings do…"

"Does the roof leak?"

"No."

"Are there lights and heat?"

"Yeah."

"Hot and cold running water?"

"Of course."

"Then we'll manage. And we'll whip it into shape in no time."

For that, he gave her a slow, sexy—and relieved—smile. "You're a good sport, Jordyn Leigh."

A good sport. It wasn't the kind of compliment that made a girl blush with pleasure, but she felt his sincerity, and that warmed her heart. "Come on," she said, and pulled on her door handle. "Let's get my stuff and get moving."

After they'd hauled everything out to the vehicles, Jordyn introduced Will to Melba and Old Gene, and handed over her key.

Old Gene shook Will's hand. "You're a very lucky young man. You take care of this sweet girl, now."

Will played the sincere groom to perfection. "Yes, sir. I certainly will."

Melba tugged Jordyn aside for a last hug. "I do hate to see you leave us…"

Jordyn promised her again to keep in touch. She thought of Claire and whispered, "I saw Claire at Country Kids today. She told me that she and Bekka are staying here with you for a while."

"She told you about her troubles?" At Jordyn's nod, Melba clucked her tongue. "I'm telling myself that she and Levi will work it out."

"I know they will," Jordyn replied with maybe a little more confidence than she felt. It never hurt to keep things positive.

Will said goodbye to Old Gene and ushered Jordyn out the door.

She paused once they were down the porch steps to look back at the old boardinghouse. "It's so weird, walking away this time, knowing I really don't live there anymore…"

He pulled her close to his side, just like a real husband might do. "You going to be all right?"

She took comfort from the warmth and strength of his sheltering arm. "Yeah. I will. I'll be just fine."

He gave her shoulder a squeeze. "Next stop, Crawford's. We need to grab a few things."

She left him to get in her Subaru as he climbed into his truck.

He drove the few blocks to North Main and pulled into the parking lot at Crawford's General Store. They parked side by side, and then got out and stood between the vehicles while he explained what they had to shop for.

"Foodwise, we need the basics. At least enough for tonight and tomorrow morning."

"What about furniture? Will we be sleeping on the floor?"

"There are a couple of old beds left behind by the previous owners, and some dusty-looking mattresses. I saw a beat-up table and some mismatched chairs in the kitchen. The living room is empty. Like I said before, it's pretty sparse."

"Pillows, sheets, blankets, towels?"

"We'll have to buy them—and you know, maybe we ought to just stay at the Manor for another night. Tomorrow I'll head for Kalispell and spend the day getting everything we need to set us up."

"Will."

He eyed her sideways. "You're looking obstinate, Jordyn Leigh."

"You're a Clifton. I'm a Cates. We come from sturdy stock. Crawford's has the basics. Let's get what we can't do without and head for the ranch."

"It's too much to ask. You have to get up early and get to work in the morning."

She knew that he would rather be out at his new place, and she intended that he should have what he wanted. "What did I just tell you, Will?"

He was weakening. "You're sure?"

"Positive. Now let's go."

They walked into Crawford's and right away, Will spotted those two middle-aged ladies from Sunday afternoon. Apparently, the two of them spent a lot of time shopping.

The two caught sight of him and Jordyn and instantly started whispering together.

Will gave them a friendly wave. They nodded and smiled—and went right back to whispering again. About then, it occurred to Will that he and Jordyn needed to play this thing right.

Jordyn pulled a cart free from the row by the doors and wheeled it around toward him. "Let's get the linens and some cleaning supplies first, then we'll get food for tonight and tomorrow." As she came even with him, he reached out, grabbed her fingers from the cart handle and reeled her in close. She made a small, breathless sound, braced her hands on his chest and stared up at him, wide-eyed. "Will! What are you—?"

He bent his head and nuzzled her shining, sweet-smelling hair. "Haven't you noticed?"

"What?"

He rubbed his nose against hers and whispered, "People are watching. And we *did* just get married."

She gave the cutest little sigh. "Oh. Well. I see…"

"Do you?" He tipped up her chin with a finger and settled his mouth gently on hers.

Chapter Six

Jordyn let out a little squeak, a squeak that turned into another soft sigh. And then she slid her hands up and wrapped them around his neck, pressing her slender body close to his. They were a great fit, just right.

And by then, she was kissing him back, stirring vague memories of Saturday night, reminding him that he really liked kissing her. She smelled so good, and she tasted like a ripe peach.

Little Jordyn Leigh Cates. Who knew?

When he lifted his head, he whispered, "We're newly-weds, remember? We're newlyweds who can't keep their hands off each other."

"Ah," she whispered back, her cheeks pink, a soft smile on those plump lips he would be only too happy to kiss every chance he got. "You mean we need to provide a public display of affection for the benefit of anyone who might doubt how very much in love we are?"

"Exactly."

"Or we could just ignore all the gossips and go about our business, not caring in the least what small-minded people might say." She started to pull away.

He caught her arm. Gently. "Jordyn…"

"What?" She gave him one of those challenging looks—the kind she'd been giving since she got out of diapers.

He didn't let that look of hers stop him. "I think you really need to kiss me again."

She giggled, a happy, playful sound. It caused an ache in the center of his chest. A really good ache. And then she scrunched up her eyebrows, pretending to think it over. Finally, she agreed, "Only one more. We have a lot of shopping to do."

"I guess I'd better make it good."

"Yes, you'd better."

So he kissed her again. Not too deep. It was a public place, after all. He made that kiss slow and tender. It wasn't hard—kissing her felt so right.

Too right? Oh, yeah. But now wasn't the time to get all tied in knots because he just possibly might be developing a too-powerful attraction to his childhood friend and temporary bride.

When he lifted his head that time, they shared a knowing smile. And when she pulled away, he didn't stop her—even though he really wouldn't have minded kissing her some more, just standing there by the carts in Crawford's, with Jordyn Leigh in his arms, his mouth pressed to hers.

For maybe a lifetime or so.

The ranch was a beauty, Jordyn thought. Acres of rolling green land, dotted here and there with stands of cottonwood and pine. Fall Mountain, a local landmark, could be seen in the distance, with the snowcapped peaks of the Rockies looming even farther out.

The ranch compound included the main house, the foreman's cottage, a bunkhouse, a barn and corrals, with a series of fenced pastures close in. The stock pond, over a rise not far from the circle of buildings, was fed by a creek, which meandered through the property.

Will stopped to open the driveway gate, and she pulled in behind him. He leaned in her window before he got back in his truck. "Did you see the creek?"

"Yeah."

"Good trout fishing in that creek." He pointed at the gate. "Picture an arch overhead with *Flying C* in wrought iron."

"Sounds perfect."

"But one thing at a time…"

They shared a quick smile. He tapped the side of her door and took off at a jog back to his pickup. They went through the gate and drove on to the circle of buildings. She parked next to him in a bare spot in front of a two-story, white-sided, blue-shuttered farmhouse with a wrap-around porch.

"It's charming," she said when he pulled open her door for her.

He made a low, rueful sound. "It will be, in time."

She got out and they went up the weathered steps to the door, which was painted a tired blue and had a fan-shaped window at the top. He had the key in his hand.

The door creaked on its hinges as he pushed it inward onto a foyer, with stairs in the center leading to the upper floor, a bare living room on the left and an empty dining room to the right. He hung his hat on a peg by the door.

"The bones are good," she said. The walls had been whitewashed, and heavy, beautiful old beams crossed the ceilings. The floor was scuffed and dusty, but made of good wide-planked hardwood. The windows were the old-fashioned sash kind.

"Master bedroom's here, with separate bathroom," he said, as they moved deeper into the first floor and passed by it on the left. He took her to the kitchen, which had a battered gate-leg table and three mismatched chairs, wood counters, a great old farm sink, an avocado-green range leftover from the seventies and a refrigerator to match.

She pulled open the fridge. It was working, and it was empty. And wonder of wonders, it was clean. "We can start loading this puppy up right away," she told him happily.

He chuckled. "You are so easy to please."

She met his fine blue eyes. They crinkled at the corners with his wonderful smile. She felt the sudden, lovely echo of his kiss on her lips and had to stop herself from raising a hand and brushing her fingers against her mouth.

This wasn't bad, her and Will, playing at being married. It wasn't bad at all.

In fact, it was really, really fun.

Maybe too much fun...

She could almost feel guilty.

But, hey. Wait a minute. They had a plan, and she intended to follow it through. No reason to beat herself up over the choice she'd made. Might as well make the best of it.

And with Will as her short-term husband, making the best of it wouldn't be all that tough. He was so easy to look at, and he kept a good attitude.

Plus, there were bound to be opportunities for more of those lovely PDAs...

He said, "Let's move along."

And they did. They passed the half bath, which had a cute pedestal sink. She glanced in the utility room. It had an empty space where the washer and dryer should be.

They poked their heads out the back door, and she admired the wide back porch. From there, they returned to the front hall and climbed the stairs.

The second floor offered two bedrooms, a shared bath and a sitting area that overlooked the bare backyard and had a great view of the barn and the creek and the stock pond shining in the afternoon sun.

"Do I get my choice of these two bedrooms up here?" she asked.

He turned from the view out the sitting room windows. "Unless you want the master..." They shared another long look.

She liked that, too, sharing long looks with him, feeling as if they were keeping a really good secret, just between the two of them.

"Forget it," she said. "I'm not kicking you out of your bedroom."

"Whichever one you want, Jordyn, it's yours." His voice had that rumble to it, a rough, manly sound that sent sparks flashing along the surface of her skin. For a long moment, she just stared at him, because it was no hardship, looking at Will.

Wake up, woman. Choose a room. "I'll take the one over the living room. It already has a bed." The bed in question was an ancient cast-iron affair, with a rolled-back mattress braced against the head of it. It didn't look all that comfortable. But at least she wouldn't have to sleep on the floor.

She followed him back downstairs and out to the vehicles.

They unloaded everything. As soon as they had it all inside, they got to work. By a little after seven, they had the kitchen wiped down, the fridge stocked with the basics, the other food put away and the two beds made and ready for bedtime.

Jordyn got to work on dinner, which consisted of ham sandwiches, potato chips, Crawford's amazing dill pickles and cold cans of beer. They were just sitting down to enjoy the feast when Will's cell rang.

Will glanced at the display before answering. "It's Cece. She's called more than once since Sunday, so I'd better answer this time." He took the call.

Jordyn set down her half-finished pickle and listened to him tell his sister the story they'd agreed on. "Yep. That's right, Cece…Uh-huh, we are…I know, I know. It's a surprise, but it's real. Me and Jordyn Leigh are in love and married and damned happy about it." He winked at her across the table.

She forced a smile for him, but she felt a stab of regret that she hadn't called Cecelia before now. They'd been friends forever, she and Cece. Maybe they didn't get together as much as they used to, now that Cece had married Nick Pritchett and they'd moved out of the boardinghouse and into their own place. But still. Jordyn had married Cece's brother, for heaven's sakes. The least Jordyn could have done was pick up the phone and share the news.

Share the lies is more like it…

And really, that was what bothered her, wasn't it?

She might be having a ball, playing house with Will. But she needed to get real with herself, at least. She hadn't called Cece because she hadn't been looking forward to telling her lifelong friend the same lies she'd been telling everyone else.

Lot of good not calling had done. In the end, she would be telling the lies, anyway.

"She's right here," said Will. "Love you, too. Hold on." He offered the phone.

Jordyn took it. "Hey," she said weakly.

"Jordyn. How *are* you? Why didn't you call?" The familiar sound of Cece's voice made her throat clutch.

She gulped to loosen it and got on with the excuses. "I'm fine. Wonderful. And Cece, I know I should have called. It's been total craziness. I hope you'll forgive me for being so thoughtless."

"Oh, stop. There's nothing to forgive. Just as long as you're happy…"

"I am." She gave Will another big, bright smile. "*So* happy. I know, it's sudden. But it's, um, what we both want. Did Will tell you? We're at the ranch now. We moved in just this afternoon."

"I hear it's rustic."

"Yeah, but it's beautiful. I can't think of any place on earth I'd rather be than here at the Flying C with Will." Across the table, her for-the-moment husband nodded his approval.

"Well, then, congratulations to you both."

"Thanks so much, Cece. Love you."

"Love you, too—and we missed you last night."

With a sigh of dismay, Jordyn remembered. "Omygosh. I don't believe it. I missed the Newcomers Club." She and Cece had formed the club a year before to help recent transplants to the community find friends and get involved in their new hometown. Jordyn hadn't missed a meeting all year. "I'm so sorry. It totally slipped my mind."

"Don't beat yourself up over it. It's not a big deal. You *are* a newlywed, after all."

Yeah, but not for long. "I should have been there."

"Oh, come on. There's always next month."

Which would be her *last* month. By the September meeting, she would be settled in Missoula. Why did that make her sad? It was her new life, after all. And she was looking forward to it.

Cece seemed to read the direction of her thoughts. "Are you still running off to Missoula now?"

"I am not *running off* anywhere, thank you very much."

Cece made a humphing sound and Jordyn could just picture her rolling her eyes. "Don't get so sensitive. Let me rephrase. Are you still moving to Missoula to pursue your degree?"

"Yes, my plans are the same. Will won't hear of my backing out on the education I've worked so hard for." Across the table, Will saluted her with his beer can. She puffed out her cheeks and crossed her eyes at him and then went on. "It'll only be for two semesters, and Missoula's just a couple of hours away."

"So you'll be back often," said Cece. "I know I can count on that, now that your husband's here."

Defensiveness curled in her belly. "Now, what is that supposed to mean?"

Cece released a slow, careful breath. "The truth is, I was worried that you'd take off for college and I'd hardly ever see you again. But now that you're married to my brother, I know you have to come home. And that's a very good thing."

Home. Strange how Rust Creek Falls really did feel like home now.

However, when she left for Missoula, she had no plans to return. And by then, she wouldn't be married to Cece's brother anymore...

"Jordyn Leigh," Cece prompted. "Are you still on the line?"

Jordyn shook herself. "I'm right here. I...well, I was just thinking that I don't know how I'm going to bear being away from him. It's going to so *hard*." When she said that, Will put his hand against his heart and mimed frantic beating. She picked up her half-eaten pickle and threatened him with it. He played along and put up both hands in mock surrender. She stuck out her tongue at him, set the pickle back down and said to Cece, "He's one of a kind, your brother."

Cece groaned. "He's a pain in the butt."

Jordyn laughed. "But in a good way—the *best* way."

"Wow, Jordyn Leigh. Look who's changed her tune. He used to drive you crazy."

"Oh, he still does. He really, really does..." She said that with over-the-top breathlessness. Will arched a brow and looked at her sideways. She should have left it at that, but she didn't. She was kind of on a roll. "He's so amazing, Cece. He's so good and kind. And hot looking. And helpful. His kisses just blow me away. And when we're alone, he—"

"Enough," Cece warned. "I know you're in love with him. I get that. But don't give me too many details. He *is* my brother, after all."

Jordyn winced. "Sorry. I think I got carried away..."

Across the table, Will sipped his beer and watched her through suddenly unreadable eyes.

Cece said, "Okay, I'll let you go. I just had to check in, congratulate you both and tell you I love you."

"Thanks. We're fine. Happy. Glad to be here in our new home."

"If you need anything..."

"I will call you if I do, I promise. Love you."

"Bye."

Jordyn turned off the phone and pushed it across to Will. She sipped her beer then picked up the other half of her sandwich. She felt...edgy now, her skin all prickly and hot.

Will leaned back in his chair and stretched a muscular

arm out on the table beside his empty plate. "Wow, Jordyn Leigh. That was…impressive."

All at once, she was totally annoyed with him. "Don't get on me, Will. I'm just doing my best, playing my part."

"Never said you weren't."

She plunked her sandwich back down without taking a bite. "If you've got something you want to say to me, well, you just go ahead and say it."

He turned his beer can in a slow circle on the scarred surface of the old table. "Now you're pissed off at me. Why?"

"*I'm* pissed off? No. Uh-uh. *You* are."

"On the phone with my sister, you sounded way too grown-up. You almost had me convinced that you and I are good and…intimate. But now, three minutes later, you're acting like a ten-year-old."

I hate you, Will Clifton, she thought, but somehow managed not to say. Talk about childish behavior. She drew in a long breath and let it out slowly. "I'm sorry. It's what I said to Cece. I just kind of got carried away. You and me, we're so busy fooling everyone, holding hands, kissing in Crawford's, telling the world how *happy* we are. Sometimes it feels like I'm fooling myself, too."

He stared at her for a long, very uncomfortable string of seconds. Then he shoved his plate aside, leaned toward her and stretched out his hand across the table. His lean fingers beckoned.

She gave him her hand. It felt good to have her hand engulfed in his big, rough, warm one.

Too good.

She ought to pull away.

But she didn't. "Oh, Will. Should we really be doing this? I mean, it's just a big lie."

He scowled. "No, it's not. We *are* married."

"Let's not go through all that again. Please."

"Jordyn, if you're having second thoughts, you need to tell me. We'll deal with them."

"It's only... Sometimes it seems so real, you know, you and me? So natural, so right."

"And that's bad?"

"Well, it does kind of scare me. I get all confused between what's real and what isn't."

He turned her hand over, smoothed her fingers open and drew a slow circle in the center of her palm. Talk about intimate. Her breath tangled in her throat, and a flush stole up her cheeks. She wished he might just keep on doing that for a very long time, keep holding her hand, brushing a sweet circle onto her skin.

And then he said, "This isn't the first time you've acted like you want to call it off."

"Call it off?" she repeated in a stark whisper.

He nodded. "I don't like it, but I can accept that maybe this just isn't something you're willing to do. You can move back to the boardinghouse. We'll tell everyone we realized it wouldn't work, after all. But then, if there's a baby, I want you to promise me that you'll come back."

Call it off...

Did she want that?

They'd been "married" for just three days. Not only did she have to deal with her guilt over the lies they were telling, but sometimes when she told a lie, it came out seeming way too much like the truth.

The stuff she'd just said to Cece, for instance. About how wonderful Will was, how superhot and protective, how when he kissed her, she melted...

Well, she found it easy to tell those lies because those lies felt so very true.

It didn't seem possible. She didn't know how it had happened. But somehow, Will Clifton was beginning to look like her dream man.

And that was scary. That made her wonder if this temporary marriage could turn out to be way more dangerous than she'd realized at first—dangerous to her tender heart.

"Jordyn Leigh," he prompted softly. "Are you ever going to answer my question?"

"Yes. Yes, I am."

"*Do* you want to call it off?"

"No, Will," she confessed in a small voice. "I don't want to call it off. I don't want to move back to the boardinghouse."

He smiled at her then. *Bam!* That smile reached out across the table and wrapped itself around her heart. "All right, then. We're still on."

"Still on," she answered in a voice that only wobbled a little.

"We get along," he reminded her.

She agreed. "Yeah."

"We *like* each other."

She chuckled and gave his fingers a squeeze. "Well, most of the time."

He remained completely serious. "We are married and it's *our* marriage, the way *we* want it, for as long as it lasts."

"Yes, Will."

"We have an agreement."

"We do," she replied solemnly. "And we'll stick to our plan..."

Chapter Seven

Will woke at the crack of dawn the next morning to the sound of a baby crying. The wailing seemed to be coming from the backyard.

"What in the…?" He jumped out of bed, yanked on his jeans and ran for the bedroom door that opened on to the back porch.

Three goats stood at the base of the back steps. One was a gestating doe. She was silent, gazing at him through big, wet, hopeful eyes. Another doe calmly nibbled at a sad-looking bush tucked up close to the steps. The third, a big, bearded billy, stared calmly at Will—and cried like a baby.

Literally. The damn goat sounded just like a wailing infant. And somehow, that critter managed to look damn pleased with himself as he did it.

Jordyn, wearing pink track pants with *Juicy* printed in silver foil across her butt, a Thunder Canyon Resort T-shirt and fat socks, bumped through the door from the kitchen. She gaped at the trio of animals and then groaned, "Goats?"

Will explained, "I think they may have been left by the previous owners. I heard they kept goats. These three probably got loose when they were trying to load them up to haul them away." He grinned at her. She looked so cute in her pink pants and faded T-shirt, with her gold hair all tangled from sleep. "Good morning."

"Mornin'. So will you call the previous owners to come and get them?"

"I will, yes."

"Do you think they'll come?"

"No idea."

The billy kept bawling.

"He's hungry," she said. From the fence by the barn, a rooster suddenly crowed. "And don't tell me. The previous owners kept chickens, too."

"Yep."

"What are we going to feed them?"

"I'll corral the goats and buy them feed today—and I'll get something for that rooster, too, and whatever other chickens might be wandering around."

She wasn't satisfied with that. "But that big one keeps crying. He's hungry *now*—and you know they're vulnerable to predators, just wandering around loose like that."

"I can only do what I can do."

She braced her fists on her hips and gave him one of those disgusted looks she'd been giving him practically since the day she was born. And then she mimicked, faking a deep voice, "*I can only do what I can do.* What is *that* supposed to mean?"

He just kept on grinning. Even cranky, she really did kind of brighten up the day. "It means they don't appear to be starving. They'll last on whatever they can forage until I feed them. And so far, they've done an okay job of avoiding any animal who might want to eat them."

The billy must have figured out that Jordyn was the soft touch. He turned his knowing eyes on her and wailed all the harder.

"You are a heartless man, Will Clifton." Jordyn went down the steps, her hand outstretched.

"You know you ought not to encourage them."

She sniffed his suggestion away and plunked down on the bottom step. The goats moved in close, butting her hand, nuzzling her shoulder. She petted them and cooed, "Yes, you are nice guys. Will says he'll feed you. You just have to be patient until he gets around to it, because he's a big meanie, oh, yes, he is…"

"Watch out. One of them will eat those pink pants right off you."

She sent him a cool glance over her shoulder. "Go put on a shirt."

Stifling a laugh, he ducked back into his bedroom, where he grabbed a quick shower, put on his work clothes and ambled out to the kitchen. He found Jordyn loading up the coffeepot.

Yesterday at Crawford's he'd bought the minimum to outfit the kitchen, including the coffeemaker, a set of sturdy pottery dishes, basic glassware, some flatware and utensils, two fry pans, three mixing bowls and a cute red toaster.

They whipped up breakfast together—well, she fried the sausage and scrambled the eggs. He set the table and burned the toast.

The billy goat serenaded them with baby wails as they ate, his bleating punctuated several times by the rooster's crowing.

"I'll clean up," he said when she carried her plate and

mug to the sink. "I know you need to get ready and get to town."

She put down her dishes and turned to him. "Is there anything I can pick up at Crawford's on the way back from work? I know you've got an endless list of stuff to buy and things to do."

He shook his head. "I've got it all handled."

She braced her hands on the sink rim behind her and crossed one stocking foot over the other. Her pretty breasts poked at that faded T-shirt, and he had to remind himself not to stare. "You paid for everything yesterday. It was a lot. I saw the bill when Mrs. Crawford rang it up."

"I planned to buy that stuff. It's all in the budget and not a problem."

"It's a huge undertaking, Will, outfitting a ranch."

He realized he'd better make his situation clearer. "That money Aunt Willie left me? It was a lot. Plenty to buy this place and fix it up, build my herd, whatever I need, even a few luxuries if I happen to want them. And I have investments now, believe it or not. With what she left me, plus what I had saved up over the years, I'm doing just fine. You don't need to worry if I can afford the feed for those freeloading goats out there."

China-blue eyes widened. "Really?"

He nodded. "God's honest truth."

"Will Clifton, rich guy," she said in a musing tone.

He looked her up and down, because she was a pure pleasure to look at, with pink in her cheeks and all that mussed-up yellow hair and that plump mouth he liked kissing. A lot. "You treat me right, little lady, and I'll feed your goats for you."

She blinked. "Oh, great. Now they're *my* goats."

"You were the one sitting on the step out there, talking baby talk to them."

She gave him one of her why-do-I-put-up-with-you looks. "I think I'd better go get ready for work."

He watched her go, the silver letters on her shapely butt bouncing with every step—not a lot, just enough to give any red-blooded man ideas. All those years, he'd thought of her as a baby sister, someone he needed to look out for. He'd always known it bugged her no end that he treated her like a kid.

Now, well, he still knew how to give her a bad time. However, he didn't feel brotherly toward her in the least. Protective, yes. But it wasn't the same as before. Not since those first moments by the punch bowl on the Fourth of July, when it hit him like a bolt from the blue that little Jordyn Leigh Cates wasn't so little anymore. Uh-uh. Jordyn Leigh was all grown-up and looking mighty fine.

He might as well be honest with himself, at least. He was having a great time playing newlyweds with Jordyn Leigh.

But he knew he had to watch himself. If there was no baby, she would be gone before September. She had a dream, and she was going to fulfill it.

He wouldn't stand in her way.

But he *did* wish he could remember all of Saturday night. Whatever had actually happened when they got back to Maverick Manor that night, he wanted those memories of her. He wanted to keep them for himself when she was long gone from Rust Creek Falls.

And thinking about Saturday night reminded him. He needed to make time to have a talk with someone at the sheriff's office about his suspicions concerning that unknown cowboy in the white hat.

After Jordyn left for town, Will made some calls—to his Realtor concerning the abandoned goats and chickens, and to the local satellite company, who promised they could be out the next day to get him set up with TV and internet.

Once he'd handled the phone calls, he drove to Kalispell. He visited a grocery store, a feed store and a couple of department stores. By the time he was finished, he had another pickup load of stuff they needed right away at the Flying C. Basic living room furniture, a wide-screen TV and a washer/dryer combo would be delivered first thing in the morning.

He drove back to Rust Creek Falls and stopped in at the sheriff's office, where he talked to a Kalispell detective named Russ Campbell. Campbell, Will learned, filled in at the sheriff's office when Sheriff Gage Christensen needed him.

A few minutes into his interview with the detective, Will realized he had zero real evidence for his suspicion that an unknown cowboy had put something in Jordyn's drink. He'd seen that cowboy once, and all the guy had done was wink at Jordyn. It was hardly proof that the stranger had tampered with her punch.

Plus, Will's best argument that a mind-altering substance had been slipped in the punch was his on-the-fly marriage, which neither he nor Jordyn could clearly recall. Will wanted the detective—and everyone else in town—to believe that his marriage was the real deal. He didn't want to say outright that he and his bride had been in no way a couple before July Fourth.

He did admit that both he and Jordyn had become strangely intoxicated that night and that they'd both suffered serious hangovers the next morning. They'd each downed several cups of punch, yes, but that had been over a seven-hour period. And Jordyn had been reassured by the bride that there wasn't enough alcohol in the punch to get anyone drunk, anyway.

The detective nodded. "That was my understanding, too. The punch contained only a very small amount of sparkling wine."

Will began to wonder if the detective knew more than he was telling. "So you were there that night?"

"That's right." Campbell said he'd been recruited by the sheriff to provide a police presence at the wedding reception—not because anyone expected trouble, but because the venue was a public park. Campbell said he'd seen the way people behaved that night. He reminded Will that lots of folks had gotten wild.

And Will asked, "Are you saying you suspect that someone put something right in the punch bowl?"

"I'm not saying anything," replied the detective. "Not at this point. But I'll talk to Sheriff Christensen about what you've reported. I promise you, we'll check into it."

Will left the sheriff's office with no more answers than he'd had when he went in. But Russ Campbell had definitely seemed interested in why so many people had behaved so strangely that night. Will believed the detective when he said he'd look into it.

He went back to the ranch. Jordyn drove up while he was still unloading his pickup, so she helped him haul the rest of the stuff inside. They put the perishables away together, making fast work of everything.

In the meantime, the goats showed up at the back steps, and the billy started wailing again.

"We *really* need to feed them," Jordyn said.

So they lured the goats into the smallest of the nearby pastures, which was next to the barn and pretty overgrown. They fed them, filled the water trough and left them to graze on the weeds. They also scattered feed in the back-yard for any random chickens.

Jordyn carried the rest of the chicken feed to the barn. Will went inside and opened a beer.

Five minutes later, she bustled back in, washed her hands and grabbed the roasted whole chicken he'd bought at the store for their dinner. She took the bird out of its plastic container, plunked it on the pull-out cutting board, grabbed a big knife and sawed it in half.

"Jordyn?"

"Hmm?" She tossed half the chicken back into the container.

"What are you doing to our dinner?"

She rinsed and dried her hands. "There's a mama cat with five kittens in the barn." She rolled off a long strip of paper towel and scooped up the other half of the chicken in it. "She needs protein to feed that litter."

"If there's a mama cat in the barn," he helpfully explained, "she's supposed to catch mice for her protein."

Jordyn ignored his remark and headed for the door. "I'll pick up some cat food tomorrow on the way home from work," she said as she went out.

Will let her go. She had that look. He knew damn well she would feed that cat no matter what he said to try and talk her out of it. He finished his beer and made a mental note to ask his Realtor if the former owners had left a pregnant cat behind along with the goats and the chickens.

Jordyn came back inside ten minutes later. By then it was after five.

Will made a decision. "It's only a half hour to Kalispell. Let's go there for dinner."

She started in with all the reasons that going out was a bad idea. "It's a waste of money."

"I'm a rich guy, remember?"

"We've got a lot of stuff to put away. And I'm sweaty from wrangling goats."

"The stuff isn't going anywhere. You want a shower, take one. Ten minutes and we're out of here."

"Ten minutes! Are you crazy?"

He suggested, "You'll never make it if you waste your time arguing with me."

Fifteen minutes later they were on their way.

They'd both liked that Italian place where they'd eaten the other day, so they went there again.

As they ate, he told her about his visit with Detective Campbell. "The detective did remind me that a lot of people acted out of character on Saturday night. It got me thinking that maybe your punch wasn't the only punch someone tampered with."

She twirled spaghetti on her fork. "Now you think someone tried to poison the whole town?"

"I don't know what to think—except that maybe I ought to leave this case to law enforcement."

"So now it's a *case*, is it?"

"Campbell's going to be looking into it."

She ate the forkful of spaghetti. "So we've got the law after the nefarious punch poisoner."

"Yes, we do."

"Now we just need to find out whoever writes Rust Creek Ramblings and blow their cover. We can think of it as a public service to the whole town." She pulled garlic bread off the loaf. "Then again, we all love Rust Creek Ramblings…"

He chuckled. "You're right. It's funny and full of heart. We only hate it when one of the columns is about us."

She leaned toward him, eyes alight. "But seriously, Will. Who do you think writes that column?"

"I'm the new guy in town. How would I know?"

"It's someone who's scarily observant, someone who has a way with words. Maybe a teacher, like Willa Traub, the mayor's wife. Or Kristen Dalton. Do you know her?"

"I don't think so…"

"Daughter of Charles and Rita Dalton? Has a twin sister, Kayla?"

"Sorry. Not ringing a bell."

"Well, Kayla's quiet, shy as a mouse. Kristen, though, she's really feisty. She loves acting and she's involved in a little theater here in Kalispell. Kristen never met a party she wouldn't crash. Being a secret gossip columnist is something Kristen might do because she's a rebel at heart."

"How do you know the columnist isn't a guy?"

"You're right." She laughed. "Maybe it's Homer Gilmore."

"Never heard of him."

"He was at the wedding reception Saturday. In his eighties, rarely shaves, has a strange look in his eye?"

Will sipped from his water glass. "Nope. Don't remember him, either."

She playfully wagged a finger at him. "You need to get to know your neighbors."

"Give me time, woman. I've lived here less than a week."

"Homer's actually kind of sweet. He's originally from Whitehorn, came to town last year. I heard they found him wandering in the woods, claiming he was the ghost of Christmas past."

Will grunted. "You're not serious."

"Oh, yes, I am."

"I hope he got help."

"He's fine, really. Just quite a character—and then again, no. I don't think he could be the mystery columnist. Maybe he has literary talents I'm unaware of, but someone was already writing the column when Homer showed up in town." She shook her head. He watched her, thinking how cute she looked, her hair pulled up in a loose ponytail, twirling another bite of spaghetti.

In fact, he was so busy admiring his temporary bride, he didn't notice the woman approaching their table until she spoke.

"Will? Jordyn Leigh Cates? I don't believe it..."

It was Desiree Fenton from Thunder Canyon, of all people. He and Desiree had dated a couple of years back. It hadn't ended well.

Will put on a smile. "Desiree. This is a surprise." And not really a good one.

Jordyn set down her fork and gave the other woman a little wave. "Hey, Desiree. How've you been?"

Desiree played it perky. "Terrific." But then she frowned in thought. "Wait a minute. I remember now—Jordyn, you moved up here after the flood, didn't you?"

"That's right. Rust Creek Falls needed help with reconstruction."

Desiree asked Will, "Didn't your sister move here at the same time?"

He nodded. "They came together, Jordyn and Cece—and Jordyn's sister, Jasmine, too."

Jordyn put in, "We were looking for a fresh start, I guess you could say."

"I heard all about it." Desiree was smiling now, a knowing sort of smile. "So many Thunder Canyon girls, heading for Rust Creek Falls looking for work—and maybe for love. They called it the Gal Rush, as I recall..."

The Gal Rush. Will remembered those awful ladies in Crawford's Sunday morning. He would not forget their snide remarks about the "Gal Rush women" descending on Rust Creek Falls to catch a cowboy.

But if the reference got to Jordyn, she didn't let it show.

She only shrugged and agreed with Desiree, "That's right. We were part of the Gal Rush—Jazzy, Cece and me."

Desiree swung her too-bright smile on Will. "And what about you, Will? What brings you to the area?"

He went ahead and told her. "I live here, too, now. I recently bought a ranch not far from Rust Creek Falls."

Desiree blinked. Twice. "You bought a ranch? Already?" Sudden tension vibrated in her voice, and her fake smile had fled. Jordyn glanced from Desiree to him and back to Desiree again.

Will fervently wished that Desiree would give it up and go away. He answered gently, "Circumstances change."

"Oh, well. I guess they do." She gave a quick shake of her dark curls, and her lips tipped up in that too-bright smile again. "I'm here for a week or two, helping my aunt Georgina pack her things." She flicked out a hand in the direction of a table by the window, where a sweet-looking gray-haired lady sat happily working her way through a big plate of pasta. "Aunt Georgie's been failing lately. She was having trouble looking out for herself, so we're moving her back to Thunder Canyon and into assisted living."

Jordyn's blue eyes were much too watchful. Will figured she'd probably heard from Cece that he and Desiree once had a thing. And right now Jordyn had to have gotten the picture that Desiree wasn't exactly at peace with the way it had all turned out. "It's, um, good you could come and help your aunt." Jordyn nervously smoothed a loose strand of hair back up into her ponytail.

That was when it happened: Desiree spotted Jordyn's ring. A tiny gasp escaped her. She shifted her narrowed gaze on Will again. He went ahead and lifted his left hand to grab his water glass for a leisurely sip, giving her plenty of time to confirm her suspicion that he wore a ring, too.

Desiree asked, "Why do I get the feeling that congratulations are in order?"

Will set down his glass. "Thanks, Desiree. Jordyn and I were married last Saturday."

"Oh, really?"

Jordyn sailed into the breach. "That's right. Will and I are newlyweds."

A silence. Desiree hovered on the brink—of what, he wasn't sure. But in the end, she only said, "I...hope you'll both be very happy."

"Thanks," Jordyn replied softly. "We are."

Desiree's red lips twisted. "Well, um, great to see you both. You take care now."

"You, too," Jordyn said.

Will nodded. "See you, Desiree."

And that was it. Desiree turned away at last. She marched across the room and rejoined her aunt.

The rest of the meal went by fast, with hardly another word shared between him and Jordyn. She seemed not to know what to say. And he didn't want to get into all that old business, anyway.

They finished. He paid the check, and they left for home.

Once they were on the road, Jordyn asked softly, "Are you all right, Will?"

"Fine."

She sent him a quick, unhappy glance. "You don't seem fine."

"I *said* I was fine. Can we leave it at that?" He said it harshly, taking the offensive when she didn't deserve it, a ploy to end this conversation before it really began.

At first she was quiet. He dared to hope he'd been a big enough jerk that she would *stay* quiet. But she'd never lacked guts. She tried again. "I remember you went out with her. Cece mentioned you were dating her more than once. My mom mentioned it, too. And I know it was serious. Desiree seemed really upset back there. *You* didn't seem very happy, either..." Her voice trailed off. He dared to zip her a sideways glance. She had her hands folded in her lap, and she stared down at them, mouth set, soft chin tensed.

"Leave it alone, Jordyn. It's not a big deal."

She kept staring at her hands. "You're doing a crap job of lying to me right now, Will."

"Leave it." He growled the words.

Her bright head shot up. She looked straight at him. "Well, alrighty, then."

The rest of the ride was as silent as the end of the meal had been.

At the ranch she made a beeline for the kitchen.

He followed her in there. She zipped over to the counter and got to work unpacking the grocery bags they'd left there.

"Leave that stuff," he said. "I'll deal with it tomorrow. Don't you have homework you need to be doing?"

She had a jar of peanut butter in one hand and a can of cocoa in the other. "I'll just—"

"I said leave it, Jordyn." Maybe it came out a little gruffer than it should have.

She glared at him. Then she stuck both items in a cupboard, shut the cupboard door and put up her hands like he held her at gunpoint. "Fine."

"What about your homework?"

She pressed her lips together. He was certain she would say something snippy. But in the end, she took the high road. "I need to get online to do it. It's no biggie. I'll just stay at Country Kids for a couple of hours tomorrow after work. Sara has Wi-Fi." She added, defiantly, "So don't expect me until after five—or better make it six, to give me plenty of time to get it all done."

He should leave it alone. If she wanted to do her homework at Sara Johnston's, what the hell did it matter to him? But somehow, his big mouth opened all by itself, and he issued what sounded way too much like a command. "Tomorrow you'll do your homework here."

"What in the world is going on with you, Will?"

"You heard me. You can do your homework here."

"That is not what you said, and we both know it. You gave me an order, Will. You don't have any right to go giving me orders. Where I do my homework is my business. And anyway, I just told you that I *can't* do it here because there is no internet connection."

"Tomorrow, first thing, the satellite guys are hooking us up. We'll have TV and internet before noon."

Spots of hectic color flamed on her soft cheeks. "Oh. Well, great. Terrific. I'll just rush right back here after work."

"Good."

She bit her lower lip. "And right now I think I'll go out and check on the animals." She started for the back door.

He knew he should let her go. But instead he reached out and caught her arm as she tried to brush past him. "Anything to get away from me, huh?"

She froze, blinked down at his fingers wrapped around her arm and then back up at him. Something arced between them, something bright and hot. And dangerous, too. "I didn't say that."

"You didn't *have* to say it." He liked the feel of her smooth skin against his palm, liked it too much. Reluctantly, he released her.

"Are you finished?" She held her ground, waiting for him to stop being an ass and say something real.

So he did. "I just don't want to talk about Desiree."

"Then don't." She headed for the door again.

He ached to call her back. But then she would expect him to actually talk to her.

And he was not up for that.

So he just stood there feeling like ten kinds of hopeless SOB as she went out the back door.

Chapter Eight

Jordyn had a nice long chat with the goats. They agreed that Will was a great big butthead. She spent some time with Mama Kitty and her babies, fussing over them.

When she went back inside, Will had left the kitchen. The door to the master suite was shut, a sliver of light shining beneath it. Terrific. He could be a jackass all by his lonesome, locked in his room. Fine with her.

Feeling equal parts defiant and helpful, she put away the rest of the groceries he'd bought and unboxed the microwave, the mixer, the slow cooker and the electric can opener. She folded all the bags and put them under the sink next to the trash can, then broke down the boxes.

After that she went upstairs and spent the rest of the evening alone.

In the morning they ate breakfast in silence. She put a pot roast and veggies in the slow cooker for dinner and then headed for work without saying two words to him.

That afternoon when she returned, she spotted cattle grazing on the hill above the stock pond. The beginnings of Will's herd must have arrived.

A circle of dusty pickups waited in front of the house. She recognized them as belonging to Will's brothers. But inside, the house was quiet. They must all be out working, getting the cattle settled in, mending fences and who knew what all.

Which was great. She had homework to do, anyway—that was, if in fact Will now had Wi-Fi, as he'd been so sure he would last night. The big-screen TV over the fireplace seemed a good sign. And the TV wasn't the only new addition. A leather sofa, coffee table and two comfy chairs made the living room a lot more inviting. In the utility room, she found a brand-new washer and dryer, hooked up and ready to go. There was also a new table and six chairs in the breakfast nook.

When it came to getting things done, Will did not fool around. She might almost admire him—if she wasn't so pissed off at him.

The billy goat must have heard her drive up. He was crying like a baby, as usual. Chuckling to herself, she went to work feeding the goats and the lone rooster. She'd stopped in at Crawford's for cat food, so she fed the mama cat and petted all the kittens.

Back inside, she went upstairs, where she discovered a sticky note on her bedroom door. *Wi-Fi operational*, Will had scrawled in his bold hand, along with the necessary password. She kicked off her shoes, got comfy on the bed and got started on her homework.

At a little before six, she heard the men come in downstairs. She might have stayed in her room for a couple more hours just to avoid playing dueling silent treatments with

Will, but she liked his brothers, and it would be rude not to go down and say hi.

She found the Clifton men in the kitchen, each with a beer, all in stocking feet with their faces and hands freshly scrubbed. Carol Clifton had raised them right. Those boys knew to wash up when they came in the house, and to leave their muddy boots at the door.

Craig, the oldest, had the lid off the slow cooker. "Jordyn Leigh, this smells great. Will's a lucky man."

The lucky man in question sipped his beer and said nothing.

Jordyn avoided Will's eyes and told his brother, "Thanks, Craig. Great to see you."

Rob, the youngest, grabbed her and spun her around. "Are you nuts, Jordyn Leigh, to go and marry *him*?"

"Robbie!" She kissed his scruffy cheek. "I think I might have lost my mind for a moment there—and how you been?"

"Can't complain. You're beautiful, as always."

Will muttered something under his breath. Jordyn didn't hear what, which was probably just as well.

She laughed. "Oh, Rob. I know you're just after my pot roast."

Rob confessed, "Well, it does smell mighty fine."

Jonathan, third born after Will, pulled her close next. "Will gives you any trouble, you let me know. I'll adjust his attitude for you."

She hugged him back. "I can always count on you, Jonathan."

Will cleared his throat. "So. Dinner ready?"

She turned to him, really tempted to say something caustic in response. But his brothers were watching—and besides, she had another way to get under his skin. She went to him, put her hands on his big, hard shoulders and smiled up at him sweetly. "Yep. Dinner's ready. Someone just needs to put it on the table."

He kept his hands at his sides and looked down at her, suspicion in his eyes. "Great. We'll do that."

"Thanks." She couldn't resist playing the moment for all it was worth. "So, honey, how was your day?"

His eyes turned turbulent, and his square jaw twitched—and then he moved, reaching. His warm hands slid around her waist and came to rest at the small of her back. Dear Lord, for someone so annoying, he was such a big ol' hunk of pure manliness. "It was a good day," he said gruffly. "Got a lot done."

"I noticed." She smiled wider, and he volunteered some actual information. "Several head of cattle arrived. I bought them at auction last week."

"I spotted a few of them on the ridge above the stock pond when I drove up."

His right hand moved at her back, a slow glide that could only be called a caress. She felt powerful, suddenly, her blood racing swift and hot through her veins, a warm, lovely shiver moving over her skin. She let her gaze stray to his mouth. His lips were so full and soft compared to the rest of him.

Now *he* was staring at *her* mouth. She held her breath. And then those big arms closed around her, and his dark head came down. He smelled so good—a hint of soap and warm, healthy skin.

And his kiss? Spectacular. It made heat bloom in her belly and her knees feel wobbly. No wonder Desiree Fenton was still bitter that she'd lost him.

When he lifted his head, she felt branded, as though his big body had imprinted itself all down the front of hers. They stared at each other, partly in anger—but anger wasn't all of it. Not by a long shot. Heat still lingered, burning between them.

It was only a kiss, she reminded herself. A nice little public display of affection, for the sake of their newly-wed act.

Jonathan teased, "Okay, you two. Any more of that and you really need to get a room."

That broke the tension. Everybody laughed.

Jordyn pushed at Will's rock-hard chest. He let her go. She said, "All right, boys. Get the table set. I'll put the food on."

The Clifton brothers ate heartily. Once the meal was cleared off, they all sat around and visited for an hour or so. At seven-thirty, the boys headed back to Maverick Manor, promising to return the next morning. Tomorrow would be another busy day at the Flying C. The new fore-man and his wife would arrive from Thunder Canyon. Also scheduled to show up tomorrow: a moving van of Will's furniture and the three horses he owned.

With the brothers gone, the house seemed way too quiet. It was just Jordyn and Will, with the bad feelings from last night like an invisible wall between them. Jordyn got to work on the dishes.

Will grabbed the towel and started drying.

More silence. He was the one who finally broke it. "I bought a dishwasher yesterday, when I bought the washer and dryer. You see the washer and dryer?"

She didn't really want to fight with him anymore. But she didn't feel kindly toward him, either. So she answered flatly, "I did. Looks good."

"The dishwasher will be installed tomorrow."

She rinsed a soapy dish. "Great."

"You, uh, get the password all right, for the Wi-Fi?"

"I did, thanks." She handed him the rinsed dish.

He dried it and set it on the stack he'd made beside the dish rack. "Your homework?"

"All done." She washed and rinsed the last dish. He dried it and put it on the stack. She got going on the glassware. He dried each one and put them away.

Eventually, he tried again. "The Realtor called back. About the goats and the cats and that rooster?"

"Yeah?"

"The former owners have no place for animals where they live now. The Realtor said they're 'in no position' to deal with any leftover livestock. Long story short, I own three goats, a mama cat with kittens, a bad-tempered, self-important rooster—and whatever other critter shows up at the back door."

Jordyn said nothing to that. What was there to say? She felt a flicker of satisfaction at the news. After all, she actually liked the critters in question. But in the end, she reminded herself, she shouldn't get too attached. She would have to walk away from them when she left for Missoula. They were his responsibility now, and he could do with them as he pleased.

Will set down the towel, carried the dried plates to the cabinet at the end of the counter and put them away. She slid him a glance when he just stood there, staring at the cabinet once he'd shut the door, his back to her.

Then, abruptly, he turned. "How long are you gonna be mad at me?" His beautiful mouth curved down at the corners, and his fine eyes were troubled.

Sudden warmth bloomed in the center of her chest, a definite tenderness toward him. She answered honestly, "Oh, probably until you talk to me." She grabbed the terrycloth hand towel from its hook and wiped her hands.

He said, "We could go in the living room, sit on that couch I just bought..." He offered his hand.

She took it. His fingers closed around hers, and she felt better about everything.

In the living room, they sat at either end of the sofa. She kicked off her shoes and drew her legs up sideways, facing him.

He hitched one knee to the cushions, shifting his big body her way. "It's pretty simple," he said. "I was never getting married until I had my place. Desiree knew that when we started in together."

"You mean you told her that up front?"

"Yeah. And I told her how long that would be—at least fifteen years. At the time, I had no clue that we'd lose Aunt Willie in two years, so I was still working on my original schedule then. I was twenty-eight when Desiree and I started going out. And I generally tried to keep things honest and upfront with any woman I went with. I tried to have the talk with them early."

"Wow. There's an actual *talk*?"

"Yeah." He gave her a sideways look. "Does that sound bad or something?"

She blew out a breath. "I'm not sure…"

"Remember Brita Foxworth?"

Jordyn did remember. "You went with her in high school. Everyone thought you two would get married after graduation."

"Brita was planning our wedding by Senior Ball." He sounded weary. "I finally had to tell her that there wasn't going to be one. Not for years and years, anyway. Not until I got my place, which by my calculations then was going to be at the age of forty-five—maybe a couple years earlier, if I scrimped and saved and pinched every penny. Brita and I broke up right before graduation, the night that I finally got through to her that I wasn't marrying anyone for a long, long time. From then on, if I really liked a woman and wanted to see her more than a time or two, I made sure we had the talk good and early."

Jordyn shifted, stretching out an arm to rest it along the sofa back. "So you had the *talk* right at the first, with Desiree?"

"Yeah. And she said that was fine with her. She said she didn't want to get married, anyway."

"Hmm. Judging by the expression on her face yesterday when she put it together that you and I are married, she either lied or changed her mind."

Now he was the one shifting, facing forward, bracing both elbows on his spread knees. "We went out for almost a year, Desiree and me."

Jordyn winced. "I hadn't realized it lasted that long."

"Jordyn, I liked her. I had fun with her. I thought she was fine with the way things were. But then one night we went out to dinner, and we went back to her place. And suddenly, we were into this big scene. She was crying and telling me she loved me and she couldn't do it, couldn't wait anymore. She wanted to get married. She wanted us together in the way that really mattered. She wanted a ring, and she wanted it now."

"Did you…I mean, were you in love with her?" She asked the question and kind of wished she hadn't. If he said yes, the next question would have to be, *Are you still in love with her?* And Jordyn didn't know if she could bring herself to ask that one.

Okay, their marriage might be just for show, but some part of her kept growing more…invested every day. To learn that he still carried a torch for Desiree Fenton, well, that would make her feel awful on any number of levels.

And he was taking way too long to answer. "Will?" she prompted impatiently.

He finally put it out there. "I told you. I *liked* her. But I wasn't in love with her, and I didn't want to get married."

Relief. She felt relief. She decided not to think about that and to focus instead on what a thickheaded fool he'd been. "Men can be so clueless." Jordyn hadn't realized she'd said that out loud.

Not until he said, "Clueless? She never said anything for all those months and months. She acted like she was happy. And then, all of a sudden…she wasn't."

"I'm sure there were signs. You just refused to see them."

He threw up both hands. "Maybe. I don't know. I do know that I felt like a first-class jerk when it ended, and I felt like one again yesterday, at the sight of her. And right now, too, as a matter of fact. I really didn't mean to hurt her…"

She mimicked, *"I really didn't mean to hurt her."*

"Well, I didn't."

"And I need to embroider that on a sampler and hang it in your kitchen."

"All right, Jordyn. Why don't you just tell me, then. What the hell *should* I have done?"

That did give her pause. She confessed, "I don't know. Sometimes, in love, people just get hurt—and I think someone told me that after it ended with you, she went out with Roger Boudreaux and that he broke it off, too. So I'm guessing she's not real happy with your gender at this point in her life."

He braced his elbows on his knees again and hung his head. "I need a beer. You want one?"

"No, thanks."

He got up, disappeared into the kitchen and returned with a cold one. Dropping down beside her again, he took a long pull off the can. "So, you and me? We're okay now?"

She held his gaze for a moment and finally nodded. "Yeah. We're okay."

He let out a hard breath and slumped against the cushions. "That's a relief."

She considered their hasty marriage, told herself not to go there—and then went right ahead and brought it up, anyway. "Lucky you got this ranch before Saturday night, huh?"

He slid her a frown. "Why do you say that?"

"Think about it. What if you woke up married to me and you didn't have your place yet? A lifetime of big plans right down the drain."

"Jordyn…" He gave her a warning look.

Which she blithely ignored. "So after we're divorced, you'll be lookin', huh? Ready to find yourself a nice little wife—and fifteen years ahead of schedule, too. Ain't life grand?"

"Jordyn Leigh." That time he said it in his boss-man voice.

She made a show of batting her eyelashes and drawled, "What, Will?"

"I may be clueless, but even I know that finding the right person to spend my life with doesn't happen on a schedule. I know it's not like buying a couch or a big-screen TV."

She snickered in a way that she knew was nothing short of evil. "Will. You hopeless romantic, you."

"Don't mock me. I'm serious. Yeah, in a couple of years, after I've got this ranch up and running, I'll be looking. But I want it all. I'm not going to settle. I want what my folks have. What *your* parents have. Love with the one and only. I'm not taking less than that." His words made her heart hurt, which served her right for goading him in the first place. And he was watching her. "Okay. Now you look sad. What'd I do this time?"

She met his incomparable eyes and refused to look away. "Nothing."

"Come on." So sweet. So gentle. The man could coax the moon from the sky if he put his mind to it. "Tell me."

She gave in and admitted, "It was beautiful, what you just said, that's all."

His dark brows lifted, and he asked hopefully, "And beautiful is good?"

Now she felt shy and too young and way too tender. "Yeah. Beautiful is good."

A lock of inky hair fell across his forehead. Her fingers ached to brush it back.

But she didn't. That would be kind of intimate. And they didn't really do intimate—except when they had an audience.

He grabbed the remote off the coffee table. "You want to watch some TV?"

"Sure. Why not?"

The big screen over the fireplace burst into life. ESPN, of course, with a baseball game in progress. She liked baseball as much as the next girl, which was to say maybe not as much as some. But enough to sit on Will's new couch with him and cheer if somebody hit a home run.

He settled into the cushions and stretched his arm across the back of the sofa. His fingers brushed her shoulder. A little thrill shivered down her arm.

Get a grip, Jordyn Leigh.

"Come on," he said. "Make yourself comfortable."

She swayed toward him—because she wanted to, wanted to lean against him, have his arm around her, pretend...

Okay, never mind what she might want to pretend.

He aided and abetted her in her foolish desire, hooking that big, hard arm around her, drawing her against his side. She let herself lean into him.

And it felt really, really good.

Too good, she knew that. And too intimate, considering it was just the two of them on that sofa, no one else in the room to put on a show for.

"Better, huh?" he asked, giving her an extra squeeze.

"Yeah," she said, and snuggled closer still.

She woke up in the middle of the night, upstairs in her own bed, still wearing her jeans and T-shirt, with the blankets tucked in around her.

Will. What a guy.

She pushed back the blankets, took off her jeans, wiggled out of her bra, but left the T-shirt on. Then she settled back under the covers and drifted to sleep again, smiling to herself.

The next day was Friday.

When Jordyn got home from work, Will's brothers had already left for Maverick Manor. Will took her over to the foreman's cottage and introduced her to his new foreman, Myron Stevalik, and his wife, Pia. Jordyn liked them both and told Pia if she needed help with anything, just to let her know.

Pia thanked her for the offer and said that, so far, she was managing just fine. The three-bedroom cottage was a little dusty but clean, Pia added with some relief, and all the kitchen appliances worked. Jordyn and Will stayed only a few minutes, clearing out quickly so the couple could get back to putting their new home together.

The movers had come with the contents of the little house Will used to rent in Thunder Canyon. The front porch and the entry hall were crammed with furniture and stacks of boxes containing clothes and household goods.

Jordyn and Will worked together, sorting furniture and arranging it in the various rooms. They set up the king-size bed and matching dresser in the master suite and moved the bed he'd been using to the extra room upstairs.

Jordyn's room got a dresser, a couple of chairs and even a nightstand. She also got more towels for the upstairs bath and extra sheets. She helped carry the boxes of his personal stuff into the master suite, where he could deal with them whenever he found the time. And there were several boxes of kitchen stuff, too, as well as a nice big oak table and chairs for the dining room.

At a little after six, Jordyn took two servings of slow cooker chicken and dumplings across the yard to the Stevaliks. Pia called her a lifesaver and asked if Jordyn and Will might go with them to services at Rust Creek Falls Community Church on Sunday.

"It would be nice," said Pia, "to get to know our neighbors, to make some friends. And it would be so great if you and Will would introduce us to a few people in the congregation."

Jordyn reminded her, "Will's new to town, too."

"So you think he wouldn't want to go?"

"How about if I just ask him?" Jordyn did feel a little pang of discomfort at the prospect. Maybe God wouldn't approve of newlyweds with a Divorce Plan. But then again, God was all about love and forgiveness, and His doors were open to everyone. Jordyn went to church most Sundays, and she wasn't about to stop going just because her marriage wasn't everything most people thought it was.

Back at the main house, Will had the table set. They sat down, and she asked him if he would go to church with her and the Stevaliks that Sunday. He said he would, simple as that.

They ate and then put their dishes in the new dishwasher. Will went out to check on his horses, which had arrived that morning. Jordyn went back across the yard to tell Pia they were on for church on Sunday. She returned to the house and got back to work on the boxes of kitchen stuff.

When Will came inside at nine-thirty, she was putting various gadgets in drawers.

She held up a rotary egg beater, circa 1955, and spun the handle so the beaters whirled. "I think this may be an actual antique."

He came straight to the counter, whipped the half-empty box she'd been unloading out from under her nose, carried it over and plopped it on top of the dwindling stack of boxes in the corner.

"Will! I'm not finished with that."

"You are for tonight."

"But I just want to—"

"Uh-uh. You've done more than enough for one day."

They had made serious progress. The place was actually beginning to look kind of cozy. Yeah, it needed paint inside and out, and the kitchen could use a general upgrade. But still. It was comfortable now. And Jordyn felt some satisfaction that she'd pitched in to help make it so.

Will asked, "How about streaming a movie?"

A movie. That would be nice. Especially if he put his arm around her and let her use him as a pillow. She would cuddle up nice and close. And if she dropped off to sleep, he would carry her upstairs and put her to bed just like last night…

"Jordyn Leigh?" He was still waiting on her answer.

"Oh! Sorry." She realized she'd been standing there in front of the still-open gadget drawer, staring off into space.

She dropped the egg beater in the drawer and shoved it shut with more force than necessary. "You know, I'm kind of tired. I think I'll just go on upstairs."

"You sure?" Did he sound disappointed that she wouldn't stay and hang around with him? Or was that only wishful thinking on her part?

Didn't matter. Upstairs. She was going upstairs. "Uh, yeah. I could use a good night's sleep." She beamed him a huge smile—a smile that felt forced as it spread across her face.

And he knew it was forced. Twin lines formed between his dark brows. "Are you okay?"

"Fine, fine. A little tired is all."

He was still frowning, but at least he let it go.

She said good-night and went up the stairs and did not allow herself to weaken and go back down.

In the morning he was already outside tending the animals when she got up. She went to work on breakfast and when he came in, they ate.

He was halfway through his eggs and ham, when he suddenly looked up, snared her gaze across the table and asked, "So what's your plan for today?"

She sipped her coffee. "Finish unpacking the kitchen stuff, maybe get ahead on my homework…"

"How about a picnic?" He gave her that killer smile. "Just you and me. We'll go on horseback. The Flying C is the prettiest ranch in the Rust Creek Valley, and I want a chance to show you around."

It sounded like fun. And what kind of dangerous intimacy were they going to get up to on horses in the middle of the day?

She decided not to think too hard about that. "Yeah. Yeah, I'd like that."

"Wear something you can swim in. We'll be mostly

following the creek, and it's going to be hot today. I know of a great little swimming hole with its own waterfall. A swim should cool us off."

Cool them off. Yeah. She could use a little cooling off when it came to him.

"Er, Jordyn?"

She realized she was staring blankly at nothing again. "Hmm?"

"Bring a swimsuit?"

"Of course. Absolutely. I will."

At half past eleven she was mounted on Darlin', Will's dappled gray mare, with a plain lunch of sandwiches and fruit packed up in the saddlebags, wearing her swimsuit under her clothes. Will led the way on Shady, his favorite black gelding.

They circled the stock pond as several Black Angus heifers watched them from the ridge above. A curious steer tagged after them for a mile or so as they left the pond to follow the meandering ribbon of Badger Creek. At first, they rode in rolling grassland, staying beyond the stands of trees that lined the water's edge. The sun was warm on her back—a little too warm. Even after she tucked her hair up under her hat to let the wind cool her neck, she had a dew of moisture on her upper lip, and her shirt clung beneath her arms.

After a while they began to climb, following the general path of the creek up a steepening grade. Will led the way, taking them closer to creekside under the willows and cottonwoods. It was still hot, but at least the trees provided a little shade.

Ahead, she could hear a low, continuous roar. "I think I hear that waterfall of yours," she called.

He waved a hand, signaling her forward, and she moved

up to ride beside him. As they wound through the trees, he said, "It's just up ahead…"

"I could use a swim."

His mouth curled up beneath the brim of his hat. "Me, too."

The sound of the water grew louder. They rounded the next bend, and he guided them off the trail, through the trees to the water's edge.

"Here we are." He sounded pleased.

And he should be. The waterfall splashed down the giant black rocks on the other side into a clear green pool. "It's beautiful."

He looked so pleased with himself. "I kinda thought you might like it."

They hobbled the horses and drank from their canteens. Then they spread a saddle blanket on the bank and stripped down—she to her Hawaiian-print two-piece, Will to his Wranglers.

He hit the water at a run.

She was right behind him, diving in, ducking her head under, letting out a shout when she surfaced. "It's cold!"

He laughed. "Come on…" He struck out for the black rocks on the other bank.

She swam after him, following him to a spot where they could climb out of the water and up the slippery rocks. He started upward, careful of his footing. She came after him, putting her feet and hands where he put his. Twice she squealed when her foot slipped.

He stopped and grinned back at her both times. "You need help?"

"Are you kidding? I know what I'm doing."

He only shook his head and kept climbing. At the top, he boosted himself to the ledge of black rock and held his hand down to her. She almost huffed at him that she could do it herself—because old habits die hard, and she'd spent what seemed like all of her childhood telling Will Clifton that he wasn't the boss of her, and she didn't need his help.

But then she couldn't help chuckling at her own childishness. She reached up, and he curled his strong fingers around hers. He gave a tug, rising to his feet, and up she went, landing on the ledge beside him, laughing some more as she stumbled a little.

He wrapped her in his big arms to steady her. "Careful—and what's so funny?"

She gazed up into those eyes—pale blue rimmed in a blue so deep—and suddenly, it wasn't funny. Nothing was funny. His wet, slicked-back hair gleamed blue-black, and beads of water glistened on the fine, sculpted angles of his handsome face, on the powerful musculature of his broad shoulders and deep chest. She wanted to stand there for at least a century or two, caught in that shaft of warm sunlight that streamed through a gap in the trees, with his hard, wet arms around her.

"Jordyn?"

"Hmm?"

"You're doing it again."

"Um, doing what?"

"Staring. Not hearing me when I speak to you. A million miles away…"

"No," she heard herself say softly. "Really. I'm right here." She stared at his mouth, acutely aware that if she kissed him now, there was absolutely no way she could excuse the move as a PDA. No one was watching—well, maybe the horses, but they sure didn't care. If she kissed him, it would be a real kiss. It would be because she *wanted* to kiss him—and she did.

She wanted that, a lot.

Vague memories of last Saturday night seemed to swirl

in the air between them. Was it only a week ago, when they danced in the park under the moon, when they stood together in front of the judge?

Was it only last Sunday that she woke up wearing a wedding ring?

"Jordyn?" His mouth, somehow, seemed to get even softer, fuller than before, creating a sharper contrast to the rest of him, to the sexy dark stubble on his cheeks and jaw, to all those lean, honed muscles, those strong arms wrapped around her nice and tight.

And why did he always have to smell so good? That really wasn't fair.

Again, he asked, "Jordyn?"

And that time, she remembered to answer. "Will." She said it very softly, like a secret. Or a prayer. And she reached up, sliding her open hand over his beautiful, hard, wet chest, curling her fingers around the back of his strong neck, brushing the blunt, wet ends of his black hair. "Will…"

He answered her in a rough whisper, "Jordyn."

And his mouth came down to meet hers.

Chapter Nine

Will covered her sweet, tempting lips with his.

Perfect, those lips of hers. Just as they'd been the other night, when she'd kissed him in front of his brothers. And at Crawford's last week, when he'd kissed her for the benefit of those two gossiping ladies.

And last Saturday night, when he'd kissed her just because he wanted to.

Little Jordyn Leigh Cates. Best kisser ever.

He should be over his surprise at how good her lips tasted. But he wasn't. He had a feeling he might never get over how terrific kissing her felt. Every time it happened, it felt like the first time.

He hoped it happened a lot in these few weeks they had together, whether he ought to be hoping that or not.

Her slim body felt just right in his arms. And best of all, she wasn't pulling away—even though they had no audience to play newlyweds for. She was kissing him back.

His wet jeans got tighter as those fine lips parted and she let him in for a deeper taste. So damn sweet.

And *his*.

His wife.

Yeah, okay. Only temporarily.

But maybe not. Maybe more than kissing had happened Saturday night. And if it had, just maybe, she was going to have his baby.

And if there *was* a baby coming, well, they'd already agreed that they would stay together, work it out, the two of them, as a married couple.

Okay, maybe a baby wasn't all that likely, no matter what they'd done Saturday night.

But so what?

Right now life was good. He was still kissing her. And she was definitely into it.

He let his hands roam the silky, wet skin of her back. Her firm little breasts felt so good pressing into his chest—even with her swimsuit top in the way. The scent of her filled his head. Ripe peaches, spring rain. She made him dizzy in the best possible way.

He tottered on the ledge. "Whoa," he growled against her parted lips. "Come on down…"

She sighed, her breath warm and sweet across his cheek. "You mean, before we fall down?"

"Yes, I do." He covered her mouth again and drank her in, nipping at her lower lip then soothing it with a slow glide of his tongue. As he kissed her, he bent his legs and carried her down with him, turning her and settling her across his thighs on the rocky ledge—and trying not to groan as his soggy jeans pinched his groin.

She leaned back on his cradling arm and touched his cheek with her fingers, stroking so lightly. "We shouldn't be doing this…"

He caught her index finger between his lips, teased it with his tongue and reluctantly let it go. "Shh. It's okay. We're just…"

"What?" Big trusting eyes held his. "We're just what?"

"Fooling around a little." He brushed his hand down her arm, loving the silky feel of her skin beneath his palm. "No harm done…"

She made a sweet humming sound low in her throat and touched his face again, fingertips skimming the scruff on his cheeks. "You're sure about that?"

"Of course I'm sure." He sounded so confident. What a joke. He should tell her the truth, admit that he wasn't sure about anything.

Not since last Saturday night.

His jeans were tight and getting tighter. But so what?

He was only going to kiss her and hold her a little. And there really was no harm in that. It was nothing they hadn't done before.

"Will…"

By way of an answer, he captured her upturned mouth for another kiss, a long one. She stiffened at first—but then she gave in and kissed him back.

When he finally lifted his lips from hers, she cuddled against him and tucked her head under his chin. Shyly, she told him, "You're a really good kisser, Will."

"I was just thinking the same thing about you."

She giggled, an adorable, delighted little sound. "No. Seriously."

"Yeah. Seriously." He gathered the dripping coils of her long hair and wrapped them around his hand. "I think we've got chemistry, Jordyn Leigh."

She looked up at him, all big eyes and soft just-kissed lips. "I think so, too. And I mean, who would ever have guessed? You and me, like this, together? You were always such a pain in the butt."

He kissed her, a quick one. "You don't mean that."

"Oh, yes, I do. And all the girls would talk about you, about how hot you are. And I was always like, 'Oh, I know, he's really handsome, sure, and he can be so charming when he wants to be and what girl in her right mind doesn't love a cowboy? But you don't know him like I do…'"

He answered carefully, "I think I'm going to focus on the part about how you think I'm handsome and charming."

"Yeah, right. You do that." She dipped her head beneath his chin again.

With slow care, he uncoiled her hair from around his palm. "Hey."

"Hmm?"

"Look at me."

"No."

"Come on…"

"Uh-uh."

"Uh-huh."

And she gave in and glanced up.

He was ready for her. He swooped in and captured her lips again. This time she gasped a little against his mouth. He drank in that startled sound and went on kissing her, taking his time.

A long time…

By the end of that kiss, he was aching to do a lot more than kiss her.

She leaned back in his arms and stared up at him, lips cherry red, cheeks slightly flushed. "We probably should cut this out, huh?"

Cutting it out was the last thing he wanted to do. But he knew she was right. "Yes, I think we should." And he made himself follow through, gently scooping her up in his arms and setting her on the ledge beside him. "There."

She leaned her head on his shoulder. For a while they were silent together. Finally, she said, "It's nice here—the falls, the swimming hole, this spot in the sun."

"I thought you'd like it." He captured her hand and wove his fingers with hers. "Come on." He gathered his legs beneath him and stood. She rose with him. "Let's ride down the falls."

Carefully, they made their way across the slippery rocks, over to where the water poured free of the wide ledge, falling in a white, foaming spray into the pool below.

"You first," he offered.

She didn't even hesitate, just let go of his hand and picked her way through the rushing water to the middle of the stream. Once she got there, she sat down—and slid off the edge.

Holding her arms high, she squealed as she fell, landing butt first in the pool below, sinking under the surface, pink-painted toes last—and then shooting up out of the churning water with a loud, "Whoa! What a ride!"

He waited until she cleared the waterfall, all that gold hair streaming behind her. Then he made his way across the swift current to follow her down. They climbed the rocks twice more and rode the waterfall into the pool below.

When they got out on the trail side, their blanket was waiting under a tree. She took a comb from her saddlebag and corralled her wet hair into one thick braid down her back. They ate their sandwiches and munched on apples, then stretched out on the blanket side by side to let her suit and his jeans dry a little more before putting on the rest of their clothes for the ride back to the house.

It was peaceful in the dappled shade of the tree, with the soft roar of the falls across the creek. And it had been a long, busy week. He dozed for a while and woke to the sound of the wind stirring the branches above them. He rolled his head and looked at Jordyn. She lay on her back and seemed to be sleeping. He admired the soft curve of her mouth, became fascinated by the way her gold-tipped eyelashes fanned across her smooth cheeks.

And then, as if she could feel the weight of his gaze on her, she turned her head and opened her eyes halfway. "Will." She smiled at him.

He couldn't resist. He levered up on an elbow and bent over her. "Tell me not to kiss you again."

She didn't tell him any such thing. On the contrary, she lifted one hand and cupped the back of his head, her soft, cool fingers threading up into his hair. "Will..."

The invitation in her half-shut eyes tempted him powerfully—enough that he decided there really was no reason he needed to resist. He lowered his mouth and he kissed her, a long kiss, slow and deep, a kiss that tasted like apples and sunshine. A kiss that only led to another kiss.

And another after that.

With a happy little hum of sound, she turned her pretty body toward him. They lay on their sides, facing each other, her slim, cool hand moving over him, caressing his shoulder, his chest, the back of his neck. Her bare knees brushed his legs, setting off sparks even through his damp jeans. She kissed him so eagerly and murmured encouragements, "Will...yes...oh, yes..."

He touched her, too, running his hand into the dip of her waist, and up over the sleek outward curve of her hip. And he didn't stop there. On he went, his fingers gliding down the outside of her thigh—and back up again.

Her skin was so smooth, warm from the sun, dusted with baby-fine, barely there golden hair. He couldn't get enough of the feel of her under his hand. He ran his fingers down her spine, reaching the back strap of her suit top and resenting it mightily. But he was past that quickly, following her smooth skin on down—only to encounter the barrier of her suit bottom.

He really wanted her bare.

Bare. Yeah. He wanted *all* of her bare.

He went on kissing her, losing himself in the taste and the sweet, clean scent of her. And by then, it seemed the most natural thing in the world to let his hand glide back up again to the clasp at the strap of her suit top. It was the work of a few seconds to get it unhooked. Just a flick of his thumb and index finger…

Jordyn gasped, bringing up her hand between them to keep the top from falling off.

That woke him up. They pulled back at the same time and stared at each other, both of them breathing hard.

Her eyes had a dazed look, and her mouth was plump from his kisses. "I, um, really don't know if we should…" The words died in her throat.

The ability to speak seemed to have temporarily deserted him. He gaped at her, shocked at himself. Great way to look after little Jordyn Leigh. Take her for a ride and get her out of her swimsuit. What was the matter with him? He shouldn't be let out in public without supervision.

Damning himself for a low-down dirty dog, he sat up. "Get up and turn around." He said it way too gruffly.

She pushed herself up to a sitting position but didn't turn. Instead, she continued to stare at him, her eyes wide—with hurt. "Will. Why are you mad at me? What'd I do?"

"You didn't do anything." He made a real effort to speak more gently. "And I'm not mad at you, I'm mad at myself. I shouldn't have been kissing you—and I damn sure shouldn't be taking off your suit."

"It's okay." One of her shoulder straps fell down her arm. She pressed the top of the suit harder against her breasts to keep them covered. Damn, she looked good, all flushed and flustered, that mouth of hers so plump and sweet. In a sad little whisper, she insisted, "You didn't do anything wrong."

"The hell I didn't." He barked the words at her. She made a startled, wounded sound. He wanted to grab her and hold her and promise her it would be okay. But he knew where that would lead—to more kisses, more caresses, more opportunities to get her out of her swimsuit.

Uh-uh. She might be one fine kisser, but she was also a virgin. Or she had been until a week ago. He was supposed to be looking out for her and making up for whatever might have happened between them last Saturday night, not trying to get her out of her clothes.

"Turn around," he commanded, more harshly than he should have. "I'll hook you back up."

Still holding the top of the suit in place, she gathered her pretty legs to the side and turned her body, showing him her back, which was slim and soft and tempting, just like the rest of her. "I…I was just thinking that we ought to stop, is all. That things were maybe going a little further than they should—that is, I mean," she stammered adorably, "that you and me, together this way, well, it wasn't really in the plan."

"Damn right it wasn't." He got hold of both dangling straps as she reached back to catch her damp braid and guide it over her shoulder, out of his way. He hooked the straps together again. "There."

She fiddled with the shoulder straps and tugged on the front a little, adjusting it to cover her. "Thank you." Slowly, she turned around and faced him. "See? No harm done." A pretty blush flowed upward over her velvety cheeks.

He looked at her, so sweet and sexy, with her mouth still swollen from his kisses, beard burn reddening her tender skin—and all he wanted was to start kissing her again. "We should get going."

"If you're upset," she said in that prim little voice she used when she lectured him, "I think we should talk it over. You shouldn't be so hard on yourself. Nothing has happened here that I wasn't okay with."

"I'm not upset," he lied. Because there was no damn way he wanted to talk about it. What good would talking do? Except to get him angrier at himself than he already was. "Come on. Let's go."

For a minute she just sat there, watching him with a hurt and chiding expression. He knew she wouldn't let it go. She would start lecturing him about how they needed to hash it out, that communication mattered and all that crap.

But then, without a word, she grabbed her jeans from the edge of the blanket and started getting dressed. Relieved that she'd given it up, he pulled on his shirt and boots, and set his hat on his head. They packed up what was left of the lunch. He rolled the blanket and hooked it behind his saddle. They mounted up and started back.

He took the lead. The ride to the house was uneventful. And neither of them said a word the whole way.

At the house, Will told her he'd take care of the horses. Jordyn left him and went inside.

She had plenty to do. She made mac and cheese with ham for dinner and popped it in the oven. While it baked, she put away what was left of the kitchen stuff. Will never came in. Apparently, he had something important to do outside.

After what had happened at the swimming hole, she felt all edgy and strange. It had been so good, kissing Will, sitting on his lap up by the falls—lying with him on the blanket and kissing him some more. She couldn't help kind of wishing that she hadn't stopped him, that she'd just gone on kissing him, while he took away her top and then the suit bottom and then, well, wherever things had gone next. She had a feeling it would have been lovely.

But then, really, was that what she wanted? After all these years of telling herself that someday she would find someone special, someone to give both her heart and her body to?

No. Really. Making love with Will, no matter how good it felt, wouldn't be right.

Why not? asked a defiant, yearning voice in the back of her mind.

Good question. Because the really odd thing was that somewhere deep down inside herself, she had started thinking that making love with Will would be very, very right.

And that got her all confused all over again—maybe even more confused than she'd been when she woke up married to him last Sunday morning. She didn't want to feel confused, thank you very much.

So she decided *not* to think about it. She would just go about the rest of her day and forget what had happened at the swimming hole.

After she finished with the kitchen stuff, she took the mac and cheese out of the oven and left it on the stove with the lid on to cool a little. She got the salad ready and stuck it in the fridge. Then she went upstairs and did homework until she was three assignments ahead of where she needed to be on Monday.

When she came back down at six, she found the lid off the mac and cheese and a big hole in the middle of it. Half the salad was gone.

Will had left her a note on the counter. *Going into town for a beer with Craig and Rob. Back late. Don't wait up.*

Really? And to think she'd called him charming back at the swimming hole. Not to mention, let him kiss her until her clothes started falling off. She had to be out of her mind to even imagine that she might want to make love for the first time in her whole life with him—or possibly the second time, depending on what had happened Saturday night.

The jerk. He'd be lucky if she ever spoke to him again.

Will met his brothers at the Ace in the Hole on Sawmill Street. They drank beer and played pool, and he tried to forget the feel of Jordyn's soft lips on his, the scent of her skin, the joy on her pretty face as she shot down the falls.

Craig asked him why he hadn't brought Jordyn to town with him. He muttered something vague in reply. Rob pulled him aside and told him how happy he was for him.

"You got it all now, man," Rob said. "That sweet ranch and Jordyn Leigh, too."

"Thanks," Will said in a tone meant to end the conversation.

Rob didn't take the hint. "I always kind of had a secret thing for Jordyn Leigh. But you know how she is—not easy for a guy to get close to. The way she can look at a guy, like she has a pretty good idea of what's going on inside his head. That used to freak me out a little. And I always felt like she never took me seriously the times I tried to work up the nerve to ask her out."

Will suggested in a low growl, "Tell me you didn't just say you had a secret thing for my wife."

Rob arched an eyebrow and backed away. "Whoa, man. Jealous much?"

"I'm considering punching you in the face."

Rob grunted. "The hell you are. If you were gonna hit me, you'd have done it by now."

"Don't ever tell me that again."

"I was only sayin'—"

"I don't care. Don't say it again."

"Sheesh. Who put the burr under your blanket?"

Will didn't answer. Over at the pool table, Craig had missed his shot. Will picked up his pool cue, gave his baby brother one last dirty look and turned for the table.

By ten, he couldn't take it anymore. He felt like a complete SOB—probably because he was acting like one. He shouldn't have just eaten that nice dinner Jordyn cooked, left her that curt note and disappeared while she was still upstairs. What kind of guy did stuff like that?

An SOB, that's who.

"I'm heading home," he told his brothers.

Rob grinned. "Give Jordyn Leigh a big kiss for me."

Will felt his lip curl—and not in a smile. "You are just beggin' for it, aren't you?"

Rob made kissy noises.

Will turned and left before he lost it and beat the crap out of his own flesh and blood.

At the ranch the lights were still on downstairs. Will stopped the quad cab in the dark, a ways back from the house. He turned off the engine and sat there for a while, feeling like a first-class loser, knowing he had to go in and make amends, afraid he'd only mess things up worse when he tried to make them better.

But he couldn't sit out here in the dark forever. Finally, he made himself get out and go in the house.

The TV was on in the living room. He could see the big screen flickering through the front window. It went off when he let himself in the front door. He pushed the door shut behind him as Jordyn got up from the sofa and came to stand in the arch between the front hall and the living room.

"Will." She wore jeans and a little pink T-shirt, her wheat-gold hair loose on her shoulders. Her face was set, her eyes full of mutiny. She said, much too pleasantly, "You're home earlier than I expected."

He opened his mouth—and curt words came out. "I told you not to wait up."

She tipped her head to the side. Her shining hair tumbled down her arm. And then she folded both arms over those breasts he wanted so badly to see naked. "I was going to do exactly what you said in your note. Just go upstairs and not come down tonight," she said, her tone so calm and reasonable, it made him want to break something. "In fact, I was considering not speaking to you again for an extended period of time. But then I thought that would just be childish, that what I really needed to do was to wait for you to come home so we could work this out tonight."

He opened his mouth again—and shut it before he could lie and insist that there was nothing to work out.

She left the archway and came toward him, her bare feet with their pink-painted toes whispering across the plank floor. "You have something to say?"

Yeah, I want to kiss you some more. I want to do all kinds of things to you, and I want to do them now. "I…" That was as far as he got. He was an idiot, no doubt about it.

Her face softened. She was such a fine woman. Better than he would ever deserve, that was for sure. "I'm listening." She said it gently, though he'd done nothing at all to warrant her kindness. "Go ahead."

His mind went blank. Stalling for time, he took off his hat, turned and hung it on the hook by the door.

When he faced her again, she hadn't moved. She was

still just standing there, still so pretty it almost hurt to look at her—and still waiting for him to say what he had to say.

There was nothing for him to do but buck up and take a crack at an apology. "I was disgusted with myself for my behavior at the swimming hole. Instead of owning up to that, I took it out on you. That made me feel even madder at myself. I sent you inside and took care of the horses by myself so that I could have a little time to figure out how to tell you I was sorry. Then, the longer I stayed outside, the harder it got to think about facing you—so when I came in and you were still upstairs, I took the world's fastest shower, put a big dent in that excellent pot of macaroni and cheese you made for our dinner, zipped off that mean note and got the hell out."

When he stopped speaking, the front hall seemed to echo with silence. But at least she was still standing there. At least she hadn't turned on her heel and headed up the stairs.

She asked, "Is that all?"

He shrugged. "Rob has a crush on you. And I'm sorry, Jordyn Leigh. I'm really sorry for the way I've behaved."

She looked at him for what seemed like half a century. Finally, she said quietly, "I accept your apology."

His heart seemed to bounce toward his throat. "Er, you do?"

"Yes, I do." She offered her hand.

He took it, fast, before she could come to her senses and change her mind about forgiving him. He wrapped his fingers around her slim ones—and suddenly everything was right with the world. "Whew."

She chuckled. "You think I let you off too easy?"

"Yeah. Probably." He reached up, ran his other hand down her shining, silky hair. She let him do it, too, gaz-

ing up at him with trust in those beautiful china-blue eyes.
"Thank you," he said, his voice ragged and low.

"You're welcome. You want a beer or some coffee?"

"Coffee sounds good."

"Come on, then." She led him to the kitchen.

He put the water in the coffeemaker. She popped in the
filter and spooned in the grounds. They stood together at
the counter as it brewed, neither of them saying anything,
which was fine. Words seemed unnecessary right then. It
was just the two of them in the kitchen, waiting for the
coffee to brew, and that was enough.

They filled their mugs and sat in the breakfast nook.

"I'll be awake half the night," she said ruefully, "drinking caffeine at this hour." She took a big sip, anyway. And
then she set the mug down and wrapped her hands around
it the way she had last Sunday morning in Kalispell, when
he took her to that little restaurant for breakfast and they
made their Divorce Plan. "And what do you mean, Rob
has a crush on me?"

Why had he mentioned that? He had no idea. "I don't
know what you're talking about."

She drank more coffee. "There's no point in saying
you're sorry if you're only going to turn right around and
tell me a lie."

He gave in and busted to the truth. "I don't know. He
was giving me a hard time tonight, saying how I had it
all, the ranch I'd always dreamed of—and you. Then he
said he'd always had a thing for you, but you never took
him seriously."

"Rob had a thing for me?" She waved a hand in front
of her face. "Oh, come on. You know Rob. He was just
giving you a hard time."

"So I probably shouldn't have threatened to knock his
teeth out, huh?"

"Will." She sat up straighter in her chair. "You didn't…?"

"Actually beat the crap out of him? No, I only threatened to—and you're right. He was probably just joking around." Will didn't know if he believed that or not. But what did it matter? If Rob actually had considered asking her out, well, it was too late now. No Clifton alive would move in on another man's woman—especially not his own brother's wife.

But what happens when she's not your wife anymore?

Better not to even go there.

And so what if Rob had a crush on Jordyn Leigh? Who wouldn't have a crush on Jordyn Leigh? She was smart and pretty, and she had a good heart.

And he might as well face it. Rob wasn't the only one who had a thing for Jordyn Leigh. What had happened at the creek that day had forced him to admit that *he* wanted her. Bad. Odds were he was never going to have her. And that messed with his mind.

"Will?"

"Yeah?"

"Is something still bothering you?"

Now, what was he supposed to say to that? The truth would just get him deeper into territory he didn't want to explore. And a lie was plain wrong.

So he hedged. "I'm okay, really. I still feel bad about… everything that happened, that's all."

It worked. She told him softly, "Let it go. We're fine now."

Jordyn thoroughly enjoyed the rest of that evening. They took second cups of coffee into the living room and streamed a movie. Will let her choose a romantic comedy. He watched the whole thing and even seemed to enjoy it.

She kind of wanted his arm around her, but he didn't

offer. And after what had happened at the swimming hole, well, maybe cuddling up close to him was only asking for trouble. After the movie, she went upstairs to bed. And even with two cups of coffee buzzing through her system, she went to sleep as soon as her head hit the pillow.

Cece called her the next morning while she and Will were having breakfast and invited them over to her place for dinner that night. Will nodded when Jordyn passed on the invitation, so she told Cece they would be there.

They caravanned into town with the Stevaliks for church. It was nice, sitting next to Will in the pretty little community church, singing the hymns she'd known all her life. The sermon was on hope, and she found it uplifting.

Twice Will caught her eye, and they shared a smile. Both times a warm, cherished feeling bloomed within her. She decided that coming to church had been a great idea, after all.

After the service, they lingered awhile. Jordyn introduced Will and the Stevaliks to the pastor and to various members of the local Traub, Dalton and Strickland families. Then Myron and Pia went across the street to the doughnut shop, and Jordyn and Will drove to Kalispell to stock up on groceries for the week ahead.

That evening at Cece and Nick's, Rita and Charles Dalton joined them. The Daltons had five grown children, including the twins Kristen and Kayla. Before the evening was through, Jordyn and Will had an invitation to next Sunday's dinner at the Dalton ranch north of town.

Monday came, and Jordyn realized that her life on the ranch had a nice rhythm, a productive routine. She went to work. And when she came home, she helped Pia clean out and organize the barn. She fussed over the goats and the kittens, and had dinner with Will.

It was good between her and Will. They got along great.

Tuesday, as usual, she and Will had their breakfast and dinner together. They discussed her day's work and his progress at the ranch. They laughed together. He teased her, and she joked back.

They were just like any married couple, she thought, except that, at the end of the evening, they went to bed in separate rooms. She was starting to see that if there was a baby, she and Will would get along together just fine. They could have a good life, build a family, be happy. She just knew that they could.

They were actually pretty well suited, she decided— *very* well suited, as a matter of fact. Her confidence increased that they could make it work.

And if there was a baby, well, then they could be together in every way. She would finally find out what it was like to make love with a good man. It wouldn't be her dream come true exactly, but close enough.

Definitely close enough.

Wednesday very early, she woke up with an ache in her lower belly. She tried to ignore it. But it was a familiar sort of ache, a definite cramping feeling.

She turned over, closed her eyes and willed the feeling away.

It refused to go.

Finally, she sat up and threw back the covers. Even in the dim light just before dawn, she could see the blood on the white sheet.

Her period had started.

So much for having to make it work with Will.

Chapter Ten

Something was bothering Jordyn.

Will noticed it first at breakfast on Thursday. She was too quiet, and she seemed preoccupied. He asked her what the matter was. She said it was nothing, so he took her at her word.

She went off to work.

When she got home, he was still outside with Myron, putting together a lean-to to protect the goats when the weather got bad. He didn't see her until dinnertime, when she was even more withdrawn than she'd been at breakfast.

After the meal she went outside for a while—probably to spoil the goats and pet the kittens and make sure the ornery rooster had enough feed. He wandered into the living room and turned on the TV. By nine she hadn't come in to join him, or even checked in to say good-night.

That bothered him. Even if she didn't hang with him, she always told him good-night before she went upstairs.

He turned off the TV and sat there in the quiet for a few minutes, listening for a sound of her. Nothing.

So he got up and circled the first floor. She wasn't down there. He went outside, checked the barn and the goat pen. No sign of her. She must have gone up to her room without a word to him.

Back inside, the dryer alarm buzzed. He went in the utility room, pulled open the dryer door and found a load of clean sheets.

Might as well take them up to her. It was as good an excuse as any to try to talk to her again, to find out what had happened to make her start acting like a ghost of herself.

Jordyn closed her laptop and tossed it down beside her on the bed. Enough with pretending to do homework. She was too crampy and miserable to concentrate.

She really should go back downstairs and give Will the big news that she *wasn't* having his baby. She should have told him this morning. Or over dinner.

But she hadn't. She was putting it off because...

Well, she didn't know why, exactly. She only knew she felt low and depressed, and she didn't want to talk about it. Hormones, probably. Or so she kept telling herself.

She was just about to go take another painkiller to knock the cramping back a little when he tapped on the door.

"Jordyn? You awake?"

She just sat there for a second or two, staring at the shut door, considering pretending to be asleep.

But come on. She'd been blowing him off all day, and she needed to snap out of it.

"It's open," she called. The door swung inward.

And there he stood, his arms full of her sheets. "Thought you might want these."

She had others, and he knew it. He'd come upstairs to check on her, to find out why she kept saying she was fine, and then dragging around like something awful had happened—and somehow, the sight of his coaxing smile and worried eyes made her feel more depressed and miserable than before.

"Come on," he said. "I'll help you fold them."

She just sat there, looking at him, thinking how manly and handsome he was, wishing...

What?

She really didn't know what she was wishing. Just that things could be different, somehow.

"Jordyn?" He crossed the threshold, dropped the big wad of sheets on a chair and kept coming until he stood by the bed.

She heaved a giant sigh and patted the mattress.

It was all the invitation he needed. He sank down beside her, swinging his stocking feet up onto the comforter next to hers. "Okay. So, what's up with you?"

How to tell him? How to explain this bizarre, depressed state she'd fallen into because there wasn't any baby? She should be overjoyed. After all, they'd only ended up married by accident, and they had a Divorce Plan. They were not what they pretended to be when other people were watching.

"Jordyn, come on. What's up?"

She blew out her cheeks with a weary breath. "Good news?" Somehow, it came out as a question.

"If the news is good, how come you look like somebody died?"

She pressed her fingers to her temples and rubbed in a vain effort to ease her sudden headache away.

He caught her wrists in either hand and gently pulled

them away from her face. "Talk to me. Tell me what's eating at you. Give me a chance to make it better."

"You can't make it better—and anyway, it's nothing horrible. It's a good thing, it really is."

"And this good thing is...?" He gazed at her with real concern.

And that did it. He really did care, and he wanted to know. She couldn't hold it in anymore. "I got my period. There's no baby."

For about a half a second, he looked as stricken as she felt. But maybe that was only her imagination. Because a second after that, he said, "Well, that *is* great news."

"Yeah. It's great. Terrific. Wonderful."

He tipped his head and studied her. "What is it? What's wrong? Come on, you can tell me."

She let her shoulders droop. "It's cramps, that's all. And I have a headache..." Not a total lie. If the cramps and the headache weren't all of what had her feeling low, they definitely contributed.

"Come here." He did the sweetest thing then, easing an arm around her, pulling her close. She surrendered to the comfort he offered, curling her tired, aching body into him, resting her head on his strong shoulder. He asked, "You want some aspirin or something?"

She snuggled in closer, breathing in the scent of him, feeling better about everything, just to have his big arms around her. "I'll get something in a few minutes. It's strange..."

"What?" He put a finger under her chin, tipping it up.

She met those gorgeous eyes. "I don't know. I guess I was kind of getting used to the idea that there would be a baby. Is that odd or what? I mean, it was only one night— and that's *if* we actually did anything."

"Not odd," he reassured her. "Not strange. You were

preparing yourself, that's all. In case it turned out we were going to be parents."

"Preparing myself. I guess that's one way to look at it." She dipped her head and snuggled close to him again.

He wrapped his arms tighter around her and rubbed her back. "You'll feel better soon..."

"I know." Actually, she felt better already. His warm hands felt so good, stroking her shoulders, fingers digging in a little to ease out the kinks. And more than the magic he worked with those rubbing fingers of his, just having his arms around her gave her comfort. She could have sat there, snuggled up with him forever. And he didn't seem in any hurry to get away from her, either.

Jordyn closed her eyes...

Will cradled Jordyn close and listened as her breathing evened out into the shallow rhythm of sleep. He thought about the baby that they weren't going to have.

And he knew it was a good thing. The best thing. She had big plans for her life, and a baby would have changed everything.

And he, well, he had a lot of work ahead of him to get the ranch whipped into shape. It was a round-the-clock job, and he hadn't planned to start a family for a few years, at least.

Better for both of them that the marriage would end as they'd agreed. They could go forward with the plan, get divorced in August and get on with their lives.

Still, a certain heaviness dragged on him, a let-down kind of feeling. He must have been preparing himself, too. Getting himself ready to go forward as Jordyn's husband, getting ready to be a dad.

Now it wasn't going to happen. He should be glad about that. Relieved, even.

But instead, he felt a bone-deep sadness.

As though something so precious was not only lost, but had never been.

Jordyn woke alone in her bed the next morning. Will, sweet and considerate to a fault, had pulled the comforter over her before he left.

She sat up against the headboard—and burst into tears.

Which was totally stupid. She had nothing to cry about.

So she tossed back the covers, ran into the bathroom, stripped down and climbed in the shower. She stayed in there, under the hot spray, until the water ran cool.

And when she got out, she felt a lot better about everything. Will was a great guy, and there was no baby and those were the facts.

Time to get on with the plan.

She put extra effort into her hair and makeup, kind of pulling herself together, putting her depression of the night before behind her. Downstairs, she made French toast for breakfast.

Will had two helpings and told her she looked great. "Seems like you feel better today."

She beamed him her brightest smile. "Much better, thank you."

"Cramps all gone?"

She knew he was only being supportive. But still, today was a new day, and she didn't want to talk about her cramps or the lack of them. She realized that maybe she'd shared too much information with the guy.

After all, he wasn't *really* her husband. And she'd gone too far last night, crying on his shoulder because she wasn't pregnant after all, whining about her cramps and her headache, cuddling up good and close, inviting him to rub her back and hold her, and then falling asleep in his arms.

Boundaries were important, and she seemed to be crossing them constantly lately, treating Will like she owned him or something, kissing him and cuddling up to him when it was just the two of them, alone, and no displays of affection were called for.

It had to stop. "I'm feeling great," she said. "Honestly."

He gave her a sideways look, as though he wasn't quite sure what to make of her right then. "If you say so…" He sounded doubtful. Like he thought she was faking it, and she didn't feel great at all.

She almost snapped at him that she didn't like his attitude. But somehow, she restrained herself. No need to get annoyed over nothing.

It was time to move on, definitely. Time to get out the dissolution papers and fill in all the blanks. She had to stop putting off dealing with them. And she would, as of today.

But where were they, exactly? Had he even given her the ones she needed to fill out? She couldn't remember.

She sent him a covert glance across the table.

He frowned. "What?"

And she just didn't feel like getting into it with him right then. "Nothing, really. Not a thing." They were probably upstairs in her room somewhere.

Before she left for work, she went looking for them. She turned her room upside down in search of them, but they weren't there.

Didn't matter, though. At Sara's, she went on the county website and printed up a fresh copy of all the forms she needed. Back at the ranch that afternoon, before she got going on her homework, she tackled those forms.

They really were extensive. Everything she owned had to be specifically listed and claimed. Had Will started on his yet? He owned a lot more than she did, and it was bound to take him longer to get everything listed, to get all the exact amounts and the numbers of his accounts. She should probably check with him, make sure he was on top of it.

That night at dinner, when they were halfway through the meal, she said, "I started on the dissolution forms today. They're long. They want to know everything you own and its value. I mean *everything*, so that we can each claim what's ours and there's no dispute later. It's going to take a while to fill out. Especially for you, Will, with the land and all the buildings, the cattle, the vehicles, the furniture. It goes on and on."

He shrugged. "I should get going on that," he said, and kept eating.

Really, she ought to get more of an acknowledgment from him that he was on top of it. "So you will, then? You'll get them out and get going on them?"

He swallowed a bite of pork chop. "Isn't that what I just said?"

"You said you *should*, not that you *would*."

"Fine. I'll get going on it."

She sipped from her water glass, pushed her peas around on her plate and tried to figure out why he suddenly seemed so pissed off. "Okay. What's wrong? Out of nowhere, we're in a conversational minefield here."

"Nothing's wrong." He scooped up a big bite of whipped potatoes and shoved it into his mouth.

Lovely. She decided she needed to keep her eye on the prize. The point was to get him going on the papers. "I mean, do you even know where you put those papers? Because I looked for mine and couldn't find them and had to reprint them today at Sara's."

"I know where they are." He said it flatly. "You could have just asked me if you wanted them so bad."

And you could stop acting like a douche, if you don't mind.

Oh, she was tempted to say it. But she didn't. She kept her tone calm and reasonable. "I didn't want to bother you."

"You wouldn't have been bothering me."

"Great. But the point is we need to get back to the courthouse by the thirty-first at the latest. That's two weeks from now. If we get to the courthouse by the thirty-first, then we get our final court date within twenty-one business days…" She shook her head. "Actually, that's cutting it kind of close. I need to be in Missoula by the third week in August. Yes, all right, if I had to, I guess I could come back, just for the hearing. I'd really rather not, though. I'll be busy when I get there, and it's two hours each way, here and back…" She let her voice trail off and waited for him to say something.

He didn't even glance up, but just kept right on eating his dinner.

Will ate the rest of his potatoes.

He finished off his pork chop. He even ate his peas, and he'd never been all that big a fan of peas. He was seriously pissed off at Jordyn about then. She was getting to him, bugging the crap out of him with her phony behavior since breakfast that morning.

What was her problem that, all of a sudden, she had to nag him up one side and down the other about something he'd already told her he would take care of?

Would she ever shut up about it?

No. She kept talking, telling him what he already knew. He'd been there at the courthouse with her. He had a firm grasp of the time frame, and he would hold up his end. There was absolutely no reason for her to keep yammering on about it.

She nagged him some more. "So you need to get on those papers, Will."

He dropped his fork. It clattered against his empty plate. "How many times are you planning to tell me that?"

She gasped like he'd insulted her. "I just want to be sure that you're on top of it, that's all."

"I'm on top of it," he said, in barely more than a mutter. "You can be sure."

"Well, terrific, then. Let's leave it at that."

"Hey. I keep trying to."

"What is that supposed to mean?"

Let it go, he thought. But he didn't. "It means that you *won't* leave it at that. What the hell is it with you today, anyway? You came downstairs this morning with that big fake smile on your face, acting like you and me are strangers or something. And tonight you suddenly just have to tell me twenty times to fill out the dissolution papers. I don't get what's going on with you. And I don't like it, either."

Her mouth was pursed up tight. "Are you finished?"

Was he? Oh, yeah. Pretty much. "Just back the hell off, Jordyn. I don't know what's up with you all of a sudden, but you can stop about the damn papers. When the time comes, I'll have them ready."

"Thank you," she said in a tone that wasn't thankful in the least.

And then she slid her napkin in beside her plate, pushed back her chair and marched from the room. He heard her swift footsteps climbing the stairs, followed by the slamming of her bedroom door.

What? She thought she was punishing him, leaving him all alone downstairs?

Hardly.

He cleared the table and loaded the dishwasher and then he went to his office nook off the entry hall, got out the papers she wouldn't shut up about and sat down to fill them out.

She was right about them, which only served to make him even madder. He had a lot of crap to list and a lot of information to gather. But he kept after it, working well into the night, digging through the documents in his file cabinets and online for account numbers and proofs of sale. By the time he finally went to bed, he had more than half of it done.

The next morning, she was in the kitchen fixing breakfast when he came in from tending the animals. They sat down to eat in a silence as deep as a bottomless well.

He just didn't get it. Wednesday night, when she'd told him there was no baby, she'd been so sweet, reaching out to him for comfort, falling asleep in his arms. He could have sat there on her bed, just holding her, forever. He'd even considered staying there with her, cradling her slim body in his arms through the night, waking up beside her in the morning.

But he'd left her regretfully several hours before dawn.

And then faced her across the breakfast table Thursday morning and wondered what she'd done with the warm, direct, affectionate woman he'd comforted the night before.

Now it was Friday and they were not speaking. By the time she left for work, she'd yet to say a word to him.

He went to his office and worked on the forms for hours—hours he should have been out taking care of business on the Flying C. But by lunchtime, he'd done it. Those forms were ready for that end-of-the-month visit to the Kalispell Justice Center.

Feeling self-righteous and badly treated and madder than ever, he put them back in the desk drawer, grabbed a sandwich and went out to help Myron move cattle from a near pasture to one farther out.

That night at dinner, he kept waiting for her to ask him about the forms he'd spent half of last night and half of today completing. She didn't ask. She didn't say a word to him beyond "Dinner's ready," and "Please pass the green beans."

It was a cold war they were into now. So, all right. He could do that.

Yeah, he was starting to feel crappy about it, and he wasn't all that proud of his part in it. But then, well, maybe they'd been getting in a little too deep with each other, anyway, acting as if they had more going on together than they did. Maybe a little distance wasn't such a bad thing.

They loaded the dishwasher in total silence.

Once that was done, he said, "I'm going into town to the Ace in the Hole to get a beer with my brothers."

"Great." She granted him a smile so cold, it was a wonder her lips didn't crack and fall off. "I'm going into town, too. I want to see how Melba's doing."

"Have fun," he said in a growl.

"I will." Another brittle smile. "You, too."

Will had already left when Jordyn got in her car and headed for town.

She reached the boardinghouse at a little before eight. Inside, Melba greeted her with a hug and then led her to the front parlor so that she could say hi to Old Gene.

"How's married life treating you?" Old Gene asked.

Jordyn played her part. "Never been happier." As the lie passed her lips, she realized it would have been true a couple of days ago.

Melba grabbed her hand and took her back to the kitchen where they had coffee and brownies—chocolate chip–cookie Oreo-fudge brownies, to be specific. They were wonderfully rich and way too delicious. Jordyn ate one and then couldn't resist having another. Sometimes a girl really needed a gooey Oreo dessert.

She told Melba all about the ranch, about the goats and the kittens, about how the place was really coming together.

Melba told her not to work too hard, to take it easy, relax and smell the flowers. "You sure you're doing okay, honey?" Melba asked. She'd always had a sixth sense about what was really going on with people.

Jordyn kept it light. "Nothing wrong with me that another of these brownies won't cure."

"Help yourself."

Jordyn reached for another one as Claire came in carrying baby Bekka. Claire poured herself a cup of coffee and let Jordyn hold the baby.

Bekka was in a good mood, giggling, waving her fat little hands around. Jordyn cuddled her close and kissed her plump cheek and tried to ignore the sadness that plucked at her heartstrings.

The sadness made no sense, really. But still, she felt it, and strongly—a sadness for the baby she wasn't going to have, the baby she'd somehow started to love and want, even though that baby had never actually existed.

She hadn't talked privately to Claire since that afternoon at Sara's when Claire had cried and confided about her husband going home to Bozeman without her. Jordyn wanted to ask if Claire had heard from Levi, but somehow, the moment never seemed right.

Claire asked, "Did you see last Sunday's edition of the *Rust Creek Falls Gazette*?"

When Jordyn said she'd missed it, Melba filled her in. "The mystery gossip columnist reported that a certain Kalispell detective is looking into the possibility that someone doctored the wedding punch on the Fourth of July."

Jordyn kissed Bekka's cheek again. "Any speculation as to who that mysterious someone might be?"

Melba and Claire both shook their heads. Claire said, "So far, not a clue."

Eventually, Bekka started fussing, and Claire took her off to get her ready for bed. Reluctant to return to the empty ranch house, Jordyn hung around. She asked Melba how Claire was doing.

Melba shook her head again. "About the same, I'm afraid. I keep hoping Levi will show up, or at least get in touch, that the two of them can make up. So far, though, it hasn't happened."

Jordyn's thoughts—as they too often did—turned to Will. "I guess sometimes people say things they shouldn't— hurtful things. And then they let their pride keep them from apologizing and working things out."

Melba patted her arm. "I know they love each other. I stay focused on that, and I don't let myself get discouraged. Real love takes hard times, too. Real love is like faith. It grows stronger when it's tested."

Jordyn sighed. "Melba, that's beautiful. I do believe you are a philosopher."

"No, just an old woman who's lived a full life." She offered the half-empty plate of brownies. "Go on. Have another."

"I've already had three. They're so hard to resist."

"Then don't. Give in. Enjoy. You only live once."

So Jordyn had another. Melba brought the coffeepot over and refilled their mugs. It was nice. Comforting, to sit there in Melba's cozy kitchen, eating those decadent brownies, chatting about love and life and what was going on in town. She could have sat at Melba's kitchen table late into the night.

But by ten, she knew she was pushing it, keeping the older woman up past her bedtime.

Melba hugged her again at the door. "My best to your handsome husband," she said.

"I'll tell him," Jordyn promised. *That is, if I ever speak to him again.* She ran down the front steps in the gathering twilight and gave Melba a last wave as she ducked into her Subaru.

She started it up and turned the corner onto Cedar Street. The quickest way back to the Flying C was a right turn on Main Street. But she went left instead. The next street was Sawmill, where she should have gone right. She turned left again.

Two blocks later, she turned into the parking lot of the Ace in the Hole.

Chapter Eleven

Will nursed his second beer and wondered what he was doing there.

His brothers played pool and flirted with the waitresses and seemed to be having a really good time. Will wasn't. He kept thinking about Jordyn, wondering if she was enjoying her visit with the old lady who ran the boarding-house.

Wondering if maybe he'd been a little too hard on her. She was right, after all. They had a plan, and the plan included the necessity to fill out the damn divorce papers. He'd needed to get on that. And when she'd first brought it up to him, he *had* blown her off. Could he blame her that she kept after him?

When he got home, if she was there and still up, he would apologize to her for being a horse's ass. Maybe he could even get her to open up and talk to him about why all of a sudden she had to treat him like some stranger, why she had to give him fake smiles and cold, distant looks.

And if she wouldn't open up about what was really going on with her, well, so what? She didn't owe him the secrets of her heart.

He was her husband, yeah, but not in the deepest, fullest way. And not forever. They got along great most of the time. He loved having her around. She was different than any woman he'd ever been with. She took care of business, never slacked. And until the other morning, she'd always been straight with him, always spoken right up and said what was on her mind.

She didn't cling—or maybe, it was more that, when she did cling, he liked it. He liked feeling needed by her, which, with any other woman, always made him want to move on. Plus, she was quick-witted and funny and easy on the eyes.

But what they had together was stamped with an expiration date. And he had no right to blame her for maybe wanting to keep him from getting too close.

Over at the pool table, Rob looked up from taking a shot. His right eyebrow inched toward his hairline as he tipped his head at the arch that led to the main bar. Will followed the direction of his brother's gaze.

And saw Jordyn, in the same snug jeans and purple tank top she'd been wearing when he'd left her in the kitchen hours before.

Jordyn. Damn, she looked good.

All of a sudden, the night brimmed with promise. The music sounded better, the lights shone brighter.

And then he started wondering what she was doing there. Had something gone wrong?

He set down his beer and went to her.

She spotted him—and her eyes got bigger. Softer. Her lips parted slightly. She looked breathless. Excited.

Like she was really glad to see him.

Like he was the only guy in the room.

He eased his way through the crush to get to her. "Jordyn."

She tipped up that sweet face to him. "Will. I, um…"

"Are you okay? Did something happen?"

"No. No, nothing. I mean, nothing *important*. I mean, well, it's…" Her beautiful mouth trembled in the most endearing way. "I don't know. I was at Melba's. And then I was going back to the ranch—but I didn't. I came here instead. And then I drove up and down the rows of cars in the parking lot until I saw your pickup. And then I parked and told myself I wasn't going to come in here…"

He needed to touch her. So he did. He cradled the side of her head, ran his hand down the silky length of her shining hair. And she didn't jerk away—the opposite.

She stepped even closer. "I…well, I was feeling bad, you know? For getting all up in your business over those papers."

He gave it up. "I was a jerk."

And she admitted, "I was a nag."

He took her arm. "Come on. Let's go home."

She hung back. "But your brothers…"

"Don't worry about them. They're having a good time."

"Won't they wonder where you disappeared to?"

"Rob saw you. He watched me come for you. He'll tell them we went home together."

"I wasn't going to ruin your evening…"

"Jordyn. You haven't ruined my evening."

"Honest?"

"As far as I'm concerned, the evening's finally looking up."

A glowing smile bloomed. "You mean that?"

"Damn straight—now stop dawdling. Let's go."

She dawdled some more in the parking lot. He wanted her to ride with him, and she didn't want to leave her car.

Finally, he gave in. She followed him home.

They pulled into the yard twenty minutes later and parked side by side beneath the half disc of the silver moon. He got out fast and went to open her door for her, taking her hand and pulling her up from the driver's seat.

And into his waiting arms.

"Will…" She was sounding breathless again. Her eyes glowed silver, reflecting the moon. "At breakfast yesterday, when I acted so distant?"

"Yeah?" He smoothed her hair again. It was silvery, too, in the moonlight, and so soft and warm.

"I'd started thinking we were getting too intimate, you know? That we needed boundaries."

"Yeah, I get that. I can see why you would want to back off, after Wednesday night…"

She nodded. "When I told you that there wouldn't be a baby?"

"Yeah?"

"I felt so close to you, then, Will. I loved the way that you were with me, the way you held me and rubbed my back. The way you comforted me…"

"But?"

"Well, but then in the morning, I got scared."

"I should have been more understanding. I see that."

She made a soft sound low in her throat. "And I should have been more honest, should have told you that I was scared, instead of putting up walls."

"Jordyn, it's okay."

Those moon-silvered eyes searched his face. "It is? Really?"

"Yeah."

"So then, we're good again, you and me? We're friends again?"

He wanted to be a lot more than just her friend. But he

would take what he could get. As long as she didn't shut him out, didn't treat him like some stranger. "Yeah," he answered in a rough whisper. "We're friends again."

"Oh, Will. I'm glad. I don't like it when things aren't right between us."

What was it about her? The light in her eyes, the way she somehow managed to be shy and bold at the same time. She was something, all right. She was one of a kind.

She slid her hand up to his shoulder and then around his neck. Her soft fingers threaded up into his hair. "And can you maybe…?"

"Maybe, what?"

"Ahem. Um…"

He coaxed her, "Come on. Just say it."

"I, well, I like it when you hold me, Will. I like it when you kiss me. We only have so much time, you and me, together. You know?"

His chest felt suddenly tight, and his heart had set to beating hard and deep. "I know."

"I don't want to waste it. I don't want only to have your affection when someone is watching. I want…" She chickened out.

But by then, he was more than willing to help her along. "Do you want me to kiss you, Jordyn Leigh?"

She swallowed, nodded. "Yeah. That's what I'm asking. That's what I want." She tipped her chin higher, offering those soft lips to him. "Kiss me, Will."

It was the best offer he'd had since the last time he kissed her, an offer there was no way he was going to refuse.

So he gathered her closer, and he lowered his mouth to hers. He started out slow and careful, brushing his lips back and forth across hers.

Until she sighed and opened.

And then he settled his mouth more firmly on hers, settled and went deeper, stroking his tongue across the edges of her teeth, meeting her tongue, which was shy at first but swiftly grew bolder. She tasted so good, and she smelled so sweet. She felt like heaven in his arms, and he wished he would never have to let her go.

He lifted his head. She gave a small moan of protest.

Until he lowered his mouth again, slanting it the other way, and kissed her some more.

Off in the distance, a coyote howled. That ornery rooster answered, crowing at the moon.

And the next time he lifted his head, she smiled up at him dreamily, her eyes full of stars. "We should go on inside."

He made a low sound of agreement. She stepped free of her car door, and he pushed it shut. Then, their arms around each other, they turned for the house.

Inside she made popcorn the way they both liked it, in a pan on the stove. She drizzled it with melted butter. He put ice in two tall glasses and filled them with ginger ale. They went into the living room, where they settled on the sofa. He pulled her in snug against his side. She kept the popcorn bowl in her lap.

He grabbed a handful. "What do you want to watch?— wait. Don't tell me. Something romantic."

And she laughed. "No, I think tonight we need something with car chases and stuff getting blown up."

That surprised him. "You're joking."

"Car chases, Will. And at least a couple of really big explosions."

He shrugged. "If that's what you want, I can definitely set us up with that."

They streamed a thriller. And even with bombs going off and tires screaming, she fell asleep in the middle of it.

When it was over, he picked her up and carried her upstairs.

She woke up as he was carefully putting her down on the bed. "Hey…"

"Shh. Sleep."

She reached up, wrapped her arms around his neck and whispered, "Sleep *with* me…"

He answered honestly. "That's probably more temptation than I'm ready for."

She gave a happy, sleepy laugh. "I'm tempting?"

He groaned. "Do you really need to ask?"

"That's a yes, right?"

He pressed his forehead to hers and nodded. "That is definitely a yes."

She sighed. "But what if we slept the way we did at the Manor, you on the outside, me under the covers."

He'd never had a better offer. "I need to turn the lights off downstairs and brush my teeth."

"That's okay. You promise you'll come back, though?"

He kissed her cheek. "You have my solemn word."

When he returned, in an old pair of sweats and a T-shirt, with an extra blanket under his arm, she was coming out of the bathroom, her face scrubbed clean of makeup. She smelled of toothpaste and had changed into a giant yellow shirt with Bad as I Wanna Be printed across the front.

He put his arm around her, herded her to the bed and waited while she climbed in, scooted to the far side and settled the covers over herself.

"Right here." She fluffed the pillow next to hers.

So he stretched out beside her and settled the blanket over himself. "Happy now?"

"I am, yes." She turned off the light. "Night, Will."

"Sleep tight, Jordyn Leigh."

* * *

Deep in the night, Jordyn woke.

Will was wrapped around her, his big arm settled in the crook of her waist. She didn't move, hardly even let herself breathe.

It felt so good, so right, to be lying in the dark with him. *Special.* That was the word for it.

A slow smile spread across her face. Yes. That was it. It was special, what she had with him.

He was special.

All these years, she'd been waiting for that special someone.

Who would have guessed that her special man would turn out to be Will?

The next morning at the breakfast table, she couldn't get enough of just looking at him. She tried to do it subtly, when she thought he wouldn't notice.

But apparently, subtlety was not her strong suit.

It wasn't long before he demanded, "What?"

She took her time chewing a bite of toast. "Hmm?"

"You keep giving me these strange sideways looks."

"Huh? Me?" She spread on a little more elderberry jam. "This jam is so good, don't you think?" She took another bite. "Delicious."

"What is going on?"

"Nothing." She assumed her most innocent expression.

He peered at her suspiciously. "You're sure?"

"Positive. Eat your eggs."

"You're doing it again, Jordyn."

It was Saturday night. They were in Kalispell, at a Mexican restaurant that served killer guacamole. Earlier, they'd bought the groceries for the week.

Jordyn was thoroughly enjoying herself.

She dipped up a chipful of guacamole and answered innocently, "I have no idea what you're talking about." She stuck the chip in her mouth. "Yum."

He accused, "You keep staring at me."

"No, I don't."

He set down the chimichanga in his hand without taking a bite of it. "Something is going on with you."

She grabbed her margarita, stuck out her tongue and licked the salt along the rim. Will watched her do it. His eyes grew a bit glazed. She loved that. "I'm out with you. I'm having fun. *That* is what is going on with me."

He grumbled darkly, "Uh-uh. There's more."

"Honestly. You are such a suspicious man."

"You *do* keep staring at me. You're planning something, aren't you? You disappeared in the store for at least five minutes. And then, when you popped up again, you had this smirk on your face."

"I do not smirk."

"Yeah. You were. You were smirking. Where did you go?"

"I had to pick up a few things."

"What things?"

She gave him her sweetest smile. "Will, come on. Think about it. What in the world would I be planning?"

He picked up his chimichanga again. "Never mind. I don't even want to know."

Back at the ranch, they put the groceries away.

Then he said he had some bookkeeping to do in his office.

She suggested, "I'll wait up for you."

His dark brows drew together. "Uh, no, better not. It's going to take me a while."

She knew exactly what he was doing—trying to get away from her before she asked him to sleep with her again. And she *did* want him to sleep with her again. She wanted to wake up in the middle of the night with him curled around her.

But she decided not to push it. It was a lot of fun teasing him, and she wasn't quite ready yet; hadn't quite worked up her nerve to make a real move on him. They didn't have forever, but they still had more than a month left together. She didn't need to rush it.

Plus, well, she wasn't exactly experienced at seduction. Better to take it slow, kind of feel her way into it—or at least, that was what she told herself. It sure beat admitting that she had no idea what she was doing, and if she put herself out there, he might just turn her down.

She told him good-night and went on upstairs where she had a nice, juicy romance loaded up on her laptop.

The next day, Sunday, they caravanned to church with the Stevaliks again. Jordyn sat next to her temporary husband as she had the Sunday before. She tried to control her need to keep sneaking adoring glances at him.

She didn't do all that good of a job. Twice he caught her looking at him. The second time he mouthed, "What?" at her.

But she only smiled sweetly and turned her gaze toward the altar again.

That evening they went to the Dalton ranch north of town for dinner. Cece and Nick were there. So were the Daltons' identical twins Kristen and Kayla.

As always, Kayla was shy and subdued. She hardly said a word the whole evening. Kristen laughed and charmed them all with stories of how she'd played a stripper in a little theater production of *Sweet Charity*. Jordyn found herself wondering again, as she had that night at the Italian place in Kalispell, if Kristen might actually be the mystery columnist behind Rust Creek Ramblings.

After the meal but before dessert, Cece dragged Jordyn out on the front porch for a private word.

"You look happy, Jordyn Leigh. You kind of have a glow, you know?"

Jordyn gave her lifelong friend a nudge with her elbow. "Okay. I know you're hinting at something. Just tell me what's on your mind."

"Well, I was kind of wondering if maybe there wasn't a little Clifton on the way?"

Jordyn groaned and made a show of rolling her eyes. "Cece. Come on. We've barely been married for two weeks."

"Sometimes babies come right away."

Jordyn shook her head. "Uh-uh. Not happening." She said it with complete self-assurance, and tried very hard not to think about the baby she hadn't been pregnant with, after all. "Where did you get such a crazy idea?"

"I don't know. It was just…something in your expression every time you looked at Will tonight. Something happy, and a little bit secretive, too. I started thinking maybe you had an idea you might be pregnant, but you hadn't told anyone yet."

Jordyn longed to confide in her friend, to tell her that, if she had a glow, it had nothing to do with babies. If she had a glow, it was all about how she'd finally found that certain special guy. And he just happened to be her husband.

For the next month or so, anyway.

But she didn't feel right about confiding in Will's sister. She didn't want to put Cece in the middle of her Divorce Plan with Will. Later, months from now, she knew she was going to have to come clean with her lifelong friend.

Not now, though. Now she and Will had an agreement, and she wasn't going to drag anyone else into it.

They got back to the ranch at a little after nine.

The minute they were in the door, Will started in with all the things he just had to do. "I really should check on the animals and then put in a little more time on the books…"

She almost threw herself into his arms. But then, at the last second, she chickened out. She told him good-night and let him go.

It was the same the next night and the night after that.

Will always had things he just had to do in the evening. Jordyn went upstairs by herself both nights. He went outside to check on the animals, and then he locked himself in his office. She read and did homework and told herself that tomorrow night she was making her move.

Wednesday night, as usual, he went back outside after dinner. Feeling like a complete coward, she watched him go. She finished wiping down the counters and trudged upstairs, where she called her mom. They chatted for half an hour or so—about the ranch and the progress she and Will had made there, about what was going on down in Thunder Canyon.

After the phone call, Jordyn took a bath, a long one, during which she gave herself a good talking-to. She needed to tell Will what she wanted from him. The days were slipping by, and she didn't have forever to make something happen with her special guy of choice.

If he turned her down, so be it. At least she'd know that she tried.

When she left the bathroom, she heard the TV going in the living room. For once he wasn't holed up in his office. She paused at the top of the stairs and looked down at her worn pink sleep shorts, pink cami and the fat pink socks on her feet. Not an outfit made for seduction.

But she knew that if she ran back into her bedroom to look for something sexier, she might stay in there all night, dithering over what to wear.

Uh-uh. She was making her move, and she was making it now.

She descended the stairs slowly, partly out of terror at the prospect of trying to seduce her husband when she had minimal experience at tempting a man, and partly because she was so nervous that if she didn't watch it, she might trip herself and fall. She would end up sprawled in the front hall with a broken bone or two. Talk about a mood wrecker.

Somehow, she made it to the base of the stairs without incident, even though her knees wobbled and her hands trembled on the banister all the way down.

The front hall opened onto the living room. She could see him, sitting on the sofa, his back to her, facing the TV mounted over the fireplace. He was watching that comedy show where four friends challenged each other to perform embarrassing pranks in public places.

She hovered there, her hand on the newel post, staring at the back of his head and his broad shoulders, at his long arms stretched wide across the back of the sofa. His hair looked wet, and he wore that old gray T-shirt he liked to sleep in. He must have had a shower after he came back inside.

Perfect. They were both nice and clean. Always a good thing when you were going to have sex—especially for the first time.

And good gravy, what was wrong with her? She needed to make her feet move, needed to go into the living room and begin the seduction. But her feet refused to budge.

The seconds ticked by. And she couldn't stand it anymore.

If she couldn't get herself to go in there, maybe she could get him to come to her. She sucked in a big breath and called, "Will!" It came out really loud.

His black head whipped around, and he spotted her standing there clutching the newel post. "Jordyn?"

"Hey." She gave him a weak little wave. "Would you turn off the TV and come here for a minute?"

She totally expected him to shake his head and go back to watching one of the pranksters slather a middle-aged lady in sunscreen.

But he didn't.

He switched off the TV, dropped the remote on the coffee table, got up and came toward her. She watched him getting closer, her breath frozen in her throat, her pulse roaring in her ears. "What's up?"

Before he could sense what she was up to and step back, she reached out and caught his hand.

He blinked and looked down at where she touched him. "Jordyn?" He said her name with way too much suspicion.

Now or never, Jordyn Leigh. Somehow she made herself move at last, stepping up nice and close to him, wrapping his arm around her, settling his hand on her lower back.

A muscle twitched in his jaw, and his eyes grew unfocused. "Jordyn, I…" He seemed to have no clue where to take it from there.

Fine. She was ready for that, ready to lead the way. She was done dithering. Tonight she would take her chances and find out once and for all if there was any hope that her special guy thought she was special, too. "Will."

"Uh, yeah?"

"Sleep with me tonight."

His expression was not encouraging. "Jordyn, I…"

Disappointment felt like a lead weight in her belly. But

she wasn't giving up yet. She slid her hands up that amazing chest of his and twined them around his neck. "Please."

He made a low, pained sound. She only continued to stare hopefully up at him. Then he said gently, "You know, it might be a better idea if we didn't make a habit of that."

A habit? Idiotically, she asked, "A habit of what?"

He sighed. Heavily. "Of sleeping together."

She got it then. "Wait. You're thinking I meant that literally. Sleep as in *sleeping*, the way we did Friday night, and when we stayed at the Manor? And you don't want to *just* sleep with me?"

"Yeah," he said bleakly.

"You want…*more* than just sleeping?"

He looked away, muttered her name again, "Jordyn…"

She realized she needed to try to be at least a *little* seductive. So she stroked her fingers up into his hair with her right hand as she trailed the left back down to his chest, where she traced the crew neck of his shirt with a finger that only shook the tiniest bit. "So you're just going to leave me alone every night with a hot romance novel and my shower massager?"

His mouth fell open. It was so cute when he did that. "I don't believe you said that."

"Just because I'm a virgin doesn't mean I don't have *needs*—and then again, we don't even know if I'm actually a virgin, do we? That ship might have sailed without either of us even realizing it."

A low groan escaped him. "What are you *doing*?"

No going back now. "Let me make this crystal clear. It's not really sleeping I'm after from you, Will."

His whole body stiffened. He gaped down at her. "I… but…you…" Apparently, he didn't know where to start.

She needed to help him. So she said it outright. "I *want*

you, Will." And then she watched, mesmerized, as understanding finally dawned in those gorgeous blue eyes.

"This…" The word died in his throat. He swallowed, hard, his Adam's apple bouncing in an agitated manner. "It's been about sex, hasn't it?" he accused. "That's why you've been staring at me constantly for the past five days."

She felt suddenly defensive. "Oh, come on. A few glances now and then? That hardly amounts to staring at you constantly."

"You know what I mean." He said it through clenched teeth.

She traced the neck of his shirt again. His skin was hot, silky. And he always smelled so wonderful. And wasn't his breathing just a little bit agitated?

Maybe they needed to get more comfortable. She let her finger trail out onto the rock-solid bulge of his shoulder and down his arm, continuing the light caress all the way around behind her to his hand. She captured his fingers. "Come on. Let's sit down." She turned from him and dropped to the bottom step.

He loomed above her, his fingers still caught in hers. "Give me a minute."

Her face was just level with his groin. She glanced down from the hot look in his eyes and directly at the big bulge in his faded jeans.

That did it. She couldn't help it. She let go of his hand as she blushed and looked away, thoroughly embarrassed—and also gravely disappointed in herself.

For a moment there, she'd been feeling reasonably grown-up and more or less in control of the situation. "I…I'm sorry." She planted her face in her hands. "Ugh. Don't listen to me. Clearly, I have no idea what I'm doing."

A silence. Followed by a definite, if somewhat pained, chuckle.

She kept her hands over her eyes. "Now you're laughing at me. I hate you, Will Clifton."

"No, you don't. You like me. A lot."

"Now you're smug. I might have to kill you."

She still had her head in her hands, but she felt the air stir as he dropped down beside her. A low groan escaped him as he sat. That gave her at least a little satisfaction, that his jeans were too tight—and she was to blame.

"Jor-dyn..." He said her name in a singsong, the way he used to do when she was six and he was eleven.

"Don't you make fun of me," she grumbled.

And then he touched her, catching a hank of her hair and guiding it behind her ear, causing goose bumps to skitter across her skin.

"Go away." She nudged at him with her elbow.

"Jor-dyn..." Now his lips were there, touching the shell of her ear, his warm breath fanning across her cheek.

She shivered a little in pleasure, at the feel of him so close. But she still refused to look. "Leave me alone."

"Uh-uh. You started this." He kissed the words into her hair and then breathed against her temple, "And I'm not backing off until you actually talk to me." His hot fingers closed around her wrist. "Come on, look at me..."

She gave up and lowered her hands. "Fine." She turned her head and glared at him. "What do you want from me?"

He kissed the end of her nose. "You're so cute."

"Cute is not what I was going for."

"Then what?"

"More like smokin' hot and completely irresistible."

He looped an arm across her shoulders and pulled her in snug against his side. "Take my word for it. You're doing great."

She let herself lean into him. For a moment they just sat

there. It was nice, actually. Companionable. Easy, but with that little edge of excitement, the thrill of banked desire.

And then he said, "Talk to me. Tell me exactly what you're thinking."

She realized there was nothing to do but give it up. "Remember the morning we woke up married?"

He grunted. "That is a morning I will never forget."

"I told you that I wasn't *saving* myself for marriage…"

"Yeah." His voice was lower now, with a certain tempting roughness to it. "I remember that, too. You said you were saving yourself for someone special."

She straightened a little and looked right at him. "That would be you, Will. You're special to me. I want you to be my first."

He just stared at her. She couldn't tell if he was thrilled—or trying to figure out a way to let her down gently.

She forged ahead. "Look, I get it. I do. I know we're not forever. You have your goals, for your ranch, for your future. I have mine. At the end of August, I'm outta here."

"Wait."

"What?"

"You're saying that no matter what happens between us, the plan doesn't change?"

"That is exactly what I'm saying. I'm saying that this, with us, is just this beautiful, magical *accident* that happened, you know? Somebody did something to the punch, and we ended up married. For a while."

"But—"

She cut him off, sternly. "Will you let me finish, please?"

He scowled. "Go ahead."

"I want you to know that I have loved it, Will, this time with you. Loved every minute of it, even the rocky parts, even when we were barely speaking to each other—and you know what?"

"I'm afraid to ask."

"Well, too bad. I'm telling you, anyway. I say, so what if it's not forever? Life's too short and time goes by. What matters is this. I know that, with you, making love will be beautiful and every kind of exceptional I've been hoping that my first time might be. No, I don't remember much about our wedding night, but right now, I'm totally conscious. And I choose *you*, Will. I do. I choose *you*."

His face changed. His mouth and his eyes got softer somehow. He said in a rough whisper, "Jordyn, even if something *did* happen in that bed at the Manor that night, it doesn't count, and we both know that. You don't have to—"

"Shh." She pressed the tips of her fingers to those soft lips of his. "So now you know for sure why I've been sneaking looks at you, what I've been thinking about. Now I've told you, and you can think about it, too."

His lips moved beneath her touch. "My God, Jordyn. How will I think about anything else?"

She could have sat there on that stair with him all night long. But no. She'd stated her case, and she needed to give him the space to make a choice of his own. She rose. "How about this? We'll sleep on it, okay—separately?"

"Sleep," he groaned, rising to stand with her. "Like that's gonna be happening."

"Good night." And she made herself turn and start up the stairs.

She got exactly two steps before he reached out and pulled her back.

Chapter Twelve

"Don't go." He tugged her down off the stairs and around to face him again.

Her heart was going like a trip-hammer. Still, she managed to rise on tiptoe and brush a kiss against the sculpted line of his scruffy jaw. "Well, okay, then."

He gazed down at her, eyes full of questions—and heat. So much lovely heat. "You're sure?"

She didn't waver. "I am."

"You're not going to wake up tomorrow and regret…"

She put her fingers to his lips again, felt his warm breath flow down her palm. "No. I won't regret it. Ever." Her eyes filled.

He saw her tears, shook his head. "Now you're crying."

She sniffed. "It's kind of a big moment, Will—an *emotional* moment."

He lifted a hand, brushed the back of a finger down the curve of her cheek. His touch burned her, right down to the center of her. How did he do it? The man just set her on fire. "You're certain that it's what you want?"

She gazed up at him steadily. "Yeah. You and me. Lovers. I don't know how to make it any clearer than that."

He stroked a hand down her hair. And then, with the hot, rough pads of his fingers, he traced a path down from her temple, along her cheek and lower, down the side of her throat. It was a light, skating touch. And still, it seemed to lay a brand beneath her skin. "You're so beautiful."

"No."

"Yeah."

"Laila is beautiful." Her sister Laila had actually been a beauty queen.

"*You're* beautiful." He said it gruffly that time. "Stop arguing with me." His hand was on the move again, tracing the line of her jaw, sliding beneath her hair to cup the nape of her neck. He cradled her head, and then he bent closer.

Until their lips met.

Oh, my, that kiss! It curled her toes inside her pink socks, set the butterflies loose in her belly, made her whole body ache in the most delicious way.

She let out a small moan of protest when he lifted his head.

He said, "My bed."

Her mouth went dry as the Great Salt Lake. "Um. Yes. Okay. Your bed, Will—but I need to, um, run upstairs first." He just stared down at her, waiting, burning her with those eyes. She cleared her tight throat. "Ahem. I have condoms. And, er, lubricant…" His mouth twitched. He was trying not to smile. "What is so funny?" she demanded.

"Saturday," he said, "in Kalispell. When you disappeared in the supermarket…?"

"That's right. I bought them then. Just in case I ever got up the nerve to put a move on you."

"I've got condoms."

"But what about lubricant? I mean, we might not need it, but then again…"

He gave in. "Fine. Go get it."

She started to turn—but changed her mind, whirled back and grabbed his hand. "You should come with me. We shouldn't be apart now. One of us could start having second thoughts."

He held his ground. "I'll be right here waiting for you. If you don't come back down, I'll understand."

She hesitated.

He pulled his hand from her grip, took her by the shoulders and pointed her at the stairs. "Go."

"But I want you to come with—"

"Go." He was not budging.

She went—taking off up the steps at a run, reaching the upper floor in seconds, darting into her room, grabbing the tube from the nightstand drawer and racing back to the top of the stairs, where she paused and looked down to see if he'd changed his mind.

He was still there, still waiting below, just as he'd promised.

Their eyes met and locked. Heat coiled low in her belly. Her skin felt electrified, little sparks of sensation firing along every nerve.

He didn't seem to be going anywhere, so she hovered there above him, pulling herself together, allowing herself a deep breath or two.

And then, slowly, with dignity, she descended.

When she reached him, she stepped right up nice and close. "Ready," she told him.

And he moved so swiftly, reaching for her. She was high in his arms before she realized he was lifting her against his broad chest. "Oh!" She grabbed him, wrapping her arms around his neck and holding on tight.

"Kiss me again," he commanded.

She lifted her lips to him. He took them, his hot tongue spearing in, laying claim to her mouth—and more. Everything: her mind, her body, all of her senses, as he carried her past the living room and into the master suite.

He set her down on the thick rug by the wide bed. The room was dim, with only a slant of light falling across the floor from the front hall.

"Here." He held out his hand. She put the tube in it. He set it on the nightstand and switched on the bedside lamp.

She couldn't hold back a tiny gasp of dismay.

He asked, "Too bright?"

The lamp cast a soft, pretty glow across the expanse of the bed. Still, a shiver went through her at the thought of being naked with him. The light might be low, but still, he would be able to see everything. She longed to be brave and tell him to leave it on.

But it was all too new and scary. "I think for this first time…could we have it off?"

"That'll work. Let me turn back the covers first?"

"Okay." She waited while he folded the blankets down. Everything seemed strange and unreal, suddenly. She wasn't having second thoughts, exactly. But she didn't feel all that confident, either.

And then, at last, he reached out and flicked the switch again. The lamp went dark. But light still bled in from the hallway.

He was watching her face. "Darker?"

She whispered, "Yes, please."

He went over and shut the door. And it was better. There was her racing heart, her yearning body. All of her senses had gone on red alert. But the darkness helped. It was one less source of extreme stimulation. The tightness in her belly eased. She felt safer, somehow.

She heard him come back to her as her eyes began to adjust. Slivers of moonlight shone around the sides of the plain cotton curtains that had been there when they moved in.

He was a tall, broad shadow before her.

And then he touched her, gathering her into him, sweeping an arm down to press her lower body against him.

Hard. All of him.

She sighed, a slightly ragged sound. But even with her nerves on a razor's edge, the feel of him was heaven.

And then he kissed her, a slow, tender kiss. As he kissed her, he gathered her cami by the hem. "Lift your arms…" His kissed those words across her lips.

She did what he told her to do. His fingers brushed upward along her sides, creating lovely shivers of sensation. For a moment the cami came between them.

But only for a moment. Then it was gone into the darkness.

Her sleep shorts came next. His thumbs slid in at the flare of her hips. And he pushed them down until they dropped to the rug.

She stepped free of them, kicking them away. And that was it, all it took to undress her. She stood by the bed wearing only her warm socks.

He kissed her some more, wrapping her up in those steely arms of his.

"You, too," she dared to whisper against his mouth. "Your shirt, your jeans…"

He smiled against her lips. And he took her hands and placed them at the sides of his waist. She got the message, getting hold of his soft, old shirt and sliding it up over his hot, hard flesh. He raised his arms for her, and it was off.

She tossed it into the darkness. He took off the jeans himself. She heard the zipper go down, felt him moving in the darkness beside her, bending, kicking free of them.

When he rose to his height again, she reached for him, laying a palm over his heart, trailing it lower. Dark, silky hair grew in a line along the center of his chest. She knew where it led, but she didn't quite have the confidence to follow it the whole way.

He seemed to sense her shyness and clasped her shoulders. "Jordyn…"

"Uh, yeah?"

"Get on the bed. Lie down." He said it softly, gently. And so calmly. So completely in command.

In command.

She smiled a little to herself, thinking of all the years she'd known him, of how she'd always felt she had to resist, make a stand, whenever he tried to take command.

Well, not now. Not here, in the dark, with both of them naked. Tonight she *wanted* him leading the way, needed him in control.

And that struck her as funny. She let out a silly, squeaky laugh.

He pulled her against him. Oh, he felt good, so good. His body pressed to her body, without a stitch to separate them. He whispered against her hair, "You think this is funny?"

"I do," she whispered back. "And I'm nervous."

He caught her chin, tipped it up and kissed her— tenderly at first, but then more firmly, more deeply. She gave herself to that kiss, all the while aware of her bare breasts pressed to his hot chest, of his hardness poking at her belly, his big arms around her.

When he finally let go of her mouth, laughing was the last thing on her mind.

"Lie down on the bed," he instructed for the second time.

And this time she didn't hesitate. She dropped to the mattress, swung her legs up and stretched out, reaching up to position a pillow under her head.

He came down with her, taking her mouth again, kissing her for the longest time, only breaking that wet, open contact long enough to slant his mouth the other way—and kiss her some more.

As he kissed her, he touched her, light caresses, controlled. Careful.

His care helped her, relaxed her. She could feel his erection against her thigh. It seemed very large. But she tried not to think about that yet, tried not to focus on where all this kissing and touching was leading.

He didn't seem to be in any hurry to get to the scary part.

On the contrary, he was kind of feeling his way over her body, exploring her, slowly. Deliciously. As though he had all the time in the world just to touch her. His hands were rough from outside work. Rough in a wonderful way. She welcomed every brushing caress.

The first time he ran his palm across her nipple, she moaned.

"You like that?" he breathed across her cheek.

"Oh, yes, I do."

"More?"

"Please…"

His big hand settled, claiming and molding her breast. It wasn't a large breast. He completely engulfed it. "Perfect," he whispered against her parted lips.

"Uh-uh, they're too small." The words popped out, and she wanted to yank them right back.

"They're perfect," he insisted.

She smiled against his mouth. "Tonight you seem to be saying all the right things."

He brushed his lips back and forth across hers. "Just tell me, okay? Tell me what feels good and what doesn't."

"Okay…"

He flicked her nipple.

She moaned.

"Is that a good moan?"

"It is. It definitely is…"

His mouth had left hers. She wanted to order him to kiss her some more. But then she realized that he *was* kissing her some more. He was trailing those soft, clever lips of his over her chin, down her throat, pausing to lightly suck her skin against his teeth.

It felt really good, and she told him so.

So he continued kissing her. He took one breast in his mouth and then the other, doing wonderful things to them, so that she gasped and moaned and cried, "Yes! Like that, Will. Exactly like that… Oh, don't stop!"

He did just what she ordered him to do—and more. His hand skated down, stroking, caressing as it went, lighting her up like a firecracker, making her sizzle and burn.

And then he touched her. *Really* touched her. She gasped when he did that.

And he asked, "Okay?"

"Okay," she whispered. And then she groaned. "Don't you dare stop."

"Yes, ma'am." He parted her gently. Already, she was very wet. And then he eased one finger in.

Oh, it was wonderful. Better than when she did the same thing to herself. Better because she trusted him and at the same time, there was an element of surprise and of the deliciously forbidden to all this. And oh, the feel of him, the heat of him, the size and the power in his big, male body. He was all around her, touching her, holding her...

She wasn't a complete innocent with men. Now and then, she'd fooled around a little when she really liked a guy. But it had never been like this. She'd had nothing this intimate, this amazing. Not ever in her life before.

It was a first in the most wonderful way.

He slipped that finger in and then another, and he moved them in and out. At the same time, he used his thumb in just the right spot. His mouth stayed at her breast, drawing on it.

She felt the shimmer building within her—so good, so right. With Will, of all people.

Seriously. Who knew?

She barely remembered her earlier nervousness. All she felt was his big body bending over her, his mouth on her breast, his hand at the core of her, stroking her, a third finger gently easing in. She moved her hips, rocking. And he went on caressing her.

And then, just like that, hardly even expecting it, clutching his head to her breast and crying out, she came.

"Rest," he said several minutes later, in a low, rough rumble.

She still felt a certain glow, a sense of complete well-being. By then, her breathing had evened out again. She started to argue, "But I'm not tired and I want..."

He silenced her with a finger against her lips. She smelled her own musky scent. My goodness. The room smelled of sex.

She couldn't help it. She smiled in delight at the thought.

"Rest," he whispered again. "It's just you and me in this house. Nobody's going to bother us. We have all the time in the world."

All the time in the world...

No, they didn't have that, not really—not in the grand scheme of things. Yes, they had weeks yet before their marriage ended and she went off to Missoula. Weeks together. But it was all zipping by much too fast. His lips brushed her temple, his breath stirring her hair.

She just had to ask, "But what about you? Aren't you feeling a little—"

"Jordyn, I'm fine."

"You're not going to explode or anything?" For that, she got a strangled sound from him. She grumbled, "Don't you laugh at me."

"Okay, baby..."

"Will. You just called me *baby*."

"You don't like that?"

She considered. "No, I do. I think I really do."

"Well, okay, then—and no, I'm not going to explode. Or anything." He pulled the covers up over them.

For a little while, trying her best to be obedient—which they both knew was not her forte—she made herself just lie there beside him in the dark.

But there was no way she could sleep. Not yet. She was much too excited. Much too curious, too...captivated. She'd waited so very long for this night with this man. She had zero regrets that she'd waited.

But no way was she stopping now.

"Will?"

"Rest, Jordyn."

"I've been thinking."

He chuckled, the sound a lovely, low rumble. "Somehow, I'm not the least bit surprised."

"I want to see you. But I'm still not all that comfortable with *you* seeing *me*. So I'm thinking, you can shut your eyes and promise not to peek. And I'll turn on the light."

"You're not going to rest, are you?" He didn't sound all that upset about it.

"Uh-uh. Are your eyes shut?"

A silence, then, "Yeah."

"No cheating."

"Promise."

There was a lamp on her side of the bed, too. She clutched the sheet to her chest and felt her way up the base until she found the switch. Soft light pushed back the shadows.

She glanced at Will over her shoulder. He was on his back with his eyes closed, as promised. He had the covers up to his chest. She admired the sculpted perfection of his neck and shoulders, the totally tempting sight of all that tanned, healthy skin against the white sheets. "No peeking," she warned.

He tried to hide his grin. "Clear on that."

"I'm just going to peel back the blankets."

He said nothing, but his lips kept twitching.

So she pulled on the blankets, easing them down— all the way down, finally pushing them into a wad at the footboard.

Will didn't move.

And oh, my. The view was absolutely splendid. He was all hard planes and lean, strong muscles. And still aroused, so she didn't have to suffer performance anxiety over how to get him interested again.

And he looked just as large as he'd felt. She was no expert, but he seemed pretty darn big to her. She could definitely get a little performance anxiety over that, given her likely virginity and all. But then again, he was a man, and she was a woman, and the thing to remember was that the two of them were born to fit.

"Oh, Will…" She bent close to him and rested her forehead against his. "Do you believe we're doing this?"

He didn't speak, just moved his head in one slow pass from side to side.

She took the lead, kissing him, starting out slow the way he'd done with her, brushing his lips with hers, nipping his lower lip, waiting for him to open to her before dipping her tongue inside. After a little while, he reached up and banded his wonderful arms around her.

And after that, she couldn't have said who was running things. He touched her all over. And she grew bolder, even daring to reach down and wrap her fingers around him. He felt like heaven, so silky. Rock hard.

He groaned into her mouth, and then he curled his hand around hers. He showed her how he liked it, which was a lot harder and faster than she would have guessed.

And then, when she sensed he was just on the edge, he caught her hand and muttered a bad word under his breath. She took that to mean he didn't want to come that way.

And that was all right with her, because he instantly began caressing her again, parting her, stroking her, bringing her right to the point where she knew she would go over.

"Wait," she moaned. "I want…"

He made a low, growling sound and swore some more.

She pleaded, "Condom, Will. Please. I want you, all of you."

For once, he didn't argue. "Drawer," he groaned. "My side…" He let her go, and she took one from the box in the drawer and got it out of the wrapper. And then he whispered to her, guiding her, as she rolled it down over him.

She grabbed the tube of lubricant off the nightstand. "Hold out your hand."

He obeyed. She squeezed a little onto his fingers and then onto hers, and then she stroked it on over the condom.

He groaned as she smoothed it on him, at the same time

rubbing his thumb over the shiny drops on his fingers, spreading them. "It might be better if you were on top and in control," he suggested, eyes still shut as he had promised her, dark, thick lashes lustrous against his tan cheeks.

"Yes. Me on top. I think that would be perfect."

A ragged sound escaped him—but then he said gently, "All right, then."

She eased a leg over him and rose to her knees above him. He touched her then, adding the lubricant, making her wetter, slicker, more eager than ever. She rocked her hips in time with his fingers, loving every knowing stroke.

"Whenever you're ready," he whispered, sounding calm, but with a definite edge.

She drew in a long, slow breath and wrapped her hand around him, loving the way his hard belly tightened even more at her touch. Rising higher on her knees, she guided him into place. Carefully, she began to lower herself onto him. "Oh!" She froze, hovering above him as her body resisted. Already, he was stretching her. And he was hardly in at all.

"You okay?" He groaned the words.

"I…need a minute."

"We have all night." It was sweet of him to say that. But the look on his face betrayed him. That look said he was burning to get on with it. She had no doubt that this moment was as agonizing for him as it was for her. But then he whispered, "Easy. It's okay…" And he touched her again.

It helped, his caress. He knew right where she needed the stimulation. She let her head fall back and closed her eyes, sighing, as her body eased and opened around him. The discomfort passed. Heat coiled in the center of her and then began to spread, relaxing her further, and exciting her at the same time. It started to feel good again, to have him there, slick and hard and ready, almost inside her.

She wanted more. She wanted to be filled with him, joined with him, moving on him.

By slow degrees, she pressed down, taking him, pausing every time it started to hurt. Even the ache of him stretching her had a certain promise to it as they waited together, both of them breathing hard, for her body to accept him and welcome him deeper.

At the last, when they were almost there, he grasped her hips in his two hands and pulled her down to meet him.

"Will…" She groaned his name.

"Okay?"

"Oh, yes…"

"Good."

"Yes…"

He took her shoulders and pulled her down to him and pressed a string of kisses along the curve of her cheek. He nipped her chin, licked the tender skin along the side of her throat. Finally, he claimed her mouth again. She opened for him eagerly.

It lasted forever, that kiss.

Her hair fell all around them, and he gathered it up and smoothed it down her back, stroking it, then tangling his fingers in it.

Oh, it was glorious, the taste of his mouth, the breadth of his big body beneath hers, his hands in her hair, the first-in-a-lifetime feeling of him filling her below.

She began to move. Or maybe he moved first. Who could say for sure, and what did it matter, anyway? She only knew that it worked for her, to lift and come down to him, lose him and claim him again, while he let her retreat and then brought her close once more, his hands on her hips now, guiding her, holding her, making it so very good for her.

He kept his eyes closed, as promised. And the longer

he moved inside her, the more dishonest it seemed to hide from him in any way.

"Will?"

He made a guttural questioning sound.

"Would you…look at me now?"

Those black lashes swept up. And she was staring into all that blue. "Beautiful." He said it like he meant it.

She closed her eyes in pleasure and rocked on him faster, feeling her body gathering, shimmering, hitting the peak. With a cry, she went over, throwing her head back as completion cascaded through her.

And then he was sweeping his fine, rough hands up to her waist, lifting and turning her, so he was on top. Those blue eyes burned down at her. "Don't…want to hurt you…"

"You won't," she managed to whisper, though the fading waves of her climax still shuddered through her. "You never could…"

He pushed up on his fists then and powered into her, hard and fast. It shocked her a little—but she breathed deep and went with it, wrapping her legs around him, riding it out.

And then he came down to her again, gathering her into him, groaning her name. She felt him pulse within her. Oh, that was lovely. Perfect.

All of it, exactly as she'd always dreamed it might be.

She twined her arms around him and held him to her heart.

Chapter Thirteen

Jordyn moved her stuff into Will's room when she got home from work the next day. "Because for as long as we have," she told him, "I want us to be together. *Really* together."

Will knew he shouldn't let her do that, just as he shouldn't have said yes to her the night before. It was wrong to get in so deep with her. Wrong for her, because she needed to move on and follow her dream. She didn't need him dragging her back.

Wrong for him, because making love with her and sharing his room with her only made it harder to imagine letting her go. He should have made himself say no.

But he didn't, not when she moved her stuff into his bedroom. And not last night, when she'd asked him to be her first—and no, she hadn't pushed him. She hadn't *had* to push him. She'd just been beautiful and sweet and honest with him, and then asked him to think it over.

There was nothing to think over. Last night he would

have given the ranch he'd finally just got to hold her in his arms all night long.

So he went for it.

And was it worth it?

Oh, you bet.

Maybe he shouldn't have said yes. Maybe he had no right to take what she offered, to be her first.

Too bad.

He'd done it, anyway. And now he intended to enjoy every second he had with her. He was going to love every minute of it and not feel guilty about it.

And when the time came, he would let her go with a gentle word and a smile on his face.

That night when they sat down to dinner, he looked across the table at her and could hardly believe that in just a few hours, they would be together in his bed. She glanced up from her plate of spaghetti, those fine blue eyes sparkling at him.

He decided right then that a few hours was too long to wait.

The minute they had the table cleared, he took her hand and led her to the bedroom. That night was even better than the night before. He didn't have to be so careful not to hurt her. And she was more relaxed, less shy. Plus, they left the light on the whole time, and he got to look at her. Looking at her was almost as good as having his hands on her.

Friday night they made love on the sofa. He missed half the baseball game. And he didn't care in the least.

Saturday at four in the morning, the old billy set up a racket, crying like a baby out in the goat pen. When the aggravating critter kept at it for more than ten minutes, they dragged themselves from the bed, pulled on their clothes and ran out to see what the hell was going on. They got to the pen just in time to watch the nanny deliver a black-spotted kid.

Jordyn made a fuss over the kid—and praised the old billy for calling them out there. The billy talked right back to her, bleating out a cry every time she finished a sentence.

Will grunted. "You know, you shouldn't encourage him."

"But he's a sweetheart, and I *love* him," she argued, and then she told the billy, "Oh, I am going to miss you when I go…"

The billy bleated at her, a pitiful sound, as though he couldn't stand the thought of her leaving.

Will couldn't stand it, either. At that moment, he felt like she'd kicked him right in the gut.

Which was all wrong. What was his problem here? They knew where they stood, and she hadn't said anything he didn't already know.

He turned away to pull himself together. Lucky for him, she was busy playing kissy-face with the goat and didn't notice that he was acting like a fool.

When he could look at her without scowling, he said, "I guess I'll just go ahead and tend the horses, get the morning chores out of the way now that I'm up."

She offered, "I'll help."

"No need." He turned and headed toward the barn and the horse pasture on the far side.

"Will. Wait up!" She came right after him.

He had to restrain himself from turning on her and ordering her to leave him the hell alone. Instead, he stopped and drew in a slow breath and faced her and made himself say calmly, "Go on in and get the coffee started, why don't you?"

She caught her lower lip between her teeth, and he wanted to bite that lip himself, to grab her and kiss her until neither of them could see straight, then to lift her up in his arms and carry her back to his bed.

And never let her go.

She asked in a small voice, "What's wrong?"

Somehow, he pulled himself back from the brink of saying or doing anything too stupid. He schooled his voice to gentleness. "Not a thing. I won't be long."

She studied his face. He knew that look in her eyes. She didn't believe him and she wanted to keep after him.

But miracle of miracles, she let it go. "Okay. See you inside…" And she went.

He stood there in the predawn darkness, watching her walk away, and tried to congratulate himself on not losing his cool over nothing. But congratulations didn't come easy when he just felt like crap about everything.

The weekend went by with a minimum of idiocy on his part. They went to Kalispell for dinner and a movie Saturday night. When they came home, they made love for hours. Sunday night, they had Cece and Nick, Rita and Charles Dalton, and the Stevaliks over for dinner. That got a little iffy for him—because it was so good.

Good to have friends and family and neighbors over. Good to sit at the head of his own dining room table and look at Jordyn Leigh down at the other end. Good to realize that right at that moment, he had everything he'd worked for since he was ten and had decided that one day he would have a ranch of his own.

He'd done it. He had what he'd wanted for so many long years. He had his ranch and a house to call home. And for the moment, anyway, he shared his dream with a woman who had somehow turned out to be everything he hadn't even known he was looking for. Everything he wanted— and she'd been in his life all along.

He watched her chatting with Cece and promising Rita Dalton to help out with the church's summer food drive. And when she passed Myron the vegetables, he had a revelation. She handed over the big bowl piled high with corn on the cob, and Will realized that he'd been waiting all his life for her.

All his life, he'd been moving toward that Saturday four weeks ago, when he'd spotted her at the punch table in Rust Creek Falls Park and couldn't get to her fast enough. For so many years, she'd been too young. And then he'd been too wrapped up in his dream of having a ranch to call his own.

He'd almost missed out. But fate had stepped in. He'd woken up on July 5 married to her.

And now, here they were, husband and wife, sitting at either end of the Sunday dinner table.

There was only one problem. It couldn't last. Because her dream wasn't his dream.

Or did that even matter? Why couldn't she have her dream and be his wife, too?

After all, she wanted him—since last Wednesday, she'd proved that every chance either of them got. And she'd chosen him for her first. Would it be so impossible that she might want him for her one and only?

They got along great and worked together like they'd been doing it all their lives. And when they fought or things got rocky, they worked through it. They got to the bottom of the problem and found a way to resolve it.

She was perfect for him.

And maybe she thought he was all right with her, too. Maybe, just like him, she was sitting down there at her end of the table trying to think of a way to tell him that she didn't want to be his temporary wife anymore. That she wanted those vows they'd exchanged on the Fourth of July—the vows that neither of them could exactly remember—to be legal and binding before God and the world.

For the rest of their lives.

* * *

That night, after everyone left, he was just about to tell her what he felt in his heart.

But then she kissed him. And he ended up doing more showing than telling.

On Monday, as usual, she went off to work in town. He drove into Kalispell to pick up a few things. While he was there, he ran into Elbert Lutello on the sidewalk outside the feed store.

Elbert shook his hand. "How's that beautiful bride of yours?"

"She's amazing," he answered, and meant it.

"The assistant county clerk told me you two came in to pick up dissolution papers." Elbert gave him a stern frown. Before Will could decide how to respond to that, Elbert was all smiles again. "But you never brought them back, so I'm guessing it's all working out for you two lovebirds, after all."

"You're right, Elbert," Will replied and refused to feel bad about not revealing the whole truth. "I'm the happiest man alive."

"Excellent. Wonderful. That is just what I wanted to hear. Carmen will be so pleased."

"Tell Her Honor that I said hello."

"I'll do that," Elbert promised.

They shook hands again and wished each other well.

And before he left Kalispell that day, Will took a big step in the direction of claiming what he wanted most. As he drove home, he promised himself that he was going to take his chance. That night, he would make his move.

But then, at the dinner table, she reminded him that they really needed to get over to the Kalispell courthouse by the end of the week and turn in the dissolution papers so that their court date would come before she left for Missoula.

In a cautious tone that set his teeth on edge, she asked, "Um, have you made any progress on getting everything filled out yet?"

That question made his belly burn with acid and his heart beat a sick rhythm under his ribs. He wanted to punch something. "I'll get to it," he told her in a voice that had *back the hell off* written all over it.

She kept after him. "I don't mean to push, Will, but you really need to deal with those. It's a lot of information, and you need to give yourself time to pull it all together."

The damn things were completely filled out and waiting in the desk drawer in his office. He should have just said that, just eased her mind that he'd held up his end.

Instead, he jumped down her throat. "You *are* pushing, Jordyn. Will you back the hell off? I don't need you nagging me."

That shut her up. She pressed her lips to a thin line and just stared at him, big eyes full of hurt and confusion.

He felt like an ass, which made perfect sense because he was acting like one. With effort, he gentled his tone and promised, "I'll have them ready by Friday. Will that do it?"

"Uh, yeah." She forced a trembling smile. "Friday would be great. I'll get the day off, and we'll take them in."

So that pretty much settled it. She'd made it clear what she wanted—for it to go the way they'd agreed from the first. He needed to enjoy the time they had together and let her go without fighting it when the moment came.

A little while later, he apologized for being a jerk about the papers. She kissed him and forgave him. He should have told her he had the papers filled out, but he didn't, though he knew very well that was mean-spirited of him. Somehow, he couldn't bear to admit to her that he had everything ready to make that trip to the courthouse.

Because he *wasn't* ready, and he would never be. And

maybe, deep inside, he kept hoping he would find a way to tell her what was in his heart.

And then, on Thursday while she was still at work, he picked up the mail. It included a fat packet in a big gray envelope from UMT. He could guess what was inside: housing options and meal plans, public transit information—all the student living stuff she needed settled before she started her new life.

In the post office, when he pulled that packet from his box, he had a bad urge to turn and toss it in the wastebasket a few feet away. But what good would that do, except to prove he was a horse's ass?

That packet held the next step on her road to fulfilling her dream. No damn way he would ever do anything to mess with her dreams. He tucked it under his arm and headed for his truck.

At the house, he got out his dissolution papers. He left them on the breakfast nook table for her, next to the college packet. Then he changed his clothes and went out to work.

Jordyn spotted Will in the distance, on the rise above the stock pond, as she drove down the dirt driveway to the compound on her way home from work.

She saw him—and then she quickly turned her eyes to the dirt road again. The sight of him reminded her too sharply that tomorrow was the day. They would go into Kalispell and file the divorce papers.

If he'd filled them out.

But he'd promised her that he would. And he always kept his promises. She needed to stop stewing about it.

What was the worst thing that could happen? He'd fail—for the first time ever that she could remember—to keep his promise. And they would stay married for a while longer.

Staying married to Will…

It was exactly what she wanted.

Only not.

Uh-uh. No. She didn't want him like that. She truly didn't. She didn't want to just wander into staying married because he hadn't bothered to fill out the paperwork that would make them divorced.

She wanted his love. She wanted him to *want* to stay married to her. And she wanted him to say so in no uncertain terms.

But he hadn't.

Then again, neither had she.

And she'd gone not declaring herself one better, now, hadn't she? She'd nagged him about the papers until he'd growled at her to back off. And what message was he supposed to take from that, except that she must be pretty eager to get their marriage over with?

She needed to step up. And she needed to do it right away.

It was only…

What if he said no? What if he told her that he liked her a lot and enjoyed having sex with her, but as far as the two of them staying married, well, that wasn't in his plans? What if he said that he wouldn't be looking for a *real* wife for at least a couple of years yet?

She didn't know if she could bear that—not that he would be so brutal about it. He would find a way to say it gently and sincerely, with kindness and care.

But it didn't matter how he said it; her heart would end up in shreds. She just hadn't managed to buck up and take a chance on a shredded heart. Not as of yet.

And time was running out.

She drove up to the house and parked in the cleared space next to Pia's blue pickup. Inside, she went straight to the kitchen to check on the slow cooker. The pork stew was ready, so she turned the dial to the warm setting and moved on to the breakfast nook table where Will always left the mail.

Her student living packet had arrived.

And right next to it, he'd left a stack of papers.

It took her a moment to process what she was looking at, because suddenly her eyes brimmed with hot tears, and everything went blurry. But then she swiped the moisture away. She could see all too clearly again and had to admit what was right in front of her eyes: Will's dissolution papers.

Her silly hands shook as she picked the damn things up and rifled through them. He'd filled in every blank in his bold, forward-slanting hand.

Damn him all to hell. He'd filled in all the blanks!

She yanked out a chair and fell into it and stared at the papers clutched in her hand. Oh, she did yearn to crumple them up in a wad and throw them in the trash, to tear them to tiny pieces, to strike a match and burn them to cinders.

Which was ridiculous.

She was ridiculous.

It wasn't the papers' fault if Will didn't want to stay married to her.

And, please. How could she even know what Will might want? Had she asked him? Had she gone to him and told him honestly what *she* wanted?

No, on both counts.

Because she was a coward. A ridiculous coward. A wimpy, gutless, chickenhearted fool.

It had to stop. It had to stop right now.

She shot to her feet, dropped the papers on the table and stormed out the back door, banging the screen good and hard behind her. In the goat pen, the billy heard her coming. He set to crying like a baby. For a second or two, she was tempted to take a moment and go to him, to check on the kid, maybe see how Mama Kitty and her brood were doing in the barn.

But no. Uh-uh. No excuses. She was doing this. She was not letting herself back down or be distracted. She was letting the billy cry for now. And the kittens could wait. She'd visit them later.

The ornery rooster strutted toward her. She zipped around him and kept going. He crowed as she went by, but she didn't turn.

Will was no longer in sight up on the rise. She kept going, anyway, clambering over a fence, breaking into a run up the slope, ignoring the cattle that lifted their heads to watch as she raced past.

At the top of the hill, she paused and put her hand to her forehead to block the sun's glare. She scanned the rolling land before her—and spotted him.

He was down below, thigh-deep in the stock pond. He had a rope around what appeared to be a heifer and he struggled, pulling, trying to haul the animal to dry land. Both the critter and the man were covered in mud.

She took off at a run down the slope, wanting to get to him, needing to get it over with at last, to tell him what was in her heart, get it out there between them, whatever the consequences. He had his back to her as he towed on the rope, and he didn't see her coming.

About ten feet from the muddy bank, she halted. Her breath tangled in her throat, her heart beating madly against the walls of her chest. She waited, giving him the time he needed to finish a tough job. She put her hand against her mouth to keep from distracting him as he coaxed and pulled and coaxed some more while the half-drowned heifer stared at him through dazed eyes and bawled in hopeless exhaustion.

He almost had the animal out of the thick mud at the edge of the water when the heifer's legs gave out, and she plopped down with a sad bellow of complete surrender, sending mud flying every which way.

At that point, Jordyn figured she ought to do more than just stand there. "Need some help? I can get her tail."

Will's head whipped around. "Jordyn? How long have you been standing there?"

"Too long. I'll take the tail."

She got exactly three steps closer before he put up a mud-caked glove. "No." His gaze swept over her good jeans and town boots. "You haven't even got gloves."

Right then, the little red heifer, with a loud moo of effort, dragged herself upright again. Will braced with the rope and pulled.

Four steps and the critter cleared the mud.

"Atta girl, there you go." Will piled on the sweet talk as he stepped in close and eased off the rope. The heifer let out another long, tired cry.

And Jordyn's heart was just too full. She couldn't wait another minute. She shielded her eyes to cut the sun's glare and she announced, "Will Clifton, I saw the divorce papers you left on the table, and I am so sorry I nagged you to get them filled out. It was nothing but cowardly of me, to push you to do that. Because the real truth is that filling out those forms is the *last* thing I wanted you to do. Will, I love this ranch. I love our life together, I love the goats and the barn cats, that big nasty rooster—and even that muddy heifer you just pulled from the pond. I love my job and Rust Creek Falls and all the friends I've made here. But most of all, I love you. So, if maybe it's possible that you might feel the same way, I really don't have to go to Missoula. I can take the rest of my classes online just as well. So, I um…"

Was she blowing this?

She feared she might be. Will just crouched there at the edge of the pond, mud all over him, his arm around the heifer's neck, watching her under the shadow of his hat.

Oh, dear Lord, was he trying to figure out a way to turn her down gently?

She wavered in her purpose. And then she caught herself. No way was she backing down now.

If he didn't feel what she felt, well, she'd just have to deal with that. She was through hiding her true feelings, through pretending she wanted to go when she only longed to stay. She was taking a stand, following her heart. And she was doing it now.

Jordyn yanked her shoulders up, hitched her chin high and cried, "Please, Will. I love you. Would you just think about not divorcing me, after all?"

Relief made Will's knees weak. He staggered against the heifer's mud-caked side. Hot damn, Jordyn loved him.

She wanted to stay with him.

He eased the rope off the heifer. He let her go, pushed to his height and slapped her on the rump. She bawled at him. So he slapped her again and gave her a shove. That did it. She staggered forward, found her feet and trotted off, still bawling.

Up the bank, Jordyn hadn't moved. She stood way too still, watching him, her plump lower lip caught between her pretty teeth, her hand shading her eyes.

He took off his hat and dropped it, along with the muddy rope and gloves, right there at the edge of the water. "Jordyn," he said, because his mind and heart were so full of her, he couldn't manage any more at that moment. Just her name. And that was everything.

"Will?" She let her hand drop, and she stared at him, tears filling those big eyes.

"Baby, don't you cry."

"Oh, Will…" And she started crying, anyway.

He lunged up the bank for her. She fell toward him, reaching. He gathered her in. "I'm getting mud all over you."

She gazed up at him, a smear of mud on her chin and tears on her cheeks. "Will Clifton, I do not care about a little mud."

At least his hands were reasonably clean. He wiped those tears with his thumb. And then he kissed her. He put everything into that kiss—his heart, his dreams, all his love. And when he lifted his head, he said, "I love you, too, Jordyn Leigh. And what I want is exactly what you want, for you to stay here on the Flying C and be my wife for the rest of our days."

"Oh, Will. You do? You really, really do?"

"Yeah. I do. I want that more than anything." And then he bent to kiss her again.

But just before his lips met hers, she let out a cry.

He frowned. "Jordyn, what in the…?"

And she pushed him away from her. "Oh, Will. Tell me the truth, now. Are you *sure*?"

His arms were empty again, and he didn't get it. "What the hell, Jordyn. Didn't I just say so?"

She fisted her hands at her sides and tipped her golden head up to the wide, clear sky. "Oh, Will. I know you. I know what a good man you are. And I can't help but wonder if you're just being your usual upright self, just agreeing to stay married to me because it's what *I* want and you believe in the sanctity of the vows that we took—whether either of us can actually remember them or not. I'm afraid you just feel honor bound to stay with me because it's the right thing to do."

Yeah, he loved her. But right then he kind of wanted to strangle her. He muttered, "That was a mouthful you just said, and all of it crap."

She sniffled. "But can you blame me? I won't take advantage of you. I admit that it's tempting. But no. I have to be certain. I have to know for sure."

Will swore. "That does it." He grabbed her hand. "Come on."

"But Will, I—"

He whirled on her and put a finger to her lips. "Jordyn. Wait. I mean it. Not another word."

She gulped. And then she nodded.

And then he turned and started walking, forging up the rise, towing her behind him. He kept going, never breaking stride, down the slope on the other side, through the pasture to the fence. He stopped there and hoisted her up. She got down on her own, and he came over right after, capturing her hand again, leading her through the yard in back.

The billy wailed in the goat pen.

He hollered, "Shut up!"

Damned if that goat didn't actually fall silent. And then that fat rooster strutted right in front of him. He stepped over the rooster and kept on walking.

He didn't even stop on the back step to get out of his muddy boots. He just yanked the screen open, pulled her through and kept going, through the kitchen and the dining room, to his office at the front of the house.

"Stand right there." He positioned her in a splash of sunlight by the window. "Don't even move."

Eyes wide, mouth agape, she did what he told her to do.

He went to the desk, yanked open the drawer and took out the little velvet box he'd stuck in there Monday after his trip to Kalispell. His hands were all thumbs at that point, but somehow, he got that box open and took out two rings.

Jordyn caught on then. A soft gasp escaped her, but she kept her peace. She did not say a word.

And then he went to her and dropped to one knee. "Give me your hand."

Those blue eyes were filling again, but he knew her well enough to tell the good tears from the bad. She held out her hand.

He slid off the cheap band she'd been wearing since that morning in Kalispell when they made their Divorce Plan. And in its place he slipped on an engagement ring thick with diamonds and a matching platinum wedding band.

"Will," she said. Just his name. And it was more than enough. He knew by the sound of her voice that she believed him at last.

He said, "I saw Elbert Lutello in town on Monday."

"No…"

"Yeah."

"What, um, did Elbert say?"

"Just that he knew we'd been in and picked up dissolution papers. But then he assumed we'd decided to stay together because we hadn't brought the papers back. He said his wife would be so pleased to know that we were happy."

She gazed down at him tenderly. "I love you, Will."

He had a boulder-size lump in his throat. He swallowed it down. "After I talked to Elbert, I found the nearest jewelry store and bought this for you."

"Monday," she marveled. "You did that on Monday. And I never guessed…"

"For days now, I've been trying to find a way to ask you to stay with me, to be my wife for the rest of our lives. I *do* want what you want, Jordyn. You're the one for me. I think you always have been. I took one look at you on the

Fourth of July in that blue dress with your shining, pinned-up hair coming loose on your shoulders, and I knew something good was going to happen between us."

Her cheeks flushed with pleasure. And she teased, "I think the doctored punch played a part—and those romance-loving Lutellos, too."

"Maybe a little. But I swear to you on my life, Jordyn, eventually the end result would have been the same—and I don't really care *how* it happened with us. I'm only grateful that it did. I just didn't want to hold you back or keep you from your dreams."

"You're not. Oh, Will. *This* is what I want. You and me and our life, here, together. Yes, I want my degree. And I'm going to get it. I just…don't need to run off to Missoula to make that happen. I was leaving town mostly because I thought I needed a fresh start. And then I woke up married to you—and what we have together has turned out to be all the fresh start I need. So I'm not leaving. I'm staying here. With you."

He got to his feet then. "Jordyn…"

She put her hands on his shoulders. "I goaded you about those papers. I was such a coward. I hoped that when I pressured you, you'd just burst out with how you loved me and you wanted me to stay."

He admitted, "I had those papers ready for weeks."

"No."

"Oh, yeah. But I refused to admit I'd finished them. I was stalling, trying to find the right moment to ask you to stay. And then, Monday night, just when I was about to go for it and whip out that ring, you got on me again about the papers. I took it as more proof that you really did want to go, and I needed to stand down."

She groaned. "We were such a couple of idiots."

He tipped up her chin. "But we're not idiots anymore."

And then he couldn't wait. He swooped down and claimed her sweet mouth, bending to scoop her up in his arms at the same time.

She laughed against his lips—and then went on kissing him as he carried her out of his office, through the front hall, past the living room, into his bedroom and straight to the bathroom for a shared shower to wash off all the mud.

More than washing went on in that shower.

And from there, he took her to bed, where they properly celebrated the end of the Divorce Plan and the beginning of the rest of their lives.

* * * * *

5_ST14

Join our *EXCLUSIVE*
eBook club

FROM JUST £1.99 A MONTH!

Never miss a book again with our hassle-free eBook subscription.

★ Pick how many titles you want from each series with our flexible subscription

★ Your titles are delivered to your device on the first of every month

★ Zero risk, zero obligation!

There really is nothing standing in the way of you and your favourite books!

Start your eBook subscription today at www.millsandboon.co.uk/subscribe

MILLS & BOON®

Cherish™

EXPERIENCE THE ULTIMATE RUSH OF FALLING IN LOVE

A sneak peek at next month's titles...

In stores from 17th July 2015:

- **The Texas Ranger's Bride** – Rebecca Winters *and* **His Unforgettable Fiancée** – Teresa Carpenter

- **The Boss, the Bride & the Baby** – Judy Duarte *and* **Return of the Italian Tycoon** – Jennifer Faye

In stores from 7th August 2015:

- **Do You Take This Maverick?** – Marie Ferrarella *and* **Hired by the Brooding Billionaire** – Kandy Shepher

- **A Will, a Wish...a Proposal** – Jessica Gilmore *and* **A Reunion and a Ring** – Gina Wilkins

---